THE ALPINE SCANDAL

AN EMMA LORD MYSTERY

THE ALPINE SCANDAL

MARY DAHEIM

THORNDIKE
CHIVERS

This Large Print edition is published by Thorndike Press, Waterville, Maine, USA and by BBC Audiobooks Ltd, Bath, England.

Thorndike Press is an imprint of Thomson Gale, a part of The Thomson Corporation.

Thorndike is a trademark and used herein under license.

The text of this Large Print edition is unabridged.

Other aspects of the book may vary from the original edition.

Set in 16 pt. Plantin.

LIBRARY OF CONGRESS CATALOGING-IN-PUBLICATION DATA

Daheim, Mary.
   The Alpine scandal : an Emma Lord mystery / by Mary Daheim.
     p. cm.
   ISBN-13: 978-0-7862-9585-2 (alk. paper)
   ISBN-10: 0-7862-9585-6 (alk. paper)
   1. Lord, Emma (Fictitious character) — Fiction. 2. Newspaper publishing — Fiction. 3. Washington (State) — Fiction. 4. Women publishers — Fiction. 5. Large type books. I. Title.
PS3554.A264A839 2007
813'.54—dc22   2007011541

BRITISH LIBRARY CATALOGUING-IN-PUBLICATION DATA AVAILABLE

Published in 2007 in the U.S. by arrangement with The Ballantine Publishing Group, a division of Random House, Inc.
Published in 2007 in the U.K. by arrangement with The Random House Publishing Group.
U.K. Hardcover: 978 1 405 64166 1 (Chivers Large Print)
U.K. Softcover: 978 1 405 64167 8 (Camden Large Print)

Printed in the United States of America on permanent paper
10 9 8 7 6 5 4 3 2 1

THE ALPINE SCANDAL

ONE

Ed Bronsky was leaving a strange trail behind him on Alpine's grapevine. *The Alpine Advocate*'s former ad manager was creating a stir with his unusual behavior. He'd been spotted at the Grocery Basket stuffing bananas in his raincoat pocket, at Cal Vickers's Texaco station putting only three gallons of gas into his Mercedes, and leaving the Burger Barn without paying for his double deluxe bacon cheeseburger with extra fries. Indeed, I had noticed him in church at St. Mildred's dropping coins into the collection basket instead of waving a check with his usual flourish.

My House & Home editor, Vida Runkel, was sorely tempted to put some of those occurrences into her weekly gossip column, "Scene Around Town," but even she felt there might be something seriously wrong with Ed. Many years earlier, he'd quit his job at the *Advocate* after inheriting a pile of money from an aunt. Ever since then he and his wife, Shirley, and their five children had lived the high life — or as high as you can get in Alpine, with its four thousand residents living in semi-isolation eight miles from the Stevens Pass summit.

I was about to discover the answer.

Ed had wedged himself into one of my two visitors' chairs on this first Monday morning in January. He looked more pugnacious than crazy.

"I want my old job back," he said without any preamble.

I was aghast. "What?"

Ed nodded once, his three chins settling into his Burberry muffler. "That's right. I'm — we're — broke."

Given the rumor mill, I wasn't completely bowled over. But I was still flabbergasted. "What happened?" I asked, pretending I hadn't heard his request to be reinstated. "I thought you had a financial adviser."

Ed cleared his throat. "I do. But . . ." He averted his eyes. "The dot-com disaster, 9/11, the whole downturn thing . . . plus, I made a few investments on the side. They didn't turn out so good."

I had to ask. "What kind of investments?"

Ed shot me a swift, furtive glance. "Prune-based fuel. Plastic tires. Paper shoes."

I didn't know what to say. "Those sound like kind of far-fetched ideas, Ed."

He pounded his pudgy fist on the table. "No! Think about it! We're ruining the planet by relying on traditional natural resources. We've got to find other solutions. We have to seek unusual means to maintain our quality of life. Was Ben Franklin flying a kite far-fetched? You bet. But look what happened."

I sensed that this spiel wasn't Ed's but had come from whoever had conned him into his bad investments.

He sighed and swiped at the comb-over that hid part of his bald dome. "There goes Stanford. Shirley and I really wanted to send at least one of our kids there."

It would have been unkind to point out that even if the Bronskys could have *sent* one of their five children to Stanford, that didn't mean that child would get in. I figured Ed would have had to endow most of the Bay Area to get his offspring accepted at the academically challenging Palo Alto school.

But I had to say something. "I'm so sorry, Ed."

He shrugged, the powdered sugar on his cashmere overcoat sprinkling the air of my cubbyhole office like tiny snowflakes. "You

9

got any more of those doughnuts?" he asked.

"I think you ate the last three," I said.

"Oh." Ed frowned. "Maybe it's just as well I never got that bond issue on the ballot last fall," he mused. "Even if it'd passed, I'd probably still have had to invest some of my own money for the Mr. Pig Museum and Family Fun Center."

Ed was referring to his harebrained scheme for an amusement park that would feature the Mr. Pig characters from a Japanese animated TV show that had been loosely based on his self-published autobiography, *Mr. Ed.*

"Yes," I agreed. "And it certainly would've been a lot of work." *Work.* It was a word with which Ed had only a passing acquaintance, as I'd learned to my sorrow when I inherited him from the *Advocate*'s previous owner, Marius Vandeventer.

"So what about it?" he asked, burying his chins deeper into his muffler. "I mean . . . that is . . . what's the chance of getting my old job back?"

I grimaced. "We have an ad manager, Ed. Leo Walsh has done an outstanding job ever since you quit."

Ed looked at me as if I were dumb as a rope. "Emma, Emma," he said in a condescending tone, "Leo came here from California. *Southern* California," he added, emphasizing the part of the state to make it sound even worse, like having pulmonary pneumonia instead of simple bronchitis. "I'm an Alpine native. Who knows commerce around here better than I do? Who hobnobs with all the business and civic leaders? Who plays golf with Mayor Baugh?"

I honestly didn't know what to say — except, of course, to refuse Ed's request to return to work. "Why didn't you run for county commissioner in November?"

Ed grimaced. "I missed the filing deadline." He paused and looked away. "And I forgot there was a fee, even for a write-in candidate."

I'd known that, of course, but I wanted to hear Ed admit it. "That's too bad," I said. "You could have added something to the board." I was sincere. Our trio of doddering old coots should have been voted out of office long before, but nobody sane enough to replace them had ever offered any opposition. Even Ed would have been an improvement. At least he didn't drool at meetings.

But I had to deal with reality. "Have you any income?" I asked.

Ed looked wistful. "A little. Not enough to cover the mortgage and everything else."

I nodded sympathetically. "Given your close association with the business community, surely you can find a job."

Ed bridled. "Not just any job! Not after what I've been . . ." He leaned forward, his stomach pressing against my desk. "I'm an ad man. I'm not an auto mechanic or a building contractor or anything like that. I need to do what I've always done."

And done halfheartedly, I thought. I sighed. "I simply can't replace Leo. He's earned his keep."

Leaning back in the chair, Ed jiggled one leg up and down. "Right. I understand. Okay." The chair creaked under his weight. "If . . . never mind." He got to his feet, huffing and puffing a little. "I never thought I'd have to put my kids to work."

"Why not?" I said. "They *should* work. They're old enough except for the two youngest. Jobs would be good for them. They need to take responsibility."

Ed shuddered. "They won't like it."

I was tempted to say that was a hereditary trait, but it would have been cruel to kick Ed when he seemed down. My phone rang. I hesitated in answering it, but Ed waved a hand.

"Go ahead. I'm out of here." He opened the door to the newsroom. The last I saw of

12

him was a mound of cashmere overcoat scurrying past Vida's desk.

The call was from my brother, Ben, who was still in town after spending the holidays with me. On Christmas Eve day he'd driven over two thousand miles in two and a half days from his temporary parish in East Lansing, Michigan, and he was taking an extra week's vacation after New Year's. My son, Adam, who is also a priest, had come down from St. Mary's Igloo in Alaska December 19 but had to go back to his ice-bound outpost on the third. Adam had stayed with me; Ben was bunking at St. Mildred's rectory.

"Sluggly," Ben said, using his childhood nickname for me, "who's Anna Maria Della Croce?"

The name rang only the faintest of bells. "Am I supposed to know?"

"Den's not here this morning," Ben said, referring to St. Mildred's pastor, Dennis Kelly. "Remember, he was taking a long weekend in Seattle to recover from all the Advent and Christmas hoo-hah."

"Oh, right." I saw Vida's imposing figure heading in my direction. "Anna Maria what?"

Ben spelled her last name. "She called the parish office at seven this morning, asking for Den. I thought she said *Ben,* so I got her confused."

The confusion was understandable, since my brother had filled in for Father Den during his six-month sabbatical. "What about it?" I asked as Vida stood behind the visitor's chair that Ed had recently vacated.

"She started telling me her troubles as if I should know," Ben went on, "and I finally figured out she thought I was Kelly. I don't recall her from the six months I served here, and I couldn't find her in the parish directory file. She needs to talk to Den, not me."

I looked up at Vida, whose face was puckered with curiosity. "Does the name Anna Maria Della Croce mean anything to you?"

Vida repeated the name several times, very fast. "It should." She frowned. "Really, I can't place her. Are you sure she lives in Alpine?"

I started to relay the message to Ben, but Vida's trumpetlike voice already had reached his ear.

"If Vida doesn't know her," Ben said dryly, "nobody does."

My brother was right. Vida was the font of all knowledge in Alpine, having been born and raised in the small logging town some seventy years earlier.

"Did she give you a local phone number or address?" I asked.

"Yes," Ben replied. "A number, that is."

"Is her situation dire?" I inquired as Vida leaned over my desk to try to hear Ben on the other end of the line.

"No. Naturally, I can't tell you what the problem is even if it's not under the seal of confession," Ben said. "Anyway, she rattled on like a steam engine, and I'm not sure what she was talking about, except that it's something she seems to have discussed with Kelly. Got to go. I have to take Holy Communion to a couple of sick people at the nursing home."

"Well?" Vida said after I'd hung up. She was leaning on the desk with both hands, and her felt hat with the feather looked like something left over from a B movie version of *The Three Musketeers*. "What's going on with that ninny Ed? He wouldn't even talk to me just now."

It was useless to keep information from Vida. She'd find out eventually, even if she had to tap every one of her considerable resources. "He says he's broke. I gather he's been doing some investing on his own and it hasn't turned out well."

"Of course not." Vida sat down. "So foolish. But I'm hardly surprised. Why doesn't

15

he sell that ridiculous house of his?"

"Who'd buy it?" Casa de Bronska was an Italian-style villa that Ed and Shirley had built at the east end of town above the river and the railroad tracks. It was complete with swimming pool, marble statuary, and Tuscan tiles featuring likenesses of the Bronsky family and their dog, Carhop. "There's no market for that kind of house in Alpine."

"True," Vida allowed. "So silly to have such a house around here. The only thing it's fit for is some kind of retreat center, or perhaps an inn."

"That's not a bad idea," I said. "You should suggest that to Ed."

Vida shot me a disgusted look. "He wouldn't listen to good sense. That's undoubtedly how he got himself into this mess in the first place."

"I'm afraid so," I admitted, and paused. "He wanted his old job back."

Vida's jaw dropped. "No! What nerve! Leo can be aggravating, especially when he smokes, but he's ten times the ad manager Ed ever was. I hope you told him no."

I nodded. "I wouldn't jeopardize Leo for the world, and certainly not for Ed Bronsky."

"Honestly." Vida thought for a moment, shaking her head and folding her arms across her jutting bosom. "Who is this Anna Maria person? I'm trying to remember where I've heard the name. There aren't that many Italian families in town."

I shrugged. "Father Den will know when he gets back tomorrow. From what I gathered, whoever she is, she's not standing on a chair with a noose around her neck."

"I've no patience with people who do that sort of thing," Vida declared. "So selfish, to the very end." She turned as our office manager, Ginny Erlandson, came into the newsroom with the mail. "I should see what's piled up over the weekend." Vida rose and walked in her splayfooted manner to her desk.

As usual, Ginny delivered my batch first; it was one of the few perks I had as the *Advocate*'s editor and publisher.

"It looks like the usual," she said, putting the stack into my in-basket. "PR and news releases, ads, and a couple of bills."

"Nobody does much between Christmas and New Year's," I noted. "How was your weekend?"

"Fine," Ginny replied. "We took the boys up to the summit so they could go sledding. It's so weird not having snow in Alpine this time of year."

It *was* weird. The Pacific Northwest was

suffering from drought. While it might be convenient to not have to dig out from under a couple of feet of snow during the winter, the freezing level in the Cascades had receded above Alpine's three-thousand-foot altitude. Despite the off-and-on-again rainfall, the lack of snow meant there would be no reserve come spring and summer. I'd written a couple of editorials on the subject, but Mother Nature didn't subscribe to the *Advocate*.

"Your boys are getting so big," I remarked, sifting through the dross of mail in search of gold. Nothing even remotely glittered.

Ginny nodded, her single red braid bouncing over her shoulder. "They grow up so fast. Rick and I wonder if we should try for a girl."

It wasn't up to me to offer family planning advice. Over thirty years earlier, I'd given birth to Adam while not married. "You can't guarantee gender," I pointed out. "Vida had three girls."

"I know." Ginny gazed at the piece of mail that lay on top of the pile that still had to be delivered. "Vida's getting a shower invitation today from Julie Nelsen. I got one, too."

I tried to look pitiful. "Not me?"

Ginny, who is quite bright but lacks a sense of humor, looked embarrassed. "I didn't think you knew Julie."

I grinned, hoping Ginny would realize I was teasing her. "I don't. I mean, I know who she is. Julie works at Barton's Bootery. Her folks are Gustavsons, right? And she's married to . . ." I blanked.

"Nels Nelsen, from Index," Ginny said helpfully. "This is their first baby. They've been trying for years."

I decided not to say that they must be really worn-out. Ginny would take me literally. "That's nice. The Gustavsons are related to Vida, but I'm not sure how."

"Sometimes I think Vida's related to everybody in Alpine," Ginny declared. It wasn't much of an exaggeration. "She's amazing. I'd better take her the mail."

I polished off my share of the delivery in less than five minutes. The next day was the deadline for the weekly edition. I had no inspiration for an editorial. Maybe I could write a stirring piece asking our readers to donate money to a fund for the Bronsky family. I wondered how many of the locals would be gloating over Ed's decline and fall. I knew he'd rubbed a number of Alpiners the wrong way with his conspicuous consumption.

I strolled out into the newsroom, where Leo Walsh had just returned and was already on the phone. He gave me a high sign as I passed his desk on the way to the coffee-maker. My only reporter, Scott Chamoud, was scouring the streets for news. Or, I should say, *street.* Alpine had only one main east-west artery, which was where most of the local government and business offices were situated. Scott had had some news of his own before the holidays when he and his longtime girlfriend, Tamara Rostova, had gotten married in October. The wedding had been celebrated at the Russian Ortho-dox cathedral in Seattle. Our entire staff had attended, along with many of Tamara's Skykomish Community College colleagues. I couldn't give Scott a raise, but I ran up my much-abused credit card by giving them four settings of their china pattern. It was akin to a bribe, since I feared that the newlyweds might make good on their mild threat to move out of Alpine.

Vida was scowling at a single sheet of typewritten paper. "This is bizarre," she declared. "There must be some mistake."

"What?" I asked, perching on her desk.

"People get crazier by the day," she de-clared, handing me the paper and the envelope in which it had arrived. "Here. Read this for yourself. And check the post-mark."

I looked at the postmark first. It was dated Saturday, January 4, from Alpine. My eyes shifted to the typewritten sheet. There was no heading, only the date, which was the same as the postmark. I read it aloud to let Vida know I wasn't missing anything:

"Elmer Edward Nystrom, longtime Alpine resident, died Monday, January sixth. Elmer, sixty-one, was born in Williston, North Dakota, the son of Oscar and Alma (née Engelman). He moved to Washington State in 1970 and worked as the service department manager at Nordby Brothers General Motors dealership for the past thirty-four years. Mr. Nystrom was a member of the Rotary Club, the Kiwanis Club, the Alpine Chamber of Commerce, the Elks Club, and Trinity Episcopal Church. He is survived by his loving wife of thirty-six years, Elizabeth (Polly), and his son, Carter. Funeral arrangements are pending."

I stared at Vida. "Will we know when the funeral is by the time we go to press tomorrow?"

Vida's scowl deepened. "Emma! Didn't you pay attention to what you read?"

I looked again at the typewritten envelope with its canceled stamps and no return address. "Oh! Good God — this was mailed *before* Elmer died! It's got to be a mistake

21

— or a joke."

"A nasty joke — and a stupid mistake," Vida said, retrieving the letter and the envelope from me. "I'm guessing that the son, Carter, wrote it and that he was rattled. From what I know of Polly, she's probably gone all to pieces. I'll call the house. Carter lives with his parents, you know."

I didn't know. But I was aware that Carter Nystrom had returned to Alpine two years earlier after having finished dental school and getting his orthodontist's degree at the University of Washington in Seattle. Our longtime dentist, Bob Starr, was glad to have a local orthodontist he could refer patients to instead of shipping them off to Monroe or even Everett. I knew all three of the Nystroms by sight but had never had any personal contact with the family. When Carter had returned to Alpine, Scott had interviewed him for a feature story. His office was in the Clemans Building on Front Street.

Vida had dialed the Nystrom number, but it was busy. "Not unexpected," she said, hanging up. "I think I'll drive over there. They live just this side of the college."

"I'll go with you," I offered. "That is, I'll follow you. I have to admit I'm curious about the obit, too, and I've scheduled an interview with May Hashimoto about a couple of new programs they want to introduce at Skykomish Community College."

Vida glanced at her watch. "What time?"

"Eleven," I replied. "It's ten-ten, so I might as well tag along."

Vida gazed at me through her big glasses. "Why?"

I grimaced. "Maybe I'm afraid Ed will come back. I'd rather not be here."

"Ed?" Leo had just hung up the phone. "What's he up to now?"

"You don't want to know," I said. "But I'll tell you when I get back. In fact, want to have lunch with me at the Venison Inn? I'll treat. I just decided it's Ad Manager Appreciation Day."

Leo grinned in his off-center manner. "Sure, why not? See you there around noon?"

"Right." I scurried into my cubbyhole to grab my jacket and purse. Vida was fastening the black galoshes that she hadn't bothered to take off. It had been raining all morning, steadily if not heavily.

Before we could make our exit, Ethel Pike limped into the newsroom. "Burl Creek Thimble Club Christmas pictures," she announced to Vida in her somewhat glum manner. "Got room?"

Vida looked as if she were trying to be patient. "Perhaps. You should have brought them last week."

"I couldn't," Ethel said. "Me and Pike were out of town for Christmas. Pike's sister invited us to Hoquiam for the holiday. I don't know why: She can't cook for sour owl's sweat, and Pike and her always get into it over some crazy thing that happened when they were knee-high to a gopher. But where else would we go, with our kids and grandkids all the way down to Orlando?"

Pike was her husband, Bickford, but he was known by his last name. Vida accepted the packet of photos. "I'll see what I can do," she said. "I noticed you were limping. Not bunions, I hope. Such a nuisance."

Ethel glared at Vida. "Not bunions. Circulation, 'specially in this damp weather."

"Ah." Vida nodded. She and I both knew that wasn't the whole story. Ethel suffered from diabetes but was too proud to let on. Even some Burl Creek Thimble Club members didn't know about her health problems.

Vida was smiling stiffly at the other woman. "If you'll excuse me, I was about to leave."

"So was I," Ethel retorted. "Pike's out and about on his errands, and I got to run him down so he can fix the electrical. The fuses

24

all blew this morning. I won't touch electrical. Too risky. Pike don't even wear gloves when he does it."

"Very foolish," Vida murmured.

" 'Course it is," Ethel agreed. "He'll blow himself up one of these days. Serve him right, the crazy old fool." On that cheerless note, she stalked out of the newsroom.

We waited a few moments until we were sure Ethel was gone. Vida's Buick was parked two spaces down from my Honda. She carried a plaid umbrella; I simply put up the hood on my car coat. Like many Pacific Northwest natives — Vida notwithstanding — I didn't own an umbrella. They were a nuisance, especially in Alpine, where winds blew through the Skykomish River valley and down the mountainside from Tonga Ridge.

Skykomish Community College was a little over a mile from the newspaper office, nestled among tall cedar, fir, and hemlock trees. Between the college and the commercial area there were scattered homes, some old, some new, and some originally farmhouses or loggers' shacks. An occasional gnome or St. Francis sculpture stood forlorn in the rain. Several residents' idea of garden décor was an old tractor or a rusted pickup in the front yard. There were tree stumps and even a toilet that during the summer months served as a planter for perennials. But on a dark January morning, everything looked a little bleak.

Ahead of me, Vida turned into a gravel driveway. A half-dozen mail and newspaper boxes stood slightly askew. I saw NYSTROM on one of them, a miniature red barn on top of a steel post. Pulling up behind the Buick, I studied the white one-story craftsman house set away from the road. It appeared well tended. The property probably once had been an orchard. A few bare fruit trees remained. Two of them sported large bird nests in their gnarled branches. A chain-link fence ran between the driveway and a newer, if faded blue house next door. There were fruit trees there, too. I suspected that the former orchard had been subdivided at one point.

But what struck me most as I got out of my car was the absence of activity. A death in the family — especially in Alpine, where everyone knows everybody else — usually brought visitors offering condolences along with casseroles and salads and an occasional dessert. There were no cars except Vida's and mine in the driveway or even alongside the road. The double garage's doors were closed. It almost looked as if the Nystrom house was deserted.

I said as much to Vida.

"Very odd," she agreed. "Odd, too, that I haven't heard about Elmer's passing. The Nystroms should be Lutheran with that Scandinavian surname, but they go to Trinity Episcopal."

I translated that to mean that Vida wouldn't have heard the sad news at Sunday's Presbyterian church service. But it also indicated that her grapevine somehow had withered. There'd be hell to pay for the slackers involved.

A dried huckleberry wreath hung on the front door, appropriate not just for the Christmas season but for the entire winter as well. Vida punched the doorbell. I could hear a soft chime inside. We looked at each other expectantly.

A few moments passed before the door was opened. "Vida?" said the stout little woman I recognized as Polly Nystrom. "What a nice surprise! Come in out of the rain."

As usual, I felt like the caboose on Vida's train. But Polly collected herself as we entered a sunroom filled with bookcases. "You're the newspaper lady," she said to me. "I know you by sight." She put out a pudgy hand. "I'm happy to finally meet you.

Let's go in the living room where we can be comfortable. I've just been putting the Christmas decorations away in the basement, and a cup of tea sounds good."

"Lovely," Vida said, her gray eyes swiftly appraising the tastefully appointed room with its whitewashed brick fireplace, framed French Impressionist prints, Oriental carpeting, and Duncan Phyfe–style furniture.

Vida sat down on a richly textured traditional sofa with coordinated throw pillows. I decided to join her. Polly smiled at us.

"I won't be a minute," she promised. "I'll put the kettle on."

"Polly," Vida said in a solemn voice, "before you do that, please tell us about Elmer. What happened?"

Polly looked mystified. "I'm sorry. What do you mean?"

Vida whipped off her glasses and began rubbing her eyes in a familiar gesture of frustration. "Ooooh! This is so . . . awkward!" She stopped beating up her eyeballs and sighed. "It must be a prank. I received Elmer's obituary in the mail this morning."

Polly's blue eyes grew enormous. "No!" She stared at Vida. "I don't understand."

"Neither do I," Vida admitted. "But Emma and I felt we should call on you. Obviously, an explanation is needed. If you have one."

"Oh, dear." Polly pressed her thick lips together. She was close to sixty, with short blond hair going gray, and probably had been a pretty girl, though her features had coarsened with age and weight. "I can't imagine." She twisted her hands as she stared into the carpet. "A prank. Who would do such a thing? Maybe Elmer knows. Shall I call him?"

Vida shook her head. "No, no. Don't bother him at work. He *is* at work?" she added.

"Yes, certainly," Polly replied, her composure returning. "He left at the usual time, right after he fed the chickens. We still keep chickens, you know. Would you care for some eggs? I'm watching my cholesterol and can't eat them very often, so we always have some extras."

"How nice," Vida replied. "Fresh eggs are such a treat."

"I'll put that kettle on now." Polly attempted a smile. "What a way to start the new year! Goodness, I hope it all isn't going to be so . . . strange." She bustled off through the dining room and into the kitchen.

I looked at my watch. "It's almost ten-thirty," I said to Vida. "Maybe I should leave. I don't want to be late for my appointment with May Hashimoto."

"Then let's skip the tea," Vida said, getting up. "Polly," she called out, "don't trouble yourself. Emma and I should be on our way. We both have work to do this morning."

Polly met Vida in the kitchen doorway. "Are you sure?"

"Yes," Vida asserted. "Tomorrow is our deadline. I'm just so glad this turned out to be a farce."

Polly's smile seemed genuine. "So am I! Elmer will be upset, of course. But Carter will make him laugh about it. Our son is so clever at always finding the funny side of things."

"Really." Vida sounded skeptical.

"My, yes," Polly declared, bristling ever so slightly. "He has to be clever — and amusing — when he's dealing with teenagers who don't want braces, not even the new kind you hardly notice. They're so self-conscious at that age."

"Expensive, too," Vida said, never willing to give an inch. "Thank goodness my grandson, Roger, had his braces removed two years ago. His teeth are now perfect."

Roger's teeth. I considered them briefly. They were good, if not perfect. There were few positive things I could say about the spoiled-rotten kid, but maybe I could allow that his teeth weren't as bad as the rest of him.

"I'm going now," I said in case Vida and Polly had forgotten that I'd ever come.

Polly stepped forward. "Goodbye, Emma. It was nice to meet you."

I wasn't searching for sincerity, which was a good thing. The comment was perfunctory at best, even though Polly smiled politely.

Vida also announced her departure, wheeling around on her heel and heading toward the front door.

"Ninny," she remarked after we reached the driveway. "No wonder I've never enjoyed Polly's company. She constantly brags about Carter. So irksome."

I wouldn't have dared point out that Vida bragged a great deal about Roger, and with far less cause. Carter Nystrom was ten years older and had completed a rigorous education. Roger was still dawdling his way through community college.

Vida stopped just before reaching her Buick. "I wonder . . ." she murmured.

"What?" I said, taking the car keys out of my purse.

"Ohhh . . ." Vida made a face. "We didn't

get any eggs."

"So?"

"I wanted to make an omelet for dinner tonight," Vida said. "My mouth is set for one. I'd only need three eggs. You run along. I'm going to the henhouse."

"Vida," I objected, "that's stealing."

Vida glowered at me. "Nonsense! Polly offered them to us. It'd be wrong *not* to take them. She said they'd go to waste."

"Then I'll go with you," I declared. "If Polly calls the sheriff, I want to be at your side when Milo Dodge comes to arrest you for egg burglary."

"Oh, for heaven's sake!" Vida gave me a reproachful look. "Very well. But you should take an egg or two for yourself. Do you know how to candle eggs?"

"You hold them up to a light and make sure the center is clear."

"Correct," Vida said, opening the wooden gate that led to the chicken coop behind the main house. "Or you can put them in a basin of cold water. If they sink, they're fine."

I hadn't known that, but I didn't admit it. I was too busy trying to keep to the intermittent brick path that led to the henhouse. I noticed a fishpond tucked in one corner of the garden. The lily pad–dotted pool was shaded by an apple tree in front and several azaleas and rhododendrons around the far rim. We had to pass through another gated fence before we reached our goal.

Chickens do know enough to stay out of the rain. But even though none of them were outside, their leavings were, causing an unpleasant smell and making it even more difficult to walk on the soggy ground.

The door was shut, and that made Vida frown. "Odd," she murmured. "Why does Elmer keep the henhouse closed up? Chickens should be free to roam."

"Maybe they have another way out," I suggested.

"Perhaps," Vida said, lifting the latch. "Oh, well. People don't use good sense."

There were at least a couple of dozen hens pecking around on the ground or sitting on nests. Two roosters perched on a rafter that ran the width of the henhouse. The chickens were all a handsome red-brown color. Despite being city-bred, I was able to identify them as Rhode Island Reds. The hen closest to the door seemed distressed. She was flapping her wings and moving from one foot to the other.

"Don't bother the ones sitting on their nests," Vida warned. "They may be broody, though this is not the time of year I would think they'd be hatching chicks."

"I know, I know," I said, stepping carefully toward a vacant nest on my right. A couple of the other hens clucked nervously at us. One of the roosters moved back and forth on his perch as if he might be preparing to attack. I eyed him warily. "Sometimes hens sit on their nests and sort of pretend they're hatching," I remarked. "Like women who want to have a baby but can't."

Vida was removing an egg from a nest just ahead of me. "Such a lovely light brown color. It may be nonsense, but I think the darker eggs have better flavor."

I collected two eggs and put them in a pocket inside my purse. Vida had confiscated her trio for the omelet. "I don't think Elmer collected eggs this morning."

"Let's go," I said as the rooster flapped his wings. "I think that one is at the top of the pecking order."

Vida had stopped almost at the far end of the aisle between the two sets of nests. She gasped. "Oh, dear!"

"What?" I asked, still keeping watch on the rooster.

"Elmer."

"Elmer? What about him?"

"He's here."

"What?" I was right behind Vida, trying to

look around her.

"There." She moved aside a few inches. "You can see his shoes."

I saw them — black work shoes with the toes pointing straight up. The rest of Elmer was hidden under haphazard piles of golden straw.

"Holy Mother," I whispered.

"Call for help," Vida snapped, bending down. "I'll try to find his pulse. He may have had a stroke. Or a heart attack."

I rummaged in my purse for the cell phone. Of course I couldn't find it right away, and of course I broke both eggs in the process. Finally I retrieved the damned phone and was about to dial 911 when Vida spoke again.

"Tell them there's no rush." Vida paused, rubbing at her forehead. "I'm afraid that obituary was correct. I can't find a pulse or a heartbeat. Elmer's dead."

Two

As usual, Beth Rafferty maintained her composure when I called 911. "Help is on the way," Beth said in her most professional dispatcher's voice. Then, because she knew it was me, she added, "We've got the fire-fighters and medics tied up at the Tall Timber Motel with some guy who may have had a heart attack, so Dodge is coming in person."

"Thank goodness," I said, and rang off.

"I don't suppose," Vida said, tapping her cheek, "I should move any of this straw." She shot me a knowing glance. "Just in case. This all seems very fishy to me."

I nodded. "We should tell Polly."

"No. Let Milo do that. It ought to be of-ficial. I'll stay with Elmer. You go get the sheriff. Otherwise, he might not know where to meet us, men being so dense when it comes to finding anything."

I was used to Vida taking charge as if she

were the boss and I the slightly dim-witted employee. Traipsing outside into the rain, I hoped Polly wouldn't notice me — or our cars, which remained parked in the driveway. More than that, I hoped Elmer's death had been a natural one. Murder was no stranger to Alpine. On the other hand, it'd give us a lead story. Journalists have to be realistic — and crass.

The rain was dwindling to a drizzle. I stood by the mailboxes, waiting for Milo Dodge. No siren wailed in the distance. That was good. Milo knew there was no urgency, and he didn't use the siren unless it was absolutely necessary. Unlike the other Skykomish County emergency personnel, the sheriff had bought an English-style *gagoo-ga* siren that was unmistakable and drove me a little crazy. Still, it was one of the sheriff's very few eccentricities. I could live with it.

His red Grand Cherokee was easy to spot. I saw it coming down the road after a wait of less than five minutes. Out of the blue, I remembered to call May Hashimoto and tell her I'd be late and hurriedly dialed the college president's number on my cell phone. Her secretary answered, and I relayed the message just as Milo pulled up on the verge by the mailboxes.

"What the hell's going on now?" he demanded as he unfolded his six-foot-five frame from the vehicle.

"Elmer Nystrom's dead — I think — in the chicken coop."

Milo made a face. "That sounds like a line out of a bad movie."

"It's not very good for Elmer, either," I retorted. "Come on, follow me. Vida's in the coop."

"A good place for her," Milo muttered. "Is she clucking her head off?"

"No." It seemed to me that the sheriff was unusually cranky, even for a Monday morning. "Polly Nystrom doesn't know yet."

"Doesn't know what? That her old man croaked?"

"Right. We're waiting for you to make it official." I'd entered the chicken area and was walking carefully. "Mind the poop."

"Right, right. I'm a rural type, remember?"

I could hardly forget. Our different backgrounds had been an obstacle in our off-and-on-again romance. Being friends was better than being lovers, but it wasn't an easy relationship.

The chickens fluttered and cackled as Milo and I entered the coop. Vida was leaning against a rail that supported the nests.

"Well, now," she said. "You made good time."

Milo grunted. "Where's Elmer?"

Vida pointed. "Is Doc Dewey coming?"

"Doc's busy," Milo said, getting down on his knees. "He still hasn't gotten around to making Sung his deputy coroner."

"Can't you do that?" Vida asked. "You're the sheriff."

"It's a courtesy thing," Milo replied. "I let Doc decide when it comes to medical-related stuff." He paused. "Hunh."

"What?" I said.

"There's blood," Milo answered. "It's on the straw behind his head. Maybe I should wait for Doc or the medics."

"A hemorrhage?" Vida asked, trying to see around the sheriff.

"No," Milo said, still examining the body. "More like a blow to the back of his head. Oh, hell!"

"Don't curse," Vida warned. "Are you talking about . . . foul play?"

Milo didn't look up. "Maybe."

Vida was incredulous. "Elmer Nystrom? Who on earth would murder Elmer? He's one of the most harmless people I've ever met, even if he was a bit of a nincompoop."

Since most of Alpine's population fell into the nincompoop category as far as Vida was concerned, that part of her comment didn't matter. I wasn't acquainted with Elmer, so I couldn't make any judgments.

"Shovel," Milo murmured, standing up and looking around. "Two-by-four. Anyway, something heavy and blunt."

But none of us saw anything that might have served as a weapon. "You're sure he didn't hit his head?" I asked.

Milo frowned. "On what?" He raised his hand to touch the rafter, which was a couple of inches above his regulation hat. "Elmer was six feet, maybe six-one. He'd have to have been wearing stilts. I don't see anything else he could've banged into. The platform for the chickens? I doubt it. It's plywood. The floorboards are a possibility, but they only run down the aisle and then stop. There's no sign of blood on them. But I'm guessing — and you know I don't like doing that — Elmer was dragged over here and then bled out. Look at the area between the nests."

Vida and I both stared at the raised wooden floor. It was no more than two or three feet wide, built on top of dirt. The well-worn boards were covered with pieces of straw and chicken droppings. But the last couple of yards between the nests were comparatively bare.

"You figure someone conked Elmer and hauled him out of sight?" I asked.

Milo shrugged. "Could be. In fact, we'd all better move away toward the door. There may be some other evidence. C'mon, let's hit it."

Vida scowled at the sheriff but obeyed. I reached the door first and opened it. Fresh air seemed like a good idea.

Polly was on her back porch, and that unsettled me. She looked upset. "Where's Elmer?" she called in a shrill voice. "Sheriff?" She started down the half-dozen stairs with an uncertain gait. "What is it?"

Milo met her halfway across the backyard. Vida followed him, though I kept my distance. The sheriff faced a heartbreaking announcement. It wouldn't be the first time he'd had to deliver bad news, but such situations weren't easy for him to handle. There was nothing touchy-feely about Milo Dodge.

Still, he did his best.

"I'm afraid something's happened to Elmer," he said. "I'm sorry, Polly. He's dead."

"Oh!" Throwing her apron over her face, Polly rocked back and forth. The sheriff steadied her. "I knew it!" she cried. "Trout's been trying to call me all morning!"

Trout Nordby was one of the two brothers who owned the GM dealership. The other sibling was known as Skunk. Even after over thirteen years in Alpine, I wasn't sure of their real first names.

Vida stepped forward. "Here. I'll take her in the house," she said to Milo. "I'll make that cup of tea now, Polly. Please, let me help you get inside. It's very wet out here."

Polly leaned on Vida, who half dragged her into the house.

I looked at Milo. "Well?"

"I'll have to interrogate her after I find out what happened to Elmer," he said.

"So we stand here in the rain until Doc Dewey finishes whatever he's doing?"

"It's not raining that hard," Milo said, taking a pack of Marlboro Lights from the inside pocket of his regulation jacket. "Want one?"

I shook my head. "I'm still in my quitting phase."

He gave me a lopsided grin. "What's this one? Number forty-five?"

"Ha ha." I gestured at the partial view of the house that sat just beyond the Nystrom residence. "Who lives there?"

Milo lighted his cigarette and pondered the question. "It's an Italian name — or Spanish. They moved in about . . . six years

42

ago, maybe. Quiet people. Husband, wife, teenaged daughter. One of the deputies — Sam Heppner, I think — went out there last summer when a cougar came into their backyard. Other than that, no trouble."

I looked in the other direction. Through some cottonwood and fir trees I could make out part of a roof and a chimney. "Whoever lives on the other side couldn't see anything going on at the Nystrom house. But this other family might. I wonder if they're home."

"I'll check." Milo scowled at me. "Are you nagging?"

"Not really. But I keep wondering when Spencer Fleetwood is going to show up so he can get the story on KSKY before I have it in the paper."

"Spence went to Hawaii," Milo said. "Or Mexico. Did Vida's pipeline spring a leak?"

I grimaced. "No. I forgot she had a mention of Spence's vacation last week in her 'Scene' column. Maybe his fill-in doesn't pay as much attention to the police scanner as Spence does."

"Rey Fernandez is still working at the station," Milo said. "He got his AA degree in December but agreed to stay on in Alpine until Fleetwood got back." The sheriff used one hand to smoke and the other to dial his

43

cell phone. "I'm checking to see how long Doc's going to take before he gets here. I've got — Doc?" he spoke into the cell phone.

I wandered over to the fishpond while the sheriff related the unfortunate news. I couldn't see any fish, but maybe the Nystroms didn't bother. Until the past couple of years, the temperature had always dipped below freezing during most of the winter. I'd heard stories, however, including one old-time classic about a fisherman who caught a big rainbow trout and tossed it into a water barrel to keep it alive until his wife was ready to cook it. That night an early frost covered Alpine, and the water in the barrel froze over until the spring thaw. Come early April, the fish was still alive and swimming around like crazy.

"Doc's on his way," Milo said.

I walked back toward him. "There's something you should know," I said.

The sheriff's sandy eyebrows lifted almost imperceptibly. "Like what?"

"Like Elmer's obituary came in the morning mail."

"Don't bullshit me," Milo retorted. "I'm not in the mood."

"It's true," I asserted. "In fact, I'll bet Vida has it in her purse. Even I wouldn't joke about something like that with the poor guy lying dead in the henhouse."

Milo swore for at least a quarter of a minute. "Who the hell sent it?" he finally asked.

"We don't know," I replied. "That's why we came out here to see Polly."

The sheriff swore some more. "Don't let anything happen to that obituary," he warned me. "It might be evidence. Come on, I think I heard Doc's car."

We walked around the side of the house. Doc already had gotten out of his new Mitsubishi sedan. He'd once confided that he'd love to own a big, expensive automobile but thought it wouldn't look good to his patients, who'd figure he was overcharging them.

"How's the patient?" Milo inquired as Doc started up the driveway.

"Which one?" Doc responded.

"The guy at the motel," the sheriff said, opening the first gate for Doc.

I was loitering behind the men, studying the faded blue house on the other side of the cyclone fence. Two large windows, probably in bedrooms, flanked a smaller window with frosted glass that looked like it was in the bathroom. As I passed by the second bedroom window, I saw movement behind the voile curtains. Someone was watching.

Vida wasn't the only curious person in Alpine, and the arrival of so many cars at the Nystrom house naturally would have aroused interest.

Doc shook his head. "False alarm. All in his head — or his stomach. People on the road eat too much grease, sleep in strange beds, get their nerves frayed by traffic — and then wonder why they have chest pains. Which," he continued as we headed for the henhouse, "are often abdominal pains and caused by digestive tract problems." He paused at the second gate. "Not the case with Elmer, I take it."

"Afraid not," Milo said, waiting for me. "This may require an autopsy."

"Well." Doc Dewey sounded only mildly surprised. He had reached a time of life when nothing surprised him. As a physician, he'd had his share of failures and disappointments. When I had been at my nadir after Tom Cavanaugh's death, he'd told me that he considered the greatest virtue to be hope, not charity. "Without hope," he had said, "the rest is impossible." Like his father before him, Doc practiced what he preached.

Inside the henhouse, I stayed by the door, petting a chicken that seemed quite agitated by the proceedings. "If only," I whispered to the distressed fowl, "you could talk, you'd be a good witness."

Doc didn't take long to examine Elmer. "The ambulance will be along any minute," he said, rising from his crouched position by the body. "After the motel call, they went to Starbucks for coffee."

I stepped forward. "Was it a blow to the head?" I asked.

Doc tucked his glasses back into an inside pocket of his raincoat. "That's my preliminary finding," he said. "Poor Elmer. He was a decent fellow."

"Meek as milk," the sheriff remarked. "Not a classic victim."

"I'm not ruling out an accident," Doc cautioned, "though I don't see exactly how. That's your line of country, Sheriff."

"Freaky stuff happens," Milo said, looking out through the open door. "Here come the ambulance guys. No siren. Not necessary." He looked back at Doc. "You going to talk to Polly?"

"I'd better," Doc agreed. "She has high blood pressure. I'll check her out. Poor woman. Has anybody called their son?"

"Vida, probably," I said as we trooped back through the rain. I stopped at the outer gate. "I should head for the college. I'm supposed to interview May Hashimoto, and

47

I'm already twenty minutes late."

"Go for it," Milo said.

I did, noticing on my way out to the road that Vida's Buick was still parked by the house. I was opening the Honda's door when I heard someone call out. I looked at the Nystrom porch, but no one was there. Then I turned toward the neighboring house and saw a dark-haired woman wearing baggy gray sweats in the doorway.

"What's going on?" she asked in a carrying voice.

I walked over to the cyclone fence that ended at the mailboxes. "I'm afraid Mr. Nystrom has passed away."

"No!" Her hands flew to her face. She was middle-aged, a rather large woman wearing glasses on a jeweled chain. "That's awful! He was such a sweet man!"

"Yes," I said, realizing that the woman looked vaguely familiar. "Were you close friends?"

The woman shook her head. "Not really. But I always talked to Mr. Nystrom when I saw him out in the yard." She hesitated. "I suppose I should call on Mrs. Nystrom. Later."

"That would be very kind," I said.

"Of course." She backed inside and closed the door.

I looked down at the mailbox in front of me. The name was gracefully lettered in red: DELLA CROCE.

I'd already heard it that morning. It was the same name as that of the troubled woman who had called my brother asking for counsel.

The college president was shocked and sympathetic when I explained why I'd been almost half an hour late for our interview.

"I don't know the Nystrom family," May Hashimoto said, "but I feel for them. I lost my own father when he was in his early sixties."

"My parents were both in their fifties," I told her. "They were killed in a collision coming from my brother's ordination."

"That's even worse." May shuddered. "On the other hand, I've known of couples who can't live without each other, and the survivor dies not long after the husband or wife goes." She shook her head. May's hair was distinctive, with a natural white streak growing among the short ebony tresses. "I have trouble understanding that, since my one attempt at marriage ended abruptly in divorce."

"I've never been married at all," I said, "but I lost my fiancé not long before our

49

wedding."

"That was terrible," May declared. "I wasn't here yet when it happened, but I heard all about it. Violence. It plagues our times."

"It's plagued most times," I noted. "In other centuries we didn't have CNN."

May smiled ironically. "You're part of the media, Emma."

"I know." I smiled, too. But the clock — stylized metal hands on pine paneling — was ticking away. I knew she wanted to go to lunch soon, and I'd promised to treat Leo, though I'd given him a quick call to say I'd be a little late. May and I got down to business, which didn't take long. Unlike many educators, May didn't use lengthy, sometimes incomprehensible discourse or speak in what I termed "Educationese." She tended to be blessedly brisk.

I arrived at the Venison Inn by twelve-fifteen. Leo was waiting in the bar, where he could smoke, a habit that wasn't permitted in the main dining room except for the sheriff, who simply ignored the NO SMOKING sign and refused to arrest himself.

"Well?" Leo said as I sat down at a small table for two. "What happened to poor old Elmer?"

"Autopsy pending," I said, catching my breath.

Leo's weathered face grew curious. "Oh? I wondered. Your tone of voice implied that something was off."

Mandy Gustavson, who was somehow related to Vida, came to take our order. Leo already had a mug of black coffee. I asked for a Pepsi and the rare beef dip with fries. "Go for the steak sandwich," I urged Leo. "It's my treat, remember?"

Leo, however, ordered the same thing I'd requested. "Never get a steak sandwich on a Monday," he said after Mandy had left us. "It'll be something left over from the weekend and taste like a spare tire."

"Good advice," I said, my eyes wandering around the dimly lighted bar with its deer, elk, and moose antler motif. Although the dining room had been remodeled awhile back, the serious drinkers preferred the original décor. Thus, the trophies from the long-dead animals had endured far longer than had many of the patrons who'd decorated the bar stools.

"Nice guy, Elmer," Leo remarked, leaning back in his chair. "If I didn't like my Toyota so much, I'd have bought a GM car just to get the good service Elmer always gave his customers. The Nordby brothers have been lucky to have him all these years."

I agreed. "I really didn't know the family," I admitted. "It's amazing that despite the fact I've lived in Alpine for going on fourteen years, there are still some longtime residents I barely recognize."

Leo shrugged. "Some people don't mix much. The Nystroms are like that. At least," he went on, extinguishing his cigarette, "Elmer and his wife weren't active in the community. He did his job and went home. She kept house. The son's more outgoing, but he's been pretty involved in getting his orthodontist practice up and running."

"Do you know Carter?" I asked after Mandy had delivered my Pepsi and the small salads that went with our entrées.

"I've met him a couple of times," Leo replied, sprinkling salt and pepper on his greens. "He bought a two-by-four-inch space with us when he first opened his practice. Then he took out a standing ad with the rest of the professionals on page five." He gave me a slightly mocking look. "You do occasionally read the *Advocate*'s ads, don't you?"

I laughed. "Occasionally. But I trust you enough to not go over them with a fine-toothed comb." That was the perfect opening to segue into Ed's problem. "In fact, we're having lunch because I want to make sure you know how much I appreciate your contribution to keeping the newspaper solvent. I know it's not easy. The print media often seems like it's in the death throes."

Leo munched on iceberg lettuce. "So," he said after he'd swallowed, "just seeing Bronsky on the premises suddenly made you grateful for my existence."

"Yes." I scoured the bar to make sure no one could overhear us. "Ed's broke. He wants to come back to work. I use that term loosely."

Leo laughed out loud. "I wondered. I've heard the stories, too. Ed pilfering a DVD from Videos-to-Go. Ed giving a rubber check to Pete Patricelli for the family-size Super Lollapalooza pizza. Ed trying on a pair of shoes at Barton's Bootery and walking out into the mall wearing them — without paying, of course. It's a wonder he hasn't been arrested."

"Everybody probably thinks he's gone goofy," I noted. "The eccentric millionaire. They probably believe — or want to believe — that no matter what he swipes, he's good for it down the line."

Mandy brought our beef dips and fries. "Word will get out," Leo remarked after

Mandy once again had left us. "I actually feel sorry for the poor slug. At least he's got his kids mostly raised."

"Three of them are still in high school and junior high," I said. "This must be terrible for Shirley. Vida had a good idea about selling Casa de Bronska." I told Leo about turning the place into a commercial site.

"Not bad," he responded. "Good for Alpine, too. Ed could probably fetch at least a million bucks right there. It'd take time, though. Do you suppose he's considered a line of credit on the house?"

"I've no idea," I admitted. "It'd see them through until they found a buyer."

"Let me talk to him," Leo said. "You know, one ad guy to another. He'll know damned well that you had to tell me about his troubles. I'll give him a call after lunch."

I smiled fondly at Leo. "You're not just a good employee, you're a really good person."

"Right, right." Leo seemed uncharacteristically embarrassed. "I'm a prince. Too bad you're not a princess." He paused for just a beat. "What's going on with you and the AP wire service guy?"

Despite my affection and respect for Leo, I'd never felt genuinely attracted to him. In the beginning he'd wished otherwise. Leo had come to me with Tom's blessing as an ad man but seemed like a poor substitute for my longtime lover. Everybody did, of course, including Milo. Going to bed with Leo would've been like sleeping with Tom's proxy. Fortunately, Leo had understood. Or at least he had accepted my lack of response to his overtures.

Rolf Fisher of the Associated Press was another matter. I'd met him after Tom died. Rolf was a smart, good-looking widower who lived in a condo near the Seattle Center. We'd dated for about a year, though it was difficult for us to be together, being separated by eighty-five miles of highway. Then I'd managed to screw up the burgeoning relationship by completely forgetting about a weekend date we were supposed to have in Seattle. Eventually I'd made amends, but in the four months that had followed, we'd seen each other only twice.

"Let's say that Rolf and I seem to have plateaued," I said. " 'Madly in love' does not describe us. Let's stick with 'warily fond.' We have a tentative date to go to the opera to hear *Norma* toward the end of the month."

Leo nodded. "I get it. He's gun-shy. Who burned him?"

The question startled me. "No one that I

know of. His wife died of cancer."

"Okay." Leo resumed eating.

I wasn't sure I wanted to know what he was implying, so I changed the subject. "Tell me about Carter Nystrom."

He shrugged. "Not much to tell. Ask Scott. He did the interview. All I know is that Carter's bright, smooth, good-looking. He's a little taller than Elmer and broader, too. Maybe he resembles his mother more than his father, although I've never met Mrs. Nystrom. I imagine he's got a very good chairside manner."

I tried to picture the young man. Fair-haired, I thought; glasses, a pleasant, earnest face. I must have seen him since he'd returned to Alpine after completing his studies, but somehow I remembered a much younger version.

Leo seemed to be reading my mind. "I suppose he's been away at school for most of the time you've lived in town. It takes several years to complete the orthodontist courses, not to mention the prerequisite dental degree. I'd never met him until he came back to set up a practice."

I'd dated a would-be dentist briefly in my younger years. He'd flunked out of school because he couldn't carve teeth. His professor had told him his efforts looked like pinto beans. Maybe he was highly suggestible. He'd gone on to get a business degree, and the last I heard of him, he was the head produce buyer for a grocery store chain in California. Unfortunately, I couldn't remember his name.

Our conversation drifted away from the Nystroms, back to Ed, and on to the newlywed Chamouds. Tamara taught at the college; she was contracted to stay through the spring quarter. Sadly, Leo and I figured they'd move on when June rolled around. Scott and his bride possessed marketable skills, and lately he'd shown signs of wanting to stretch his journalistic muscles. Both he and his bride were originally from the city. Unlike Leo and me, who were old veterans of the small-town weekly wars, they were young and ambitious.

As we walked back to the office, I noticed how ordinary Front Street looked: cool but fresh air, steady rain, rugged tree-lined mountains rising up into the low-hanging gray clouds above the town. A trickle of cars and trucks moved through town. Other working stiffs like us also were returning from lunch. No one seemed in much of a hurry. A driver at a four-way stop honked and waved at a middle-aged man crossing the street. A young woman bent over a squawking infant in a covered stroller by the dry cleaners. An empty school bus made its way up Sixth Street toward Alpine High.

Everything seemed normal, even peaceful. Life was going on at its usual mundane pace. Except, of course, for Elmer Nystrom, who was lying in the morgue at Alpine Hospital. But what was more mundane than death?

Unless, I thought, Elmer had been murdered.

THREE

Vida didn't get back until after one-thirty. "Honestly," she said, stripping off her fuzzy woolen gloves, "some people are no good in a crisis. Polly Nystrom is one of them."

"Did she fall apart?" I asked as our production manager, Kip MacDuff, came into the newsroom from the back shop.

"My, yes!" Vida exclaimed. "Especially after Carter got there. I waited until he could come from his office. He, I might add, was quite calm and composed."

"What happened?" Kip asked.

Vida related our discovery of Elmer Nystrom's body. I went over to Scott's desk to see if I could tell from his calendar when he'd be back in the office. I'd write the main story, but I'd need him for any sidebar articles. Vida, of course, would handle the obit.

"You want me to call the Nordby brothers?" Leo asked.

"I'll do it," I said, seeing that Scott had scheduled a one-fifteen meeting with Rita Patricelli at the Chamber of Commerce. "Just tell me how I can differentiate Skunk from Trout."

"Easy," Leo replied. "Trout has fish lips. Skunk's got fur on his back."

I stared at Leo. "He goes shirtless in January?"

"I'm working off of rumors," Leo said with a grin. "Trust me."

Kip was shaking his head. "I've known Elmer ever since I got my first car. It was a seventy-nine Chevy Impala. I thought I'd have an emotional meltdown when I got that car. It was really *hot,* even if it was ten years old at the time. I blew the engine two years later racing a buddy up one of those logging roads near Martin Creek. Elmer gave me a bad time about that. But in a nice way."

"Everybody liked Elmer," I murmured as I approached Vida's desk. "Let's hope it was an accident."

Kip's earnest face expressed disbelief. "What do you mean?"

Vida frowned at Kip. "Precisely what I told you. The sheriff's investigating to make sure foul play wasn't involved."

"That's bunk," Kip declared. "Only a nut

case would hurt Elmer."

"Let's hope so," I said. "Vida, we must turn that obit over to Milo."

"Oh." She put a hand to her cheek. "Y-e-s. Of course we do. I'll get it out of my purse." She stopped in midreach. "No. I'll take it to him right now."

"What obit?" Kip inquired.

Putting her gloves back on, Vida looked disgruntled. "I didn't mention that part to you. We got an obituary for Elmer in this morning's mail."

Kip looked even more incredulous. "Weird!"

"Very," Vida agreed. "Or prescient. I won't be long. I have to go through Elsie Overholt's retirees column when I get back. Such an editing job she requires! My, my!"

Leo watched Vida leave. "How long will it take her to put Bill Blatt on the rack?" he asked in a bemused tone.

Deputy Blatt was one of Vida's numerous kinfolk. He often served as a source, albeit a reluctant one, for law enforcement information. I often wondered what cajolery, what flattery, what threats, what dark family secrets Vida used to wrench confidential facts out of the poor guy. If anyone but Vida had forced an employee to spew out unofficial pronouncements, that deputy would have been canned long ago. But Milo knew my House & Home editor too well. She was irresistible when it came to getting others to spill secrets.

Still looking dismayed over the news of Elmer's sudden death, Kip returned to the back shop. Leo was on the phone again — his usual mode of coddling advertisers when he wasn't meeting them in person. I felt adrift. There was no point calling on the Nordby brothers until I knew how Elmer had died. Maybe I should begin work on my weekly editorial, I thought. All I needed was a topic that wouldn't put the readers to sleep.

Roads. I could always write about roads. Even if we weren't getting much snow, the roads would need repairing in the spring.

No. I'd beaten that subject to death.

Flood control on the Skykomish River. But the thaw wouldn't be as bad this year because there shouldn't be a dangerous runoff from the mountains.

Skip flood control.

The Alpine Wilderness bill that had been stalled in Congress for years. Despite efforts to safeguard a wide swath of forest in the adjacent area, the nation's governing body didn't seem to care. My previous editorials hadn't done one jot of good.

Shut up, Emma.

When I had bought the paper from Marius Vandeventer, one of the pieces of advice he'd given me was to avoid writing essays that enlightened and informed. Stick to changing people's minds, make them move in the direction you want, stir the pot, show some passion. That, he said, was what good editorials accomplished.

But week after week, that wasn't easy. My brain felt arid. Maybe I had the postholiday blues.

My phone rang, making me jump in my swivel chair.

"Hey, Sluggly, let's get the hell out of town."

"Where?" I asked my brother, whose crackling voice had exploded in my ear.

"What about that very fine French restaurant out on the highway?" he inquired.

"Not open on Mondays," I replied. "Try again."

"Monroe? Everett? Hong Kong?"

"You can't have cabin fever," I pointed out. "You've only been here ten days."

"It's not cabin fever," Ben explained. "It's that I need to taste some really good food. Tonight's the night. I've got nothing on my slate, and I'll bet you don't, either."

"How true," I admitted. "I am not Alpine's

party girl."

"If not French, then seafood," Ben said. "Why is the ski lodge the only place where you can get decent fish in this town?"

"Alpine's a raw beef kind of place," I replied. "All those loggers."

"Most of the early ones were Scandinavians," Ben pointed out. "They like fish."

"So they go to the ski lodge. Or catch their own. When they get lucky." I flipped open the phone directory for Everett and went to the restaurant section. "How about Anthony's Homeport? It's on the water, by the naval shipyard and the marina."

"Sure," Ben said. "If you don't mind driving. Or do you want me to?"

"No!" I was emphatic. For years I've regarded my brother as the craziest driver I know, not counting Durwood Parker, retired Alpine pharmacist, who'd had his license pulled by the sheriff years earlier. Nothing was safe in Durwood's path: not pedestrians, not other vehicles, not concrete sidewalk planters. He could mow anything and anybody down, though, thank goodness, he'd never caused a serious injury. One of the worst accidents had occurred when he drove through the Bank of Alpine — before they had a drive-through window. The debacle had given the bank's officials the idea of creating a drive-up. According to Ginny Erlandson's husband, Rick, who worked at the bank, it was cheaper than making the full repair.

As for Ben, I don't know how he managed to keep from killing himself in East Lansing. My brother drove a beat-up Jeep that he'd owned since moving to Tuba City, Arizona, where he ministered to the Native American population. He had gotten used to rocky dirt roads and almost no traffic. When he'd come to Alpine the previous year to fill in for Father Den, I was sure he'd kill somebody — or himself — before he got out of town. I had been horrified when he'd informed me that he planned to drive to Alpine from East Lansing, but somehow he and the Jeep had survived.

"It's about an hour's drive to Everett," I said. "A little over fifty miles. But it's probably our best bet for a really good meal, especially seafood."

Ben told me he'd be ready by five. I didn't bother to make a reservation, since it was a Monday night, which usually is slow in the restaurant business. I saved my question about the Della Croce family for our preprandial cocktail time.

Vida returned to the newsroom shortly before two. There was no news from the sheriff's office.

"Doc Dewey will have preliminary results later today," she informed me with a disgusted expression. "He admits, however, that he'll probably have to send Elmer to Everett's medical examiner's office. You know Doc — he's even more cautious than Milo. Not a bad thing, of course, but sometimes frustrating."

"Especially when Everett gets busy and has to put us at the end of the waiting list," I remarked. "Any word of funeral arrangements?"

Vida shook her head. "The Nystroms go to the Episcopal church. Polly's choice. She was a Carter before marrying Elmer. Their son was named for his mother's family — English ancestry, I assume."

Scott still wasn't back from his meeting, and Leo had gone out to hustle ads. "Maybe," I said, as much to myself as to Vida, "I'll write an editorial on how strapped the sheriff's office is for personnel. This county's growing. Our population's over seven thousand. Milo's been shortchanged forever."

Vida frowned. "Are you suggesting a bond issue?"

I shrugged. "For now, I merely want to make readers aware of the sorry state of affairs. It affects the voters' safety."

Vida seemed skeptical. "They know," she said softly. "Look how narrowly the last school levy passed. People here believe in thrift."

"Thrift — or lack of vision?"

"Call it what you will." Vida turned to look at something on her desk. "I do wish Elsie Overholt would type and not write in longhand. She's very spidery."

"Elsie's ninety, at least," I noted. "She's earned the right to be spidery or any other thing she wants to be. Don't her reports make sense?"

"Usually," Vida conceded. "But this paragraph about Maud Dodd moving into the retirement home's indecipherable. I'll have to call on Elsie to see what she means."

"Call on? Or call?"

"Elsie's deaf as a cedar stump," Vida explained. "She won't get the kind of phone that will amplify her ability to hear. It's not really a problem to visit her. The retirement home is close to my house, so I'll stop in after work. Perhaps she'll invite me to dinner there. The meals are bland but wholesome."

Vida neglected to mention that the retirement home's food was also better than what she'd fix for herself at home. My House &

Home editor dispensed recipes and offered cooking advice on her page in the *Advocate,* but the truth was, she couldn't create a decent meal. I would rather graze on grass in my backyard than eat a casserole from the Runkel kitchen.

The afternoon dragged along. I did some research in our files for facts and figures to bolster my editorial about the sheriff skating on thin financial ice. Then I wrote an unsatisfactory first draft. By four-thirty I figured there'd be no news from Milo or Doc Dewey. It was pointless to write even a boilerplate story about Elmer's death. Most of the other loose ends were tied up for the weekly edition.

Scott still hadn't returned, and I was beginning to wonder what he was doing. Maybe a story had broken somewhere else after he'd finished his meeting at the chamber.

He walked in at four thirty-five, looking embarrassed and disheveled. "The sink blew up. At home, I mean. Tammy was in water up to her ankles."

"So now you're a plumber?"

He looked askance. "Not a very good one. But I can bail."

"What was the problem?" I asked, putting on a sympathetic face.

"That's the good news," Scott said. "For you. The water main broke at Alpine Way and Stump Hill Road. About three dozen households were affected. I've got the story and some pictures."

"Excellent," I declared, ignoring the misery of others for the sake of a newsy page one article. "The cause?"

"Roots got into the main line from a weeping willow in a corner house across from our condo," Scott informed me. "The Stuart place, in The Pines."

The Pines was Alpine's upscale development, built on acreage that originally had been a stump farm. The Stuarts owned what was once called Stuart's Stereo but had been rechristened Stuart Sound when technology rushed forward.

My own little log house was on Fir, four blocks directly east of the trouble spot. "Did the flooding go past Alpine Way?"

Scott grinned. "Not in your direction. But some of the houses in The Pines have problems."

"The people who live there can afford them," I said crassly. "Nancy and Cliff Stuart have made a pile of money."

Scott left my office to write the water main story. The mention of Nancy Stuart, who was Doc Dewey's sister, spurred me to call

Milo and check on the medical findings, if any.

"Doc won't rule on Elmer's death," Milo informed me. "He shipped Elmer off to Everett about an hour ago."

"Thanks for the heads-up," I said sarcastically.

"I told Vida that's what'd happen," the sheriff replied in an irritated voice.

I spoke in my most formal journalist's tone. "You did — but we didn't get confirmation."

"Shit. You want it in writing?"

It was useless to argue with Milo about media protocol. I got frustrated when he went by the book in a law enforcement investigation; he became irked when I stuck by my journalist's rules. And after all these years, he seemed to have no grasp of the deadline concept.

I just had time to hurry home and change clothes before I picked up Ben at the rectory. My brother was in civvies, a red sweater over a navy blue shirt and jeans. He didn't bother with a jacket. After all those years in the Arizona desert, and before that on the Mississippi Delta, he insisted he was getting acclimated to cold weather because his last two temporary assignments had been in Wisconsin and Michigan. I wasn't sure I believed him. He hadn't spent a full winter in either state.

The rain let up just before we crossed the flat, fertile sloughs outside of Everett. It was dark, of course, the sun having set beyond the Olympic Mountains at least an hour before we left the Cascades behind us. I mentioned to Ben that it was always better to drive the late afternoon and early evening westerly route in fall and winter. Otherwise, the sun can blind you when it suddenly appears from around the many bends of Highway 2.

"I miss the mountains," Ben said as traffic slowed just before we finished crossing the flats. "I didn't miss them that much in Arizona because of all the formations in the desert country. But the Middle West — that's different."

It took us another fifteen minutes to drive through Everett's rush-hour congestion. Shortly after six we reached Anthony's. I was right: The restaurant had several vacant tables, including one by a window where Ben and I could sit and watch the well-lighted marina.

"Some day," Ben said after we'd ordered a cocktail, "I'd like to live on a boat. Monks can have their spartan cells and all that — not that they always do — but I think I'd find true solitude on a boat. A small boat, of course."

"Where would you find your flock?" I asked. "On bigger boats?"

Ben shook his head. "No. I'd serve an island community like the San Juans. Maybe I can do that when I retire."

Through the window, we saw a young couple walking up the pier. Maybe they'd been working on their own boat. Maybe they were dreaming about having one of the bigger, more splendid craft that lay at anchor about thirty yards away.

"The San Juans would be wonderful," I said. "You'd be close."

Ben didn't say anything, but he smiled slightly.

We were comfortably silent for a moment or two, still staring outside. I hated having my brother go off again, probably for several months. Even though he didn't say so, I sensed he dreaded it, too. A priest's life is lonely. So was mine. There were times when I fought loneliness — for Ben, for Adam, and still, once in a great, sad, self-indulgent while, for Tom.

"Speaking of your flock," I said, breaking the silence, "I saw one of your Della Croces today."

"Oh?" Ben suddenly seemed wary.

"Who?"

"The wife," I said. "And the mother, I guess."

My brother sipped his drink. "They're not my Della Croces," he retorted. "They're Father Den's."

"You don't have to get grumpy about it," I snapped.

"I'm not grumpy." He looked at me with the same brown eyes that I possess. "I'm not here long enough to get involved in town gossip. If you want to talk about the Della Croces, yak it up with Dennis Kelly."

I waited until I was calmer. Even in middle age Ben and I had the ability to raise each other's hackles. I resented the ever-present if subtle sense of superiority that he claimed by right of being two years older; he had no patience with the pesky little sister who constantly invented new ways to badger and annoy him.

"Did I mention that Elmer Nystrom may have been murdered?"

Ben was still staring at me. "Yes. You talked about that on the way over here. So?"

"So the Della Croces are the Nystroms' next-door neighbors. That's how I happened to see Mrs. Della Croce today. She came out on her front porch while Vida and I were at the house."

"And," Ben said, apparently not reluctant to rile me again, "you played the perfect ghoul and announced that Elmer had been butchered in his own backyard."

"He wasn't butchered," I declared. "He may have been bashed to death. I'm a professional ghoul, by the way, and rarely perfect."

"Okay, okay," Ben said, and sighed. "I didn't mean to make you mad." *Yes, he did.* "But whatever's bothering Mrs. Della Croce isn't my business. She should talk to Kelly. She should also attend Mass regularly instead of four or five times a year."

Maybe that was why the woman had looked familiar. Perhaps I'd noticed Mrs. Della Croce on one of her rare visits to St. Mildred's. "I might do that," I said.

Ben's smile was sly. "Kelly may have his own ethics to shove in your face."

"If whatever problem Mrs. Della Croce wanted to talk about when she phoned the rectory wasn't under the seal of the confessional, Den will cooperate in a murder investigation," I pointed out somewhat stiltedly.

Ben chuckled. "Dismount from that high horse and order some food," he said. "I can tell when you're hungry. You get ornery."

My brother was right. I chose the yearling

Quilcene Bay fried oysters; he went for the alderwood planked salmon. We spent the rest of the meal talking about things that wouldn't evoke anger. What really bothered us, of course, was that we soon would be separated. Our family had dwindled to three: Ben, Adam, and me. Two celibate priests and a woman past the childbearing years meant we had only one another, and we were usually far apart. The years were flying by. There were far fewer of them that we could spend together.

Ben insisted on paying for dinner. "You've cooked for me on this trip; you fed me dozens of times when I was here for the six-month stint," he argued.

I agreed to let him play host. I noticed he didn't say how soon I might have a chance to repay him.

My cell phone rang while we were waiting for the return of his credit card. I was surprised to hear the sheriff's voice on the other end of the line.

"Vida told me you'd gone to Everett with your brother," Milo said, sounding uncharacteristically benign. "Have a nice dinner?"

"Very," I replied, suddenly on guard. "What's happening?" Milo wasn't one to make casual phone calls.

He paused. "They've stuck us into tomorrow afternoon."

"What?"

"SnoCo. The medical examiners. They won't get around to Elmer until tomorrow afternoon. And that's an optimistic prediction. A lot of people die this time of year after the holidays."

This was bad news for Milo, and it wasn't good for me, either. I had a deadline to meet.

"Damn," I said, glancing at Ben, who was watching me with curiosity. Suddenly I was curious, too. "How come you're calling to tell me this?"

"Well . . . you're in Everett, right? The head guy over there tonight is Brian McDonough. I hear he's pretty religious. Catholic, I mean. I thought maybe if you and your brother stopped by . . ."

Priest in tow. Milo must have been pretty desperate to ask such a favor. I wondered what had galvanized him into action. It wasn't his usual style.

"You think Ben — who, I should tell you, is wearing his civvies and looks about as clerical as you do — can just show up, make the sign of the cross, and presto! SnoCo's good Catholic McDonough will start carving Elmer up before our very eyes?"

"It can't hurt." Milo sounded strained.

"Okay." I made a face at Ben. "We'll try."

"Thanks. I'll let them know you're coming. Remember," Milo went on, "the morgue is at Paine Field. You need directions?"

I did, taking them down in the notebook I always carried in my purse. Ben and I left the restaurant five minutes later, headed back to the freeway. Paine Field was south of downtown, home not only to the county airport but to the Boeing Company — and the morgue. Milo knew how to approach it only coming from Alpine. It turned out to be a ten-mile detour from Anthony's Homeport. I was no longer in a good mood by the time we arrived.

"This is stupid," I declared as we got out of the car. "I'd like to know what Milo told the ME's office when he let them know we were on our way — that Elmer had spoken from beyond, asking to convert?"

My brother didn't say anything.

After identifying ourselves and proving we weren't carrying concealed weapons, we were directed to the morgue by the guard on duty. I steeled myself as I entered the large, brightly lighted room with its accents of functional stainless steel and odors I had no wish to identify. Two bodies were being subjected to God only knows what kind of dissection. I didn't look but followed Ben as we made our way to an office with a large window that looked not outside but back into the work area.

Brian McDonough was fiftyish, with thinning fair hair and a round, rubicund face. He looked up from his paperwork when Ben stood in the doorway while I hovered behind him.

"Father?" the ME said, taking off his rimless glasses and standing up. "Sheriff Dodge told me you were coming. What can I do for you?"

"Nothing," Ben replied. "We're here on a fool's errand."

McDonough looked puzzled. "I don't understand."

Ben shrugged. "Sheriff Dodge is under the misapprehension that my presence would expedite Elmer Nystrom's autopsy. As a Protestant, he somehow thinks that all Catholics must be conspiring either against him or, in this case, for him. By the way, this is my sister, Emma."

I stepped forward to shake hands with McDonough, wondering whether Milo had told the ME that I was the *Advocate*'s editor and publisher. I hoped the sheriff had been discreet. Very few public officials liked to have media types barging into their work-place.

McDonough put his glasses back on and eyed both of us with curiosity. "In other words, Dodge thinks I'll move your SkyCo deceased up on the slice-and-dice list?"

Ben shrugged. "I guess so. You'd think he wouldn't be so naïve."

McDonough fingered his chin. "Did you know the dead man, Father?"

Ben shook his head. "Only by reputation. He seems to have been a very decent kind of guy, especially for somebody who worked for a car dealership. You know how that goes with repair bills."

"Don't I, though?" The ME groaned. "You wouldn't believe what it cost the last time I went for an annual checkup on my SUV. They found more alleged problems than I could ever imagine. It came to over a grand. But what can you do?" He spread his hands helplessly.

"Nystrom wasn't like that, I gather," Ben said. "My sister here tells me everybody sang his praises."

Cue Emma. "That's true," I put in, discovering that I could talk, after all. Between Ben and Vida, I was feeling more and more like a finger puppet. "Elmer was honest — and kind, too."

McDonough nodded thoughtfully. "So Dodge thinks there may have been foul play? That doesn't sound right. I mean, why is it the good guys who get whacked?"

"A fair question," Ben said, and left the query hanging in the air.

"Justice," McDonough said. "Dodge is a good lawman. It's not his fault he lives in a small county and doesn't have any money behind him. God only knows — and I mean that literally — we could use more funding right here. SnoCo is growing like crazy."

"Then we shouldn't take up any more of your time," Ben said, taking a backward step. "I can't apologize for Dodge. He meant well."

"Oh . . ." McDonough smiled sheepishly. "Why not? A couple of the cases we've got on the list are old coots whose families are a bunch of fussbudgets. Some people can't grasp the idea that their parents or grand-parents just die of old age. They have to know how and why. Well, they can wait. Tell Dodge I'll have his report by noon tomorrow." He held out his hand again. "And say a prayer for me, will you, Father? I could use it."

"We all can," Ben said. "Just don't tell those non-Catholics how cliquish we really are."

McDonough smiled broadly, revealing a slight gap between his front teeth. "It's our little secret, Father. *Pax vobiscum.* Hey — I remember that much Latin, anyway."

McDonough shook hands with both of us. He stood in the doorway as we made our exit. "I'll get started right away," he called after us. "Remember, news by noon."

I could hardly forget.

FOUR

By late Tuesday morning I still had to leave a big hole in the front page for the Nystrom story. Vida had written the obituary, and Scott had done an interview with the Nordby brothers as a sidebar. Skunk and Trout extolled Elmer's virtues as a loyal, hardworking employee and "a true friend to Alpine's General Motors customers."

I asked Vida if she'd been in touch with Mrs. Nystrom or the son.

"No," she replied. "I did call the Episcopal church but was told they hadn't scheduled the funeral yet. I wrote 'services pending' at the end of my obituary. I can change that at the last minute if we hear anything before deadline."

"That figures," I said, going over to the coffeemaker and refilling my mug, "though the autopsy is supposed to be done by noon. I'll check in with Milo before I go to lunch. At least he called to say he was grateful to

Ben for moving things along."

"Very shrewd of your brother," Vida declared. "He understands human nature rather well. On the other hand, I've found Catholics *are* quite cliquish."

I held my tongue. It was useless to argue with Vida about religion or politics or any other topic on which she held strong opinions. Since that included everything under the sun, I'd learned restraint long ago.

She wasn't finished talking, however. "As for Elsie Overholt, she had some interesting gossip, though I don't dare let her include it in her column or even allude to it in 'Scene.' "

"What was it?" I asked, carrying my coffee mug over to her desk.

"Well, now," Vida began, with her usual smug expression when dishing the dirt, "I mentioned to you how I couldn't decipher what she'd written about Maud Dodd moving into the retirement home as of New Year's Day. Of course she didn't actually move on the first, it being a holiday, but settled in last Monday, the thirtieth."

I nodded. "You said Elsie's handwriting was spidery."

"Correct. I *thought* she'd written 'Maud couldn't want to move out of her family home because of the fossil at Chuck.' That made no sense, of course, but what she'd scrawled was, and I quote," Vida continued, reading from Maud's original submission, " 'Maud couldn't *wait* to move out of her *familiar* home because of the *gossip* at *church*.' "

"Aha." My interest meter registered high marks. "What was the gossip?"

Vida scowled at me. "I wish I knew. Elsie didn't know, and Maud had company. I *will* find out, given time and opportunity."

"Which church?" I asked.

"Trinity Episcopal," Vida replied. "I'll go to the source, that is, Maud. Regis and Edith Bartleby are far too holier-than-thou to reveal anything," she added, referring to the Episcopal vicar and his wife.

Back in my cubbyhole I toyed with the idea of calling Dennis Kelly and asking him about the Della Croces. But the more I thought about it, the more I realized that I was going beyond the call of journalism and being just plain nosy. The fact that the Della Croce family lived next door to the Nystroms wasn't a good enough reason to pry into the private lives of my fellow parishioners. Father Den probably would cut me off as Ben had done, although my pastor would be more tactful than my brother.

Instead, I polished my editorial urging more funding for the sheriff's department. Just before I shipped the finished piece off to Kip in the back shop, I called Milo.

"I'm beating your drum," I told him. "By the end of this week you're going to owe me big time, big guy. How about leaning on somebody to fix those potholes in front of my little log house?"

"What's landed on your brain this time?" The sheriff sounded slightly less than enthusiastic.

I explained about the editorial I'd just written. "What more can I do?" I asked in a plaintive tone.

"I could tell you," Milo responded in his slightly laconic voice, "but you'd say no."

"You're right." I wasn't in the mood to flirt, even over the phone. "Instead, I'll say, 'How about that autopsy report?' "

"Not in yet," he replied. "It's only ten to twelve."

"Where are you having lunch?"

"You want to stalk me?"

"If need be. I have a deadline, remember?"

"Thought maybe I'd stick around in case McDonough or whoever called after twelve. Maybe I'll send Lori over to the Burger Barn to pick up something."

Lori Cobb was Milo's new receptionist

85

who had replaced the Alaska-bound Toni Andreas. Lori was also the granddaughter of one of our aged county commissioners as well as a recent graduate of Skykomish Community College. She seemed brighter than Toni, although not quite as decorative. Lori was a long, lean blond with plain features but a pleasant manner.

"Maybe I'll wander down to join you," I said.

"Fine. Bring your own grub."

I told him I would and hung up immediately as the light on my phone flashed to indicate I had another call.

"Is this Bel Canto?" Rolf Fisher inquired. "I've got the tickets, if you've got the time."

"Good," I said. "I've never heard *Norma* in the flesh."

"There's usually plenty of that with bel canto singers," Rolf said. "They need the padding to get through all those vocal gymnastics."

"What night?" I asked, paging through my daily calendar.

"Saturday, the twenty-fifth," he replied. "You'll come Friday? We can have a leisurely dinner and then . . . a leisurely evening with my dog, Spree."

"Sounds lovely," I remarked. "Pray for rain."

"Of course. I don't want you getting stranded up in the mountains." He paused. "Anything interesting in your next edition?"

I told him I wasn't sure; we might have a big story developing. "What about you?" I asked. "Are you awaiting breaking news on the AP wire?"

"We always are," Rolf said. "We play the waiting game. I'd like to get out in the field more, frankly. I miss the reporting part. I used to think I was too old for it, but I get stale on the desk."

At that moment I saw Scott come into the newsroom. A strange idea popped into my head. "Do you mean that, or is it just the postholiday doldrums?"

"No," Rolf insisted. "I'm serious. For once. I know — not my style."

Leaning forward, I watched Scott take a brown paper bag out of his desk drawer. He removed a plastic bag containing a sandwich. I realized he'd been bringing his lunch to work more often since he'd gotten married. Maybe he couldn't afford to eat out. If he and Tamara moved on, could I dare ask Rolf to work for the *Advocate*?

But how would he like brown-bagging it? How could he endure small-town life? How could he stand working for me? And how far might he go to become a reporter again?

Probably not as far as Alpine. I dismissed my odd idea.

"I hate to tell you this," Rolf said, "but I'm off to the Union Square Grill for lunch with an old college buddy. Advertising type, but decent all the same."

"Wish I were there."

"Where?"

"Never mind." I rang off.

The Burger Barn was about as far from the Union Square Grill as any gourmand could imagine, but that was where I headed. I was forced to stand six-deep in line for takeout. Lori Cobb was being waited on at the counter, probably getting Milo's standard cheeseburger, fries, and coffee. At least the coffee tasted better than what the sheriff's office served. But now that I thought about it, I hadn't tasted Lori's attempts at coffee brewing. It had to be an improvement over the swill Toni had made.

Seven minutes later — I clocked it on my watch — I requested a hamburger dip au jus with fries and a pineapple malt. They were out of pineapple, so I asked for vanilla instead.

I was heading for the door when I saw Milo coming in.

"Changed my mind," he said. "Changed my routine, too. I want a double bacon burger. I gave my order to Lori. She could use some meat on her bones."

"What about McDonough?" I asked as Milo steered us toward a booth that had just emptied.

"Wait till we sit," he said as a waitress began to bus the vacated table.

We waited. Finally I put down my take-out bag, complete with its red barn logo showing a cow going in the door and coming out as a hamburger on the other side.

"Well?" I said, unable to hide my impatience.

"I got the call right after I talked to you," he replied, signaling for coffee. "Blow to the back of the head with something metal. Elmer's skull was crushed. He probably died quick. Not much blood loss, no hemorrhaging, just a smallish cut from whatever he got hit with."

"Which was . . . ?"

Milo shrugged. "Farm or garden implement. Shovel, hoe, even a rake. Possibly a tool. I told Erskine that I didn't see anything like that in the henhouse. McDonough had left after he'd performed the autopsy and put in his report. Bill Blatt and Dustin Fong went out there this morning to look around the rest of the place. They'll be back as soon as they've had lunch at the Bourgettes' diner."

"Your deputies didn't call anything in to you?"

Milo shook his head. "No. But that doesn't mean they didn't find something. In fact, they could have bagged a whole bunch of stuff. They wouldn't know offhand what was a weapon and what wasn't."

I'd removed my food from the bag and brushed some hard roll crumbs off my lap. "Your official pronouncement?"

The sheriff munched on a couple of fries. "Possible homicide."

"You aren't sure?"

He shrugged. "It could be an accident. But a pretty freaky one. Whatever bashed in Elmer's head was metal. Steel, to be exact. If there wasn't any sign of the weapon — if you want to call it that — inside the chicken house, then it'd be pretty weird if Elmer had banged into the thing outdoors and come all the way back inside."

I agreed. "But 'possible homicide' is a bit weak."

"You want headlines? Why don't you just run a big skull and crossbones on the front page?"

"I like that," I said.

"You would."

I ignored the sarcasm. "Estimated time of death?"

"Seven-fifteen, seven-thirty yesterday morning. That's when Elmer usually went out to the henhouse before he headed for work."

"Nobody saw or heard anything?"

Milo shot me a dirty look. "We only found out we had a homicide on our hands about five minutes ago. Anyway, you know damned well I wouldn't tell you any details so soon in the investigation. Go with the facts. You've got enough for your front page."

I feigned typing on the Formica countertop. " 'Sheriff Dodge has no suspects, no motives, no weapon, no understanding of the public's need to know.' "

"You're a pain in the ass, Emma." He sipped more coffee.

I knew that — at least as far as Milo was concerned. There was certainly a big story in the bare bones of the case. If murder wasn't sensational enough, Elmer Nystrom apparently had been well liked, well known, and well respected. I shut up and resumed eating.

It's a wonder my lunch stayed down. I'd barely finished when I saw Spencer Fleetwood stroll into the Burger Barn. The sheriff had already gotten his bill and was getting out of the booth when Spence spotted him.

"The lovely Lori told me you were here with the equally lovely Emma," Spence said to Milo, having the gall to wink at me. "I just got in town about an hour ago. Rey Fernandez told me something was afoot."

"We're working on it," Milo said, putting on his regulation jacket. "We can talk later." He squeezed past Spence and loped toward the entrance.

"I think," my nemesis said, "I've just been given the brush-off."

"I do believe you're right," I said, digging into my purse for my wallet. I'd get my own bill from our waitress and hightail it out of Spence's purview.

But Mr. Radio wasn't going to make it easy for me. He had the nerve to slide into the booth beside me. I was trapped.

"What's this about Nystrom?" he murmured in that mellifluous voice so familiar to KSKY's listeners. "Do I sense foul play or a nasty accident with the chickens?"

While I was grateful to Milo for stalling Spence, I knew that the story would break over the radio before we could go to press. Elmer's death was a matter of public record, as was the medical examiner's report. But that didn't mean I had to offer up the facts on one of the Burger Barn's serviceable white platters.

"Did you have a nice trip?" I inquired in my sweetest tone.

"Very," Spence replied. "Maui, Kauai. Very nice this time of year."

"I've never been to Hawaii," I said, trying to avoid looking at Spence's hawklike profile. Adam had gone to school there for a short time, but his impoverished mother had never made it to the island paradise.

"No? You should go. It's a great vacation spot." Spence reached in front of me to remove one of the plastic-covered menus from behind the napkin holder. "Of course, it can get crowded, especially at Kaanapali Beach. I did get in some golf there, though. Wonderful course — Robert Trent Jones design. But Kauai isn't quite as popular. Next time I'll try Molokai. It's getting to be quite a destination place."

"What'd they do with the lepers?" I asked.

"That's not worthy of you," Spence said, glancing at the menu. "Same old, same old." He sighed. "Really good seafood, too. You ought to treat yourself. I mean it. You can go on and on about how much you like the rain, but you've got to admit that gray skies for six months in a row can get you down."

"No, they don't."

Spence chuckled. "You're a hard case, Emma Lord." He turned as the waitress, a strawberry blonde named Bunny — or so her name tag stated — came to give me my bill and take Spence's order. "I'll have the cold turkey sandwich on multigrain bread, lettuce, tomato, mayo, sprouts. All white meat," Spence informed Bunny. "Black coffee and maybe a slice of the apple pie if it's really good today." He dropped his voice. "Is it, Bunny?"

"Oh, yeah," Bunny replied. "It's great."

He offered her his most ingratiating smile. "I trust your sound judgment, Bunny. Thanks."

Giggling, Bunny hopped away.

"Move it," I said to Spence. "I have to get back to work."

"Deadline day, right?" Spence didn't budge. "You're not going anywhere until you tell me why I should hire Ed Bronsky."

"What?"

"Rey tells me Ed came by this morning to apply for his job," Spence explained, looking serious. "Rey's leaving Alpine at the end of the month or whenever I can find a replacement. He finished his AA degree in December and wants to try a larger radio market. Ed wants Rey's spot. He said you recommended him. What does he know about radio, and why does he want to work?"

"Because he's broke," I said bluntly. "As for what he knows about radio, I can't tell you. He can turn one on, I suppose. But I certainly didn't recommend him for a job with you. Ed's dreaming."

"That's what I figured," Spence said. "I have to get — or train — a replacement who can act as an engineer as well as do the on-air stuff. I plan to get somebody else from the college."

I didn't blame Spence. Students, especially older ones like Rey, were a good investment. They needed the experience and were willing to work for meager wages. I'd thought about hiring a journalism student if and when the time came for Scott to move on. It'd be taking a chance, but maybe I'd get lucky as Spence had and find someone who was more mature than your average nineteen-year-old.

"I can't help you," I said, "when it comes to Ed. I feel kind of sorry for him, but I'm not recommending him for a job at your station."

"Not even to solicit advertisers?"

I managed to keep a straight face. The best thing that could happen to me when it came to competing for ads would be having Ed work for KSKY. He'd send potential merchants running like deer during hunting season.

"That'd be up to you," I said. "Come on, Spence, let me out of here. It's one o'clock."

He hesitated. "You won't tell me about Nystrom?"

"Do your own digging," I snapped as he finally got out of the booth. "After all," I added, standing in the aisle, "I did my share. I found the body."

It was a great exit line, but I knew Spence would scoop me anyway. Back in the office, I wrote the lead story. After I'd sent it off to Kip in the back shop, I walked up Front Street to the Nordby Brothers GM dealership between Sixth and Seventh.

The showroom faced Front; the car lot was on the other side of the main building next to the railroad tracks. As usual, a couple of men were browsing around the display models, especially a hot yellow Corvette. They were unmolested by sales personnel. In fact, I didn't see any sales personnel on the floor. Behind a glass partition I spotted the brother who must have been Trout, talking on the phone. He definitely had fish lips.

"A beauty," I heard one of the men remark.

I knew they weren't talking about me. They meant the 'Vette. I had, however, caught Trout's eye. He was putting down the phone and smiling in my direction.

"Emma Lord," he said, coming out from behind the partition and offering his hand. "Don't tell me you fired Leo and are doing the ad job yourself."

"Never," I asserted, shaking his hand. "But I am here on business. I'm very sorry about Elmer. It's a loss for you and your brother."

Trout's fish lips turned down. "Hell, yes. So damned sudden. Come on in." He led the way into his office.

"Looky-loos," he said, nodding at the two men in the showroom. "Some guys spend their lunch hours in here, just staring at the vehicles. Down the line they might actually buy one. But it won't be that Corvette."

"Out of my price range," I remarked, sitting in a customer chair that was far more comfortable than what I provided for visitors at the *Advocate*. But then, I wasn't catering to people I necessarily wanted to feel at ease. "Who would you sell that car to in Alpine?" I inquired.

Trout smiled wryly. "Ordinarily, nobody.

Some of the small-town dealerships borrow a really hot car just for show purposes. Having a 'Vette like that on the floor brings in potential customers who can't fork out fifty, sixty grand but may buy something a lot cheaper. But in this case, I may have a buyer. Or did, until today. We'll see."

I hadn't come to discuss car sales, but I wanted Trout's cooperation. "That one's a convertible. Isn't it sort of impractical for Alpine?"

"Hey," Trout said, leaning closer in his padded swivel chair, "when it comes to a car like that and a buyer who can't live without it, I could sell the danged thing practically without an engine. It's like true love. There's no way to get over it."

"True enough," I said, recalling the secondhand Jaguar I'd owned for years simply because I'd always wanted one. What I hadn't considered was the frequent and expensive repair bills. "You and your brother have a good reputation in this community. So did Elmer. Was he as wonderful as everyone says?"

Trout made a clicking noise with his tongue. "You bet. We were so lucky to inherit him when Skunk and I bought the dealership from Old Man Jensen almost twenty years ago. My brother and me were pretty green: We thought we should start fresh, can everybody, hire our own people, especially guys we'd grown up with who knew about cars. But ol' Jensen, he said Elmer came with the dealership. If we didn't keep him on, the deal was off." Trout shrugged and chuckled. "So we did like he told us, and never been sorry for it."

I assumed that Trout hadn't yet heard that Elmer might have been murdered, so I had to skirt the obvious questions. "Did customers ever get mad at Elmer?"

"Heck, no." Trout hooked his fingers in the empty belt loops of his polyester pants. He wore wide brown suspenders over a bright yellow shirt. "Nobody could get mad at the guy. He treated the customers like royalty. Oh, he'd give 'em the occasional lecture about maintenance and taking pride in your vehicle, but that was always for their own good. But never any shuck-and-jive about when your car was ready or ordering a wrong part or screwing with an estimate. Organized, too, and his work area was always neat as a pin. He was tops. Look . . ." Trout pushed his chair away from the desk and folded his pudgy hands in his lap. "We got Nissan across the street, Honda and Toyota in town, too. You drive a . . . Honda, right?" He saw me nod. "That's fine. Those

Jap cars are good. Danged good. But we manage to keep right up with 'em in this town, and a truckload of the credit goes to Elmer. Owners know they can trust him when it comes to parts and repairs." Trout hung his head. "*Knew* they could trust him. Dang it, I can't believe he's gone. What'll we do without him?"

I asked if Elmer had someone working directly under him.

Trout made a face, which emphasized his big lips. "Yeah — half a dozen over the years. The one we got now is Dink Tolberg's son, Alex. He's young, just out of that auto mechanics course they got at the college. But you know these kids nowadays." He shrugged again.

"It can be a problem," I allowed.

Trout was looking out into the showroom. "The looky-loos are gone. Maybe they decided to go eat something. Here comes Skunk. I wonder if I should call Carter," he said, more to himself than to me.

"That would be very considerate," I said, also getting up.

"Oh, I already talked to Polly," Trout said, walking slowly out of the office. "She was holding up better than you'd expect. I meant calling Carter about that car. I suppose it's bad timing."

"What car?" I asked, nodding at Skunk, who was tending to a smudge on a dark green Saab.

"The 'Vette." Trout jerked a thumb at the classy sports car. "Carter's the one who's interested in buying it. I wonder if he's changed his mind now that his father's dead."

FIVE

Vida was requesting items for her "Scene Around Town" gossip column from her colleagues. "I have one Christmas tree thrown away with several ornaments still on it at a house on Cascade Street," she said as she gazed through her big glasses at the computer screen she'd grudgingly learned to use in recent months. "The latest Gustavson, Rikki, aged fourteen months, refusing to relinquish his Baby New Year top hat after the family holiday brunch — I ought to know, I was there. That awful child pulled the hat down over his head and it got stuck on his enormous ears, and he shrieked like a banshee. Furthermore, the food was perfectly dreadful, especially that ridiculous couscous."

Leo looked up from the floor where he'd dropped his matches. "Duchess," he said, using the nickname Vida loathed, "you subscribe to a recipe service. Couscous has been in for years."

"Then it's time for it to be out," Vida declared. "It tastes like postage stamp glue, and it's just an exotic name for rice. Where was I? Oh — Valentine's already on display at Alpine Stationers, Blue Sky Dairy delivering the last of this season's eggnog, Francine Wells showing off the redesigned diamond and platinum wedding ring Warren gave her for Christmas. Come, come — who has something?"

I considered the two men ogling the yellow Corvette at Nordby Brothers, but I didn't know their names. Besides, the dealership was already getting news coverage in this week's edition, even if it was of the unwelcome sort.

"Two goldfish floating upside down in a bowl at the pet store," Scott offered. "Or is that too grim?"

"It is," Vida informed him. "Something more cheerful, please."

"That leaves out Ed," I remarked.

Vida shot me a dirty look. "It's always good to leave out Ed."

Leo snapped his finger. "I saw something. The Reverend Poole riding his tractor lawn mower down Fourth Street yesterday afternoon. Don't ask why. I didn't. But this is a weird time of year to mow your grass.

Maybe it's a Baptist thing."

"Very well," Vida said. "I'll use that. One more."

"I've got one," I said suddenly. "Stella and Richie Magruder's grandchildren — the twin boys — standing at the top of First Hill with a brand-new sled and no snow."

Vida passed judgment. "Poignant but acceptable."

I'd been standing in the doorway to my office. As Vida entered the latest tidbits, I walked over to her desk. "What did Milo make of that obit on Elmer? I didn't ask him at lunch because I was verging on being a nag."

Vida looked disgusted. "He thought it must be a very unfortunate joke." She paused and pursed her lips. "Of course that was his initial reaction. You know Milo — like most men, he needs to think things through and come to his own conclusions."

"A joke seems unlikely," I pointed out.

"Of course it does," Vida agreed. "But you must admit, it's very strange. Surely Milo must realize that the only person who knew in advance that Elmer was going to die would be the person who killed him."

"Yes. Or Elmer himself," I said. "Maybe he had a premonition."

"Elmer doesn't strike me as a fanciful

person," Vida noted. "Perhaps he had been threatened. On the other hand, he must have been a very careful and well-organized man. Polly might know if he'd written his obituary to save her — or Carter — the trouble by doing it himself."

"Possibly," I allowed. "A trustworthy and conscientious service department manager would want to help customers prevent problems before they happen. Elmer probably was the type who considered all sorts of contingencies. But he wouldn't have mailed it to you."

Vida sighed. "I regret in some ways I didn't know Elmer better. Except for anything complicated, my nephew Billy has always been kind enough to work on my Buick. He's quite handy with cars, you know."

"He's probably saved you a bundle of money," I pointed out.

"Oh, my, yes. But I always buy him ice cream afterward."

I didn't comment. Bill Blatt was now over thirty, but that didn't mean he had lost his taste for ice cream. I was about to say something else, but Vida had craned her neck to look around me as someone came into the newsroom. "Tara, how nice to see you! Have you brought us a news item just before deadline?" The hint of reproach in Vida's voice may have been detectable only by me.

Tara Wesley, who owns Parker's Pharmacy along with her husband, Garth, approached Vida's desk. The usually unruffled Tara seemed tentative, as if she were approaching the prison warden, begging for special privileges.

"Hi, Vida, Emma," she said with barely a nod at me but her eyes fixed on my House & Home editor. "I have a favor to ask."

"Of course," Vida said smoothly. "What is it? Do sit," she urged, indicating her visitor's chair.

I backed away, going over to Scott's vacant desk to see if he'd left any loose ends in his stories or photos before we went to press. He was a good writer, an excellent photographer, and a better-than-average interviewer, but he still had trouble meeting deadlines.

Tara had sat down, though she obviously wasn't relaxed. "This morning on my way to the drugstore I mailed you a story about Jessica."

"Oh, yes," Vida said. "Your pretty daughter."

Out of the corner of my eye, I saw Tara nod. What I wasn't seeing was any problems

Scott had left on his desk or in his in-basket. But Tara had aroused my curiosity. I stalled to listen in, pretending to concentrate on my reporter's work area.

"Ordinarily," Tara went on, "I would have dropped the little story off, but I had to mail three Christmas cards to people I didn't expect to hear from and whose greetings didn't get delivered until Friday or Saturday. You know — every year you hope to eliminate some names from your list, but they pop up anyway."

"Of course. So awkward," Vida said in her most sympathetic tone.

"I put the cards and a couple of bills and the article all in the mailbox by our house," Tara continued. "But it turns out that I should have held off. The story's no good."

"Oh?" Vida was giving Tara her most owlish expression.

"You see," Tara said, leaning forward in the chair, "Jessica quit the UW at the end of the winter quarter. She doesn't want to follow in our footsteps and become a pharmacist, after all. She's decided to take some time off from school."

"Very sensible," Vida said. "There's no point in wasting money on tuition these days when you don't have a goal."

"Yes, right," Tara agreed. "Jessica's only

eighteen. Anyway, she decided to get a job here in town. So yesterday she started work for Dr. Nystrom as a receptionist. That's what I wrote the little story about because I know you like to print that sort of thing."

"Yes, always of interest to our readers," Vida said, shifting slightly in her chair, which I recognized as a sign of impatience. "And?"

"She quit this morning."

"Oh?"

"So would you please just toss the thing out when it comes?"

"Of course," Vida assured her. "My, my — this hasn't been a very good day for Dr. Nystrom. Not, certainly, that Tara quit because his father passed away. Or was your daughter terribly upset by the news?"

Tara had gotten to her feet and was putting the hood of her jacket up over her salt-and-pepper hair. "I'm not sure Tara knew about that when she gave notice. I haven't had a chance to really talk to her. Both Garth and I are working today. Frankly, this is embarrassing. I expected better of Tara. When she worked for us at the pharmacy, she was very reliable."

"A mismatch, perhaps," Vida said. "Personalities sometimes clash. I must confess my grandson, Roger, had a bad experience this past summer working for Sky Dairy. He and Norm Carlson simply never hit it off. Norm can be very unreasonable and demanding. That's terribly hard on a young person, particularly when it was Roger's first job."

And his only one so far, I thought. Along about August 1, Roger had finally gotten off of his fat rear end and gone to work at the dairy. He'd lasted less than a week. Leo insisted the kid had fallen into the ice cream vat, but I wasn't sure I believed him. It was more likely that he'd gone to sleep on the job or simply not shown up.

Tara said goodbye, remembering to include me as an afterthought. I was used to it when Alpiners came calling on Vida.

"Drat," Vida said, using her strongest oath. "I wish I'd gotten to know Carter Nystrom better. His name keeps cropping up."

"Of course it does," I said, walking back toward her desk. "His father died this morning. Though I admit, I was surprised to hear it in another context when I was at the car dealership."

Vida regarded me with interest. "Oh?"

I told her about the yellow Corvette that Carter was interested in buying. "I suppose he can afford it," I said, "though he's only been in practice a couple of years."

"Orthodontists charge the world," Vida remarked. "Still, you'd think he'd have student debts. I've always understood that doctors and dentists and such have to pay off some very large loans before they actually start making money."

"Did Polly ever work?" I asked.

"Heavens, no!" Vida's expression was disparaging. Upon becoming a single mother in her forties, she had begun her career with the *Advocate* to support her three daughters. "I've always thought of Polly as a hothouse flower. Pampered. Catered to. Husband and son only too eager to wait on her hand and foot. You wouldn't believe the fuss that was made a few years ago when Polly had hammertoe surgery. You would have thought she'd had all of her extremities amputated. Elmer and Carter were running around like chickens with their heads cut off." Vida clucked her tongue, sounding appropriately like a noisy hen.

"I sort of recall that," I said. "It happened not long after I moved to Alpine."

Vida nodded. "That's right. Carter hadn't yet started college. It's no wonder I've never been particularly friendly with Polly. I did try when they moved here. I had an ice cream social for her. But I heard afterward that she'd complained about the cookies I served. Imagine! Talk about an ingrate."

Maybe that was why Carter had decided to go into dentistry. If Vida had made the cookies, his mother might have broken a couple of teeth trying to chew them. But I merely nodded sympathetically.

"Very critical," Vida murmured. "And inclined to embroider her tales. That serves no purpose with gossip. The truth is always sufficiently damaging. When it's told, of course."

I left Vida to ponder Polly Nystrom's errant tongue. I had some loose ends of my own to clear up before five o'clock. One of them was the sheriff. I called him around four.

"Anything on that obit Vida gave you?" I asked.

"Like what?"

"Invisible ink. Poisoned paper. A secret code." I paused. "What do you think, Sheriff? Fingerprints, DNA, how it was generated — what you law enforcement types call *evidence*."

"Get real," Milo said in a tired voice. "We don't have expensive forensic testing equipment in SkyCo. The damned thing went over to Everett. And what kind of DNA do you expect? A long blond hair?"

"The envelope," I snapped. "Whoever licked it would leave DNA." Did Milo think I never watched TV?

"Maybe, maybe not. The sender could have moistened the flap with water." He sighed into the receiver. "Frankly, I don't know what to make of it unless we're dealing with a nut case. You're not going to print anything about the obit, are you?"

"No," I replied. "It can wait until we — you — find out who might have sent it to Vida."

That was fine with Milo. "By the way," he added, "Spence broke the homicide story on the three o'clock news."

"Of course."

"Sorry."

"You can't help it," I said. "Who'd he get to?"

"Dustin," Milo replied. "You know how damned polite he is. Anyway, he couldn't lie."

"What did he and Bill find at the Nystrom place?"

"What you'd expect," Milo answered. "Lots of garden tools, all the usual hardware. They kept that place up, I guess. Hard to tell this time of year, when nothing's in bloom."

Since I was fond of puttering in my own sloping patch of mountainside, I sensed who was good at gardening and who was not. "I imagine their yard is very pretty during the spring and summer. Shrubs, a fruit tree, probably lots of flowers. If a place looks tidy in January, you can bet it's lovely during the growing season."

"I'm not much good at that stuff," Milo confessed. "Old Mulehide used to nag me about pruning this and planting that on my days off. All I wanted to do was veg out in front of the TV. She never figured that law enforcement was hard work."

I'd often heard that complaint about Milo's ex-wife, who'd finally left him for a high school teacher. Fortunately, I'd never met Old Mulehide, or Tricia, as she was known to the less bitter. Maybe it was just as well that we hadn't crossed paths. I might have liked her.

"Give me a quote," I said.

"About Old Mulehide?"

"Of course not. Something to wrap up the front-page story."

"Make one up," Milo drawled. "That's what you usually do, isn't it?"

In the past, I had put words in Milo's mouth, but never without running them by him first. "Okay. How about 'The victim

113

was a well-respected and a well-liked member of this community. The sheriff's office is expending every effort to solve this tragic murder.' How's that?"

Milo didn't respond immediately. "Ditch the 'expending.' It doesn't sound like me."

That was accurate. I suggested "will exert"; Milo quibbled briefly but gave in. I rang off and finished the article.

After conferring with Kip MacDuff about the *Advocate*'s layout and checking the wire for any last-minute news that might have had a local tie-in, I shut down my computer and got ready to go home.

But I was antsy. As much as retreating to my little log house appealed to me on a winter night, I felt there must be something I could do to help move the Nystrom investigation forward. It wasn't conceit. Over the years, I'd become so involved in various homicides that I couldn't dismiss this one just because we'd met our deadline. Instead, I felt compelled to act.

But I didn't know what to do.

When in doubt, ask Vida.

She was putting on her raincoat when I went into the newsroom. "What are you doing this evening?" I inquired.

"As a matter of fact," she replied shamelessly, "I'm having the Bartlebys to dinner."

I was startled. "Is this a date you made in advance?"

"No," she admitted. "I called this afternoon." She had the grace to look sheepish. "They're going to England next month for some sort of Episcopal — or Anglican — I can never quite understand the distinction — convocation or such. I decided to do a pretrip article."

"You're a fraud, Vida," I said.

"Yes, but they don't know that." She buttoned her raincoat. "I was fortunate that they didn't have a previous commitment."

"You really don't expect Regis and Edith to gossip about their parishioners, do you? They're the soul of genteel discretion."

"Yes, yes," Vida said, gathering up her purse and gloves. "Nor will they gossip in the way that most people do. But they'll say things, and discreet or not, interesting information can slip out." She peered at me through her big glasses. "Do you want to join us?"

I hesitated. Revealing comments about the Nystroms versus Vida's awful cooking. Me as interloper versus my role as editor and publisher. Two non-Episcopalians versus the vicar and his wife.

"No, but thanks all the same," I said. "I should e-mail Adam. Besides, if there's any information to be had, you'll get it on your own." *And my stomach won't have to suffer.*

"That's true," Vida allowed. "Nor would we want them to think we were ganging up on them, as the phrase goes."

I agreed. Still, I was left at loose ends. After Vida left, I remained alone in the newsroom. Maybe it was time to talk to Dennis Kelly, after all. I started to pick up Vida's phone to call the rectory but remembered that the first Tuesday night of each month was reserved for my pastor's meetings with the parish council. Another dead end. Frustrated, I grabbed my handbag and deserted the *Advocate.*

But I didn't head for my Honda. Instead, I walked down the street to Parker's Pharmacy. There are always items to buy at an all-purpose drugstore.

Tara was working the front end, checking out a customer. I dodged her on my way in and went straight to the pharmacy section at the rear of the store. Garth Wesley was behind the glassed-in area, reading a prescription. He saw me right away and smiled, exhibiting uneven but very white teeth.

"Hi, Emma. What can I do for you?"

I asked if he had any of the Band-Aids that stopped bleeding almost immediately. "They're hard to find," I said, "and they

116

really work."

"Paper cuts, huh?" he said.

I chuckled obligingly.

"If they aren't with the rest of the first-aid items," he said, no longer smiling, "then we don't have them. Maybe I can special order some."

"That'd be great," I enthused. "I'll make do with the antibiotic ones in the meantime." I fumbled around in my handbag, stalling for time. "I thought I had a list in here," I fibbed. "Oh, well. I'll remember what I need most. Say," I said, as if the idea had just popped into my head, "how come kids these days don't go into journalism? If Jessica was interested, I might be able to hire her someday. Tara says she doesn't like being a receptionist."

Garth made a face. "Who knows what this younger generation likes? Jess wanted to be a pilot at one time, then a lawyer, and after that some kind of environmental type. The one thing Tara and I are sure of is that we aren't spending money on tuition and room and board for her to go to the UW and mess around without any real goal."

"Good thinking," I said. "I went through that with Adam. He changed majors and colleges so often that I wrote his address in pencil. And then he stunned me by becoming a priest. I never saw that one coming."

Garth slid his hands into the pockets of his white lab coat. "At least our Aaron figured it out. He's still over at Pullman, studying to be a veterinarian. Of course, we figure he'll go into practice some place other than Alpine. Jim Medved's got this town sewed up."

"The county's growing enough that we could use two vets," I pointed out. "Look how overworked Dr. Starr is with his dental practice. At least now he doesn't have to refer patients to an orthodontist out of town."

Garth looked rather pained, as I figured he might. "Right. It's too bad Jess couldn't have stayed with Nystrom. He's got a good thing going for him. His patients aren't just kids but adults, too." He bared his own uneven teeth. "I've thought about having him straighten these. But it'd cost quite a bit, and I've lived with them this way for over forty years."

"You wouldn't look like you," I remarked. "Of course I assume Carter Nystrom does good work."

Garth shrugged. "As far as I know. If he didn't, I'd hear complaints by now. Patients tend to gripe to their pharmacists if they're not satisfied with a doctor or dentist — or even a veterinarian. We fill plenty of prescriptions for animals, too."

I didn't seem to be getting anywhere, so I decided to play the frustrated mother. "Oh, Garth," I said, shaking my head, "raising kids gets harder all the time. I'm so glad Adam made a good choice — and that he's over thirty. I don't know how your peer group manages to parent these days. Young people seem to drift even more than they used to."

"Well." Garth leaned on the counter. "To be honest, Jess and Aaron have been darned good kids. Both of them have worked for us — and that's not easy, having Mom and Dad as your boss. That's why this thing with Jess quitting after just a day seems weird. Granted, it was her first full-time job, but Bree Kendall had worked there ever since Nystrom opened the practice. Tara and I are going to have to have a real sit-down tonight with Jessica."

"Why did Bree quit?" I asked.

Garth frowned. "She's not from here, you know. As I recall, Carter hired her out of Seattle. Maybe she didn't like small-town life. Bree gave it two years. I suppose she missed the city."

Vaguely, I could visualize Bree. We'd run her picture a couple of times: once when she started working for Dr. Nystrom and again when we had a co-op ad featuring our professional people and their staffs. She was blonde and rather good-looking, as I recalled.

"The personnel change could've been the problem," I said as Mary Lou Blatt strode up to the pharmacy counter. "Dr. Nystrom must've been used to a routine with Bree. Maybe he was a little hard on Jessica. It'd be an adjustment for him, too."

Garth shrugged. "It's possible. But darned if Tara and I won't find out. We've raised our kids so that they talk to us. Usually."

Mary Lou harrumphed. "Talk *to* but not talk *back,* I hope. If there's one thing I can't abide, it's youngsters who sass. I need a refill on my blood pressure medicine. I had to see Vida over the holidays."

I bit my lip to keep from smiling. Mary Lou was the widow of Vida's brother, Ennis Blatt. The two strong-minded women had never gotten along.

"I don't know how you put up with that windbag," Mary Lou declared, her sharp eyes pinned on me. "A know-it-all if there ever was one." She turned back to Garth. "Let me tell you, and don't I know, having taught school for many years, that parents are spoiling their children something terrible these days. Thank goodness I'm retired. I'd take a ruler to most of these kids — and then get sued by their silly parents. *If* they have parents, that is, with half the population either divorced or living together without benefit of clergy."

I waved faintly and walked over to the first-aid section. Mary Lou could give as good as she got when it came to windbaggery.

Twenty minutes later, I was emptying my shopping basket for Tara. Band-Aids, Super Glue, Excedrin, liquid eyeliner, toothpaste, mouthwash, a sympathy card for the Nystroms, shampoo and conditioner — I had it all.

"Thirty-eight dollars and twelve cents," Tara announced.

I ran my debit card through the machine, doing it right the first time, which was unusual for Emma the Inept. "What time do you get off?" I asked.

"We're both working until we close at eight," Tara said, sounding tired. "Our holiday help has gone back to the classroom. I guess we'll have Jessica fill in until we get someone else. Aaron has a semester break coming up. We can put him to work, too." She glanced across the wide front aisle at Mary Lou Blatt, who was studying the marked-down holiday candy. "I can't believe it," Tara said, lowering her voice. "Ed Bronsky came in this afternoon asking about a job."

"Oh, dear."

"Right." Tara smiled at Barney Amundson, who had just entered the store. I smiled, too. Barney headed for the camera section. "Has Ed really lost his money? Or his mind?" Tara inquired.

"Yes. Yes." I sighed. "He wants his old job back at the *Advocate.* It's impossible, of course."

"He wasn't asking for himself here," Tara said, handing me my receipt. "It was for Shirley. What do you think?"

"How strapped are you for employees?"

Tara grimaced. "We are a bit strapped. But *Shirley?*" She nodded in Barney Amundson's direction. "His niece Carrie worked for us last summer and did fairly well. Maybe I could ask Barney if she'd consider coming back. She's dropped out of college, too."

"Jessica plans to stay in town, I assume."

Tara nodded as Mary Lou headed for the checkout counter. "I hope so. I don't want her at loose ends in the city."

I signed the receipt and picked up my purchases. "Say, do you know if Bree Kendall is still in town?"

Tara looked surprised by the question. "I think so, but I really don't know. I hardly knew her."

I admitted I didn't know her at all.

But I intended to correct that situation as soon as possible.

I used my cell phone to call directory assistance from my car. Bree Kendall still had a listing. I jotted it down and asked for the address. Dr. Nystrom's former receptionist lived on Alpine Way. Judging from the street number, she was probably a resident at the Pines Villa Apartments.

I sat in the car staring out into Front Street. At five-thirty it was busy by Alpine standards. I had no excuse to call Bree Kendall. I didn't even know why I wanted to talk to her. She'd apparently given notice to her employer that she would quit at the end of the year. That didn't sound precipitous and thus couldn't be construed as sinister. Like just about everyone else connected to the Nystroms, Bree was a stranger to me. So far, I knew only the Nordby brothers, and Trout hadn't been much help when it came to moving the murder investigation forward.

Still, I decided to take the long route

home and headed for Alpine Way instead of going up Fourth Street. Two blocks away from Fir, where my little log house stands, and a block shy of Pines Villa, I decided to stop at the Grocery Basket. The Christmas turkey had been recycled once too often, the larder was low, and I was hungry.

I treated myself to a Kobe beef steak, Brussels sprouts, and a Yukon Gold potato. Guilt came over me. It was a perfect dinner for Milo, except that the sprouts would have been replaced by green beans. When it came to food — and other things as well — the sheriff's tastes were pretty basic. I would've liked to ask Ben to dinner, but I knew he had an invitation to dine with Bernie and Patsy Shaw from the parish. Having spent six months in Alpine, Ben had gotten acquainted with many of the locals. Many of them insisted on offering him hospitality during his short holiday stay, and that meant I wasn't getting to see him as often as I'd have preferred.

I also selected a few items from the frozen food case. I'd put them in reserve for nights when I didn't feel like cooking. I was wheeling my cart toward the front end when I saw Betsy O'Toole coming out of the far aisle. She was wearing her coat and carrying her purse, indicating that she was finished with her co-owner's duties for the day.

"Emma!" she shouted. "What's this about Ed?"

I reined in my cart by a soda pop display. "Not you, too?" I said.

"He was in here half an hour ago, trying to talk Jake and me into hiring a couple of his kids," Betsy said. "It's not a good time. Business slows down in January. The snow-birds all head for Arizona and California. Or they take a cruise. I can't believe Ed's broke."

"Believe it," I said. "But I'm glad to hear he's trying to get his kids to work. It'll be good for them."

"Better if Ed got his own butt out of that stupid mansion and did something besides show off," Betsy asserted. "Oh, I feel sorry for the guy, but he's been such a pain since he inherited that money. Did he blow it all or what?"

"Bad investments," I said. "Say, do you know Bree Kendall?"

Betsy laughed. "Of course." She jerked a thumb toward the express checkout stand. "That's her, right behind Edna Mae Dal-rymple. Bree shops here all the time. She lives just up the street at Pines Villa."

"Do you mind if I roll in behind her?"

125

Betsy shrugged. "Go for it." But before I could move the cart, she blocked my way. "What are you up to, Emma? Does this have something to do with poor Elmer Nystrom having his head bashed in?"

I tried to look innocent. "Why do you ask?"

"Because Bree worked for his son," she said. "You know that, of course."

"Move it, Betsy," I said. "Edna Mae can't dither forever. It's an express lane, remember?"

Betsy got out of the way. "How can I forget? This morning I had to tell Darla Puckett that twenty-seven items are seventeen too many. That woman either can't count or can't read. See you."

Betsy breezed off.

Edna Mae was trying to make exact change. "I'm sure I have another dime," she insisted as the redheaded checker exhibited strained patience. "Dimes are so small. They get caught in the lining of my coin purse." Edna Mae, our local head librarian, kept digging.

I stood behind Bree, studying her appearance. She was several inches taller than I was, probably was twenty-five years younger, and her shoulder-length blond hair looked like it might have been the original color. Her tan all-weather hooded coat was lined with black faux fur. She wore black boots with heels so high that I wouldn't have dared wear them to walk farther than from my bedroom to the front door. Bree already had placed her purchases on the checkout counter: prosciutto, provolone, a small baguette, a yellow bell pepper, and a bottle of Pinot Gris.

"Trade you," I said, leaning over my cart.

"What?" Bree turned around.

"I think I like your choices better than mine," I replied with a friendly smile.

Bree gave me a cool look. "Oh."

Edna Mae hadn't found a dime, but she'd dumped the entire contents of her purse on the checkout stand and was counting out five pennies and a nickel. "There!" She beamed at Cara, the redheaded clerk. "I knew I had exact change! I hate making people wait while I write a check or give you a ten-dollar bill for five dollars and some odd cents worth of purchases." She must have seen me out of the corner of her eye. "Emma? How are you? I meant to call you this evening. Can you substitute for bridge tomorrow night? It's short notice, but the flu's going around. Charlene Vickers and Francine Wells are both sick. Francine phoned me just before I left the library."

"That's fine," I said, pressured not so much by Edna Mae as by the half-dozen people who were now lined up behind me. "Where is it?"

"My house," Edna Mae said, carefully collecting each of her items one at a time and putting them back in her purse. "Seven-thirty, of course."

Of course. I nodded. I'd been a regular member of the bridge club for several years, but for a short time a couple of the members had boycotted me for reasons that still rankled. The rest of the group finally had rallied and invited me back, but I'd played hard to get and told them I'd substitute only when needed.

Edna Mae finally pulled herself and her belongings together. Bree moved quickly, credit card and pen already in hand. My chance to get acquainted was slipping away as fast as a rock rolling down Tonga Ridge.

I leaned closer to Bree. "Can you tell the difference between the yellow and the red peppers?"

Bree, whose eyes were a mesmerizing blue, regarded me as if I were the local loony. "I find the yellow a bit more mild," she replied through tight, glossy lips. She turned away and gazed at Cara, who had finished totaling up Bree's groceries.

I was undaunted. Journalists are used to rejection. "Say," I said in my most engaging voice, "aren't you Bree Kendall?"

Bree all but glared at me. "Yes. Why do you want to know?"

"I'm Emma Lord," I said, still friendly as I could be. "We've run your picture a couple of times in the *Advocate*." I became somber. "I'm very sorry about your employer's father."

"He's not my employer," Bree snapped. "I resigned last week."

"Oh — yes, I'd forgotten." Bree had signed off on her purchases and turned away from me. "Then I guess you're not a suspect," I said loudly.

She almost dropped her plastic grocery bag. "What?" The deep blue eyes stared. Cara, who was already starting to tote up my items, also gave me a startled look.

I shrugged. "That's how it works with a homicide investigation."

Bree took two steps toward me. Menace can distort even the most attractive faces. "If I ever hear you or anybody else even mention my name in connection with that Nystrom bunch, I'll sue for every cent I can get. You hear me?"

I blinked. "I hear you." I steeled my nerve. "But you don't realize what you're saying."

Bree may not have heard me. She was already stalking resolutely toward the exit in her mile-high boots.

And she was not aware that she'd told me what I wanted to know.

SIX

"They're gone," Vida said over the phone. "I'm so glad. The Bartlebys are very difficult to entertain. Regis said grace, and it must have lasted ten minutes. My casserole got cold and didn't taste as it should."

Maybe the vicar had been praying for something edible. Hot or cold, Vida's casserole would have tasted like newspaper pulp. "Was your social gesture worthwhile in terms of information?"

"Oooh . . ." Vida paused. I could imagine that she'd taken off her glasses and was rubbing her eyes in frustration. "The Bartlebys are so maddeningly discreet! You'd think all those Episcopalians led blameless lives!"

"Including the Nystroms?"

"Oh, yes!" Vida's sigh carried over the phone line. "Elmer was practically a saint. Polly is such a dear woman, 'bless her heart,' and I quote. Carter is a paragon of virtue. 'Bless his heart,' too. Elmer was an usher. Polly made tea towels for the church bazaar. Carter has very flexible payment plans for patients who are financially embarrassed. That's the way Regis put it. So tactful. Whatever happened to — and now I must quote myself — 'broke,' 'lazy,' or 'spending paychecks at Mugs Ahoy'?"

"You didn't expect them to dish the dirt," I pointed out.

"I expected *something*," Vida declared. "And I must say, there were some very small tidbits of interest, if one interprets them properly."

"Such as?"

"Edith described Polly as 'taking an interest in other people.' Yet at another point in the conversation, Regis mentioned that the family kept to themselves. 'A close-knit trio' — those were his exact words. The two things don't go together."

"Meaning . . . ?"

"Meaning, of course," Vida explained, "that someone who takes an interest in others usually has many friends. That person is a good listener and probably is sympathetic. However, if that person — Polly, of course — is merely encouraging people at church — and I don't think the Nystroms had a social circle beyond Trinity Episcopal, because I certainly never ran any items about them entertaining guests — then I must conclude that Polly was pumping the other parishioners for information. Which, of course, is perhaps what Maud Dodd complained about. Polly is a *gossip.*"

I was glad Vida couldn't see my expression. *Pot, meet kettle,* I thought to myself. "There are worse things," I remarked.

"That may be so," Vida allowed, "but it depends on whether or not Polly adhered to the truth and refrained from malice. I intend to visit Maud Dodd tomorrow on my lunch hour."

With the cordless phone propped between my ear and my shoulder, I had wandered into the living room where I stood before my favorite painting. *Sky Autumn* hung above the sofa, replacing a Monet print I'd moved to my bedroom. I never tired of my recent acquisition. The tumbling river seemed to change color and movement with the light. Just then, with only one lamp burning on an end table next to the sofa, the rushing water looked dark and dangerous. It struck me as a metaphor describing Elmer's killer.

"Is that all you found out?" I asked.

"Almost," Vida replied. "Elmer's funeral will be Friday morning at ten. I called that in to Kip so that he could add it to my obituary and your story. But," she went on, "there was one other faintly curious comment by Regis. He mentioned that as an usher, Elmer always stood in the rear of the church during the service. Polly and Carter sat together in the third row and nudged each other frequently during the sermons. Regis was puzzled as to whether they were quibbling with Scripture or with his — that is, Regis's — interpretation."

"That's a clue?" I said, leaning so close to my painting that I could see the signature of the artist, Craig Laurentis.

"Well, no," Vida admitted, "but it obviously disconcerts Regis. He wonders if he's becoming too pedantic as he grows older."

I sat down on the sofa and put my feet up on the matching ottoman. "At least he's not senile like our poor old Father Fitzgerald. When I first came to Alpine, he was giving homilies about loose women with bobbed hair and short skirts doing the Black Bottom and drinking bathtub gin."

"Yes," Vida said. "I recall the St. Mildred's people complaining about that sort of thing. Living in the past, poor soul. Of course it always seems a safer place."

"By the way," I said, "I ran into Bree Kendall at the Grocery Basket."

Vida didn't respond immediately. I sensed

that she was checking Bree's name in her prodigious memory bank. "Oh, the young woman who worked for Carter Nystrom. Really, Emma, you did not just happen to run into her."

"In a way," I said. "I didn't follow her to the store. She was ahead of me in the express lane." I related our brief encounter.

"Well, now," Vida said, "Bree's the first person I know who's been openly critical of the Nystrom family. I wonder why."

"I'd say it was because she and Carter didn't get along," I said, "except that she definitely referred to all of them. I wonder if Milo will talk to her."

"He should," Vida asserted. "He must. Disgruntled employees have motives. Though why Carter's receptionist would kill his father seems very odd. I'm ruling out a mistake. Except for both men being fairly tall, they don't look at all alike."

I told Vida that I'd drop Bree's name in Milo's lap. On that note, I rang off. It was after nine. The Wesleys would be home from the drugstore. They'd probably spend the dinner hour having their little talk with Jessica. I gave them another twenty minutes before I dialed their number.

Tara answered the phone.

"I'm sorry to bother you," I said, "but I

need some background for a follow-up article on the Nystrom tragedy." Like most people, Tara wouldn't stop to think that I had an entire week to write the article. If she thought about it at all, she'd figure I was still working on this week's edition. "How many employees does Dr. Nystrom have in his office?"

"Not counting our daughter?" Tara said dryly.

"Right." I couldn't resist the opening Tara had given me. "Did you find out why she quit?"

"Jess didn't like the environment. Whatever that means." Tara sounded annoyed. "Hang on. Maybe I can get a straight answer out of her on your question." I waited. I could hear voices in the background but was unable to understand what was being said. "Two assistants," Tara finally informed me. "Jess doesn't know their last names and doesn't think they're from around here. The dark-haired girl is Christy, and the one with blond highlights is Alicia. You'll have to check with the office to get their last names. Sorry."

"That's okay," I assured Tara. "I know the environment bit with the younger set. It can be anything from not liking the workplace's computer keyboard to hating a co-worker's shoes."

"Exactly," Tara said. "Still, I expected better of Jess. It's not like her to be vague. Got to go, Emma. I was just loading the dishwasher."

After hanging up, I checked my e-mail to see if Adam had responded to the message I'd sent to him in Alaska. He hadn't. As usual, I worried that he'd been kidnapped by marauding polar bears.

An hour later, I was brushing my teeth in the bathroom. When I was ten or so, our family dentist suggested that I get braces because I had an overbite. The cost was out of my parents' price range, and I didn't ever want to wear those ugly metal things. I'd preferred the overbite despite the dentist's dire warnings that I'd do all kinds of damage to my jaw and teeth. By middle age, I had never suffered any such problems, nor was I self-conscious. Still, I wondered if I couldn't use my slight deformity as an excuse to see Dr. Nystrom.

I stood there looking in the mirror and trying to tell myself it was a dumb idea. For one thing, Carter Nystrom might not be taking appointments until after his father's funeral. And, I asked myself, why was I trying so hard to play detective? Didn't I trust

Milo? Or had I gotten into the habit of helping solve murder cases over the years?

I turned away from the sink and flicked off the light switch. *None of the above,* I thought as I went into my bedroom. My rationale was quite different and very simple: The prehomicide obituary had been sent to the *Advocate.* Had it been a warning? An attempt to stop the murder before it happened? Or was it a cruel hoax to play on my staff and me? If Vida hadn't known the Nystroms, we might have run the obit and looked like idiots. Or, even worse, gotten slapped with a lawsuit. Whatever the answer, I had to find it. *The Alpine Advocate* was already involved, and that meant I was, too.

Pub day — Wednesday to the rest of the world — usually meant the pressure was off. It was a good day for haircuts, doctor and dental appointments, or whatever else had to be done during the week between eight and five. But this time there was no letting up for me on the day the newspaper came out. As soon as I reached the office, I dialed Carter Nystrom's office.

After four rings, a recorded message came on, informing me that the office was closed for the rest of the week due to a death in the family.

Shot down again.

I went out to Vida's desk. "Alicia and Christy, Carter's orthodontist assistants. Do they have last names?"

Vida had just turned on her computer. "A moment. I'm still never sure if I've done this right." She gazed at the screen, which was black. "Oh, dear. Now what did I do wrong?"

I leaned over her chair and poked the button on the monitor. "See if that helps."

"Ah," she said. "Yes, it's doing something now. You're very clever, Emma."

"Hey," I responded, "plugging things in and turning on switches are as clever as I get. As far as I'm concerned, the computer is just a typewriter with pictures. Now, what about Alicia and Christy?"

Sadly, she shook her head. "I know at least two Christys and one Alicia, but none of them work for Carter Nystrom. Like Bree, they must be out-of-towners he hired when he went into practice. Very foolish of him, really. Alpiners prefer dealing with people they've known a long time. Strangers can be so off-putting."

Having been a stranger in Alpine, I knew that Vida spoke the truth. I pointed out, however, that Carter was a local.

"True," she said slowly, "but he'd been away for many years completing his studies. He'd grown up in Alpine and should have known better than to hire outsiders."

Scott had been assigned to the morning bakery run. "I'll talk to him as soon as he gets in," I said. "If Scott met any of these young women when he did the feature article on Carter, they might thaw a little if he talks to them again."

Vida nodded. "Just because he's married now doesn't mean he's lost his appeal to the fair sex."

Leo entered the newsroom, looking grim. "I got a call from Carter Nystrom at seven-oh-five this morning. He wanted to know if it was too late to place a paid obit in this week's paper. I had to restrain myself from telling him he couldn't put it there but I knew somewhere else he could shove it."

"There's no need to be crude, Leo," Vida chided. "The poor man has just lost his father."

"He's also lost track of time," Leo grumbled. "I was just getting into the shower. Why the hell did he have to call me at home?"

"He probably thought we hadn't printed the paper yet," I put in. "So many readers don't get it."

Leo glanced at the coffeemaker, seeing that the red light hadn't gone on yet and that the baked goods hadn't arrived. "So I'm supposed to stand there buck naked listening to Carter natter on about how his mother knows for an absolute certainty that Elmer wasn't murdered but just had a freak accident? Talk about denial!" He glared at the coffeemaker, as if he could compel it to finish the brewing process.

"An accident?" I said. "How can Polly believe that?"

Vida made a disgusted face. "Polly doesn't want to think that their perfect little family could be involved in anything as messy as murder."

"Then Polly is an idiot," Leo declared, lighting a cigarette.

"Perhaps," Vida allowed. "And please don't blow that smoke in my direction."

"Right, Duchess, right. I'll blow it up my —"

"Leo!" Vida wagged her finger. "You are out of control this morning! Please overcome your foul mood so that the rest of us don't have to suffer."

The red light came on. "Yeah, okay, fine," Leo grumbled. "Carter talked so much that I didn't have time to get my first jolt of caffeine at home. He got me off to a bad start.

141

You don't need caffeine, Duchess. You never sleep. All that hot water you drink must have a magic potion in it."

Vida ignored the comment. "Did Carter say anything of interest?"

Leo poured mugs of coffee for me and for himself. "Damned if I know. I told you — I wasn't really awake and I was stark —"

"Yes, you've mentioned all that," Vida interrupted. "Please drink some coffee, stop cursing, smoke your awful cigarette, and try to remember. I'll give you five minutes." She turned away, fiddling with her computer.

I was about to retreat into my cubbyhole, but just then Scott made his entrance, purple Upper Crust box in hand.

"Apple slippers and pear boats," he announced. "The new hot items from the Upper Crust. Almost literally. They're still warm."

I pounced, all but ripping the box to get it open. Leo waited until he'd finished his cigarette. Vida shook her head. "They sound very fattening. I'm on a diet."

Vida always claimed that she was on a diet, yet she never seemed to gain or lose an ounce. Her large frame supported her weight, not to mention her hat, which she was still wearing this morning. It was a

142

bright green turban with a large brooch of multicolored fake gems.

Ginny and Kip appeared, as if popping out of a genie's bottle. After eating a bite of the delicate pastry layers surrounding the pears, I sat down on the edge of Scott's desk.

"Tell me everything you know about the people who work for Carter Nystrom."

"Hang on." Scott waited for Ginny and Kip to make their selections, then chose an apple slipper and poured out a mug of coffee. Vida, who had heard my query, came over to stand by my reporter's desk. "You mean the two assistants and the receptionist?" Scott said, sitting down in his chair. "Bree quit last week."

"We know," Vida said impatiently. "Jessica Wesley took over but stayed only one day. She resigned yesterday morning for reasons that don't satisfy her parents."

"I didn't know that," Scott said, looking apologetic. "Anyway, the only one I knew was Bree Kendrick."

"Kendall," Vida corrected, edging a few inches along the front of the desk.

"Oh." Scott shrugged. "Sorry. Anyway, I knew her because she lived at Pines Villa and knew Tammy from the UW. They were in the same sorority."

"Ah." Vida looked pleased and moved to the corner of Scott's desk. "So your bride and Bree are friends?"

"Not exactly," Scott said, using a paper napkin to wipe some of the apple substance from his fingers. "Tammy and Bree were three years apart. I don't know much about the Greek sorority and fraternity scene, but Tammy felt she should at least ask Bree to dinner. That was before we were married, when Bree first got here. They've seen each other a few times since and going in and out of the apartment, but I wouldn't call them close. We had Bree to our place a year or so ago and told her to bring a date." He paused to take a sip of coffee.

"Did she?" I asked, noting that Vida was now at the side of the desk.

Scott nodded. "She brought Carter Nystrom."

Vida stopped just short of the coffee and baked goods table behind Scott's chair. "Scott! You should have told us this sooner!"

"I didn't know it mattered," he said. "Honest, I'd kind of forgotten about it. The dinner wasn't a social highlight on our calendar. Tammy didn't even invite Bree to the wedding. At least she wasn't there. As I recall."

"Men!" Vida shook her head and snatched

up a pear boat. "I'll save this for later," she murmured, wrapping a napkin around the pastry. "Emma, we must talk to Tamara. Or," she continued, looming over Scott's chair, "can you tell us if this was a serious romance between Carter and Bree?"

Scott was looking annoyed. "They weren't pawing each other, if that's what you mean. How would I know?"

Ginny, who had been observing the exchange, lifted her hand as if asking permission to speak. "I saw Carter and Bree once having dinner at the ski lodge last summer. They looked friendly but not what I'd call in love. I told Rick I thought Carter was kind of a stick. He said Carter was a nice guy and always very pleasant when he came into the bank. In fact, he always asked for Rick to help him instead of going to one of the tellers."

"No doubt Carter's carrying a box full of money," Leo put in, finally finishing his cigarette and coming toward the baked goods. "Those orthodontists make a killing."

"Ginny," Vida began, "you must tell Rick I'll be coming by for a private chat."

Kip, who had been silently munching away, announced that he felt left out. "I don't know Carter Nystrom or any of these people. Except Elmer, I mean, and he's dead."

"That's the problem," Vida asserted. "Not Elmer being dead — which he is, and that's a different sort of problem from what I intended to say. It's that nobody really knows the Nystroms except on a professional level. That's very odd, since they've lived here forever."

Leo gave Vida his crooked grin. "You can cure that, Duchess. I have faith in you."

But for once Vida seemed uncertain. "I'm not sure I can. I don't think the Nystroms want to be known."

Vida, however, was as good as her word. As soon as the Bank of Alpine opened, she headed off to talk to Ginny's husband, Rick Erlandson. I called Tamara Rostova Chamoud to set up a lunch date. She couldn't take a break until one, as she had to meet with some of her students after her eleven o'clock class.

After Ginny delivered the mail at around ten, I left for the sheriff's office. It was a mild January day with fog that would lift by noon. The damp air was invigorating despite the smell of diesel trucks and the faint but unpleasant odor of pulp from the only surviving mill in town, Blackwell Timber.

The law enforcement staff seemed to be holding an informal meeting behind the curved mahogany counter that separated the public from the employees. Dustin Fong, Jack Mullins, and Doe Jameson were huddled around Lori Cobb, who was seated at her console. None of them looked happy.

"What's going on?" I asked.

Jack Mullins, who had seniority among the group, gave me a woebegone look. "The sheriff's sick."

This was shocking news. Milo never got sick except for the occasional cold that he always toughed out in his usual macho fashion. "What's wrong with him? Why didn't Scott tell me when he checked the police log?"

"The boss man was okay then," Jack said, his customarily puckish face as grave as I'd ever seen it. "It happened about half an hour ago. He had terrific chest pains, and Dwight Gould took him to the hospital."

"A heart attack?" I gasped, leaning against the counter to steady my suddenly weak knees.

Doe Jameson, Milo's recently hired deputy, shrugged her broad shoulders. "We don't know. Dwight's still there with him. Both Doc Dewey and Dr. Sung are checking him out."

Milo wouldn't allow himself to be taken to the hospital unless he thought he was dying. Even then, he was the type of bearlike man who'd prefer to crawl into his cave and let nature take its course.

"I can't believe it," I said faintly. "Are you sure this pain was sudden?"

Dustin Fong shed his lost-child demeanor long enough to answer. "I didn't think he seemed quite right when he came in this morning. He hardly talked at all, just went straight into his office."

Lori nodded in agreement. "I haven't worked here long enough to know Sheriff Dodge that well, but he looked kind of . . . what my grandma would call 'peaked.' "

"Is Dwight still at the hospital?" I asked, putting some steel into my spine. I, too, could be tough — or at least in control of my emotions. God knows, I'd had plenty of practice.

Lori nodded again. "He told us he'd call when he found out anything."

My cell phone rang inside my handbag. Could someone be calling me from the hospital? Had Milo asked for me in his final hour? I excused myself and took the call a few feet away from the counter.

"Hey, Sluggly," my brother said in his most chipper voice, "want some grease for lunch? It's your turn to treat. I'll let you off easy at the diner or the Burger Barn."

"I don't know," I said. "Milo's in the hospital with chest pains. I'm going over there now."

"Damn!" Ben's tone changed immediately. "I'll meet you there. How bad is it?"

"I don't know that, either."

"You don't know much for a newshound. See you." He clicked off.

I didn't bother saying goodbye to the sheriff's employees. I raced out the door, terrified that I might have to say a permanent goodbye to the sheriff.

SEVEN

The hospital was on Pine, only a block uphill from the sheriff's office. I walked hurriedly across Front Street. Through the drifting fog, I spotted Vida down the block, coming out of the Bank of Alpine. I thought of calling to her, but she had turned in the opposite direction, apparently going back to the *Advocate* office. She wouldn't be pleased to find out that I hadn't told her about Milo's catastrophe right away, but I was in a panic.

The emergency room was virtually empty except for a couple of older people I didn't recognize and Grace Grundle, whom I intended to ignore.

But Grace wouldn't let that happen. "Emma," she called to me, struggling to get out of the waiting room chair. "Are you under the weather, too?" She didn't wait for an answer. "It's this terrible cough. I can't get rid of it. I've had it since before Thanksgiving. Doc Dewey gave me some kind of medicine, but really, I don't think it helped a bit. I was awake half the night coughing and coughing. My poor kitties couldn't get any rest, either. It's not fair to them to have to put up with me."

I was trapped and tried to calm myself enough to be civil. Grace was the kind of senior citizen who spent half her time at the doctor's for herself and the other half at the vet's with her cats. As far as I was concerned, the Grace Grundles of this world share the guilt for the high price of medical premiums. I know that elderly folks get lonely, and if people like me would take time to visit them once in a while, we might alleviate the problem.

"These germs seem to hang on forever," I said rapidly, watching Grace as she rummaged through her well-worn purse. "Excuse me, but I —"

"Just a moment, Emma. I have something to show you." She kept rummaging; I shifted from one foot to the other. "I stopped to pick up my Christmas pictures from Safeway on the way over here. You must see them. You might want to run one in the newspaper. They are absolutely adorable!"

Finally she took out an envelope and began removing the photos. One by one.

The first three were so dark, I couldn't see much except for glowing feline eyes. Or so I assumed.

"This one is much better," Grace informed me. "I remembered to use the flash button."

A fat gray cat wearing a Santa Claus hat stared malevolently at the camera. "Cute," I said. "Very cute."

"That's Snickerdoodle," Grace said. "He's almost four. This next one is Tiddlywinks. What do you think?"

Tiddlywinks looked feral to me. The cat was baring its teeth, and its eyes were wild. Clearly, he didn't seem to like the mistletoe that was tied around his neck with green and red ribbon.

"Colorful," I said weakly, suddenly realizing that Grace hadn't coughed once despite her bountiful flow of words.

"I rescued him last spring, poor thing," she informed me. "He was out in the backyard, eating a crow, and I —"

Ben came through the double doors. "Emma." He spoke softly, but his voice was urgent.

Grace shut up and turned to stare at my brother. "Oh! Aren't you . . . uh . . ."

Grace wasn't Catholic and probably didn't recognize Ben in his Levi's and parka.

Ben smiled and nodded. "Yes, I'm that priest from out of town. Also known as Emma's big brother. Could you excuse us for a moment?" He steered me away from Grace. "How's Milo?" he asked in a whisper.

"I wouldn't know," I retorted. "I haven't had a chance to find out."

At last, I was able to approach the reception desk. I gave a start. Sitting warily in wait was Bree Kendall. She didn't look very happy to see me. Maybe she thought I was being committed to the mental ward. If Alpine had had one.

"Can I help you?" she asked frostily.

"I've come to inquire about Sheriff Dodge. My brother is a priest." I turned to look at Ben, but he wasn't behind me.

"What brother?" Bree inquired, looking as if she wished she had a straitjacket at hand.

I moved a few steps away, spotting Ben on the floor, where he was helping Grace pick up some of the cat photos she'd apparently dropped. I realized Bree couldn't see him from her seat behind the desk.

"There," I said, pointing out of her range of vision. "He's helping Ms. Grundle."

Ben stood up. Bree saw him. "Did the sheriff request a priest?" she asked, her query sheathed in ice.

"No. My brother and I are friends of his.

The deputies told me he'd been brought here with chest pains."

Ben finished helping Grace and joined me at the counter. "I don't want to offer up prayers for Sheriff Dodge unless I know what's wrong with him," he said quietly to Bree. "After all, this is the feast day of the baptism of our Lord, Jesus Christ."

I didn't know that, and I'm sure Bree had no idea what my brother was talking about. But the frost melted slightly. "He's stable," Bree said, "but that's all I know."

At that moment Dwight Gould came out through the double doors that led to the two examining rooms. He was scowling, but Dwight was negative by nature.

I hurried over to the deputy. "What's going on?" I asked.

"Damn it, Emma, are you putting this in the paper?" Dwight growled.

"The paper's already printed," I snapped. "How's Milo?"

"What do I look like?" Dwight retorted. "Dr. Kildare?"

Dwight looked more like Dr. Killjoy to me, but I tried to be patient. "Well?"

Again, Ben was covering my back. "Does anybody know anything yet?" he asked.

"Hi, Padre," Dwight said, his attitude softening slightly. "You been fishing since you got here?"

Ben shook his head. "I'd like to, but I have to leave Sunday. How about you?"

"Caught a ten-pounder over the weekend near where the Tye comes into the Sky," Dwight said.

"Nice," Ben commented. "The river looks off-color today, though."

Dwight shrugged. "You can't always tell by that. The steelhead can't tell, either, if you ask me." He chuckled.

"So how's Dodge?" my brother asked, having bonded with a fellow fisherman. Fishing, after all, was almost as good as religion when it came to male relationships.

"Doc's doing some tests," Dwight replied. "Dodge is pretty pissed."

"Then he's not dying," I said.

"Hell, no," Dwight replied. "It could be a heart attack, but Elvis Sung isn't sure. I'm going back to the office."

Dwight stomped through the waiting room, but not before Grace stopped him, brandishing her cat photos. "Not now, Miss Grundle," Dwight said, though his tone was more kindly with Grace than it had been with the Lord siblings.

"Thank you again," she called after him, "for saving Chubbins last fall when he got wedged in the fence."

"No problem." Dwight hurtled out through the door.

Ben drew me over by the aquarium, as far as we could get from the others without climbing out a window. "Now what?" he asked.

"We wait?"

"That could be quite a while," Ben pointed out. "Believe me, I know. I've had to sit with plenty of anxiety-ridden parishioners in emergency rooms and hospitals in my time."

I knew Ben was right, but I couldn't leave without making sure that Milo wasn't in danger. Dwight might describe his boss as "pissed," but I'd expect that of the sheriff on his deathbed.

"I'm going back there," I declared, waving in the direction of the examining rooms.

"Okay." Ben came with me. Bree called out to stop us, but we ignored her.

"What's with her?" Ben asked as we went through the double doors.

"I'll tell you later," I said. "She must be temping."

"What?"

"Later."

Constance Peterson, LPN, was coming out of the room on the right. She saw us and frowned.

"May I help you, Ms. Lord?"

"I come with clergy," I said, taking Ben's arm. "I'm inquiring about Milo Dodge. This is my brother, Father Ben."

"Oh." Constance's frown eased a bit. "I remember you. When your church's organist became ill a year or so ago, you came to visit."

"Yes," Ben replied. "I was filling in for Dennis Kelly."

"Sheriff Dodge isn't a Catholic," Constance said.

"That's not a problem," Ben said dryly.

"I mean . . ." Constance's usual professional aplomb teetered a bit. "I thought maybe you came to . . . do whatever priests do when somebody's . . . very ill."

"We're here as friends," Ben said. "How is he?"

"He's stable," Constance replied, resuming her usual efficient manner.

"Is it his heart?" I asked.

Constance's round face was expressionless. "The doctors are doing tests."

Ben sensed my frustration. "Nurse Peterson," he said quietly, "can you assure us that Sheriff Dodge is in no immediate danger?"

"I don't know. Medical personnel don't own crystal balls, Father," Constance replied primly. "As I've already told you, the most I can say is that the patient is listed as stable. I'm in no position to second-guess Dr. Dewey or Dr. Sung. Excuse me." She glanced above the door on the right. "The light is on, summoning me. I must go."

Nurse Peterson opened the examining room door only enough to allow her to slip inside. I couldn't see a thing; neither could Ben.

"Foiled again," Ben murmured.

I scowled at the closed door. "If Milo's in that examining room, what kinds of tests are they taking? Shouldn't he be where they have the specialized equipment?"

Ben shrugged. "Some of it's mobile these days. You'd know more about what Alpine Hospital has than I would."

"They don't have as much as they need," I said. "Like everything else in a small town and a small county, they're short of the expensive new high-tech stuff. I've written plenty of editorials about those problems, from the sheriff's office, to the hospital, to the highway and transportation departments." I turned as Olga Bergstrom, RN, bore down on us from the far end of the corridor.

"Ms. Lord," she called out. "You can't wait in this part of the emergency area."

She studied Ben for a brief moment. "I know you — you're Father Lord."

Ben nodded. "I've been here so long, I feel like Grandfather Lord. Is the sheriff going to be released or hospitalized?"

The direct question seemed to catch Olga off guard. "I don't know. That's up to the doctors. Really," she went on, "you must go into the waiting room."

We had no choice except to move on. But there wasn't much point in sitting around looking at the rest of Grace Grundle's cat photos. "We'll go out the back way," I said.

"Fine." Olga stepped aside to let us pass.

We exited on Cedar Street, catty-corner from St. Mildred's. Ben decided he might as well go back to the rectory and catch up on any messages from East Lansing. We agreed to meet for dinner at the diner, since I already had a lunch date with Tamara Chamoud.

I steeled myself before entering the newsroom. The only staff member present was Vida, with her steely gray eyes fixed on me as if I were an enemy target and she were a bombardier.

"Well?" The single word shot out of her mouth like a bullet.

"Marje Blatt?" I said, moving slowly toward her desk.

"Of course." She cleared her throat. "You could at least have called me from the hospital. How is Milo?"

"I don't know," I replied, standing by her in-box. "They're running some tests. Did Marje know anything?"

Vida's lips were pressed tightly together. She shook her head. I waited. "All she could tell me," Vida finally said, "was that Doc Dewey had been called away from the clinic to tend to Milo. It's a good thing I have reliable *relatives* to keep me informed."

The reproach stung, as it always did when coming from Vida. Marje was Doc's receptionist and Vida's niece. I was surprised that Bill Blatt hadn't alerted his aunt from the sheriff's office. But maybe Bill wasn't on duty that morning.

"I'm sorry," I apologized. "Frankly, I panicked."

Vida sighed. "Yes, perhaps you did. Word is getting out. Ginny's telling callers that we have no information. That's very galling for a newspaper to have to admit."

It was even more galling for Vida to admit such a thing. I eased myself into her visitor's chair. "Did Rick Erlandson have anything interesting to say at the bank?"

"No," she retorted. "Bankers! So closemouthed! It was as frustrating as dealing with the Bartlebys." She paused, her eyes darting up to the window above her desk. Vida kept watch on that window, able to identify most pedestrians by their feet and legs. "It was what he didn't say that intrigued me."

"Which was . . . ?"

"Reading between the lines, Carter Nystrom wasn't making large deposits to the Bank of Alpine," Vida explained. "He has a checking account there but apparently doesn't deposit much of his income. That's very puzzling, since it's the only bank in town."

"But not the only bank in the area," I pointed out. "Sultan, Monroe, Snohomish — they all have bank branch offices. Who knows? Maybe Carter's using a Seattle bank he set up during his student days."

"That's not very wise," Vida declared. "He's from Alpine, he lives here, he has his practice here. I'd consider his banking elsewhere as disloyal."

Naturally. "Well, maybe. But it could be more convenient for him. Anyway, what I'd like to know most is what Rick thought of him — and his family."

Vida literally rolled her eyes. "The same old story. Elmer and Polly have banked with BOA forever. Lovely people. Or at least

161

Elmer is. *Was.* Polly apparently didn't handle the money. I'm not surprised. She's one of those helpless females who's probably never written a check in her life and now will have to hire a CPA to keep her accounts balanced. Ninny."

I held my head. "This is getting tiresome. Let's face it, somebody didn't think Elmer was so lovely or kind or decent or whatever. Otherwise he wouldn't have gotten his head bashed in with a shovel."

Vida frowned at me. "A shovel? Did you hear that from the sheriff's office?"

"No. I'm guessing. It could've been a brick or a board or . . . who knows?"

"We certainly don't," Vida asserted. "We know very little."

I remembered to tell her about Bree working behind the emergency room desk. "Temping, maybe," I suggested.

"Or it's her new job." Vida looked thoughtful. "Who's been at the desk in recent months? They seem to change personnel quite often. Stress, I would think. That is, I wouldn't find it stressful, but so many people take the problems of others to heart. It's not a healthy approach. One should keep a certain amount of distance. That's far more sensible in dealing with demanding situations."

162

I translated that as allowing Vida to meddle and criticize without guilt. "I wouldn't think the hospital job would pay as well as working for Dr. Nystrom," I remarked.

"Perhaps not," Vida said as Leo came into the newsroom carrying an inflated snowman. "Goodness! What's that for?" she inquired.

"Alpine Ski is praying for snow," Leo replied, placing the snowman behind his desk. "So's the ski lodge. This is a leftover from Safeway's Christmas decorations. It's also our new god. Should we call him Baal?"

"How about Bald?" I suggested. "Snowmen never have hair, only hats."

"True," Leo said, tapping his lower lip as he studied the plastic figure that didn't want to stay upright. "I'm going to take a picture for an ad. Nobody at Alpine Ski had a camera. Can you believe that?"

"Maybe they can't afford a camera," I remarked. "The ski industry has been hit hard the last couple of winters."

"Money," Vida said. "Leo, if you were Carter Nystrom, where would you bank?"

Leo looked at Vida. "What?"

"You heard me. He must make a great deal of money," Vida asserted. "Heavens, it cost the earth when Amy and Ted got braces for Roger. Of course they had to have it done in Monroe because Roger needed his braces before Carter set up practice. I must say, Roger has the most engaging smile. But it certainly set his parents back several thousand dollars."

I felt like saying that I'd never seen Roger smile. He was usually sulking or sullen when I encountered the wretched kid. But I kept quiet and waited for Vida and Leo to finish their conversation.

"I'm not sure," Leo said, "what you're getting at, Duchess."

"He doesn't bank in Alpine," Vida responded. "That is, he doesn't use the local bank for payroll and such. I find that very strange. And how many times do I need to tell you to stop calling me 'Duchess'?"

"As many times as I keep doing it." Leo shrugged. "I can't answer your question about Nystrom. Maybe he has some elaborate financial setup with a bank in Seattle. Maybe that's how he's paying off his student loans. Or," he went on, finally getting the snowman to stop bobbing and weaving, "maybe he's laundering his money in the Caribbean like a lot of professionals do."

Vida thought a minute. "To avoid taxes?"

"I guess," Leo replied. "When I was living in southern California, there were several doctors and dentists who sent their money offshore or even to Switzerland and Liechtenstein. I wouldn't know, being a poor newspaper ad man." Leo glanced at me. "I'm not complaining. It's my choice. Besides, I wouldn't want you to get mad and fire me so you can bring back Ed Bronsky."

"Ease your mind," I murmured, going into my office. It was almost eleven-thirty. I wondered if I should call the hospital to check on Milo. But surely someone from his office would let me know what was going on. Maybe I'd stop by the sheriff's headquarters on my way to lunch with Tamara. We'd agreed to meet at the new Pie-in-the-Sky Café by the Alpine Mall. The six-block walk would be good exercise.

Just before noon Ginny came into my cubbyhole. "There's a whole bunch of rumors going around town," she told me, her plain face looking worried. "People are calling to say all kinds of things about Sheriff Dodge, including that he's been shot and that he tried to commit suicide."

"Jeez." I shook my head. "What are you telling them?"

Ginny straightened her shoulders and assumed a virtuous air — easy for her to do, being a staunch adherent of virtue. "That he's been admitted to the hospital for observation."

"That's good." I smiled kindly. "You don't need to say anything else. I assume Fleetwood will carry the story on the noon news."

"Was he at the hospital?" Ginny asked.

"No, thank goodness," I said. "But for all I know, he may be there now, doing one of his breaking news remote broadcasts." I poked the button to turn on the transistor radio I kept on the filing cabinet by my desk. "We'll find out. Or I will. You go ahead and have lunch."

KSKY aired two commercials before the newsbreak, the first for the Upper Crust's new "flaky, fruit-filled European-style pastries" and the second for Bernie Shaw's insurance agency, where "your agent is your neighbor."

Spence was at the mike, greeting his listeners in his mellifluous baritone. "It's noon in SkyCo, and here are the latest headlines from KSKY-AM, the voice of the Cascade slope."

That phrase was an innovation. Of course I didn't usually listen to Spence's station except for the Wednesday night broadcasts of *Vida's Cupboard.* Everybody listened to my House & Home editor while she presented her weekly shelf full of homely gossip, helpful hints, and an interview with a local personality.

Spence's lead story was about the ongoing investigation of the Nystrom homicide. Spence didn't seem to know any more than we did. Or so I thought until he paused ever so briefly and said, "Later this afternoon around three o'clock I'll be interviewing someone closely connected to the case. Stay tuned for the exact time of our live and direct broadcast."

I was stupefied. Who did Spence have up his well-tailored sleeve? But his next words grabbed my attention. "Meanwhile," he said, "Sheriff Milo Dodge was taken to Alpine Hospital with an undisclosed illness. Doctors Gerald Dewey and Elvis Sung are conducting medical tests to determine the cause of Dodge's illness. The hospital has listed his condition as stable. KSKY will be reporting breaking news when further word is released."

Spence broke for another commercial. I turned off the radio and fumed. With Milo confined to the hospital, could my archrival have coerced one of the deputies into being interviewed? Was Carter Nystrom willing to go on the air because Spence had convinced him a public forum might help catch Elmer's killer? Or had Mr. Radio dredged up some friend or neighbor who wanted to be in the limelight?

But the Nystroms didn't have any friends as far as I could tell. They were a world unto themselves. Or were they? I wondered.

When I stopped at the sheriff's office on my way to meet Tamara, Jack Mullins was the only one up front behind the mahogany counter. He was eating a sausage pizza, drinking a Diet Coke, and not answering the phone that was ringing as I entered.

"Screw 'em," he said with his mouth full. "They're just a bunch of snoops."

"What if someone is reporting a crime?" I asked.

Jack shrugged and swallowed. "Then they can call 911, just like regular victims do. I don't mind sitting in for Lori, but I'll be damned if I'm going to play phone operator."

"Any word on Milo?"

Jack shook his head. "Doe stopped by the hospital just a few minutes ago. They're still doing their damned tests — or waiting for the results. Dodge must be feeling better. Doe said Doc Dewey told her that Boss Man was being a pain in the ass. Or words to that effect."

"Milo's not used to being sick," I said. "Or when he is, he's the type who never talks about it."

"That's the problem," Jack said. "For all we know, he's been having these pains for a while. That bothers me."

It bothered me, too. "You've got my cell number," I said. "Call me whenever you hear anything. Please?"

"Sure." Jack finished the last bite of pizza.

"By the way," I said, "did you hear Spence on the noon news?"

"Hell, no. I don't listen to the radio unless I pick up KJR with the sports bullshit. But with all these mountains, the reception sucks in the patrol car." He gave me a curious look. "Why're you asking?"

I told Jack about Spence's mystery interview. "Any ideas?"

"Not any of us," Jack said staunchly. "Maybe one of the Nordby brothers, looking for some free advertising. Or one of the girls from Carter's office. Who knows with Fleetwood? Maybe he came up with some guy who was in tooth school with Carter. Or some kid who just got new braces. I'll bet he's reaching."

"You're probably right," I allowed.

The phone rang again. Jack ignored it. I said goodbye and left. I never could resist a ringing telephone. If I hadn't made my exit, I would've answered the call myself.

Tamara was a couple of minutes late, though she floated into the café in the customary graceful manner that always made me think she could've been a ballerina with the Bolshoi. Her ebony black hair was pulled away from her face to reveal a classic profile, and her fair skin was flawless. If I didn't like her so much, I could've hated her.

"Students," she said, joining me at the counter where we could place our orders. "They're so helpless."

"Helpless or hopeless?"

She grimaced. "Sometimes I'm not sure. I used to be so enthusiastic. Ever since I turned thirty, I seem to have less patience. Shouldn't it be the other way around?"

"Not necessarily," I replied. "In some ways, I'm not as patient as I used to be. I suffer fools less gladly. Life gets shorter as we get older."

"That's a sobering thought," Tamara murmured. "In that case, I think I'll order cheesecake along with my sandwich and salad."

I liked her style. "Why not? You're very slim."

"It's my genes," she said.

"Mine, too." I noticed the young clerk in a white apron staring at me. "I'll have the pastrami on light rye with Havarti cheese, sprouts, mayo, and butter, the house salad with honey mustard, and the mocha cheesecake." Late lunches always found me ravenous.

Only three of the dozen tables were still occupied past one o'clock. Tamara and I chose a window setting that looked out into Alpine Way.

"Scott told me I was going to be grilled, just like my panini," Tamara said as we waited for our meals. "That sounds exciting."

"It's not," I admitted. "It's pretty mundane. I understand you know Bree Kendall."

Tamara laughed softly. "In a way. The way, I mean, that sorority sisters know each other. When she moved up here with Carter Nystrom, I thought I should contact her. She was bound to be lonely. I know I was when I first started teaching at the college."

"You say she moved here 'with Carter.' Do you mean . . . what?"

Tamara laughed again. "I don't mean they were a couple," she explained as the white-aproned lad strolled over with our salads. "He'd hired her and the other two girls in Seattle. That caused some hard feelings, you know."

"I didn't," I said. "In what way?"

"There were at least a couple of girls — well, women, actually — who were trained orthodontist assistants already living here. That's unusual, because there's a shortage of them in the profession. Anyway, they'd sent their résumés to Carter when they heard he was coming back to Alpine to set up a practice. He never responded."

"Who were they?"

Tamara lightly salted her salad. "Jeanne Hendrix, who's married to Keith Hendrix, one of our science profs. Jeanne was really annoyed. She worked for an orthodontist in the Bay Area for years before she was married. Jeanne and Keith don't have kids — it's a second marriage for both of them — and she's been at loose ends in Alpine ever since they moved here three years ago. She figured she was a cinch for a job with Nystrom. But that never happened."

When Tamara stopped to take a bite of salad, I posed the obvious question. "Who was the other persona non grata?"

"Someone I don't know, but Jeanne heard she lived here," Tamara replied. She tapped a long, slender finger on the wooden tabletop. "It's an Italian name . . . Della Something-or-other."

"That's her first name?"

Tamara shook her head. "No, her last name." She paused. "Della Croce, I think."

I stared. "Anna Maria Della Croce, by any chance?"

"Yes." Tamara stared back. I must have registered surprise. "Do you know her?"

"Not exactly," I said, recalling my brief encounter on the porch next door to the Nystrom house. "But I certainly intend to get to know her better."

EIGHT

After explaining that the Della Croces were the Nystroms' neighbors, I asked Tamara if she knew anything else about Anna Maria.

"Not really," Tamara said, licking panini crumbs off her lower lip. "Jeanne Hendrix mentioned that she was older by a few years. I'd guess Jeanne to be in her early forties, so maybe this Anna Maria is fiftyish."

That fit the description of the woman I'd seen on the front porch of the house next door to the Nystrom residence. "The Della Croces are supposedly members of St. Mildred's parish," I pointed out, "but I don't know them. They aren't regular churchgoers."

Tamara brushed panini crumbs off her red sweater. "I wouldn't know anything about her if it weren't for Jeanne. Somehow she knew there was somebody else in town who was qualified to work for Dr. Nystrom. Jeanne figured this Anna Maria was the only competition. It turns out nobody here was in the running." Her eyes widened. "Surely that's not . . . oh, Emma, you aren't thinking . . . are you?"

I shrugged. "Not seriously. But the Nystroms seem to be a very isolated family. I can't imagine who'd want to kill any of them, especially Elmer. Tell me more about Bree. Scott said she brought him to your place for dinner, and Ginny Erlandson saw them together at the ski lodge one evening."

"I don't know if they ever were a serious romance," Tamara said as she scrunched up her paper napkin and put it on the table. "I thought — maybe I'm wrong — that Bree seemed a little starry-eyed when they had dinner with us. Carter acted polite — he has terrific manners, I might add — but not what I'd call romantic. For all I know, he squired the other two girls who work for him around town. Or maybe he took them into Seattle on dates. He struck me as having outgrown small-town life."

"Interesting," I remarked. "How do you mean?"

"He talked quite a bit about different cultural and sporting events in Seattle," Tamara related, discreetly checking her watch. "Apparently he went to Mariner baseball games and Husky football and basketball games and the symphony and the opera and . . ." She stopped, looking wistful. "I'll admit, we get shortchanged up here when it comes to events like that."

I sensed what was going through Tamara's mind. She wanted out. And she'd take Scott with her. "Yes," I agreed. "It's not easy to make that hundred-and-seventy-mile round trip into Seattle, especially in the winter. And traffic is so bad once you get beyond Sultan."

Tamara nodded vaguely. "Of course," she said, perhaps to make amends for speaking of Alpine's shortcomings, "it's very expensive to live in Seattle."

"That's true," I said, then steered the subject back to the Nystrom matter. "If Carter is so enamored with city life, I wonder why he didn't go into practice there. I suppose it was because there's no competition here, though I'd think in the long run he could make more money in Seattle."

Our cheesecake slices finally were delivered. Despite the lateness of our lunch hour and the few customers who remained in the café, service was slow. But then, Alpine was slow. I still missed that upbeat big city tempo despite all the years I'd led a small-town life.

Tamara, however, had picked up her own

pace and was practically devouring her New York cheesecake. "I'm sorry," she said between mouthfuls, "but I have a two o'clock class. I'm afraid I haven't been much help."

I disagreed. "You have, actually. You've filled in some of Carter's background and even his personality. Now if I could learn more about Polly, that would add several brushstrokes to the family portrait."

"Fascinating," Tamara said, sounding as if she meant it. "I never realized until I met Scott that journalists get so involved with the stories they write. You're like detectives."

"Crusaders," I said with a grin. "For truth and justice. Or so we tell ourselves when we're prying into other people's private lives. It's a good excuse for being nosy."

"That's not quite fair," Tamara said seriously. "The media is a watchdog for society."

"The media can be not only self-righteous but self-serving," I responded. "One trend that bothers me is that contemporary reporting is often more about the reporter than the subject. I hate that. We should be invisible communicators. Ego shouldn't enter the picture." I laughed. "Sorry. I'm preaching."

Tamara assured me that she didn't care. "The more I know about what motivates

Scott in his work, the better. I want him to understand why I teach, that I hope — maybe without reason — to make some kind of impression on at least a few students. Frankly, it's an uphill battle."

"Life's like that," I said. "By the way, I wanted to treat you to lunch. This was a genuine business meal, approved by the IRS. I didn't realize we had to pay when we ordered."

"Next time," Tamara said, getting up. "It was a nice break from eating in the college cafeteria or bringing a sack lunch."

I smiled. But I knew that Tamara was telling me that sooner or later I'd lose my only reporter.

There was still no news about Milo, according to a disgruntled Vida. I called Father Kelly as soon as I got back to my cubbyhole. Fortunately, he was in.

"With your brother hanging out with me," Father Den said, "I actually have five or six free minutes a day to be at my desk. I'm thinking of holding him hostage from the Lansing diocese."

"I think of Ben as a freelancer, these days," I said. "A mercenary priest or a migrant worker in the fields of God."

"That fits," my pastor agreed. "Are you

sure you don't want to talk to him and not to me?"

"Yes. I'm snooping, but in a good cause. Do you know the Della Croce family?"

"Yes," Father Den said. "Do you?"

"No." I'd rehearsed what I intended to say. "Did Ben tell you that Milo Dodge is in the hospital?"

"He did. Any word on how he's doing?"

"Not so far. It's really frustrating, but I suppose they're waiting for the test and lab results. But," I went on, soothing my soul by reasoning that most of what I was about to say was true, "with the sheriff under the weather, the Nystrom murder investigation is going to stall. The Della Croces live next door to the Nystroms, but I've never seen any of them at Mass."

"They're not regulars," Father Den said. "I've only met them a couple of times, Easter and Christmas. But they're registered parishioners, and I think they've been in town for a few years." He chuckled. "Are you fishing for an invitation to their house?"

"Well, yes. I also thought you might know them better, since apparently Mrs. Della Croce called the rectory the other day."

"Emma." Father Den's tone was reproachful. "Why don't you come right out and say it? Obviously, your brother mentioned that call. Now you figure that Anna Maria or Maria Anna or Chiquita Banana or whatever her name is murdered Elmer Nystrom and was calling the rectory to make her confession. Which, even if it were true, I couldn't tell you without violating the seal of the confessional. If you want to go snooping around the Della Croce place, you have my blessing."

"I do?"

"Yes. Go with God — and good luck. Just don't mention my name, okay?"

I agreed that I wouldn't — and, as soon as I hung up, realized that he wanted to find out what was going on with the Della Croces and felt it wasn't his place to ask. It made me think that maybe there was a connection to Elmer's murder.

If so, he should have gone to the sheriff. Or, for the moment, one of the deputies. Whatever my pastor's motivation, I was the chosen vessel — or goat, as the case might be.

Around two forty-five, I grudgingly turned the radio back on to listen to Spence's mystery interview. Vida heard it from the newsroom and tromped into my office. "What's this?" she demanded, gesturing at the radio where fifties rock 'n' roll music

180

was blaring. " 'Great Balls of Fire'?" Are you reliving your youth?"

"I was a mere child when this song came out," I said. "I'm waiting for Fleetwood's interview with someone connected to the Nystrom murder."

Vida leaned forward so abruptly that she had to grip my desk to stay upright. *"What?"*

"You heard me. He mentioned it on the noon news."

"Oh, for heaven's sake!" She steadied herself and flopped into one of my visitor chairs. "Who on earth can it be?"

"That's why I'm listening," I replied. "It's not anybody from the sheriff's office, according to Jack Mullins."

"I should think not!" Vida exclaimed.

Jerry Lee Lewis was followed by Little Richard's "Tutti Frutti." I turned down the volume and told Vida about my luncheon conversation with Tamara.

"Well, now," she said thoughtfully. "You're going to follow up on this Della Croce woman and perhaps the Hendrix lead as well?" She frowned. "Didn't you ask me about the Della Croce family even before we went to the Nystroms' house?"

I wouldn't mention the phone call to Father Den, not even to Vida. "Yes. Do you want to take on Jeanne Hendrix?"

181

Vida ruminated. "Do I know her? I think not. But certainly I can call on her. I'll use the pretext of a faculty wife angle. The phone directory, please."

I handed her the SkyCo directory. Vida looked for the address, which turned out to be on Cascade Street, not far from her home. "Perhaps I'll call on her after work. If Jeanne still hasn't found a job, she may be lonely, as well as frustrated. That will be my news peg — the educated woman in a small-town market." Vida winced. "Ugh. That's very negative. I shall think of another angle."

It was almost three. The Platters were singing "My Prayer." KSKY often played three songs in a row before a commercial break. "How about the informal group of faculty spouses and partners? They've done some fund-raisers along with their social gatherings. Why not use the postholiday season as your hook? Everybody locks up their wallets after the feel-good, do-good Christmas season. You can tie it in to any local needs that get neglected the first part of the new year. Maybe the women's shelter would be a —"

I shut up as the music ended and turned the radio volume back up. "Appropriately enough, it's a Platters-in-the-Sky ad," I murmured. "They're having a big inventory sale. We carried the ad in today's paper."

Vida nodded. "A co-op ad, I believe."

I nodded back at her. Spence and I had common ground when it came to advertising. We had worked together on many occasions, offering discounted rates to advertisers who would buy both airtime and newspaper space. Usually, the radio ads ran the same day the *Advocate* was published.

Rey Fernandez had recorded the music store's commercial, but it was Spence's voice that uttered the words that followed:

"This is Spencer Fleetwood with a live news report on KSKY-AM. As we promised our listeners on the Cascade slope, the voice of Skykomish County is bringing you an interview with an Alpine resident who has some exclusive insights into the brutal, unsolved slaying of Elmer Nystrom. Here with us at the microphone is a longtime friend and a loyal fan of KSKY, Ed Bronsky."

I thought for a moment that Vida would fall out of her chair. She opened her mouth to say something but quickly clamped her lips shut and glared at the radio.

"Ed," Spence was saying, "I understand that you were in the vicinity of the Nystrom house Monday morning, probably about the time that Elmer was killed. Can you tell us what you observed?"

I heard Ed clear his throat. "It was a gloomy winter morning," he began, sounding pretty gloomy himself, the way he used to sell — or *not* sell — advertising for the *Advocate.* "I was out driving around, sort of contemplating life in general, and I happened to pass by the Nystrom place. I knew it was their house because once, a long time ago, when I was working for *The Alpine Advocate,* I had to drop off an ad for Elmer, who was home with a bad cold."

I remembered that incident all too well. With Elmer sick in bed, Ed had composed his own copy for a Nordby Brothers ad on brake maintenance. He'd written "fiction materials" instead of "friction materials," listed "rooters" rather than "rotors," and referred to calipers as "caliphs." At the time, even I knew Ed had screwed up beyond misspelled words, but I didn't know how to correct the ad. Only the ailing Elmer could rescue us.

"What time was this, Ed?" Spence asked in his usual smooth style.

"Seven-seventeen," Ed replied promptly. "I knew that because I'd just glanced at the digital clock in my Mercedes. And, of course, I was listening to KSKY."

"Good for you, Ed," Spence said, the faintest hint of impatience in his mellow voice. "What did you see while you were passing by the victim's home on the Burl Creek Road?"

"A hamburger?" I whispered to Vida.

She smirked.

"I saw a car." Ed spoke dramatically and paused for effect. "The car was coming from the other direction — from the center of town — and it slowed down when it got near the Nystrom house. Naturally, I figured whoever it was intended to turn in there at the driveway. I thought it was kind of early for visitors, so I slowed down, too, and watched the car in my rearview mirror. It almost stopped, right there by the Nystrom place. But I had to go around that bend in the road, so I lost sight of it. But it definitely struck me as suspicious."

I didn't dare look at Vida, who I knew was about to bust a gusset.

"Can you describe the car or the driver?" Spence asked.

"Like I said, it was still pretty dark. The car was dark, too, like black or brown or blue. One of those dark colors. I'd guess it to be an American-made midsized sedan. Of course, these days, so many cars look alike."

"And the driver?" Spence persisted.

"A man." Ed cleared his throat again. "I'm pretty darned certain it was man. Or a woman with short hair."

"Have you reported this sighting to the authorities?"

"Not yet," Ed said quickly. "You know how it is — you see something that doesn't mean much at the time — and being a trained media type, I see plenty — and anyway, later you realize maybe it was important after all. I've been mulling over what I saw and finally decided this morning I should go public. Sheriff Dodge, of course, is in the hospital, so I thought, well, maybe I should do this over the air because it might alert somebody else who saw something suspicious, too, and then they'd come forward."

"Sound thinking," Spence said with less than his usual conviction. "Thank you, Ed Bronsky, for bringing this information to light over KSKY. Now let's hear from one of our local sponsors."

"Ed's job hunting," Vida declared. "Ed's a ninny. And Spencer Fleetwood has been his dupe."

"Incredible," I said, shaking my head. "How could a sharp guy like Spence let Ed talk him into that so-called interview? Was

186

it Spence's way of getting out of hiring Ed?"

"If so, it was a very stupid thing to do." Vida turned in her chair as Leo came through the newsroom. He looked at us and kept coming.

"What's up?" he asked.

I signaled for him to be quiet. The commercial had ended. But it wasn't Spence's voice that came out of the radio; it was Rey Fernandez, announcing the continuation of the rock 'n' roll programming. I wondered if Spence was pummeling Ed into the station's cinder-block wall.

I switched off the radio while Vida started to explain what we'd just heard. Leo, however, interrupted.

"I know," he said. "I heard it in my car. What a jackass!"

"Which one?" I said in disgust.

"Good point." Leo leaned on the back of my empty visitor's chair. "What if Ed's telling the truth?"

"What if he is?" Vida snapped. "It means nothing. A car driving on the Burl Creek Road — it could have been headed to the college, the fish hatchery, anywhere along that route. Maybe the driver slowed down to see who was driving a Mercedes. There aren't many of them in town."

"True," Leo allowed.

"Besides," I put in, "if Ed really saw anything suspicious, even he would've told the sheriff before this. For that matter, why didn't he tell *me?*"

Leo smirked. "Because you'd already turned him down for a job?"

Vida uttered an exasperated sigh. "Really! This is all too ridiculous! Can't Ed be arrested for bearing false witness? Or something like that? At the very least, there should be a law against such nincompoopery!"

"I think," Leo said in mock seriousness, "the word has to be invented by someone other than you, Duchess. I'd better get back to work, or maybe Ed *will* replace me."

Leo went back into the newsroom. Vida rose from the chair.

"Maybe," I muttered, "I should talk to Ed."

"Don't," Vida ordered. "It's a waste of time." She tromped away in her splayfooted manner.

My phone was ringing. I answered it to hear Cal Vickers's voice on the other end of the line.

"Say, Emma," he said, "I was just listening to Ed Bronsky on KSKY. How's the sheriff doing?"

I assumed this wasn't a complete non

188

sequitur. "I don't know anything you don't," I said. "Why do you ask?"

"Well . . ." Cal's conversation meandered when he wasn't talking about fuel pumps or tire pressure or any of the other subjects connected to his Texaco service station. "I had an early morning tow job Monday out by the Burl Creek Bridge. Gus Tolberg had a little too much beer at Mugs Ahoy Saturday night, and he went off the road. He wasn't hurt, but his pickup got banged up and had to be towed back into town."

I thought back to Scott's weekly listings from the police log. "I don't recall that item. Did Gus report it?"

"Uh, no. Being a bailiff, Gus didn't want to get into trouble." Cal lowered his voice. "I shouldn't have mentioned his name. Can you keep a lid on this one, Emma?"

"I have no choice," I said. "If it's not in the log, it's not in the paper."

"Okay. Good. Thanks," Cal said, sounding relieved. "Anyway, this was just before seven because I wanted to get the pickup out of the way before all those college kids came down that road. You know teenagers — they don't always pay attention, especially on these dark mornings when they're still half-asleep."

I was getting impatient, but I knew there

was no hurrying Cal unless he was presenting me with a large bill for doing a brake
job. Even then he stalled, probably savoring
the moment. "Right," I said.

"So I went out to the bridge and hooked
up the truck and started back into town,"
Cal continued. "I had to go pretty slow past
the part of the road near the Nystrom place
because — wouldn't you know? — a couple
of kids were riding their bikes to the college. I mean, I guess that's where they were
going. The high school is in the opposite
direction."

"Right," I repeated as Cal paused for
breath.

"Oh, they had lights on their bikes, but
still, that time of day in January and the
road being kind of bumpy — well, you have
to be careful, especially if you're driving a
tow truck with a load. So I was only doing
about fifteen miles an hour when I passed
the Nystrom place. The lights were on —
most working people are up that time of
day, of course."

Cal paused again. "Of course," I agreed,
filling the void and letting him know I was
still conscious.

"But there was another light out back,
near the henhouse," Cal went on. "I didn't

think much about it until I heard Ed on the radio."

I was mystified. "How do you mean?"

"Well, Elmer always took care of those chickens before he went to work. When he'd stop by to get gas, he'd talk about feeding those chickens. They had names — like Alice and Ruthie and Hazel. Elmer called them 'his girls.' Elmer could go into details, you know. Anyway, when Ed mentioned that he was going by the Nystrom house at seven-seventeen, that didn't sound right to me, not from how Elmer talked about his chicken schedule."

"I see," I said, though I was not completely enlightened.

"So this was a couple of minutes before seven. Now, how long does it take to feed the chickens and collect the eggs?"

"I've no idea," I admitted.

"Not long, not with the few chickens Elmer had," Cal said, sounding on almost as firm ground as if he'd been discussing wheel alignment. "So I started to wonder. Was somebody else out there by the henhouse?"

I was still puzzled. "What makes you think that?"

"Because there wasn't any light on in the henhouse," Cal said slowly. "The light I saw

191

was bobbing around off to the left of it — away from the main house."

"Oh." I thought for a moment. "It still might have been Elmer. Maybe he'd heard an animal on the prowl. Maybe he liked to check things out before he went to work."

"What things?" Cal asked.

"I don't know," I confessed. "This time of year, cougars and deer and even bear come down from the mountains. I'm sure Elmer was very fussy about keeping his chickens safe."

"Well, maybe. But do you think I ought to tell the sheriff? Or one of the deputies if Dodge is still in the hospital?"

"Why not?" I sounded flippant and was immediately sorry. "That is, any information connected with the investigation is worth mentioning."

"That's kind of what I thought," Cal said. "On the other hand, I don't want to be an alarmist."

"I'm sure that they'll be glad to hear what you have to say, Cal."

"Okay. I'll wander over to the sheriff's office when things slow down at the station." Cal rang off, though not before I remembered to ask him if his wife, Charlene, was feeling better. He said he thought so. I took that typical male response to mean that

Char was still breathing.

My other line blinked, indicating a call on hold. I pressed the button, and Ginny put the caller through.

"Emma!" It was Janet Driggers, the wife of the funeral home's impresario, Al Driggers. "Are you playing bridge tonight at Edna Mae's?"

"Yes," I said. "I'll go over there as soon as I finish listening to *Vida's Cupboard.*"

"Oh, sure," Janet said. "Nobody skips Vida. But why doesn't she ever have any *really* juicy gossip? I could fill her ear if I wanted to."

No doubt Janet wasn't kidding. If there was ever anyone who could learn — or invent — the most salacious sort of dirt, it was the ribald wife of our local funeral director. "Vida doesn't want to get sued for slander," I said. Furthermore, Vida didn't consider Janet a reliable source. My House & Home editor insisted that Janet embroidered her gossip with lurid details that weren't fit to repeat.

"I could add something to this Nystrom whack job," Janet asserted.

"Such as?"

"Check out the next-door neighbors," she replied.

"The Della Croces?"

"The very same. Their teenage daughter, Gloria, is known as SuperSlut. I've heard that she's got all kinds of boys coming to their house at all hours. I figure one of the Nystroms complained about all the moaning and groaning and other cries of sexual ecstasy, so Gloria or one of her adolescent studs got revenge by killing poor old Elmer."

"No kidding," I said.

"I never kid when it comes to sex. Well . . . I do, but that's part of the fun. Anyway, I thought I'd spill this to you now because sometimes our fellow bridge club members are easily shocked. Or pretend to be. But," she added in an insinuating tone, "you know how that goes."

I did, which was why I'd been exiled from the club several years earlier. My own alleged affairs had branded me with an *A*. As far as I was concerned, the letter stood for *Absent.*

As for Janet's assertions about Gloria Della Croce, her theory concerning a motive for Elmer's murder seemed far-fetched. But the problem was that no better reason had come to light. This seemed to be a murder without a motive. Random, perhaps, senseless, a terrible waste. Yet it had happened. I knew that from experience, especially when I'd worked for *The Oregonian* in a bigger city like Portland.

But I didn't think that was what had happened to Elmer.

NINE

The afternoon, however, was dwindling away. Shortly after four, Vida returned to my office, looking annoyed.

"I just fielded a complaint over the phone," she declared.

"About what?" I asked.

"Amer Wasco's distant cousin," she replied, tucking her blouse with its bright red amaryllis pattern into the waistband of her black pleated skirt. "Jan Wasco died in Seattle last week, and we didn't run his obituary in today's paper."

The Wascos owned the local cobbler shop. "Oh?" I remarked as Vida paused to rearrange the black sweater vest that she wore over her blouse.

"Yes. Amer — well, having emigrated from Poland, he doesn't spell terribly well, though he's certainly a fine shoemaker — so he asked his niece — this Jan Wasco's grand-daughter — to send us an obituary. Amer and DeeDee thought the death notice should appear in the *Advocate* because he — the deceased — and his wife, Irena, visited here once in a while. Anyway, he called to find out why we hadn't run it. I told him it was because we never got it. He was very put out."

"Of course," I said. "Is Amer certain his niece sent us the obit?"

"She told him she'd mailed it last Friday," Vida replied. "I told Amer we still might get it, and we'd run it next week. I also suggested that his niece resubmit it, just in case. Marlow Whipp isn't always the most dependable postman, and I don't think the other carriers are much better."

To dissipate Vida's annoyance at our alleged oversight, I divulged the gossip that Janet Driggers had passed on over the phone.

"Janet!" Vida said scornfully. "Everything and everybody is all about sex with that woman! Really, I'm not sure I believe this tale."

Because of my promise not to mention my pastor's name, I still couldn't elaborate about Mrs. Della Croce's phone call to the rectory. But the incident — and Father Den's reaction — strengthened the plausibility of Gloria Della Croce's wanton behavior. Maybe the mother needed pastoral advice on how to handle her wayward daughter.

"I'd still like to call on the family," I said, "if only to find out how miffed Anna Maria is about not being hired by Carter Nystrom."

"By all means," Vida urged. "Will you go tonight?"

"I can't," I said with regret. "I have to meet Ben for dinner and then play bridge."

"You could go now," Vida pointed out.

"We still haven't heard anything about Milo."

"I know." Vida looked solemn. "That worries me. I'm going to call Doc Dewey directly. My niece Marje will put me through to him unless he's in surgery."

Vida returned to my cubbyhole five minutes later. "Honestly! It's impossible to get a straight answer out of anyone in the medical profession! You'd think that being a practitioner was some sort of secret society, like the Black Hand."

"Did you talk to Doc?"

"Of course." She made a face. "He says they still don't know for sure. Doc thinks that because Milo smokes it could be a minor heart attack. Dr. Sung is leaning toward gallbladder. Marje told me on the

QT that it sounds like a virus to her."

"Are they keeping Milo overnight?"

"Yes. For observation. Naturally, Milo is very angry. That's probably because he can't smoke in the hospital."

"Then I should visit him instead of the Della Croces. I can see them tomorrow, maybe in the morning."

One of the things I wanted to do before I left work was to call Spencer Fleetwood. Luckily, he was at the station. But he wasn't very happy to hear my voice.

"Look," he said before I could get started, "don't you think I quizzed Bronsky before we went on the air? He made it sound as if he'd actually seen something or someone he could identify. Of course I cautioned him that he couldn't suggest he'd seen who killed Elmer, but he felt that whoever this figment of his imagination was would be a useful witness."

"Sucker," I said.

"I know, I know." Spence paused. "Frankly, I felt sorry for Ed. I'd had to turn him down when he asked about a job here. Then he came up with this so-called information, and I caved. No matter what you think, I'm not totally heartless."

I didn't think that. Not anymore. I'd seen Spence when he was at his lowest ebb. Mr.

Radio had turned out to be as vulnerable as the rest of us.

"Have you gotten any calls about the interview?" I asked.

"Oh, sure. At least a half-dozen other people have phoned in to say they saw something suspicious, including Averill Fairbanks, who insisted that cloven-hoofed aliens from Neptune wearing LA Lakers uniforms killed Elmer."

Averill was our resident UFO spotter. Two days before Christmas he'd phoned me to report that Santa's sleigh had been hijacked by terrorists from a distant star called Scroogii.

"Maybe," I said, "I share some blame in this. I rejected Ed's offer to come back to work for me a couple of days ago."

"Good thinking," Spence said. "Got to go. I'm doing the five o'clock news."

"Got anything good?"

"Would I tell you if I did?"

"Of course not. But I will be listening to *Vida's Cupboard.*"

"So will everybody else. Her ratings are sky-high. If she could extend her grapevine to Monroe, I might apply to the FCC for more power." Spence hung up.

Great. That was all I needed — Spence acquiring outside ad revenue because he'd snagged my House & Home editor for KSKY. On the flip side, however, that might mean more co-op deals with the station. I decided not to look for trouble where it hadn't yet happened. I had enough already.

I finished a few more minor tasks and drove to the hospital shortly after four-thirty. Milo was on the second floor, where Debbie Murchison, a young RN, was at the nurses' station.

"We're about to serve dinner," Debbie said with a big dimpled smile. "Turkey. Yum."

I wondered if the turkey was left over from Christmas. "Isn't dinner a little early?"

"Oh, no," Debbie replied, still smiling. "We have to let our patients digest their food and take their meds and get settled in for the night shift."

"By the way," I said, "when did Bree Kendall come to work in the emergency room?"

"Monday." Debbie couldn't seem to stop smiling. "Isn't she a doll?"

I wanted to say that the last doll I'd seen that acted as ornery as Bree was a miniature of the Wicked Witch from *The Wizard of Oz*. Instead, I mused that she must have found her previous employment unsatisfactory. "I assume," I said humbly, "that Bree wanted to be in a situation where she could do more for patients with serious problems."

Debbie's smile faded. "You mean . . . but she's not a nurse."

"I meant," I explained as Elvis Sung came out of one of the patient rooms, "that she could assist with medical cases rather than cosmetic care. I assume that's why she quit the receptionist's job with Dr. Nystrom."

"I wouldn't know about that," Debbie said. "Bree just wanted a change."

Dr. Sung greeted me with a friendly expression. "I'm guessing you're here to see the sheriff."

"That's right," I said. "How is he?"

Dr. Sung grimaced. He was a square-built, good-looking young man of mixed Korean and Hawaiian ancestry. "I understand you've known Sheriff Dodge a lot longer than I have. You can probably figure out how he is, being confined to bed rest for twenty-four hours."

"Mean as a bear in a bee's nest, I suppose," I said.

"That's not a medical definition, but it'll do. Enter at your peril," the doctor said, stepping aside. "Second room on your right."

Bravely, I walked across the threshold. Milo was sitting up in bed, watching an NBA game. His six-foot-five frame seemed to overflow the narrow hospital bed, and the covers were a tangled mess. He took one look at me and said, "Oh, God." It wasn't a prayer.

I came closer, standing at the foot of the bed. "You don't look too bad," I said. "How do you feel, besides lonesome, ornery, and mean?"

"Just like Waylon Jennings's song," Milo muttered. "I could use a dose of ol' Waylon's music about now. The Sonics are getting their asses kicked by the Spurs. That figures."

"Any news?"

Milo turned the volume off on the TV set. "That's a funny question coming from you, Emma. How would I know? Nobody tells me a damned thing. Maybe I should go AWOL. To hell with them. Give me a ride home." He started to get out of bed.

"Hey!" I gave him my fiercest look. "Don't even think about it! Sung's outside in the hall. He'll call the" — I almost said "cops" — "somebody to make you stay here."

"Shit." Milo retreated. "Sung was a college wrestler. I don't want to tangle with him. My sidearm's back at the office."

I sat down in the plastic molded visitor's chair next to the bed. "In lieu of a professional medical opinion, what do you think is wrong with you?"

"Food poisoning," Milo replied. "I picked up one of those precooked chickens at the Grocery Basket last night. Except it wasn't cooked all the way through. I should sue the O'Tooles."

"You mean salmonella," I said, adding quickly, "which is a form of food poisoning. But chest pains?"

"Indigestion," Milo said. "You can get a gut ache even up high."

"Okay, Dr. Dodge. That's as good an explanation as I've heard. Is there anything I can do for you?"

"Sure. Close the door and crawl into bed with me."

"I must decline," I replied in a mock prim voice that would have done Vida proud. "I have to meet my priestly brother for din-ner."

"Dinner." Milo made a face. "What kind of slop are they feeding the inmates here tonight?"

"Turkey," I said. "Cooked through and through. And over and over and over."

"Shit," Milo said again. "Go away, Emma. I can't stand looking at people who are free to come and go. I might as well be locked up in one of my own frigging jail cells."

"Okay," I said, getting up. "You're too

crabby to be really sick. You aren't even hooked up to any IVs."

"That's because I yanked them out," Milo retorted. "Beat it."

I did. But I was still worried about the sheriff. He hadn't asked any questions about the Nystrom murder. That seemed very odd.

Ben was ten minutes late arriving at the Bourgettes' diner. I'd secured a booth for us and told Terri Bourgette, the hostess, to show my brother where to find me.

"Rush-hour traffic," Ben said blithely when he showed up at five-forty. "All those four cars and two trucks on Alpine Way."

"Very funny," I shot back. "Why don't you get a watch that works?"

"It does work," he said reasonably. "It just doesn't keep time very well."

"I should've bought you a new one for Christmas."

"I wouldn't wear it if you did," he replied, picking up the menu. "What does Lucille Ball recommend tonight?"

Ben referred to our booth's décor with its still photographs of Lucille Ball and Desi Arnaz in scenes from their fifties TV series *I Love Lucy.* "Terri mentioned the meatballs," I said. "Personally, I'm going to have the crab club sandwich." Suddenly I leaned forward. "Damn it, Ben, why do you have to leave? It's so wonderful having you here in town. Why can't you get posted closer to Alpine?"

Ben didn't look up from the menu. "I go where I'm sent. You know — the vow of obedience."

"Yes, yes." I tried to look contrite. "But sometimes I'd like to have family around. I feel like an orphan with you and Adam so far away. It's selfish, but I get lonesome."

"Who doesn't?" Ben said, putting the menu aside. "I'm rootless these days, but you've lived in Alpine for . . . what? Thirteen years? You have a family of sorts. Vida and the rest of your staff. The sheriff. Your bridge-playing pals."

"It's not the same. They're not blood."

"No." Ben gazed at a black-and-white picture of Lucy and Desi, who in turn were gazing at the baby who had been born to them during the height of their TV fame. They looked like a happy family. It turned out later that they weren't. But they had put on a good enough act to fool most of America. "Happiness is an illusion," Ben said.

"You mean the superficial kind," I responded.

"I mean any kind."

I quibbled. "I wasn't talking about being happy. I know the difference between *un-happy* and *lonely.* I know the difference when you or Adam is with me. I feel . . . more complete, like being whole, because I'm part of somebody else."

Ben shrugged. "Yes, I understand that. But you know as well as I do that families aren't always happy, whether they're to-gether or apart. And in the end, we're all alone. Except for God."

"Thanks for making me feel better," I snapped. "Maybe I'll order the strychnine sandwich and be done with it."

"Go ahead," my brother said cheerfully. "It's my treat, remember."

It was impossible for me to stay angry with Ben. He made me feel good even when he was trying to make me feel bad.

We finished eating a little after six-thirty. Ben followed me to my house so we could listen to Vida's program together.

"You're only doing this because I bitched about you leaving," I said as we went inside.

"True," Ben said. "On the other hand, I'm not the one who's running off to play bridge instead of watching mindless television with her dear sibling."

"I assumed you had things to do," I said, turning on the kitchen light. "You usually do, even when you're on vacation."

"As a matter of fact," Ben replied as he opened the refrigerator, "I have a late date with Sherry at eight our time, eleven in Lansing."

"Who's Sherry?" I asked. "And what are you looking for?"

"Whatever it is, I'm not seeing it. I was in the mood for crab dip."

"I don't keep that on hand. If you were still hungry, why didn't you have dessert?"

Ben closed the fridge. "I'd rather have crab dip."

"So who's Sherry?"

"She's a seventy-six-year-old parishioner who's still working to support her father, who's a hundred and one. I talk to her every week after she gets home from her shift at the local convenience store. She's been held up twice but ran off the would-be thieves with her .38 Smith & Wesson."

"Good Lord," I said.

"Family." Ben smiled as we went into the living room. "Not always a bundle of fun."

"You've made your point." I turned on the radio before sitting on the sofa. KSKY was playing its usual oldies-but-goodies show that preceded Vida's program. The

208

music was most appropriate.

Ben was admiring my river painting. "Has this Laurentis done anything recently?" he asked.

"Not that I know of," I replied. "That is, Donna Wickstrom hasn't shown a new work lately at her art gallery. I'll ask her tonight. She joined the bridge club a few months ago."

Ben sat down in the easy chair just as Connie Francis finished singing and a station break was announced.

"Now," Spence's recorded voice said, "stay tuned for KSKY's weekly edition of *Vida's Cupboard,* featuring all the news that's not fit to print. Hot off the gossip griddle is *The Alpine Advocate*'s House & Home editor, our favorite friend and neighbor, Vida Runkel."

The sound of a cupboard door being opened came across the airwaves. A couple of months before, it had been followed by a crash and a clatter reminiscent of Fibber McGee's closet on the old radio comedy show. Vida had pitched a fit and threatened to box Rey Fernandez's ears for his practical joke. Later, she'd confided to me she was secretly pleased that anyone as young as the almost-thirty Rey would know about a radio program that had been popular during the thirties and forties.

Vida's slightly braying voice was always amplified over the microphone. She began with a roundup of holiday parties that she hadn't had space for on her page. "Clancy and Debra Barton revived an old Irish custom on St. Stephen's Day — the twenty-sixth of December — by forming a Wren Boys procession. They planned to go from door to door, begging money for the penniless wren they carried on a stick. The wren was made of papier-mâché, and unfortunately blew away in the strong December wind before they got to the first home on the block. Darla Puckett's golden retriever, Noodles, mistook the bogus bird for the real thing and swallowed part of it, resulting in an emergency trip to Dr. Jim Medved's clinic. The money the Bartons intended to collect for the local food bank will go instead toward the Pucketts' veterinarian bill. Very generous of the Bartons, I'm sure."

Ben looked up at the ceiling and groaned softly.

Vida continued: "Two of our fine community college students who have Egyptian ancestry, brothers Anwar and Naguib Tabak, celebrated Christmas on Monday, January sixth, with traditional food and drink. They ate a form of shortbread called *kaik* — that's spelled K-A-I-K — and drank a beverage known as *shortbat*. Some student pranksters apparently put a little extra something in the *shortbat*. Happily, the Tabak brothers were treated and released from Alpine Hospital early Tuesday morning."

"Roger, the prankster?" Ben said.

I shrugged. It sounded like the kind of stunt Vida's grandson would pull.

Barely pausing for breath, Vida rattled off a number of other parties and open houses held over the New Year's holiday. "Now we must pause for a word from one of our fine sponsors. But I'll be back with a very timely and informative guest who has some fond memories of the late Elmer Nystrom."

Ben stared at me. "Who is it? Did Vida give you a heads-up?"

"No." I was annoyed. "She'd better not be scooping herself."

After the Itsa Bitsa Pizza and Parker's Pharmacy commercials, Vida returned. "Originally, I'd planned to interview Charlene Vickers about what to do with those wilting poinsettias after Christmas, but Charlene has come down with flu. We hope she has a speedy recovery. We wish the same for Sheriff Milo Dodge, who was hospitalized this morning but has been upgraded to satisfactory condition and is resting comfortably."

"Ha!" I said. "*Un*comfortably."

"Now," Vida said, "I take great pleasure in bringing you one of Alpine's fine young men, who is following in the footsteps of his father and his uncle, Bryce Nordby. Bryce, won't you tell us how you came to know and admire the late Elmer Nystrom while working at the Nordby Brothers GM dealership?"

"Ah," I said. "Not quite scooping herself."

"I've always been crazy about cars," Bryce replied, "so I decided to become a mechanic. I was going to go away to school to learn the trade, but Elmer told my dad, Trout, he could teach me everything I needed to know. So I stayed in Alpine and learned from Elmer, and now I'm a full-fledged mechanic."

"That's a wonderful story," Vida said in her most unctuous manner. "Staying in Alpine was so wise — and mature — of you. I'm sure Elmer was an excellent teacher. He seemed like a very kind, patient man."

"Right. Totally. But he wouldn't let anybody cut corners or cheat on the job. He was real strict about that. Like, when I was learning to drive five, six years ago, he really got on me for going too fast up and down Front Street. Stuff like that. He was the

212

same way with my brother, Brad, when he learned to drive a couple of years ago. You had to do it Elmer's way because it was the right way."

I tried to picture the younger pair of Nordby brothers but couldn't come up with any images. Of course I must have seen them around town, but I hadn't made any connection with Trout and Skunk.

"I'm sure," Vida was saying, "that Elmer will be very hard to replace. I know you're still quite young, but do you have any aspirations to become head of the parts department?"

"Naw," Bryce replied. "I like being a mechanic. That'd be more in Brad's line, but he's only eighteen and wants to become a billionaire."

Vida's chuckle seemed forced. "Ha, ha. I'm sure most young people would like to do that. But money isn't everything, you know. It's very important to get satisfaction from your work. I'm sure Elmer taught you that."

"Oh, wow, yeah, totally. And I do. Guess I'm just a grease monkey at heart."

"And a very fine thing it is," Vida declared, "with Americans so dependent on their vehicles these days. I wish every young person felt as you do about your job, Bryce."

"Me, too, but they don't sometimes. I mean, like, I try to tell Brad — my brother — that, but he doesn't listen. All he wants to know is how to make big money."

"Perhaps he will someday." She paused. "Thank you, Bryce, for being my guest this evening. That's all we have time for tonight, dear friends. I'm closing my cupboard until next week at this same time. Stay tuned to KSKY for more easy listening."

I turned off the radio. "That was a dud," I remarked.

"Vida's heart was in the right place," Ben said. "She wanted someone who knew Elmer, and Bryce definitely did. Besides, he's from the younger generation. It speaks well for Elmer that he could communicate with a teenager."

Both Ben and I stood up. I glanced at my watch. "That's odd. It's only seven-twelve. Vida's show didn't run for the full fifteen minutes."

"Maybe *your* watch doesn't work very well, either," Ben said.

I checked the digital clock on the VCR. "It just switched over to seven-thirteen. Vida cut at least a couple of minutes off of the program."

"Is it prerecorded?" Ben asked.

"No. It's live. Except I think there's a five-second delay during the interview portion in case somebody says something libelous or obscene. There was an incident a few months ago when Vida had the Dithers sisters on and they talked — actually *talked* instead of neighing and whinnying like their horses. One of them — I forget which — started to explain about giving their sick stallion, Tubby, an enema. Vida had to pull the plug — so to speak — when it got too graphic."

Ben grinned. "Yes. I'm glad I missed that one."

"I'll try to call Vida after she gets home," I said, putting my jacket on again and grabbing my purse. "I can do it at bridge club when I'm dummy."

"In the interest of my eternal soul, I'll skip the smart remark on that one," Ben said as we went out the front door. He noticed that I wasn't going to my car in the carport. "You want a lift?"

"With you in your Deathmobile? No thanks. I'll walk. Edna Mae lives only a block away."

We parted company. Ben shot out of the driveway in his Jeep and roared past me before I could get to Fir Street. I moved fairly fast along the unpaved verge. It was raining harder, heavy cold pelts that hinted at snow later in the night.

Edna Mae greeted me at the door. "Come in, come in, it's nasty out there," she said, taking her usual birdlike steps to make way. "Dixie Ridley and Molly Freeman got here early to listen to Vida's show with me. The others should be along any minute. Would you like some hot cocoa?"

"Oh — no, thanks." Edna Mae used water instead of milk for her low-fat cocoa despite the fact that she didn't carry more than a hundred pounds on her five-foot frame. The other hostesses usually served wine, which always required the pulling of drapes to keep out prying eyes that might spot two of the high school faculty wives — Dixie and Molly — imbibing spirits. Janet Driggers, however, offered a wide range of adult beverages and ended her hospitality offerings with "Stroke him if you got him." Edna Mae always pretended she didn't understand the remark. Or, come to think of it, maybe she wasn't pretending.

Molly, who was married to Karl Freeman, the high school principal, and Dixie, the wife of the football coach, Rip Ridley, greeted me cordially. Neither was among my staunchest supporters, but at least they hadn't tried to run me out of town.

The rest arrived in quick succession: Darlene Adcock, whose husband, Harvey, owned the local hardware store; Mary Jane Bourgette, mother of the diner clan and wife of Dick, a local building contractor; Donna Wickstrom, who ran a day-care center along with her art gallery and was Ginny's sister-in-law; and last, but certainly not least, Janet Driggers.

Edna Mae might dither and fidget, but she was organized. Her career as a librarian had given her plenty of experience. Tally cards were handed out. I drew Mary Jane as my first partner, opposing Dixie and Janet. We seated ourselves at the two tables and cut the cards.

"King of spades," I announced, flipping my card into the middle of the table. "It's my deal."

Dixie, who had been a marching band majorette in her younger days, bounced in her chair and bid one heart before turning to me as I began to deal out the hands. "How's Sheriff Dodge, Emma?" she asked.

Though her expression was ingenuous, she might as well have said, "How's the sheriff you sleep with now and then, you snooty little tart?"

I shrugged. "According to Vida, he's been upgraded to satisfactory condition. But you must have heard her program."

"Oh — of course." Dixie smiled, showing off her dimples.

Mary Jane, who was a fellow Catholic, shot Dixie an arch glance. "So you have a heart after all, Dixie, dear. I mean, *hearts*. Then I'll bid one spade."

"The better to dig the dirt with," Janet murmured, and passed.

Since I was holding a mediocre hand, the best I could do for Mary Jane was to bid one no-trump. "Since we can't provide much support, it seems as if Dixie and Mary Jane have all the high cards," I said to Janet.

Janet's expression was unreadable. "Mmmm," she said.

Mary Jane passed. Dixie scowled at her cards and then rebid her hearts. The rest of us passed. As dummy, Janet laid down her hand, showing a high card count of fifteen. Dixie shrieked.

"Why on earth didn't you respond to my opening bid?" she demanded.

Janet remained inscrutable. "I don't know. I thought you were fishing. You know, just trying to get some information."

"I'll bet we have at least a small slam," Dixie said angrily. "Since when did you get to be so cautious?"

I didn't know where to look. I knew that Janet was being ornery to spite Dixie for her query about Milo. Janet — and Mary Jane, for that matter — tended to take my part in any situation.

"I've had a bad enough day as it is," Dixie grumbled as I led a low club.

"Not getting any?" Janet said, batting her eyelashes.

"Oh, stop it, Janet!" Dixie exclaimed. "Could you stop talking about sex for once? Frankly, it gets tiresome. You'd think you were still in high school!"

"Sorry," Janet deadpanned. "I just thought maybe you hadn't had any since you were in high school."

Dixie raked in the trick with the king of clubs from her hand. She glared at Janet. "Don't even mention high school to me! That's all I hear about from Rip — those damned football and basketball players! It's one thing after another with those kids. I get sick of listening to him gripe about who broke curfew, who was caught drinking beer, who is smoking weed — and most of all, who's knocked who up! What's wrong with parents these days?"

"A fair question," Mary Jane said mildly. "Dick and I've raised six kids, and heaven knows they're not perfect, but we had rules. Even if children are lucky enough to have two parents who are married to each other, they either neglect them or spoil them rotten. There doesn't seem to be any middle ground."

Mary Jane's little speech seemed to help Dixie simmer down. "Don't I know it!" Dixie exclaimed. "So many of them get too much too soon. Cars, computers, all these high-tech gadgets — they have everything. No wonder they won't come to practice and can't take criticism."

Molly Freeman, who was sitting with her back to Dixie, turned in her chair. "Now, Dixie, don't be talking about our students out of school. Literally."

Dixie shifted around to glance at the high school principal's wife. "Okay, okay, I'll shut up. But maybe Karl should use a heavier hand with some of the students. You know who I mean." She scooped up another trick.

Molly leaned halfway out of her chair. "You know darned well that if Karl did anything to the students, he'd get his rear end sued off by the parents. Come on, Dixie — don't blame my husband for today's sorry state of affairs when it comes to the younger generation. Rip's in the same boat, and they're both rowing as well as they can."

Dixie sighed. "I know. I just get frustrated." She took the last trick, making a grand slam. But the steam seemed to have gone out of her. "At least," she said, "we got a part score."

"Right," Janet agreed. "I'll do better next time." Her green eyes darted around the table. "We can all do better."

Her words signaled some kind of truce. The rest of the evening went smoothly enough, except for Darlene Adcock knocking over the bowl of mixed nuts, Donna Wickstrom dealing with one card short that was later found under Molly's foot, and Edna Mae getting hiccups for at least fifteen minutes, causing her partner, Janet, to misplay a hand that had been doubled and redoubled, setting them back a thousand points. But as Janet announced at the end of the evening, there were no deaths and only a few wounds.

I'd tried to call Vida a couple of times while I was dummy, but her line had been busy. I left messages, and when I got home a little after ten, I noticed the red light blinking on my phone.

"I know why you're calling," her recorded voice said. "I also know you must be calling from Edna Mae's. Ring me as soon as you get home."

Quickly, I dialed her number. Vida answered on the first ring. "Goodness! I thought you'd never call! Did you realize I had to censor that dreadful Nordby boy?"

"Yes. You cut almost three minutes off of your program," I replied. "How come?"

"Right after Bryce mentioned his brother, Brad, a second time wanting to be a billionaire, I said something about maybe he will, and Bryce replied, 'Not by knocking up Brianna Phelps. He's going to have to pay big bucks for that dumb stunt.' Or something like that. Naturally, I had to press the mute button. He wouldn't stop going on about it, so I simply ended the show."

"Ah. I knew something must've happened." I thought back to Dixie Ridley's comments about the high school students' misbehavior. "What's Brad Nordby, a senior?"

"Yes," Vida answered, "and Brianna is only a sophomore. In fact, I believe she's underage as far as the law is concerned. Not to mention that she's the Methodist minister's daughter."

"Well," I said, "that's too bad. I wonder how the Reverend Phelps and his wife will handle this."

"With profound embarrassment, I should imagine," Vida said. "But that isn't all I have to tell you."

"What?"

"After we went off the air, I quizzed Bryce

most closely about this little scandal," Vida said. "He told me that he'd confided in Elmer, and Elmer was going to give Brad a good talking to. I gathered that this wasn't the first time Elmer had pitched in with advice for Brad Nordby."

"You're suggesting that . . . ?" I let my voice trail off.

"Yes," Vida said somberly. "I'm suggesting a motive for murder."

TEN

Vida and I discussed Bryce Nordby's revelation for several minutes. It was possible that Brad Nordby had been summoned to the Nystrom home by Elmer and that they had met in the henhouse, but of course we were speculating. Milo Dodge despised speculation, especially from amateurs. But Vida and I both felt that at least we'd found a viable reason for someone to take a dislike to the otherwise lovable Elmer Nystrom.

"If," Vida said, "Dixie Ridley was including Brad in her diatribe about students, I'd guess that the Phelps girl's pregnancy isn't a complete secret. These stories run like wildfire through a high school. Dear me, I'm sadly out of touch with the younger generation. I don't see as much of Roger since he's been going to college. Maybe he and I can have one of our overnights this Friday. And I must talk to Marje and some Methodists."

"Marje and the Methodists," I remarked. "Sounds like a rock band."

Vida wasn't amused. "I can't think of what's wrong with Marje lately. My niece used to be so informative."

"Patient confidentiality bothering her?" I suggested. "Or Doc Dewey has threatened to can her if she leaks any more medical news?"

"Marje does not breach patient confidentiality," Vida declared. "She simply keeps me informed of certain vital statistics. They do run on my page, you know."

Except, of course, that Vida didn't need to know about impending births before the mother-to-be found out. But I didn't argue. My House & Home editor and her niece could struggle with their consciences. My own was enough for me.

After a few more surmises, we hung up. It had been a long day, a busier Wednesday than usual. I went to bed a little after eleven and slept soundly. I awoke to more rain but no snow, not even a hint of frost.

Vida had performed the bakery run, bringing back maple bars — her favorite — and a coffee cake covered with caramelized pecans. She began her morning's work with a call to Jeanne Hendrix. "She wasn't in when I stopped by on my way home last

225

night," Vida explained. "Perhaps she's found a job somewhere else, maybe with an orthodontist in Monroe or Snohomish."

I told her I was going to drop by the Della Croce house in about an hour. "I'll arrive unannounced," I said.

"Sometimes it's better that way," Vida remarked, holding the receiver to her ear. "Hmm. Jeanne Hendrix isn't answering. I'll try later."

As soon as I'd gotten some coffee and a maple bar, I called the hospital. According to whoever answered the phone, Milo was waiting for Doc Dewey or Dr. Sung to release him. I said that the sheriff must be feeling better.

"He is," the female voice replied. "But we're not. He's a very poor patient."

"May I speak to him?"

Long pause. "Very well," the woman finally replied. "I'll put you through."

"Yeah?" Milo's usually laconic voice was a growl.

"Have we eaten our oatmeal this morning? Have we had our bath?" I asked in my most condescending manner.

"Stick it, Emma," Milo snarled. "Why are you calling?"

"Actually," I said, becoming serious, "I have a suggestion for you. Please don't act

226

like I'm being a jackass."

"What?"

A roaring noise could be heard in the background. "You should talk to Bree Kendall before you leave."

The noise, which sounded like a machine, grew louder. *"What?"*

I raised my voice. "You should talk to —"

"Shut that damned thing off!" Milo yelled. "Do it *now!*"

Silence in the background. "Sorry," Milo said, apparently to me. "Some idiot steered a floor polisher into my room."

I explained about Bree and told Milo she should be working the reception desk in the emergency room. "As long as you're there," I added.

"Just because she quit her job —" Milo began impatiently.

I interrupted him. "Hey, you or one of the deputies will talk to her at some point, right? Or have you solved this while you're in the hospital, like Josephine Tey's policeman in *Daughter of Time?*"

"What the hell are you talking about?"

"Never mind." For a moment I'd forgotten that the sheriff never read anything except spy novels and hunting and fishing magazines. "Just do it. Please?"

"If I see her," Milo muttered. "Will you

make me dinner tonight? I'm starving."

"Sure," I agreed. "Assuming, of course, you're not going to be put on a restricted diet."

"Screw that," Milo said. "See you tonight." He hung up.

I checked the AP wire, returned a couple of phone calls, ate the maple bar, and drank my coffee before heading out to the Burl Creek Road. It was almost nine o'clock. I assumed the Della Croces would be up and about.

In fact, on this gloomy January morning, there were lights on in the modest house next door to the Nystrom property. I pulled up onto the grassy verge. The Nystrom house was dark, at least toward the front. I couldn't see the rear of the house, nor could I spot any cars. The driveway led to a garage away from the henhouse and not far from the fence that separated the two lots. I got out of the Honda and opened the front gate.

Stepping-stones had been placed at convenient intervals on the dirt path to the house. A few shrubs grew close to the front, and a big, leggy rhododendron overlapped the handrail on my right. There were only three wooden stairs to the small porch. I rang the bell and waited.

The overweight middle-aged woman I had

assumed was Anna Maria Della Croce opened the door a moment later. The glasses she wore on a chain now hung over a flowered housecoat. "Yes?" she said, eyeing me curiously.

I introduced myself. "I talked to you the other day — after Elmer's death."

"Of course," she said, but sounded uncertain. "You say you work for the newspaper?"

I guessed she didn't read the editorial page. "I'm the editor and publisher," I said. "Do you mind if I come in for a few minutes? I've been doing some background work on Elmer's life."

And death, I could've added, but didn't. Anna Maria stepped aside and led me not into the living room but into the kitchen.

"I was just having coffee," she said. "Would you like some?"

"If it's not any trouble," I replied.

"No, no. I keep a pot going most of the day." She put her hands on her ample hips. "It keeps me from snacking too much."

I sat down in one of the four red schoolhouse chairs. The chairs, along with the red wooden table, were in a nook. Anna Maria poured coffee for both of us.

"I'm not sure what I can tell you about Mr. Nystrom," she said, sitting opposite me. "We've only been here four years, since our daughter started high school. Gloria's a senior now."

"Four years is a fairly long time," I pointed out, "especially when your houses are so close together."

"Yes." Anna Maria looked away toward the small window above the table. "Yes, it is, generally speaking." She turned back to me. "But the Nystroms aren't very outgoing."

"I understand that," I said. "That's why I'm bothering you. Very few people seemed to know the Nystroms intimately, despite Elmer's fine reputation for customer service at Nordby Brothers."

Anna Maria nodded. "My husband, Nick, took his pickup there. It's a Chevy model. Nick always raved about Elmer and the service department. I suppose Nick knew Elmer as well as anybody outside the dealership. Sometimes they'd talk together over the fence."

"Then I should talk to Nick," I said. "Where does he work?"

"For the county," Anna Maria replied, her brown-eyed gaze traveling to a ceramic cookie jar on the kitchen counter. "Would you like a molasses cookie to go with your coffee?"

"No, thanks," I replied. "I just ate a big

maple bar."

"Oh." She looked disappointed. I suspected that she'd hoped I'd accept her offer so she could have a cookie, too. "Where was I?" she murmured. "Oh, yes — Nick. He's a surveyor. He's out with a road crew near the Cascade Tunnel. He won't be home until after five. They quit a little earlier this time of year because it gets dark so soon."

I recalled a news release about improving a dirt road in the area. "I would like to talk to him," I admitted. "If it's okay, I can call him this evening."

Anna Maria grimaced. "Just make sure you do it before eight. He won't talk on the phone once his favorite TV shows come on."

I promised I'd comply. "Did you call on Polly Nystrom Monday?" I inquired.

"Oh, yes," Anna Maria said. "She was terribly upset, of course, poor woman. I didn't stay long. I felt as if I were getting in the way. Her son had come home, and there were a couple of sheriff's deputies snooping around. I think their pastor — Bartleby, isn't it? — was on his way."

I knew I was about to tread on some rocky ground, but faint heart never won good newspaper story. "Do you know Carter Nystrom very well?"

Anna Maria's face grew impassive. "No."

"But you must have been quite friendly with Polly. I mean, both stay-at-home moms and living so close."

The brown eyes grew cold. "Cordial," Anna Maria said after a pause. "We were always good neighbors to them. Polly and I never really talked much. She didn't come outside unless she was giving gardening directions to Elmer or watching Carter work in the yard."

I played stupid. "But you liked her," I remarked.

Anna Maria got up from the chair. "Excuse me for a moment. I think I heard our cat at the door."

She left the nook and went to the back door but returned before a minute had passed. "My mistake. Do you think Elmer was killed by some crazy person?"

"That's possible, of course," I replied.

Anna Maria shuddered. "That's very frightening. Maybe we should get an alarm system." She sat down again and smiled. "Now tell me how you got to be a newspaper owner."

I was so used to asking the questions that I was startled. Someone I hardly knew was showing an interest in my life. I must have stared at Anna Maria.

"I think," she said, "it must be a fascinating story. I've never known a woman who was a publisher."

Of course she was trying to divert me. Still, I answered, though as succinctly as I could. "I had an unexpected inheritance. I decided to quit my job as a reporter for *The Oregonian* and buy a small weekly. The *Advocate* was up for sale."

I went on to explain the money I'd inherited was not only unexpected but undeserved. My ex-fiancé, Don, had listed me as the beneficiary on his Boeing employee insurance policy. After we broke up, he forgot to delete my name. When he died of a heart attack twenty years later, I ended up with half a million dollars. His wife had been furious, but over the years Don had risen in the company ranks and left her and their kids comfortably well off.

Anna Maria looked bemused. "How could anyone — like your fiancé — make such a mistake?"

"It wasn't a mistake," I replied. "When he first went to work for Boeing, there were so many forms to fill out, it took him most of a day. Apparently, as time passed, he forgot about putting my name down as his life insurance beneficiary. Real life was sometimes vague for Don. He was an engineer."

"Fascinating," Anna Maria declared.

"More coffee?"

"No, thanks," I said, "but now tell me if you've had a career." Turnabout was fair play, after all.

"Well." Her features hardened. "Before and after I was married, I worked for many years in Everett, where I grew up. I took several years off after Gloria was born, but I didn't like staying at home, and when she reached third grade, I went back to work. Are you sure you don't want a cookie?"

"Yes, I'm sure, but thank you anyway. What kind of work did you do?"

Her expression was faintly defiant. "I was an orthodontist's assistant."

I laughed, but I don't know if my feigned spontaneity was convincing. "That's a coincidence. With Dr. Nystrom, I mean. Two people in the same profession living side by side."

"I suppose it is," Anna Maria said dryly.

I frowned. "I heard there's an opening in the office. The receptionist quit, and so did her replacement . . . but of course that's not your line." I feigned another laugh, this time of the self-deprecating variety. "What am I saying? I don't even know if you want to go back to work."

Anna Maria shrugged. "We could use the money. Gloria will be starting college next fall. She'd like to go to the UW."

"But you're more than a receptionist," I remarked. "I assume that becoming an assistant to an orthodonist takes quite a bit of training."

"It does." The warmth hadn't yet returned to Anna Maria's eyes. "Are you trying to find out if I resent Carter Nystrom for not hiring me when he opened up his practice?"

I wasn't a very good liar. Certainly my subterfuge hadn't fooled Anna Maria. I decided to come clean. Sort of. "Sometimes when you're investigating a story like this, you have to hear the bad as well as the good. Frankly, all I've heard about Carter's dad is that he was a wonderful man. That certainly doesn't point to anybody having it in for him. So why was he murdered? I can't figure that out until I know why somebody wanted him dead."

Anna Maria's plump fist tightened on the cotton tablecloth. "Isn't that up to the sheriff?"

"Of course. But," I went on, "the sheriff had to be hospitalized yesterday." I saw my hostess nod slightly. "I don't think the doctors know what's wrong with him, which means they'll tell him to take it easy. That may leave this case up to the deputies. They're capable, of course, but any good journalist wants to help find out the truth, if only for selfish reasons, and often that takes a lot of personal questions and probing. It's called investigative reporting."

"It takes a lot of nerve," Anna Maria declared.

"Yes, it does." I paused. "Professionally, I prefer to call it courage."

My words seemed to give Anna Maria food for thought. "I suppose it does. Require courage, that is." She eyed the cookie jar once more. Temptation won. She got up and fetched herself a cookie. Comfort food was also food — and fuel — for thought. And maybe for her own brand of courage.

"Honestly," she began after taking a couple of bites of cookie, "Elmer was a very nice man. Carter was pleasant and polite but distant."

"And didn't hire you," I pointed out as she worked her way down to the last mouthful of cookie. "That might have caused the coolness. Guilt on his part."

Anna Maria shrugged. "Maybe. He must have known I was qualified. My résumé was very thorough, with excellent references. But Carter had already made up his mind and hired outsiders." She grimaced, brushing cookie crumbs off of her housecoat. "Granted, we haven't lived here all that many years, and he was away at school for much of the time. I'll bet Polly knew I was suited for the assistant's position. She's very snoopy."

"You don't talk to her often, though," I pointed out.

Anna Maria made a face. "Who needs to? Polly has her ways. Through their church, her husband and her son, the mailman, your newspaper delivery boys — you name it. Polly grills them all as if she were the police."

"But she's not a social type of person?"

"Not that I can tell. I hardly ever see any cars at the Nystrom house except for their own — Elmer's Chevy and Carter's Pontiac. Polly doesn't drive."

"Interesting," I commented. "It's peculiar for people to want to *know about* others and yet not to want to *know them.* If you see what I mean."

"Oh, I see perfectly," Anna Maria responded. "She wants the dirt, I figure. She's one of those people who has to feel better than anybody else, so she finds out all the negative stuff. I suppose it gives her a certain kind of power over others. She thinks her knowledge makes her superior — and she shows it in the way she acts, even if she is all nice-nice and polite. But the truth is, Polly has —" Anna Maria broke off and gave herself a stern shake. "Never mind. As I was saying, I've never told tales about people like she does. I'm not going to start now."

I considered urging her to finish saying what she'd started. But I could tell from the set of her jaw that she'd refuse.

Her virtuous resolution disturbed me. I was sure that Anna Maria knew something she ought to say.

But maybe she could only tell a priest.

ELEVEN

Anna Maria and I chatted for a few more minutes while she ate a second cookie. The subject moved away from the Nystroms — mostly because she seemed reluctant to talk about them anymore — and onto her daughter, Gloria, or, as I recalled Janet Driggers's description, "SuperSlut."

But Gloria's mother presented quite a different picture. "Our daughter wants to be an urban planner," Anna Maria explained after I'd asked why Gloria was headed for the University of Washington. "She'd actually be in the school of architecture, where she'd get her BA in urban design and planning. Then, if she wants to, she can get an MA and even a doctorate. She's an excellent student, but I don't think she should make such a long-range commitment at this point."

"That's probably wise," I said.

"Gloria's a very sensible girl, if I do say so

myself." Anna Maria wore a pleased expression. "People always label only children as spoiled and selfish. That's unfair. Nick and I've made darned sure our daughter didn't turn out that way." She got up from the table. "Let me show you a picture."

Anna Maria left the kitchen. I took the opportunity to look around the area. It was reasonably, if not compulsively, tidy. A few dirty dishes sat in the sink, a frying pan had been left on the stove, and a plastic bag of garbage was waiting to be taken outside. I had a feeling that the reluctant homemaker took her time in completing household tasks.

She returned with a color photograph in a silver frame. "Senior picture," she said. "They always take them in the fall."

I studied Gloria, a pretty, slightly plump girl with dark blond hair and her mother's brown eyes. Her makeup was spare: mascara, maybe, lip gloss, and possibly foundation base. She looked intelligent and happy. There was nothing in her appearance that would proclaim her as SuperSlut. But then, you can't tell just by looking.

"She's quite attractive," I remarked. "Gloria exudes brains, too."

Anna Maria laughed. "I always tell Nick that I don't know where she got them. I figure that my husband and I are both fairly average."

"Maybe you're underrating yourselves," I said. "You had to be smart to complete your training. I assume Nick needs a brain for his job as a surveyor."

"Well . . . maybe," Anna Maria murmured. She gave me a scrutinizing look. "I've seen you somewhere before. Safeway? The mall?"

"That's possible," I replied. "How about St. Mildred's?"

Anna Maria clapped a hand to her cheek. "That's it! You were at Christmas Mass."

I nodded. "I thought I'd seen you, too, probably at church."

"We don't go as often as we should," she said with a rueful expression. "I'm a slow starter in the morning, no matter what day of the week it is. And Nick . . . well, Nick never has been much of a churchgoer, even though he's a baptized Catholic, too. We don't set a very good example for Gloria."

"Sometimes it backfires," I said. "Gloria's smart. She'll figure it out. My son did, but it took him a long time."

"He goes to church?"

"He's a priest."

Anna Maria's eyes widened. "Really! That's . . . amazing, especially these days. I was so surprised to see two priests saying

241

Mass, not just Father Kelly."

I smiled. "The other priest was my brother. He's been visiting me over the holidays. He's the one who set the example for Adam — my son. It wasn't me. It was Ben."

"For heaven's sake!" Anna Maria continued to look startled. Then, suddenly, her face clouded. "I think I may have —" She stopped. "Never mind. I forgot what I was going to say."

She hadn't, of course. I was sure that Anna Maria was going to mention that she had spoken, however briefly, with Ben on the phone, mistaking him for Dennis Kelly.

I rose from the chair. "I should be on my way. You've helped fill in some gaps."

Anna Maria frowned. "Not very much. I probably shouldn't have said what I did about Polly. But I don't like people who constantly want to think the worst of others. That's the way she strikes me."

"There are people like that," I said, starting out of the kitchen. "It's a nasty habit."

"Yes, but saying those things about her makes me as bad as she is," Anna Maria insisted. "And I don't think it probably helps anybody figure out who killed poor Elmer."

I shrugged. "You never know."

We'd reached the front door. Anna Maria was frowning again. "I suppose not." She bit her lower lip. "You're right. You never know."

As I walked back to my Honda, I reflected on Anna Maria's bouts of evasion. I still had a feeling that she knew more than she'd told me.

After I recounted my visit to the Della Croce house, Vida agreed.

"So," she said, "you think Polly may have started false rumors about Gloria?"

"Maybe," I allowed.

"I must call on Maud Dodd," Vida declared, picking up the phone. "I intended to do that sooner, but I put it off. Very foolish of me. I'm going to see if she's at the retirement home or out gadding. If Maud complained about Polly gossiping, then the tales must have been spread at their church. That's what Maud complained of — the gossip."

"Go for it," I urged, and returned to my cubbyhole.

I found a message from Milo, telling me that he'd be back in his office by noon. It was ten-fifteen. Probably he was still at the hospital, waiting impatiently for Doc Dewey or Dr. Sung to sign the release papers.

"I'm off!" Vida shouted.

I glanced up to see her tromping at top speed across the newsroom. As she went out, Scott came in. He headed straight for my office.

"I was wondering if I could do any kind of follow-up on the Nystrom story," he said. "Or are you going to handle all of it?"

Ordinarily, I would, but I knew Scott wanted to have more variety on his résumé when he sent it out. Experience limited to the police log, occasional features, and photos — albeit good ones — of Mayor Fuzzy Baugh presenting an award to an Eagle Scout wouldn't excite a potential employer. "Let's play it by ear," I said. "You can do any of the stuff that doesn't put us in harm's way. That's probably most of it. But if there's ever any risk of a flap over what we run, I don't want you held responsible."

"Any leads I can follow now?" he inquired.

"Well . . ." I considered the options. "You know Coach Ridley and the rest of the high school faculty pretty well, don't you?"

The public schools, along with their sports programs, were part of Scott's regular beat. He and I shared the college reporting chores.

"Sure," Scott replied, "but Coach is having another bad season. The basketball team has no rebounding."

"Coach is always having a bad season," I pointed out. "The Buckers aren't famous for their athletic prowess. I want you to get him in a talkative mood. Buy him a beer after practice and find out what you can about Brad Nordby and a certain sophomore girl."

Scott's jet-black eyes twinkled. "Does she have a name?"

"Brianna Phelps."

Scott looked even more intrigued. "The Methodist guy's daughter?"

"The Reverend Phelps," I said. "Obviously, this isn't for publication, just background."

"Whoa!" Scott held up a hand. "What's this got to do with Elmer getting killed?"

"Maybe nothing," I admitted. "But Brad Nordby knew Elmer fairly well, and Elmer occasionally took it upon himself to reprimand both Brad and his brother, Bryce. Maybe Elmer believed that Trout Nordby and his wife weren't sufficiently strict. Certainly Elmer must've felt some kind of responsibility for reprimanding the Nordby boys, or at least knew he could give them a talking to without riling his boss."

"Trout's wife," Scott said softly. "Her

245

name's Emily, but they call her Fish."

"Trout and Fish? That figures," I said, "but how does she come by her nickname?"

"Because," Scott replied, "she drinks like one."

Vida returned around eleven. I'd spent part of the last hour having Kip MacDuff try to explain the latest production problem to me. I didn't understand what he was talking about, and he knew it but apparently felt he should at least make an attempt to keep the boss informed. "Just fix it," I'd finally said. The only thing I *did* know was that Kip was capable of fixing just about anything related to computers and high-tech newspaper production.

"Maud Dodd had quite a bit to tell me," Vida announced smugly, "once I got her past her aches and pains. She had several falls before she moved to the retirement home," Vida continued, settling into one of my visitor's chairs and removing the black felt Gaucho hat that was her *chapeau du jour.* "Maud informed me that Polly started a rumor at their church that she — Maud — was addicted to pain pills and forged prescriptions. That was why she fell so much. But of course those of us who know Maud very well are aware that she's always been pigeon-toed. It makes her clumsy and causes her to fall down rather often. Luckily, she's limber for her age."

"Lucky indeed," I murmured.

"Maud got very upset about the pain pill rumors Polly started, because Maud insists she's never taken anything stronger than aspirin in her life, as her longtime pharmacist, Durwood Parker would swear to in court."

"Durwood's been retired for years," I remarked. "Would the Wesleys also swear to it?"

"Certainly. Doc Dewey would, too. But that's not the point." Vida looked faintly piqued. "Polly can be very convincing. Maud says that after the rumor was spread, several people started giving her odd looks and even avoiding her, and one of them — Bertha Cobb — hinted that Maud should go into rehab. Maud didn't know what rehab was until she asked somebody else. She thought it was some sort of a motor home."

"Maud wasn't the only victim, I assume."

"My, no." Vida made a clucking sound with her tongue. "Shameless, really. And people are so credulous! Admittedly, Maud gets a bit muddled, but hardly any of the Episcopalians were left unscathed — not to mention anyone else Polly knew. Doc Dewey himself was a victim, though he has the good sense to ignore such prattle. Polly insisted he'd gotten fresh with some of his female patients. Imagine! That's slander!"

"Slander sounds like Polly's middle name," I noted.

"Indeed. But the woman's so seemingly sweet and so very insidious. A hint, a phrase, a gesture — she apparently never comes right out and *says* things. Really, it's enough to make me want to attend the Sunday Communion service at Trinity Episcopal. But of course I wouldn't dream of abandoning my Presbyterians." She paused and looked at the ceiling. "Or would I? Ecumenism is still in the wind."

"And the wind is blowing a mighty gust of gossip," I said. "Of course you'd be doing such a thing in a good cause."

"Of course." Vida seemed slightly indignant.

"What about the non-Episcopalians?" I asked. "Like the Nystroms' neighbors, the Della Croces, for example."

"Well, now." Vida frowned. "We didn't get off onto names — Maud had to attend her brass rehearsal. She plays the trombone, you know. The retirement home has its own band — or is trying to have one."

"If they ever get it together, write it up," I said, marveling at myself for no longer considering certain small-town activities preposterous.

"If," Vida responded. "At their age, they're a little short on air."

I leaned on the desk, propping up my chin with one hand. "So where does this rampant tongue of Polly's get us? She'd make a better victim than Elmer."

"That's certainly true," Vida said. "Polly might even have attempted blackmail, though there's no indication that she did."

"Nobody would advertise it if they were being blackmailed," I pointed out.

Scott had just returned from the rest of his morning rounds. He approached my cubbyhole and raised a hand. "Is this a private meeting?" he asked.

"No," I said. "Come in. Take the other chair."

He sat down. "I remembered something while I was at the courthouse just now. A couple of weeks ago, the police log had a call to the Nystrom house about a prowler. One of the hens went missing, but Jack Mullins figured it was probably a cougar, coming down from the mountains to get some dinner."

"Makes sense," I remarked. "I vaguely

remember the incident."

"But," Scott went on with a significant glance at both Vida and me, "cougars don't drink milk out of cartons. Two days before Christmas, they reported that their Blue Sky delivery had been swiped."

"A missed delivery, perhaps," Vida suggested.

"Not according to Norm Carlson," Scott said. "He swears he made the delivery himself. Jack figured that in the pre-Christmas rush, Norm might have skipped a house or two on his route that Monday. That's why the incident was never reported in the log, but Jack reminded me when I stopped by the sheriff's office just now after I got finished at the courthouse."

"Pranks," Vida said. "Why?"

"Harassment," I added. "Like sending Elmer's obit to us before he was dead. It seems to be a pattern. Is there anything else in the log — or Jack's memory — before the missing milk?"

Scott shook his head. "Not unless you go back a year or more. There was a trespassing report, either hunters or fishermen going through the Nystrom property. But those get reported all the time. Most people don't bother to call the sheriff unless the situation gets nasty."

"True," Vida said. "It's difficult, especially for fishermen, when the creeks and the river rise and there's no bank to walk along. And often, the trespasser knows the owner and there's no bother. Unless, of course, the two have a long-standing feud."

Feuds weren't uncommon in Alpine. They were part of small-town life, sometimes reaching down through generations and started a hundred years ago by So-and-So letting his cows wander into Such-and-Such's pasture or Mrs. A and Mrs. B getting into it over a misplayed pinochle hand.

"Okay," I said, "so who'd have a grudge against Elmer and the other Nystroms?"

"Somebody got their car repair screwed up?" Scott offered.

"Possible, but unlikely," I said.

"Bree Kendall," Vida announced with a wag of her finger. "Disenchanted employees often resort to mean-minded tricks."

"Or the would-be employees who were never hired in the first place," I said. "Jeanne Hendrix and Anna Maria Della Croce."

"What?" said Scott, looking puzzled.

Vida explained about the two applicants who hadn't been considered. "I still haven't been able to run Jeanne Hendrix down," she added. "I wonder if she's out of town for the holidays."

"Her husband teaches at the college," I pointed out. "He had to start classes Monday for the winter quarter."

"Well . . ." Vida frowned. "Perhaps she's visiting her family and he came back ahead of her."

"Maybe," I said. "Let's not forget Jessica Wesley. She quit after one day."

Scott grimaced. "I know Jess from seeing her at the drugstore. She seems an unlikely killer."

I agreed. "But we can't rule anybody out." I gazed at my handsome reporter. "Maybe you could talk to Jessica. Her parents can't seem to get her to open up about why she quit."

"Where is she?"

"Job hunting? Or she may be back at Parker's," I said. "I don't think Garth and Tara want her sitting around watching daytime TV while she postpones her college education."

"I'll wander by," Scott promised.

Vida nodded encouragement. "By all means. You realize," she went on, addressing us both, "that we can't eliminate anyone who's been harmed by Polly's naughty tongue. And don't remind me that Polly should have been the victim instead of Elmer. Not everyone is rational. For example, the person may have believed that Elmer should have controlled his wife and not allowed her to spread vicious rumors."

"That would seem to include the entire Episcopal congregation and a few others," I pointed out.

"Nonetheless," Vida said, her jaw firmly squared.

I shook my head. "For Elmer being such a wonderful guy, it seems as if about a hundred potential suspects are lurking out there."

Vida leaned forward. "What does that tell us?"

Scott turned sideways to stare at her. "Darned if I know. What?"

"That we're wrong about all of our theories," Vida said earnestly. "There's something about the Nystrom family that we don't know." She frowned, removed her glasses, and began rubbing frantically at her eyes. "Ooooh! Why don't we know? Why don't *I* know?"

The eye-grinding gesture was a sure sign that Vida was agitated. And if there was one thing that agitated my House & Home editor, it was not being in the know.

A few minutes later, after Scott and Vida had left my office, I sat deep in thought and realized I'd flunked my visit to Anna Maria Della Croce. There'd been no hint of why she might have called Father Kelly. Of course it could have been a spiritual matter, but Anna Maria didn't act like she possessed a tormented soul. Missing Mass seemed to bother her only in regard to how it may have affected her daughter. Or maybe she'd simply said that as a face-saving gesture for my benefit, since I went to church regularly and had two priests in the family.

It was possible that whatever had caused Anna Maria to consult Father Den had nothing to do with the Nystroms. Yet he had told me not to mention his name. I translated that not only as discretion on his part but as a way to help me in pursuing the homicide story. If Anna Maria was struggling with her spiritual life, Kelly would have told me to butt out. Yet he hadn't done that. Like my brother, Ben, Dennis Kelly was a commonsense type of priest.

I'd have to give Anna Maria another try. But I didn't know how.

With the problem still licking away at the back of my brain like a deer with a salt block, I dialed the sheriff's number a few minutes before noon. He answered on the third ring.

"Shall I bring lunch in?" I asked. "Or will you change your mind again and decide to eat out?"

"In," he said. "I don't want half the town asking me how I feel, goddamn it. The usual, but get me a big Coke."

"So I'm lunch *and* dinner," I said. "I'm flattered."

"You I can tolerate." He paused. "You haven't asked me how I feel. Don't."

"I won't," I replied. "I'll see you in fifteen minutes."

As I walked into the Burger Barn at five to twelve, I was surprised — but pleased — to see Scott sitting in a booth with Jessica Wesley. I avoided them, not wanting to interrupt what might be a fruitful conversation. If any man in Alpine could get a female to reveal her darkest secrets, I figured it was Scott.

"Wait till Tamara hears this," a voice behind me murmured.

I turned around in the take-out order line. It was Leo, wearing his off-center grin.

"It's strictly business," I said. "I made him do it."

"Better than the Devil," Leo responded. "I hear the sheriff got sprung from the hospital."

"I'm getting his lunch for him," I said,

moving up a place in line. "He's not ready for public viewing."

Leo put a hand on my shoulder. "Oh, Boss Lady, why don't you ever spoil me like that?"

"You're healthy, thank God," I said. "Stay that way."

"I guess I'd better," Leo murmured. "It's job security. Look who's taking the orders."

I looked. Ed Bronsky was behind the service counter, which fronted the open kitchen.

"Good grief!" I shrank down behind the large woman ahead of me, two places shy of Ed. He was wearing a white paper hat with the Burger Barn logo, a white apron, and a red-and-white-striped shirt, de rigueur for the restaurant's employees. "I'm embarrassed," I whispered to Leo. "For Ed. For me."

"And I have the poor bastard's job," Leo remarked ruefully. "Do you think he's seen us? We could check at the Venison Inn to find out if they'd do take-out."

"They don't," I replied, "unless they'd make an exception for the sheriff."

But it was too late. The large woman had dropped her cell phone, and when she bent down to pick it up, Ed spotted us.

"We've blown our cover," Leo murmured.

"Hi, Ed."

Ed nodded and waited on the woman, who had retrieved her cell before moving up to the counter.

"Have you got that?" the woman asked after Ed finished his jottings on the take-out ticket.

"Yes, ma'am," Ed replied. "One double mushroom burger, one salad with blue cheese dressing, one chocolate shake, and one giant lady to go."

"What?" the woman yelped. *"What did you say?"*

Ed looked frazzled. In fact, he was sweating. "One giant fries to go."

"That's not what you said!" the woman shouted. "Do you think I'm fat? *You're* fatter!"

Ed kept his eyes down. "Maybe so."

The woman leaned both fists on the counter. "I want an apology. I want my meal for free."

Leo stepped around me and went up to the irate woman. "Please," he said in an unusually mild tone, "allow me, madam." He removed a twenty from his worn leather wallet. "I'm a fan of Rubenesque beauties. By any chance, have you done plus-size modeling? You look familiar."

The woman seemed taken aback. "No.

I've never seen you before. I live in Leaven-worth. I'm on my way to Seattle." She eyed Leo warily. "What's this 'Ruben' thing? A sandwich?"

"Peter Paul Rubens was a famous Flem-ish painter in the seventeenth century," Leo explained, his voice still mellow as an autumn morning. "His specialty was gor-geous women with flawless, bountiful flesh." He handed the twenty to Ed. "Will this cover the order?"

"Uh . . ." Ed stared at the ticket. "Yeah, yeah, that's good. Thanks." My former ad manager couldn't look my current ad man-ager in the eye.

The woman stepped away, still watching Leo with a curious expression.

"Now," Leo said to Ed, "we're both broke." He opened his wallet, revealing a single dollar bill. "Emma will have to pay for my lunch."

"Not to mention the sheriff's," I said with a sly little smile. "Go ahead, Leo, order yours. Then I'll do mine and Milo's."

Leo made short work of his request and stepped aside in the opposite direction from the large woman. I forced Ed to look at me.

"When did you start here?" I asked.

"Today," Ed replied, finally making eye contact. "It's a job."

"One of your kids should be doing this," I declared. "For heaven's sake, get them off their butts and out hustling."

"You'd better order, Emma," Ed muttered. "There's still a lineup."

I complied, then went over to stand by Leo. "That was really good of you," I said. "Are you actually broke? Payday's not until tomorrow."

"I can go to the cash machine," Leo replied. "I may have almost thirty dollars in my savings account."

I didn't know if Leo was kidding. On the off chance that he wasn't, I didn't press him further. Instead, I stood there like an idiot and felt guilty for not being able to pay my staff higher wages. I wanted to, but the postal rates had risen — again — in June. We mailed the *Advocate* to several subscribers out of the area, including a batch of retirees in California and Arizona. What little extra money I'd put aside, I'd had to spend at the post office. For all I knew, Ed was making more at the Burger Barn than he would've earned in his old job with the *Advocate*.

Milo was at his desk, looking a trifle thinner and slightly pale. Or maybe it was my imagination. But I remembered that I wasn't supposed to ask how he felt.

"Sustenance," I said, unwrapping his order and placing it in front of him. "Real food, courtesy of your humble servant."

"You were never humble," Milo said.

I ignored his comment. "Well," I said, taking my hamburger dip from its packaging, "have you solved the Nystrom case since you came back to work?"

"Funny Emma." Milo bit into his cheeseburger with jaws that would have done credit to a killer shark.

"Do you want to know what I've found out while you were malingering?"

The sheriff looked pained. "Go ahead. I could use a laugh."

"Funny Milo." But I recapped the pertinent information Vida and I had gathered in the last couple of days — except, of course, for Anna Maria's phone call to Dennis Kelly. I did, however, mention that I thought something was bothering Mrs. Della Croce besides not being hired by Carter Nystrom.

Milo had finished his cheeseburger by the time I concluded my recitation. "The only thing I can get my hands around," he said, "is what Scott and Jack remembered about the Nystrom calls here. It's possible — I repeat, *possible* — that somebody had it in for the family. Not to mention that weird death notice you got in the mail."

"Anything new on that?" I inquired, noticing that my fries had gone cold while I talked.

"We got the lab report back from Everett this morning," Milo answered. "No fingerprints. Obit typed on a computer, probably a PC, envelope addressed the same way, font was Times Roman, which is the default typeface on Microsoft Word — as you probably know."

"Yes. I don't like it. Too tight."

"Mailed in Alpine, obviously. Educated person wrote it — no mistakes and put together like the real thing. Not to mention that whoever sent it knew the Nystroms fairly well. They had all the facts right."

"Not many people do know them," I pointed out, "even if they have lived here for years. Anybody could find out that information if they wanted to. It's easy these days with the Internet and all the standard sources. What about DNA from licking the envelope or the stamp?"

Milo shook his head. "The sender was very careful."

"Wait," I said suddenly. "*Stamps,* not stamp. There were four — a cat commemorative and four smaller stamps with a bird on them."

Milo looked vaguely amused. "The sender's secret message is that the cat is going to eat the birds?"

I was disdainful of the sheriff's reaction. "Hardly. I'll explain." But first I offered him the last of my cold fries. He accepted. I was glad to see that his appetite was hearty. "I don't know why I forgot about those stamps," I said. "I guess it was the envelope's contents that took all my attention. Whoever sent that obit to the paper doesn't use the mail much. The postage rates went up six months ago. I ran out of the old stamps by the Fourth of July."

As I'd anticipated, Milo was looking skeptical. "So?"

"So this person either is cat-crazy or didn't send out Christmas cards," I said. "Unless Grace Grundle is the perp, we've got some kind of loner."

"I didn't send out Christmas cards," Milo responded.

"You *are* a loner," I shot back, "but I'll bet you don't have any of the old-rate stamps left."

"I don't have any stamps, period," said Milo, finishing off the fries. "I mail everything at county expense. It's one of my perks."

"Maybe our perk has perps. I mean —"

Milo held up a big hand. "I know what you mean. You're getting rattled by sticking to this subject. Move on." He lit a cigarette.

I gave up. Frankly, I wasn't entirely sure what I was getting at — or even if I did, what did it mean? There were plenty of loners in Skykomish County. Isolated small towns such as Alpine either attracted or created them.

"I don't know the next move," I admitted.

"Then have a cigarette," he said, holding out the pack of Marlboro Lights.

"No, thanks," I said. "I smoked my last one on New Year's Eve."

"It's a whole new year," Milo said, still proffering the pack. "You can quit again next December thirty-first."

I shook my head. "You know I haven't smoked regularly in ages." I waited until he pocketed the cigarettes. "Look. Do you agree that whoever sent that obit is the same person who killed Elmer?"

"It's possible," Milo allowed.

"And the other pranks? The stolen chicken and milk?"

The sheriff shrugged. "That's guessing. I'm not convinced they weren't coincidences. It seems to me that Polly's called us several times over the years with reports that weren't worth a damn."

"Then we should check the log for the past year or two, right?"

Milo started to look annoyed but pressed the intercom button. "Jack? Oh — Dwight. When you get a free minute, Dwight, flip back through last year's log and see how many calls we got from the Nystroms. Thanks." Through a haze of cigarette smoke, the sheriff gazed at me. "Satisfied?"

"It can't hurt." I stood up. "I'm going away now."

"You got the steak for tonight? T-bone?"

"I've got steak in the freezer, but it isn't T-bone," I replied. "I'll stop at the Grocery Basket on the way home."

"I'll be there around six," Milo said. "I need to go home and change. I'm wearing the same clothes I wore to the hospital."

"Put on your tux," I retorted. "At the price of T-bone, this should be formal."

"I've never worn a tux in my life," Milo declared with a certain amount of pride.

"Neither have I. See you at six." I exited the sheriff's office.

"Jeanne Hendrix is working for an orthodontist in Everett," Vida announced when I came into the newsroom. "According to my niece, Marje Blatt, she started the first of the year."

"So Marje has finally proved useful," I remarked.

"Indeed." Vida paused, scowling at her computer screen. "Now what did I do? My piece on the Bartons going to Samoa for a week has disappeared. Fortunately, it was short. They don't leave until the end of the month."

"Let me see." I'm only a few rungs above Vida on the high-tech ladder, but the least I could do was try to help her. The monitor showed a blank screen. "You turned it off by accident," I said. "Let's reboot."

"Reboot, my foot!" Vida exclaimed. "Such silly terms with these computers. Mice, menus, icons — it's all so very confusing."

"Computer people don't speak real English," I said, waiting for the computer to come back on. "How well does Marje know Jeanne Hendrix?"

"Only as a patient," Vida replied. "Jeanne had some minor surgery a month or so ago. She told Marje at the time it was scheduled so that she could be up and doing by the time she started her new job. I might add that we can probably eliminate Jeanne as a suspect because in order to get to her job in Everett at seven-thirty, she has to leave Alpine long before seven in the morning. Oh, you got it started again. Good."

"Did Marje know anything about Milo as far as the tests were concerned?" I asked, watching Vida scowl at the monitor.

"No. Being a receptionist, Marje doesn't always learn of hospital patients' test results. She only finds out when they come back for a follow-up appointment. Very disappointing."

"Milo doesn't seem to know anything, either," I said, "including the murder investigation." I went on to relate my insight about the multiple stamps on the envelope containing the obit. "Milo thought I was nuts, but I still think it means something."

"Quite right," Vida agreed. "Goodness, I don't think I got a single Christmas card this year with the old postage stamps on it." She drummed her short fingernails on the desk. "A loner, you say — yes, that fits. Cat stamps. Now let me think . . ." She drummed her fingers some more. "I recall that series of commemoratives because that ninny Grace Grundle happened to be at the post office when I was there, and she was buying an entire sheet and simply had to show them to me. 'So adorable,' she said, 'but they spoiled it by putting dogs on every other stamp.' It was, I believe, an issue to foster neutering pets. I felt like saying I

266

wished her cats' ancestors had all been neutered before they ever had kittens. But of course I kept mum."

"So we may be talking about an animal lover," I conjectured.

"Or quite the opposite," Vida pointed out. "Someone who wants to obliterate pets altogether."

"What about a stamp collector?"

Vida shook her head. "A collector would have more recent stamps."

"True." I sighed. "We're not getting anywhere. Did Marje have the scoop on Bree Kendall's new job at the hospital?"

"Alas, no. Marje has been out of the loop lately for medical gossip. The holidays, you know. So busy."

I had begun pacing the newsroom. "Bree must have made some friends. She's been here two years. Somehow, we've got to talk to those other women who work for Dr. Carter. In fact," I said, "we should talk to *him.*"

"I intend to," Vida responded. "Tomorrow, at the funeral. There's nothing like a death in the family to get people to open up. Are you coming?"

"I don't know," I admitted. "One of us is enough. It's not as if we know the Nystroms."

"Nobody does," Vida said softly. "And I still think that's the key."

TWELVE

A happy Scott Chamoud went off to confer with Dwight Gould at the sheriff's office a little after two. Jessica Wesley hadn't proved to be a font of information, but she had confided in Scott by telling him that she "didn't feel comfortable working in Dr. Nystrom's office." The Wesleys' daughter was too immature to put her finger on what bothered her, alluding to "atmosphere," "tension," and "stress." Even if Jessica had a lively imagination, I suspected that she could be right. Bree Kendall's resignation might point to some kind of problem. It wasn't as if receptionist jobs grew on Douglas firs in Alpine. The fact that she already had gone to work at the hospital indicated that she needed the money. Or at least planned to stay in town. That in itself seemed odd, since Bree was a city girl. But maybe I was transferring my dream of eventually moving back to the bright lights of Seattle.

I praised Scott for his ability to conduct an insightful interview. He wasn't the moody type, but I'd certainly noticed that he'd grown restless lately. Of course it had taken me long enough to assign him more responsibility on big stories. Then again, we didn't have many of them in Alpine.

Leo, however, was unusually quiet that afternoon. Vida noticed and asked if he was ailing.

"We don't need another person rushed to the hospital," she warned my ad manager. "The doctors are overworked as it is, especially this time of year with flu season."

Leo rolled his chair around so he could look at Vida. "You know what the Bard said, Duchess: 'Now is the winter of our discontent.' "

"Piffle," responded Vida. "Unlike Shakespeare's Richard the Third, you're not deformed, nor, I trust, are you determined to play the villain. Unless, of course, you insist upon lighting another of your filthy cigarettes."

I'd just come out of the back shop, where I'd been conferring with Kip about a computer program he thought we should get for our income taxes.

"Do I hear discord among my staffers?" I asked.

"Discontent," Vida said, "on Leo's part."

Still feeling pleased about my dealings with Scott, I was taken aback. "How come?" I asked my ad manager.

Leo gestured at Vida. "Did you tell the Duchess about Ed?"

"Ed!" Vida cried. "Of course Emma told me. Are you actually fretting about him? It serves Ed right if he has to work, however menial the job. It's not your fault he's an idiot."

"Hey, there but for the grace of God — and Emma — go I," Leo retorted. "I was inches away from jumping off a ferryboat when she came along and threw me a lifeline. So to speak."

"Well," Vida said, "you're not the one working at the Burger Barn. What does that tell you? I daresay that if you'd inherited several million dollars, you wouldn't have wasted it on foolish show-off purchases or made ill-advised investments."

"No," Leo replied, the twinkle returning to his eyes. "In my bad old days, I'd have sucked it out of a bottle. An endless number of bottles. Then I'd have gone out in my new Porsche and killed myself and probably some other poor SOB."

"Really," Vida huffed, "you're getting me down, Leo. Forget about Ed. He's his own worst enemy — as people usually are."

"Yes." I spoke the word involuntarily. Vida and Leo stared at me.

"Well?" said Vida.

I shrugged. "It's true, of course. But I wasn't thinking of Ed. Elmer Nystrom came to mind."

"You mean," Vida said with her most owlish expression, "Elmer brought his murder upon himself?"

I nodded faintly. "I guess. Of course it may be a crazy notion. But hasn't it been pointed out that often you can discover the killer by knowing more about the victim?"

"Certainly," Vida agreed. "And as I've mentioned, we don't know that much about Elmer. But at the funeral I'll —"

For once, I interrupted Vida. "Fine. But now, I'm going to do some deep background of my own." I hurried into my cubbyhole, grabbed my purse and hooded jacket, then dashed back through the newsroom. "See you in an hour or so."

Vida ran after me, catching up just as I was turning the ignition key. "You can't go to the Nystroms' without me!" she shouted through the closed window.

"Get your coat," I shouted back. "And

your crazy hat," I added under my breath after she'd zipped back inside.

As soon as Vida got into the car, she insisted that we stop at Posies Unlimited and pick up a bouquet of flowers. "We can't burst in empty-handed," she said.

"How about the Grocery Basket's deli?" I suggested. "We can bring Carter and his mother a meal. The store's not too far out of our way, and I have to get some steaks for Milo anyway."

"You buy deli food?" Vida asked in a tone that suggested I might also eat small children.

"Sometimes," I replied, backing out onto Front Street.

"It can't be wholesome," she declared. "Just sitting there all day in those cases. Ugh." She leaned closer and peered at me. "You're making Milo dinner, too?"

"It's the least I can do," I said.

"Also the most, I hope." Vida sounded stern. She had never approved of the sexual relationship between the sheriff and me.

As usual, I wasn't inclined to discuss the matter with Vida, so I reverted to the original topic. "It seems a waste of our efforts for both of us to go to see Polly. Why don't you think up some excuse to talk to Carter's assistants?"

"The office is closed until after the funeral, remember?"

"Oh." I braked for the red light at Front and Alpine Way. "Did you ever find out if Christy and Alicia had last names?"

"Yes. Christy's is Millard. Alicia's is Strand. Christy lives in those condos on Spruce by the RV park, and Alicia has an apartment in that newer building on Tonga Road."

I took a left onto Alpine Way. "Anything else?"

"According to my daughter Amy, they're both around thirty, unmarried, and quite attractive. They also seem highly qualified. Amy told me they were always very patient with Roger when he was having his braces worked on."

Canonization now. I could imagine what kind of horror Roger would've been at the orthodontist's office. "I thought Roger had his braces done out of town."

"He did," Vida replied as I waited to get into the Grocery Basket's parking lot. "But he needed some maintenance work after he finished. I'd forgotten about that. Amy managed to get a referral to Dr. Nystrom for the follow-up work."

No doubt it was a referral gladly given. I had visions of his original orthodontist digging a moat around the office.

I volunteered to go get the meal for what was left of the Nystrom family. Vida said she didn't mind waiting in the car; parking lots could be very interesting. "You never know who's going to show up," she asserted. "What's even more intriguing than who goes into the store is who's left behind. Especially at night."

Inside the store, I got the T-bones first. At the deli counter, I decided that a small roasted chicken would be in poor taste, considering Elmer's demise in the hen-house. Instead, I settled on the Betsy's Buffet dinner special — the Swedish meatballs, egg noodles, and broccoli. Our ads claimed that the specials were always from "Betsy O'Toole's busy kitchen," but I knew that she spent so many hours working in the store that the family did more take-out and frozen meals than most people in Alpine.

It was raining again by the time I got back to the car. Vida was still rubbernecking.

"Lois Dewey had eight grocery bags," Vida informed me. "How often does she shop? She and Doc are alone in that big house. What do you suppose they eat? Of course they can afford the best."

I concentrated on avoiding a collision with a small car that had whipped out of a parking space without looking to see if anybody was coming.

"Kay Gould had only one bag, and she was carrying it most carefully," Vida continued. "I suspect it was wine. Why doesn't she buy it at the liquor store? Have you ever noticed Dwight being tipsy? I haven't. I don't think he drinks."

"Maybe that's why she does," I remarked, heading back down Alpine Way to the Burl Creek Road. "Dwight can be a pill sometimes."

"And the children!" Vida exclaimed. "As soon as school lets out, they go to the grocery store and buy all kinds of sodas and sugar treats! Why do their parents allow it? I must have seen a dozen of them, some as young as eight or nine. Tsk, tsk."

Vida would have made a great undercover surveillance cop if it wasn't for those wacky hats.

The rain had almost stopped by the time we reached the Nystrom house five minutes later. To my surprise, Polly answered the door.

"Oh, hello, Mrs. Runkel, Ms. Lord," she said in a subdued voice. "Come in. I was getting Elmer's pictures out for the funeral tomorrow. Would you like some tea?"

I started to decline, but Vida accepted.

"Very kind of you," she said. "We brought dinner for you and Carter so you wouldn't have to cook."

I handed over the bag containing the food. "You might want to put this in the refrigerator, Mrs. Nystrom."

"How thoughtful," Polly said softly. "I'll do that, and I'll put the kettle on. Please sit."

We both sat on the sofa. But as soon as Polly left for the kitchen, Vida rose and went to the dining room table. Several photo albums and individual pictures were scattered over the hand-crocheted lace tablecloth.

"I don't see the portrait of Elmer that we used in his obituary," she called out to Polly. "Are you using it for the service? It was very nice."

Polly didn't answer right away. The living room and dining room were contiguous, their demarcation created by a polished hardwood floor between two large Persian rugs. From my place on the sofa, I could see into the kitchen. Polly had gone first to the fridge but was now out of sight, presumably at the stove or sink.

She reappeared a moment later, stopping near Vida in the dining room. "There. The kettle's on. Now, what did you say about a portrait?"

"We had a file portrait from Nordby Brothers taken a few years ago," Vida explained. "You know, the one that hangs on their showroom walls with the other employees' pictures. It was a very good likeness, taken by Buddy Bayard. I assumed you'd use that on the altar."

Polly straightened her apron. "I don't think I have a copy of that picture," she said vaguely as I came over to join the two women. "I hadn't thought about having a picture in church. Mr. Driggers suggested having some on a bulletin board in the reception area afterward. This one's nice." She pointed to a black-and-white snapshot showing a much younger Elmer in a shirt and tie. He had hair, and I could see a grain silo in the background. "That was taken in Williston before we moved west."

"Surely," Vida said, "you have a more recent photo."

"Oh . . . Let me see." Polly pulled at her lower lip and studied the disorganized photos on the table. "There's one from a few years ago out in the garden, but his back is turned."

I stared. Carter was in the foreground, holding a rake and making a face for the camera. In fact, most of the photos seemed to be of Carter with or without Polly at his side: baby pictures, toddler pictures, kid pictures, teenage pictures, college-age pictures, adult pictures. I glanced around the living and dining rooms. There were framed photos of Carter in graduation regalia — one, I assumed, for his under- graduate degree and another for the completion of his orthodontist studies. There was also a large tinted picture of a youthful Polly, looking svelte and pretty as a prairie rose.

"Don't you have a family picture?" I blurted.

"Well . . . not really." Polly cleared her throat. "Elmer took most of the pictures, you see."

Maybe that explained his absence from the photo collection. But it seemed a bit weird to me.

Vida was flipping through one of the albums. "So many memories," she mur- mured. "I do enjoy looking at people's cherished photos. Ah!" She tapped a color photo. "This one seems to be more recent than the shot taken in Williston."

Elmer was proudly standing in front of a white Chevrolet Caprice. "Oh, yes," Polly agreed. "Carter took that one. He'd just turned twelve but was very clever with a camera. We'd got him one for his birthday."

I was looking at the picture, too. "Is that a brand-new car?"

"Uh . . ." Polly removed her glasses to stare at the photo. "I think so. It was the one that Carter learned to drive on later."

I judged the picture to be almost twenty years old. "Any Christmas or other holiday photos?" I asked.

Polly chuckled softly. "Yes, indeed. All of Carter's Santa pictures are in a special album. I didn't bring it out. Would you like to see the Christmas albums? Carter was only a few months old when he celebrated his first Christmas, but he seemed to understand what it was all about. I can get them if you'd like."

"I don't think . . ." I began as the teakettle mercifully whistled. Polly excused herself and went back to the kitchen.

Vida headed for the sofa. "Honestly!" she exclaimed under her breath. "You'd think Elmer didn't exist! If Carter was so clever with a camera, why didn't he take more pictures of his father?"

"Spoiled only child," I whispered, hearing Polly rattle cups and saucers in the kitchen. "But smart."

"So?" Vida sniffed disdainfully. "Being smart doesn't mean you can't also be a dreadful person."

I had, of course, immediately thought of Roger. But Roger wasn't very smart. Or so I'd always figured. Vida, of course, didn't consider her grandson spoiled. We all have a blind eye when it comes to people we love.

"Here we are," Polly announced cheerfully, setting a tray on the coffee table in front of the sofa. "I'll pour. I baked oatmeal cookies this morning. They're one of Carter's favorites. Do try them."

"Where *is* Carter?" Vida inquired, immediately scooping a large amount of sugar into her tea after Polly had filled two Royal Albert Lily of the Valley bone china cups.

Polly didn't answer until she'd poured herself a cup and had sat down in a side chair with a needlepoint seat and back. "He had to do some things regarding the funeral. Oh, and pick up his new car."

I couldn't keep my mouth shut. "The Corvette?"

Polly beamed at me. "Why, yes. How did you know?"

"I went to see Trout Nordby," I said, "to ask about Elmer."

Polly looked blank. "To ask what about him?"

"How he was regarded by his employers, his co-workers, his customers." I shrugged.

281

"The kind of information that readers like to know about their fellow Alpiners."

"Oh." Polly sipped her tea.

Vida leaned forward, causing her black Gaucho hat to slip back on her head. "Have you had many callers?"

"A few," Polly said.

"It's nice to have neighbors so close," Vida went on, tightening the string under her chin to secure the hat, "like the Della Croces. Very nice people, I've heard."

"They seem to be," Polly said in a noncommittal tone. "How do you like the cookies?"

Vida, who had taken a bite out of one, nodded. "Tasty," she said after she'd swallowed.

"Who're the neighbors to the west?" I inquired.

"The Tollefsons, I think," Polly replied. "They've only lived there a year or so. We don't see much of them. Their house is quite a ways from here, and the view's cut off by the trees."

"Oh, yes," Vida said. "Pamela and Russ Tollefson. I believe they both work for —"

She was interrupted by the doorbell. "Excuse me," Polly said in a surprised voice. "I wonder who that can be."

As Polly went to the door, Vida shot me a

questioning look. "Why is she surprised to have a caller?"

I knew what Vida meant. After a death in the family, visitors flocked to the bereaved. Unlike the city, Alpine's smallness in population and geography encouraged people to visit, which also gave the locals something to do.

We couldn't see who had rung the bell from our angle on the sofa, but I heard someone — a male, I thought — speak, followed by Polly voicing surprise — and pleasure. Then the door was closed, and she returned to the living room carrying what looked like a floral display.

"My goodness," she exclaimed softly. "This is certainly a lot of flowers." She put the delivery up on the fireplace mantel and unwrapped it. "Oh, how pretty! Why, I've never seen some of these before!"

Vida was on her feet. "Let me look. Is it from Posies Unlimited?"

"Yes," Polly said excitedly. "Yes, it is. There's a card."

It dawned on me that I hadn't seen any other bouquets or plants that I'd expect to find in a house of mourning. Maybe all of the floral arrangements had been sent to Driggers Funeral Home.

Vida was studying the lavish bouquet in

its wicker basket. "Alstroemeria, liatrus, along with the more common snapdragons, carnations, and roses. My, my. Very lavish."

Polly was beaming. "It's from Carter. How dear of him!" She slipped the card under the wicker basket. "He certainly knows how to treat his mama when she's feeling blue."

"Very thoughtful." Vida moved away from the fireplace. "Emma, we really must go. I have some work to finish this afternoon." She turned to Polly, who was still admiring the flowers. "Thank you for the tea. Enjoy your meal."

"What?" Polly looked startled. "Oh — the food you brought. Yes, thanks again."

I traipsed along after Vida like a pet pooch. "Honestly!" she cried after Polly had closed the door behind us. "That woman is mental! It's all Carter, Carter, Carter! What about poor Elmer? I've never known such a peculiar woman in my life."

"She's not the first one we've run into who's more obsessed with her child than with her spouse," I reminded Vida, thinking back to a recent Alpine tragedy. "I doubt that Polly has ever done anything except be a wife and mother."

"That's sufficient for many women," Vida said, getting into the car, "and they do it very well. But they also extend themselves in other ways and don't dwell constantly on their offspring."

"Polly's world does seem very narrow," I remarked, turning the key in the ignition. I paused. Vida was searching rather frantically around her person, as well as the floor and the seat. "What's wrong?"

"I can't find my gloves. I had them when we got here, didn't I?"

"I think so." I turned the engine off. "Did you drop them on the way from the house?"

She stared out through the windshield. "Yes, I may have. I remember taking them off right after we arrived. I'll go look."

Vida got out of the car and retraced her steps. In her long brown tweed coat she made me think of a giant sparrow searching for food. Except, of course, that sparrows don't wear Gaucho hats. She finally reached the porch. I saw her bend down and pick something up. The gloves. She started back down the walk but suddenly stopped and cut across the front lawn to the side of the house, peering around the corner. I couldn't see what she was looking at, but knowing Vida, it was something interesting. After a moment, she turned back and headed my way.

"Well, I never!" she huffed, getting into the car and pulling on her gloves with a fierce motion. "I heard a noise outside and decided to see what it was. How aggravating!"

"What's aggravating?" I asked, turning the engine on again.

"Polly. She was outside at the garbage can, throwing away the meal you brought her. Why would she do such a thing?"

THIRTEEN

"Maybe," I suggested as we drove down the Burl Creek Road, "Polly thought we were trying to poison her."

"Nonsense," Vida retorted. "She's one of those strange people who can't accept charity. Too high and mighty, I suspect."

"Ben would say that it's a lack of humility."

"Isn't that the same thing?" Vida demanded.

"Yes, I guess it is." I swerved slightly to avoid a big bump in the county road. "Or maybe it tells us something about Polly's level of trust in other people."

Vida shot me a sharp glance. "Meaning what?"

"I'm not sure." I slowed for a chipmunk that was racing to safety among the maidenhair and sword ferns that flanked the creek side of the road. "My problem is that I keep trying to tie everything that happens with the Nystroms into Elmer's murder. That's futile, really."

"Y-e-s," Vida said slowly, "but personalities and habits — even one's daily routine — often offer clues to how individuals meet an untimely demise."

A moment of silence followed, perhaps in memory of Elmer. "Why aren't you inviting Ben for dinner tonight?" Vida suddenly asked.

"He's been asked out to the senior Bourgettes' home," I replied. "Do you think Milo and I need a chaperone? Want to join us?"

"I can't," Vida said. "Buck is taking me to visit some old friends of his who just moved to Sultan from east of the mountains."

Buck Bardeen was Vida's longtime companion. He was a retired air force colonel and the older brother of Henry Bardeen, who ran the ski lodge. Buck and Vida didn't seem inclined to get married. They maintained their own homes, hers in Alpine, his down the highway in Startup. I was never quite sure of their arrangement, and I didn't pry, because Vida guarded her private life as assiduously as she ferreted out the secrets of others.

I tied up a few loose ends at the office before I headed home at five. Early January was always a time to take stock of the newspaper, and not just in a financial sense. I looked through the last quarter of the year's editions, paying special attention to the features we'd done. They were heavily slanted toward middle-aged and older women. Like everybody else in the print media, we needed younger readers — of both sexes. I made a note. Scott was going to be busy finding interesting eighteen- to thirty-five-year-olds.

One of whom, I realized, was Carter Nystrom. What kind of guy, I wondered, rushed out to collect his new Corvette the day before his father's funeral? Or was the car a symbol? *My parents helped me become successful so I could buy this expensive automobile from the dealership where my father toiled so long and so hard on my behalf.* That was what I wanted to think about Carter. But I had reservations.

On my way out through the newsroom, Scott told me that he was meeting Coach Ridley for a beer at Mugs Ahoy around five-thirty. I congratulated my reporter on his enterprise and wished him well. Maybe he could inveigle some information about the amoral Nordby son and the Methodist minister's daughter.

I didn't bother to change when I got home. My usual winter work attire of sweater and slacks was casual enough for cooking. It was also devoid of any come-hither appeal that might make the sheriff think about hitting the sheets after dinner.

Milo arrived at two minutes before six. Frankly, I thought he still looked drawn and tired. He insisted on making our drinks — Scotch for him, bourbon for me — but went out into the living room before I left the kitchen. Usually, he stayed around to visit while I finished the cooking preparations. I joined him as soon as I'd turned on the burner to start his steak, which he preferred cooked as tough as a logger's tin pants.

Milo was sitting in his favorite easy chair, smoking and staring up at my *Sky Autumn* painting.

"That's not bad," he remarked as I plopped down on the sofa. "At least it looks like a real river. You ever hear anything of the nut job who painted it?"

I shook my head. "Craig Laurentis? Not really. He keeps himself to himself, as they say. Donna Wickstrom thought he might be working on a picture of Mount Baldy. If he is, she wants it for her art gallery."

"Hunh." Milo swallowed some Scotch. "I guess geniuses are all pretty crazy."

"I don't think Laurentis is crazy," I said. "He's antisocial. I still think it's strange that nobody has ever found out where he lives."

Milo waved a hand. "There's plenty of forest out there. Second growth, anyway. Some of it still hasn't been explored since the Alpine Lumber Company clear-cut this neck of the woods eighty years ago. One thing, though — I'll bet this painter guy has his cabin or whatever near a creek. He'd have to have water." The sheriff paused and eyed me over his glass. "What'd you do with that other picture of the pond?"

"The Monet? I put it in my bedroom."

"Any chance I could see it after dinner?"

"Not a prayer," I said firmly. "You just got out of the hospital."

"I feel fine."

"Don't push it, Milo," I said. "Wait until your test results come back."

"Bullshit," he growled. "Ten to one they won't show a damned thing. All those tests are just a way to rake in money. It's a good thing I've got SkyCo medical coverage. Otherwise, I'd probably have to sell the house."

I stood up. "I'm going to check your steak and put mine on."

He held out his glass. "How about a refill?"

There was still some liquid covering what was left of the ice cubes. I frowned. "Well

. . . okay. But you shouldn't overdo the booze, either."

"When did I ever?" he retorted.

That much was true. The sheriff wasn't a heavy drinker. "Fine." I took the glass and went into the kitchen. So far, I'd refrained from asking him about the homicide investigation, but I couldn't keep quiet forever. Ten minutes later, after we'd sat down to our meal in the dining alcove off the living room, I tendered a query.

"Any progress concerning Elmer?"

"Those garden tools are being checked out at the Everett lab," Milo replied. "We should hear back tomorrow."

"That's taking them quite a while," I noted. "Should Ben and I rush over to Everett so we can lay some Catholic guilt on Brian McDonough?"

Milo gulped down a bite of steak. "They're shorthanded. Some of the crew scheduled vacation this week instead of between Christmas and New Year's. At least three lab people and their wives or husbands or whatever took a package cruise. Not to mention that a ton of people always croak around the holidays."

"So they do," I agreed. We'd already had five people die in Skykomish County just before and after Christmas. And that didn't count Elmer, who wasn't a typical holiday corpse. Homicide wasn't the usual cause of deaths at Christmastime in Alpine. "What about interviews with people who know the family?"

The sheriff didn't answer until he'd gnawed all the meat off the bone. "Worthless," he finally said, wiping his mouth with a paper napkin. "At least the church people are. They said all the right things — Elmer was devoted to his family, a hard worker, always willing to help out the other guy, honest, upright, blah, blah, blah."

"What did they say about Polly and Carter?"

"More or less the same kind of bullshit," Milo said, casting his eyes toward the kitchen. "That's it for the steak?"

"Lord, Milo, it was the biggest one I could find."

"Oh." He looked disappointed. "Hospital food makes you hungry for the real thing."

"You had the real thing for lunch," I pointed out. "I've got some leftover cheesecake for dessert. I froze it after Christmas."

"Sounds good," Milo said, cheering up a bit. "How about some of that sweet after-dinner drink to go with it?"

"Drambuie? Sure, I've still got half a bottle." I rose from the table, cleared away our plates, and went into the kitchen. Milo stayed put at the dining room table.

Upon my return with the dessert and liqueur, I tried to coax some more information out of the sheriff. "You can't tell me," I said, sitting down again, "that even the saintly ladies of the parish had only good words for Polly. I hear otherwise."

Milo threw me a snide glance. "You women. You just love to dig the dirt."

"You find the truth under the dirt," I retorted. "Like finding gold in the mountainside. All those bitchy little nuggets reveal far more than the hoo-hah you're getting from the mealymouths."

Milo downed some Drambuie. "Okay, so what have you heard that's so damned important?"

"Polly's a vicious gossip," I said. "She spreads false rumors."

"Who doesn't in this town?" Milo responded. "It's one of Alpine's biggest hobbies."

"That's not accurate," I asserted. "People gossip, they get things twisted, they end up exaggerating or even inventing. But usually it's not malicious, just stupid. I don't think that's the case with Polly. She's a mean-minded woman."

"Give me some evidence."

I hesitated. I couldn't tell Milo about the phone call from Anna Maria Della Croce to the rectory. But I could relate what Janet Driggers had said about the Della Croce daughter.

"Polly spread stories about her next-door neighbor's daughter, Gloria. According to Polly's rumor mill, Gloria is a tramp."

The sheriff paused with a forkful of cheesecake halfway to his mouth. "And you know that's a lie?"

"I've heard no other such tales," I declared. "Furthermore, she's an excellent student."

"So she's a smart tramp. So what?"

"Milo —" I shut up. The sheriff despised hearsay. "Never mind."

"Some goofball," he said. "Maybe a bum who holed up in the henhouse to keep warm. That's the theory we're working on. But don't go broadcasting it."

"We don't broadcast," I snapped. "That's Fleetwood's job. We print."

Milo shrugged. "Whatever. Got any more cheesecake?"

"Yes. No!" I glared at the sheriff. "Do you want to end up looking like Ed Bronsky?"

"I told you I was hungry," he said, annoyed. "I'm in a weakened condition."

"How about some fruit? Or cheese?"

"Cheese*cake*," Milo said emphatically.

I surrendered. "A sliver, that's all."

I went back to the kitchen. This time Milo followed me. "Skip it," he said, standing behind me and slipping his arms around my waist. "I'll settle for another kind of dessert. It'll work off the food."

I resisted the urge to lean against him. Milo was tall and big and strong as an oak. I'd sought shelter in his arms many times. But not now. Frankly, I was afraid for him. Even oaks can wither and die.

"Please," I said in a plaintive voice. "Let's wait."

He let go. "It's that AP guy, right?"

With a sigh, I turned around to look up at him. "No. I'm not in love with Rolf." *Not exactly,* I thought. *Not yet. Maybe some day* . . . "Honestly. I like him very much. But I'm not in love."

The sheriff was skeptical. "You're doing a damned good imitation."

I almost told him the truth. But I stopped. I knew he didn't want to hear that I was worried about his health. Milo, even more than most men, didn't want to hear his strength questioned. I also knew he wanted to prove that he was perfectly healthy.

But instead of giving in, I put a hand on his arm and shook my head. "The year's young yet." *Even if we're not.* "Next time I'll buy you two steaks — and you can name your own dessert."

I'd like to think he suddenly looked a bit more cheerful. But that was wishful thinking. Milo, in fact, looked pained.

I patted his arm. "I'm not putting you off," I asserted with my kindest smile. "I'd really like to —"

I stopped. Milo didn't look pained, I realized, but was *in* pain. One hand was clutching his chest. "I'd better sit down," he mumbled. "I don't feel so good."

I started to steer him toward the living room, but he fumbled with a kitchen chair and sat down heavily. "Shit," he murmured, still with a hand on his chest. "What now?"

"I'm calling 911," I said, hoping I sounded calm. My eye flitted around the kitchen. I couldn't find the phone. Maybe it was in the living room. When had I used it last? Not since I had gotten home. Fighting panic, I espied my purse on the counter and dug out my cell phone.

I recognized the voice at the other end of the line. It was Evan Singer, who often manned the emergency calls after Beth Rafferty went home at five.

"Emma?" he said after I'd managed to mangle my message. "Did you say the sheriff? Or do you want the sheriff?"

I glanced at Milo, who was doubled over in the chair. "I want medics. And an ambulance. Dodge isn't well. Hurry."

"Got it." Evan rang off. Unlike his big-city counterparts who often kept callers on the line until help arrived, SkyCo's 911 service was a one-person gang. The line couldn't be tied up any longer than necessary.

The sheriff was groaning and cussing. It was hard to tell which was which. I moved closer. "Where does it hurt?" I asked.

He shook his head but didn't look up.

I tried again. "Your chest?"

His only reply was a moan and a "goddamn it."

"Is it like what you had before?"

Again my question was ignored. Frustrated, I picked up the Drambuie bottle and took a big swallow. It was all fire and sticky sweetness, but it put some steel in my sagging backbone. So did the sound of approaching sirens.

I opened the front and back doors, then collected Milo's jacket from the living room, stuffed his cigarettes and lighter in an inside pocket, and watched through the front window. After only a few seconds, the street was illuminated by flashing lights. A moment later, the medic van pulled up in the driveway behind Milo's Grand Cherokee.

Luckily, the two senior medics, Vic Thorstensen and Del Amundson, were on the job.

"Where is he?" Del asked, hurrying into the house.

"Kitchen," I replied, waiting to follow both EMTs.

"Hey, Sheriff," Del said in his most upbeat voice, "you got another bellyache?"

I was standing in the kitchen doorway. All I could see was Milo's back, hunched over in the chair. He responded, but I couldn't hear what he said. It sounded like a grunt.

The phone rang from the living room. The receiver was on the end table. No wonder I hadn't found it in the kitchen.

"Where did those sirens go?" Vida demanded.

The query caught me off guard. "What? I thought you went to Sultan with Buck."

"Thelma got sick and threw up all over the table," she said. "We left. I just got home. What about those sirens? They sounded as if they were near your house."

Thelma, I presumed, was Vida and Buck's hostess. But she was the least of my problems. "It's Milo," I said. "He's had another spell."

"I wondered," Vida murmured. "Whatever were you doing?"

"Nothing!" I virtually shouted the word into the phone. "The medics are . . ." I walked back toward the kitchen. Vic was still with Milo, but Del had disappeared. Probably he'd gone out the back door to get the gurney. "I think they're taking Milo to the hospital."

"A good place for him," Vida huffed. "They never should have let him out so soon. I'll meet you there."

"Where?"

"The hospital, of course." Vida hung up.

I hadn't thought that far ahead. But of course I'd follow Milo and his merry band of medics. That silly phrase had slipped into my mind. I suppose I was trying to stay optimistic, cheer myself up, prepare to deal with a long, anxious wait.

Del returned with the gurney. I still kept my distance, not wanting to get in the way.

"You coming, Emma?" Vic asked.

"Yes. Yes."

"Want to ride in the ambulance?" he inquired.

"Uh . . . no, I'll drive."

Vic frowned. "How're you going to get your car out? The Cherokee's blocking it."

"I'll get Milo's keys and move it."

Vic nodded. Milo was making an unsuccessful effort to stand up.

"Don't," Del said. "We provide all the transportation you need."

Milo said something unprintable about what they could do with their transportation. But he stopped trying to stand. Wanting to spare the sheriff from having me observe his "lack of manliness," I grabbed his keys and went back into the living room, taking my time to put on my jacket. As soon as I heard the gurney leaving the kitchen via the back door, I returned to make sure the stove was off and everything was unplugged. I felt kind of unplugged myself. If not dying at the roots, my sturdy oak was being buffeted by the winds of ill health. I was overcome with a sense of vulnerability as unfamiliar as it was disturbing.

The medic van was out of sight if not out of hearing range by the time I backed onto Fir Street. The most direct route was to go down Third. As soon as I turned the corner, I could see the flashing red lights nearing the hospital. The steep, wet pavement in front of me was safe enough in daylight, but after dark several bumps and potholes were concealed. My editorials urging a bond issue for street improvements had gone for naught.

I parked on Pine and crossed the street to the hospital's main entrance. The emergency room was off to the right of the small lobby. Milo would have been taken in through a different entrance, near the corner of Second and Pine. Vida was already at the reception desk, badgering a stout middle-aged woman I didn't recognize.

"He's here, I tell you," Vida said, wagging a finger. "Sheriff Dodge just came in."

I sidled up to Vida, who was wearing what looked like a chocolate layer cake on her head. It was probably the hat she'd worn to her dinner party in Sultan.

"Tell her," Vida commanded, turning to me.

"You just did," I said.

The receptionist's name tag stated that she was Mona Lysander. She sure wasn't Mona Lisa, judging from her sullen expression.

"Nothing's official," she declared, "until the patient has been formally admitted." In a gesture of dismissal she swiveled her chair in the direction of her computer.

Vida leaned on the counter. "Where's Bree Kendall?" she demanded in a voice so loud that a dozing elderly man sitting by the aquarium woke up with such a start that his glasses fell off into his lap.

302

Mona glared at Vida. "She works days."

Vida didn't budge. She remained leaning on the counter, eyes fixed on Mona, who had turned back to her computer. The receptionist looked up. "Would you please take a seat."

Vida shook her head, causing the cakelike tiers of felt to sway atop her gray curls. "Not until we hear what's going on with Sheriff Dodge."

An older woman I hadn't noticed came toward us carrying an embroidery hoop and a threaded needle. "What's this about the sheriff?" she asked. "Is he dying?"

I recognized Ethel Pike's round, pugnacious face. I also saw her husband, Bickford, in a chair by the far wall, staring vacantly at the old guy by the aquarium who was still fumbling with his glasses.

Vida straightened up, towering over Ethel. "Certainly not! He's had another spell, that's all. Indigestion, if you ask me. He doesn't eat properly."

I knew that Vida was worried far more than she'd let on to Ethel. But she wouldn't start unfounded rumors or give Ethel the satisfaction of knowing that Vida was in the dark when it came to Milo's health.

"Well," Ethel said, "he'd better spend more time on the job and catch whoever killed Elmer. If you ask me, whoever did it croaked the wrong Nystrom. They should have done in his missus."

I'd forgotten that the Pikes lived on the Burl Creek Road, probably less than a quarter mile from the Nystrom house.

"You don't like Polly?" Vida asked, finally stepping away from the reception area.

"She's a pill," Ethel declared, jabbing her needle into a random spot on what looked like a pillowcase. "Polly's always complaining about Pike." She nodded in her husband's direction. "He's got the bronchitis. I had to drag him in here before it gets to be the pneumonia. Stubborn as a mule, that's Pike. Says he wouldn't be sick at all if we'd spent the winter with our kids in Florida. All he wants to do is go beachcombing, but I tell him he'd get eaten by them crocodiles. Anyways, we can't afford it."

"What did Polly complain about?" Vida asked, steering the conversation back to the Nystroms.

"Pike's truck," Ethel replied. "He hauls stuff, you know. He can't stay retired from the mill, has to run himself ragged even in bad weather, carting this and that around. No wonder he's got the bronchitis."

Anxious about Milo and impatient in my role of Vida's mute puppet, I spoke: "You

304

mean Polly complained about the truck making noise?"

Ethel glanced at Pike, who broke into a coughing fit, perhaps to prove that he was still alive. "The noise — that old Silvery-aydo truck kind of rattles when it's got a big load of junk — and because sometimes things'd fall off along the road. Like a mattress that landed by the Nystroms' mailbox. As if Pike wouldn't pick it up! You can't sell junk from the side of the road."

"Certainly not," Vida agreed, showing uncustomary commiseration for Ethel, who my House & Home editor usually deemed "an idiot." "Tut, tut," Vida went on. "Polly sounds quite unreasonable."

"That's for sure," Ethel said. "Pike picked up that mattress the very next day. Or so."

"What," I asked, "does Pike do with all his . . . collectibles?" Maybe there was a feature story in his junk business.

"He takes it to Snohomish and Everett," Ethel replied as her husband finally stopped coughing. "Snohomish's got so many of them antique places. Sometimes he gets as much as twenty-five dollars for a load."

"Yes," Vida murmured, "I've heard that Pike's quite a scavenger. So many people — hikers and campers and that sort — leave all sorts of items in the forest. Even automobiles and motorcycles."

"Boats, too," Ethel put in. "Too lazy to haul 'em back down the mountains. 'Course they're not worth much — usually good only for firewood."

I noticed that Mona had left her post and disappeared into the examining room area. Maybe she was in the process of officially admitting Milo. The bold face on the clock above the entrance showed the time as seven thirty-seven. Somehow, it seemed as if it should be much later.

Mona returned to her post and busied herself with some paperwork and the computer. I half expected Vida to reach over the counter and snatch away what I guessed was the sheriff's admittance form. Ethel, however, interjected herself between Vida and me.

"Say," she barked at Mona, "how much longer does Pike have to wait? He's coughed up half a lung already."

A still hostile Mona looked up. "He's next after Mr. Almquist."

Mr. Almquist, I presumed, was the old guy who'd gone back to sleep by the aquarium. Or maybe he'd already died.

"It won't be long," Mona said in a voice that was anything but reassuring.

Vida was about to make her move as Ethel

stepped back from the counter and barked at Pike to stop coughing. "You're driving me crazy. Keep your yap shut and just sit there!" She turned back to us. "Honest, that man'll be the death of me. Won't take care of himself, but wait and see — he'll live to be a hundred while I'll be moldering in my grave."

Before either Vida or I could respond, Jack Mullins suddenly burst through the doors that led to the examining rooms.

"There you are," he said to Vida and me. "Come outside. I need a smoke."

"You don't smoke," Vida pointed out. "How's Milo?"

Jack kept walking. "I smoke when my boss gets hauled to the hospital. I stole his cigs." He opened one of the double doors for us. "Jesus, this is getting to be a habit."

"Smoking?" Vida said, holding on to her hat as a brisk wind blew down from Tonga Ridge. "Or Milo's hospital visits?"

"Both." Jack lit up before he spoke again. "Sung's on duty tonight. Doc may get called in. No news is good news. I guess." He took a deep drag on the cigarette and blew the smoke well away from Vida. "He wants you to go home, Emma. You can't do a damned thing waiting around. You, too, Vida. Dodge didn't know you were here."

"Where did he think I'd be?" Vida snapped. "And stop swearing!"

"Knock it off, Vida," Jack shot back. "I'm not in the mood for lectures. This stuff with Dodge is getting me down. It's getting to all of us at headquarters."

For once, Vida reined in her reprimands. In fact, she appeared almost docile. "Of course you're upset. We all are, or we wouldn't be here." She tapped my arm. "Jack's right. Or, rather, Milo is. We can't do anything waiting all night for news. We should go home. Are you staying, Jack?"

He took another puff and nodded. "Unless I get called away. I'm on duty along with Doe. She dropped me off in the patrol car."

"You'll call us if you hear anything?" I asked.

"Sure." Jack's usually cheerful face looked drawn and sickly under the harsh overhead light above the emergency entrance door.

"Call," Vida said, "even if you don't hear anything."

Jack nodded again. Vida and I walked out the short driveway to the sidewalk.

"Most upsetting," she said quietly. "Milo doesn't take care of himself. He needs a wife."

"He had one," I pointed out as we stopped

at the corner. "She didn't turn out so well for him."

Vida frowned. "No. Tricia hated his work. Milo was gone too much and far too involved in his job. But that's the way it is with law enforcement. She knew that when she married him. So silly of her to have that affair with the schoolteacher. Retaliation, of course, for being left alone. I never thought she'd actually marry the man. If only . . ." She shrugged. "I'm parked over there," she said pointing across Third.

"I'm on the other side, opposite the hospital." I hesitated. "If only what?"

Vida stared straight ahead into the intersection, where a beat-up old Chevy was going far too fast for the driver's own good. Kids, I figured, with nothing better to do than try to maim themselves on a Thursday night in Alpine.

"Well, now." Vida sighed and then looked at me. "It's really a shame you aren't in love with Milo. Despite what you think about your differences, you two would do well together."

"That's hardly a reason to get married," I said.

"But you should," Vida declared. "Growing old alone isn't desirable. I've been thinking about that myself, but I don't know . . ."

She stopped and tugged at my sleeve. "It's not the same with you, Emma. You'll never find another Tommy. Don't end up like me."

She let go of my sleeve and tromped away into the night before I could speak.

But I was too stunned to say anything at all.

Fourteen

I managed to get hold of Ben shortly after nine o'clock. He offered to come over and keep me company, but I knew he was tired. His voice had lost its usual crackle.

"Stay put," I insisted. "You'll have dinner with me tomorrow night, right?"

"Sure. But I'll have to pack first. I'm leaving at eight."

"In the morning?"

"No. Friday night." Ben paused. "If I don't, I can't make it to East Lansing by Monday. There's supposed to be a snowstorm in Montana."

"Oh, Ben!" I cried. "Why did you drive out here? Why couldn't you have flown?"

"You'd rather have me die in a plane crash than on the highway?" He suddenly swore under his breath. "Sorry. I shouldn't have said that."

I knew he meant the unintentional reference to our parents' death. "I'd rather," I said firmly, "not have you die at all. I've got enough to worry about with Milo in the hospital again." I didn't mention that Vida's revelation about her loneliness had shaken me to the core.

"I'm coming over," he said, and hung up.

Naturally, I was glad. I needed Ben. I could be selfless for only so long. My inner resources were drained. Milo. Vida. My stalwarts were reeling.

Ben arrived five minutes later, looking energized. Maybe he needed to be needed as much as I needed him.

"I'll make us a drink," he said, heading straight into the kitchen.

"Fine." I remained on the sofa, staring at the phone, waiting for it to ring.

"Here," Ben said, handing me a glass of bourbon and water over ice. "I've got something to tell you."

I watched him in alarm as he sat beside me. "What? Are *you* sick?"

"No." He chuckled and took a sip of his bourbon cocktail. "I've been talking to Den Kelly about Mrs. Della Croce's phone call. He figured that since it had nothing to do with baring her soul, maybe he and I should speak up. Preferably to the sheriff, but he's not exactly available at the moment, and you're our next best bet."

My brain, which had seemed numb, began to function again. I had something to do besides worry. "This pertains to the Nystrom murder?"

Ben sighed. "Maybe not. But it does have something to do with the Nystroms, which is why Mrs. Della Croce phoned the rectory." He gazed at me with the same brown eyes I saw every time I looked in the mirror. "You know I trust you."

"I should hope so," I said with a lame little laugh. Then I frowned. "You don't trust Vida? Or Milo's deputies?"

"Except for Jack Mullins, who's a parishioner, I don't know the deputies," Ben said. "Let's face it, Jack can be a little flaky. He doesn't always think before he speaks. As for Vida . . ." Ben grinned. "I do trust her, but you're the editor and publisher, whether you always remember that or not. Besides, she's not my sister."

"Okay. I think I get it. So what did Anna Maria say?"

Ben cradled his glass in his lap. "When she thought I was Kelly, she started talking in abstract terms — about a neighbor's duty and a parent's responsibility. Frankly, I couldn't make much sense of it. I realized I was supposed to know at least something about what she was saying — or at least who she was. That's when I stopped her and said I wasn't Kelly."

I nodded. "You never met her when you did your stint at St. Mildred's."

"No," Ben agreed. "She's not a regular. The Della Croces may have gone to one of the Christmas Masses, but there was such a mob that I didn't notice them. I still wouldn't know them by sight. Anyway, she spoke to Den later. The gist of what she told him was that her daughter, Gloria, was upset about what she'd been hearing from the Nystrom house."

"Quarrels?" I asked.

Ben shook his head. "Far from it. And not recent, actually. It seems that Gloria got an assignment in her senior English class to write about something that had surprised or amazed her or somehow given her a new perspective on approaching adulthood. She'd been mulling over what she'd heard ever since school started. In fact, after that, she hadn't heard anything because the weather changed and both families closed their windows. But during the spring and summer the houses are so close to Gloria's bedroom that she could hear plenty. Not all the time, but maybe once or twice a week." Ben paused to sip his drink. "Elmer, I assume, belonged to various civic clubs around town?"

"Yes," I replied, growing impatient for Ben to get to the meat of his story. "He was a former Kiwanis president and chaired the roadside litter cleanup for Rotary. Elmer also belonged to the Chamber of Commerce."

"Okay, then we can assume Elmer wasn't home on the evenings that Gloria overheard the conversations between Polly Nystrom and her son, Carter."

"Conversations?" I stared at Ben. "A plot to kill Elmer?"

"No, no." Ben laughed again, though not with his usual gusto. "Polly and Carter talked like lovers."

"Oh, ick!" I shrieked. "What kind of aberration is that?"

Ben looked bemused. "I guess you're still a little naïve, Sluggly. There isn't much I haven't heard since I became a priest. People are damned odd. Inventive, too. They can think of more ways to sin than the old prophets ever dreamed of."

I shook my head. "It still sounds gross."

"Don't get me wrong — Gloria never suggested that there was anything more than talk," Ben explained. "In fact, she figured that Carter was either in the bathroom or his bedroom while his mother was in the other bedroom. He always called her Polly, not Mama or Mom or whatever. He'd say things like 'How's my best sweetheart tonight?' and 'Don't ever be jealous — you're the only girl in the world for me' and 'Is my true love looking as pretty as ever in the frilly pink bed jacket her devoted Carter gave her?' "

"Ick times ten," I said, making a face. "Do sons talk to their mothers like that?"

Ben shrugged. "I didn't. Our mother would've whacked me with her infamous wooden cooking spoon. But maybe some do utter endearments that sound a little off. Still, this stuff seems too far out to not exhibit some kind of obsession or kink."

"Was Gloria shocked?" I inquired.

"No." Ben smiled. "She's eighteen. Kids these days are pretty worldly. She just thought it was really weird. Mrs. Della Croce didn't think there was anything sexual, just this St. Valentine card stuff, ballad lyrics kind of thing. It was harder for Gloria to hear Polly, but apparently she'd simper and egg him on."

"It's peculiar," I said.

Ben drained his drink. "Of course it may have nothing to do with Elmer's murder."

"Maybe not." On the other hand, it might have everything to do with it. "Has Gloria written about this for her English class?"

"No. She sounds pretty smart. She decided that while it might have been unusual behavior — I'm using Kelly's interpretation of what her mother said — it wasn't really something that helped her mature. But it worried Mrs. Della Croce, who was more shocked than her daughter. Mother frets over daughter's moral corruption — or something like that. The Della Croces might try going to Mass more often instead of fussing about what the next-door neighbors are doing."

"Except," I said softly, "that the neighbors — or one of them — got murdered."

"I leave the sleuthing to you," Ben responded. "My report may be worthless."

"Maybe," I allowed. "I suppose I should tell Vida. Even if Milo wasn't sick, he'd consider Gloria's eavesdropping as salacious gossip, not evidence."

"Do what you will," Ben said with a shrug. "I know you won't put it on the local grapevine."

That was true, even if I told Vida. She could, when necessary, keep things under her bizarre collection of hats. With my thoughts turning to both the sheriff and my House & Home editor, I told Ben about my concerns for them. He shrugged off Milo's health problems.

"There's nothing you can do about that," my brother said. "Milo may have to change his lifestyle. Or it might be a virus."

"Let's hope so," I said, still fretting.

"Vida's another matter," Ben remarked. He'd refilled our glasses with Pepsi and fresh ice. Neither of us wanted any more liquor. "I'm a little surprised," he went on. "I thought she enjoyed her independence."

"So did I. But Vida's a very private person. Ernest has been gone for almost thirty years. The three daughters left home to get married not too long after that. Only Amy still lives in Alpine. Vida's in her seventies. I hope she never retires. I can't imagine the *Advocate* without her."

"Or Alpine," Ben remarked. He grinned at me. "The *Advocate*'s a bigamist. You both seem married to it."

"It's different," I said in a serious voice. "To Vida, the *Advocate* and Alpine are one and the same. For me, they're separate entities. I love the paper and my work, but the town . . . well, I still feel a bit like an outsider. That comes from not being born here."

Before Ben could say anything, the phone rang. I practically fell all over myself reaching for the receiver on the end table. Instead of saying "Hello," I barked "Yes?" and steeled myself for the worst.

"Emma?"

"Yes." I tempered my tone but still must have sounded impatient. "Who's this?"

"Scott," my reporter replied. "Are you okay?"

"Oh!" I fell back against the sofa. "Yes. I was expecting a call about Milo. He's in the hospital again."

"No kidding," Scott said in surprise. "I mean . . . well, you know what I mean. What happened?"

Briefly, I explained the circumstances. After Scott had made the appropriate commiserating comments, I asked why he'd phoned.

"I met up with Coach Ridley after work," Scott said. "I tried to call you when I got home around seven, but you didn't answer, and I didn't leave a message because Tammy and I had to go grocery shopping."

I scribbled Scott's name on a notepad to show Ben who had called. He nodded and got up to wander around the living room. "And?" I prompted Scott.

"Brad Nordby and Brianna Phelps had been dating off and on for a year," Scott said. "But they broke up just after Thanksgiving. Then she found out she was pregnant. The Reverend Phelps insists that his daughter and Brad get married ASAP. The Nordbys are dead set against it because Brad has a chance at a track scholarship to Seattle Pacific University."

"A Methodist school," I remarked. "Not good for the minister's son-in-law to show up with a pregnant bride in tow. When's the baby due?"

"Uh . . . I don't know."

Men. "Late spring, early summer," I guessed out loud. "But it's still a problem for Phelps's image around here. Did Ridley say anything about Elmer giving Brad fatherly advice?"

"A little. Just that Elmer seemed to take it upon himself to lecture kids on safety and taking care of their vehicles. Coach thought that he'd probably chewed out Brad about Brianna and how he should do the right thing. Like 'Be a man and marry the girl.' "

"That's not much of a motive for murder," I said.

"Coach told me Brad had quite a temper."

Quick tempers can lead to violence, but it's usually spontaneous. Brad would have been more likely to throttle Elmer during a lecture on good behavior. I couldn't see him biding his time and hiding out in a hen-house at seven in the morning.

"I guess," I said to Scott, but also for Ben's benefit, "we can rule out Brad Nordby as a suspect. Rip Ridley didn't think that Elmer and Brad had more than words, right?"

"Coach had some words of his own for Brad," Scott replied. "He's threatening him with suspension from the track team. That'd mean goodbye scholarship."

"I'd say Brad's in a pickle. Thanks, Scott. You've done well."

"Glad to help," my reporter said, sounding pleased. "I've been thinking. How about an editorial promoting vehicle safety in SkyCo and offering an annual award in Elmer's name? He was really hard-nosed on the subject. Elmer didn't lecture only teenagers. According to Coach, he came down hard — well, as hard as it went with Elmer — on everybody."

"That's a good idea," I said. "We'll have to figure out how a winner would qualify. Maybe AAA or the state safety council can help. But we should check with Polly and Carter first. We can do that after the funeral."

Assuming, I thought sadly, *that the wife and the son would care about Elmer's memory.*

■ ■ ■ ■

Jack Mullins finally called a little after ten. There was no real news on Milo. He was feeling better, but despite his protests, Dr. Sung was holding firm on keeping the sheriff overnight. Jack was going back on patrol, waiting for the inevitable accident along the Highway 2 corridor.

Ben went back to the rectory a few minutes after I'd hung up. I tried not to think about my brother being on the road to Michigan in less than twenty-four hours. I also tried not to think about Milo or Vida. I failed miserably and spent a restless night.

The next morning Vida was dressed in her funeral garb, which included a broad-brimmed black hat with precariously dangling jet poodles. "You're not coming?" she said, noticing my emerald-green sweater and dark green slacks.

I shook my head. "You're a keen observer. I didn't know the family at all. Just give me a full report."

"Of course." Vida looked surprised that I'd bother to make such a request. "I'm leaving early so I can stop by the hospital and see how Milo's doing. Or have you called this morning?"

I shook my head again. "I haven't had time. It's only five after eight. Sit. I've got something to tell you."

It took me only a couple of minutes to relate the Gloria Della Croce eavesdropping story. Vida made a face but otherwise showed no overt amazement.

"Such silliness," she declared. "An unnatural attachment, of course. But perhaps harmless. The question is why. Is Polly so deprived of spousal affection from Elmer that she seeks it from their son? Or is Carter unable to commit to a woman in his peer group and thus transfers his romantic notions to his mother? I'm not a great believer in psychiatrists, but I do think a good shake is often in order."

"I'm not sure that'd work," I said. "I wonder how long this has been going on."

"Well . . ." Vida considered it, tilting her head to one side and fingering her chin. The black hat's poodles danced in my drafty cubbyhole. "Carter's been back in Alpine for two years. Anna Maria's daughter might have heard similar exchanges the previous summer, but being a teenager, she paid no attention. So self-absorbed at that age. But this past summer, she was more grown up." Vida shrugged. "Who can say?"

Certainly not me. I told Vida to have Scott

relate Coach Ridley's information about the Nordby son, heir, and prospective father. She rushed off to interrogate my reporter while I sought satisfaction in coffee and a sugar doughnut. Then I called the hospital.

Milo had left without permission. Some time around two a.m., according to an indignant Constance Peterson, the night nurse had discovered that the sheriff was no longer in his bed. A search had proved futile. His clothes were gone, too. Dr. Sung had been notified about three a.m. and had attempted to reach Milo by phone. There was no answer.

"You mean he's missing?" I asked, feeling panic rise.

"No," Constance snapped. "He's in his office. We checked again this morning. He arrived there shortly before eight o'clock and refuses to talk to any medical personnel."

I didn't know whether to applaud Milo or strangle him, but after finishing my doughnut, I headed for the sheriff's headquarters.

"Is the ex-patient in?" I asked Lori Cobb upon my arrival.

She grimaced. "Yes, but he's not seeing anyone this morning."

I glanced at Dustin Fong, who was standing by the water cooler, looking uneasy.

"He's in seclusion?" I inquired.

Lori avoided my eyes. "Let's say that what he's in isn't a good mood."

"I suppose not." I gazed past Lori and Dustin to Milo's closed door. "I think I'll try anyway."

"Good luck," Lori said.

I knocked. "It's me, Emma."

"Go away." Milo's voice was muffled.

"Why?"

No answer.

"Come on, Milo. Open up."

More silence.

I tried the knob. The door was locked. "You're an idiot!" I shouted.

The idiot didn't respond. I shrugged and walked back through the reception area. "I flunked. Any news other than the sheriff's escape from medical treatment?"

"Do you want to see the log?" Lori asked.

"No. I'll let Scott handle that," I said. "Assuming, of course, that there's nothing startling in it."

Dustin had walked over to where I was standing. "Just the usual," he said. "A couple of DUIs and a fender bender by the railroad crossing at the bridge over the Sky."

"Who's going to the funeral?" I inquired, knowing that Milo usually felt that someone should show up at a service involving a homicide victim. The sheriff might stick to the evidence trail like Ponce de Leon searching for the Fountain of Youth, but he did believe that it was important to observe suspects and witnesses during a time of stress.

Dustin and Lori looked at each other, and both shrugged. "Dodge hasn't assigned anyone," Lori said. "That we know of. Maybe he forgot."

Under the circumstances, that was possible. "Is anybody available?" I asked.

Lori looked at the duty roster. "Dwight and Sam are on patrol. Doe's providing the police escort for the funeral. I suppose she could do it — except she hates funerals."

"Not many people enjoy them," I said. Except for Vida and, of course, the Wailers, a trio of older women who showed up at every funeral and memorial service to shriek and moan and carry on even if they didn't know the deceased.

"We should tell Doe to do it," Dustin said. "She's tough."

"Except for funerals," Lori put in, but she didn't argue with her co-worker.

Doe might be tough, but maybe she wasn't observant. I headed back to the office wondering if I should attend the funeral, too, or at least stop in at the reception. Vida, of course, would absorb every detail like a sponge. But even she — contrary to rumor — couldn't be in two places at once. Two sets of eyes and two sets of ears were better than one, even when one set belonged to my House & Home editor.

I had walked as far as Parker's Pharmacy when I heard my name being called. Tara Wesley was hurrying across Front Street, carrying coffee from the Burger Barn.

"I was coming to see you as soon as I delivered this to Garth," she said, stepping onto the curb. "Have you got a minute?"

"Sure," I replied. "Your office or mine?"

She nodded toward the drugstore's entrance. "Mine's closer."

"Sure," I repeated, and opened the door for her.

The Wesleys' office was only slightly larger than my cubbyhole, but it was even more crammed with cartons, most of which contained pharmaceuticals. Their security was much better, however: The door was padlocked as well as bolted to prevent theft.

"Our coffeemaker broke," Tara said after she'd delivered her husband's coffee. "I drink tea. Want some?"

I shook my head but thanked her for the offer.

"Anyway," Tara went on, "we sell a couple

of coffeemaker brands, but I don't like them." She made a face. "I shouldn't admit that. Harvey Adcock carries the kind I like at the hardware store, and we won't infringe on his exclusivity. Local merchants have to stick together — up to a point."

"Of course."

"Anyway," Tara went on, "I didn't want to see you about merchandising problems. Jessica *finally* unloaded about why she didn't like working for Carter Nystrom."

"Ah." I settled back in the folding chair, prepared to listen.

"The two assistants, Alicia and Christy, sniped at each other constantly," Tara began. "Alicia was particularly annoying because she took it out on Jess, being the new girl in the office. Apparently, Alicia was going through a bad patch — somebody in the family died or was sick or some such thing, and Christy was unsympathetic. Jess thought they were probably very competitive with each other. Then the last straw that day was when Carter's accountant from Mill Creek, or somewhere in Snohomish County, came to the office for a dinner meeting with Carter after work. He was very rude, and it made Jess nervous. She accidentally spilled a flower vase all over the CPA, and he really chewed her out. She didn't want to tell us for fear that Garth and I'd be mad at her for not sticking to the job longer. But frankly, I don't blame her. Bree hadn't stayed on to train Jess, and the assistants seemed to feel it was beneath them to help her. Naturally, Carter was too busy."

I nodded. "Did Bree leave her work in good order?"

"Not particularly," Tara said, "as far as Jess could tell. She told us the charts were so disorganized that she couldn't find a couple of them for two of their patients that day. I know kids have to learn to work under all kinds of conditions, but enough's enough. Backbiting creates a very poor atmosphere. I assume Alicia and Christy don't act like that in front of Carter or the patients."

"Probably not," I agreed. "I wonder how the assistants got along with Bree Kendall."

"Not very well, I'd guess." Tara poured hot water from a thermos and dipped a used tea bag into her Merck mug. "Jess said both Christy and Alicia made some rude remarks about Bree. Maybe that's the only thing they could agree on."

"Not a happy situation." I was thankful that my staff was usually friendly despite Vida's complaints about Leo's smoking and

Leo's ribbing of Vida. It hadn't been quite so pleasant when Ed was around, and that thought prompted a query for Tara. "Was Ed Bronsky working at the Burger Barn this morning when you went there?"

"Ed?" Tara looked startled. "No. Is he supposed to be?"

That was a loaded question. Ed was always *supposed* to be working when he was at the *Advocate,* but the reality had been quite different. "He was there yesterday," I said. "Frankly, I feel sorry for him."

"You shouldn't. Ed's a very foolish person. Shirley can't be much better. People create most of their own troubles, if you ask me."

Tara's hardheaded attitude mirrored Vida's — and probably that of most Alpine residents. Rooting for the underdog is an American pastime, but God help the person who puts himself or herself on a pedestal.

I left Tara, only slightly wiser than I'd been before she'd told me about the unhappy situation in Carter Nystrom's office. Jessica Wesley might be exaggerating, but I doubted it. Still, I couldn't see that the information did anything to help solve Elmer's murder.

Vida was gone by the time I got back to the office at nine-thirty. Only Leo remained in the newsroom, talking on the phone. I still had to come up with an editorial for the next edition. Maybe the idea for a safe driving award could be worked into an editorial. I started to look up the number for AAA. The corporate headquarters for Washington and northern Idaho was in Bellevue; the closest regional office was in Everett. But this was a job for Scott. I wrote him a note and put it on his desk. The editorial was stalled until we got some feedback on funding such an award, as well as securing approval from Polly and Carter.

At loose ends, I dialed the rectory number. Father Den answered.

"Your brother's visiting a couple of parishioners at the nursing home," our pastor informed me. "He's seen just about everybody he met while he was filling in for me. He's also buying some stuff to take on his trip back to East Lansing. I assume I can't do anything for you," he added in a self-deprecating manner.

"I just wanted to make sure I'd see him before he leaves," I said. "I'm going to miss him terribly. I'll bet you will, too."

"He's good company — and really helpful," Father Den said. "Running this parish keeps me hopping. I'm on my way to a meeting at the chancery in Seattle. I could do without that kind of interruption, archbishop or not."

"I don't blame you," I said. "I hate meetings. By the way, Ben told me about Anna Maria Della Croce's problem."

"Oh. Right. Her biggest problem is not attending Mass and receiving the sacraments, but what's the point in belaboring that one?"

"None, I guess." Who was I to offer spiritual advice?

"Got to go, Emma. I've already said goodbye to Ben since I won't get back in town until late." Den sighed. "This is my second trip this week. I had a funeral Mass Wednesday at a parish clear in the south end of Seattle."

I wished Father Den a safe trip and hung up. It was almost ten o'clock. Maybe I would go to the funeral reception in the church hall at Trinity Episcopal. After all, I hadn't yet met Carter Nystrom. I hated to think of him as a suspect, but it wouldn't be the first time a child had killed a parent.

The phone rang before I could refill my coffee to fortify me for the reception. It was Rolf Fisher, sounding chipper as usual.

"Slow news day," he announced. "I decided you should amuse me. Want to come down for the weekend?"

"I'm not a traveling circus," I declared. "We've got murder up here, remember?"

"Ah, yes — the chicken coop mystery. Which came first, the killer or the victim?"

"Not funny." I paused. "Well, it is. But I intend to stick around. In fact, I'm off to the funeral reception in a few minutes."

"How's the sheriff?" Rolf inquired. "We heard he was back in the hospital."

"How'd you find that out?" I asked in a vexed voice.

"Oh, we have our ways," Rolf said.

"Spies, you mean."

"Yes. No. Maybe. The truth is — Why am I telling you this? Don't you find me more fascinating when I'm being mysterious?"

"Yes. No. Maybe."

"One of our intrepid reporters was driving over the pass last night and stopped at your quaint fifties diner for a late dinner," Rolf explained. "Somebody mentioned it. What's wrong with Dodge? Suffering from a broken heart?"

"Hardly. But," I admitted, "the doctors haven't figured out what's wrong with him. Anyway, he walked out of the hospital during the night, and he's back at work."

"Brave fellow," Rolf remarked. "Are you sure you don't want to come down and make passionate love to me?"

"Yes. I'll be there later this month. Try to control yourself."

"Not easy. I could come to Alpine."

I hesitated. It would be extremely pleasant to have Rolf around, especially since I'd be gloomy when Ben left. It also would be a distraction. I had to stay focused, particularly since Milo's health was so erratic. Sometimes I felt as if I'd been deputized by the sheriff.

"Maybe next weekend," I said.

"Darn. We'll see. Ah. Something interesting just came across my desk. She's very blonde and very nubile. Talk to you later."

I put the phone down. Rolf had a knack for making me smile — when he wasn't driving me crazy. I still hadn't figured out whether to always take him seriously.

Still, one thing he'd said stuck in my brain: *Which came first, the killer or the victim?*

FIFTEEN

I'd been in the church hall at Trinity Episcopal a half-dozen times before this damp Friday morning. As always, I was impressed by — and a bit envious of — the good taste in both architecture and appointments. The building was small but made of granite quarried from the mountainside on which it was built.

The hall was in the basement, furnished with faux wooden folding chairs and tables. The walls were decorated with three high-quality framed prints: Dale's engraving *The Interior of the Chapel of the Holy Trinity, Leadenhall, London,* Edward Burne-Jones's *The Morning of the Resurrection,* and Dante Gabriel Rossetti's *The Annunciation.* I've always liked the Rossetti reproduction best. Mary looks very young and really leery of the wingless angel standing before her.

I'd arrived just as the service was drawing to a close. After a quick peek through the window in the door leading to the sanctuary, I'd decided not to intrude. Downstairs, two middle-aged women stood by a long table where a tray of cookies, a punch bowl, and two silver urns apparently constituted the refreshments. I didn't recognize either of the women, who I assumed were there to pour, and wondered if they were Nystrom relatives from North Dakota. I walked over to the portly one who was checking the coffee urn and introduced myself.

She put out a plump, freckled hand. "How kind of you to come. I'm Ruth Nystrom Pollard, Elmer's sister." Ruth nodded at the other woman, who was arranging cookies on a silver tray. "This is Elmer's sister-in-law, Dorothy Nystrom. She's Will's widow."

Dorothy aligned a stray chocolate chip cookie before giving me a tentative smile. "Hello," she said, but kept her hands to herself. "Will died ten years past. Liver."

"I'm sorry," I said. "Was he older or younger than Elmer?"

Ruth answered for the widow. "Two years older." She smiled slightly. "I'm the baby of the family."

"When did you get here?" I inquired.

"Yesterday," Ruth replied, inspecting a cup for cleanliness. "We're staying at that motel — Timber something or other."

"Is this your first visit to Alpine?"

Ruth shook her head. "We came out west once before, the year that Mount St. Helens blew up. Just missed it. Twenty-odd years ago. All these mountains." She shuddered. "They make me nervous. So big. So high. How do you stand it?"

It wasn't the first time I'd heard Midwest natives complain about the claustrophobia our mountains could cause. "We like them," I said, trying not to sound too apologetic. "Did Elmer and Polly visit you folks often?"

Ruth glanced at Dorothy, who shook her head. "Not them," Ruth declared. "Too busy. Too caught up with their new lives. North Dakota wasn't good enough for them." She pursed her lips. "Speak no ill . . . and so forth. But I never blamed Elmer, did I, Dot?"

Dorothy shook her head again.

Voices could be heard in the distance. The mourners were on their way down to the reception. "I'm sure," I said, "that Polly and Carter are glad you've come."

Neither woman responded. In fact, they turned away from me and posted themselves at either end of the long serving table. I snatched a sugar cookie off the tray and went over to study the Rossetti painting. Now that I thought about it, Mary looked more than leery — she appeared frightened. Perhaps the angel was about as welcome in Nazareth as the Nystrom kinfolk were in Alpine.

The Nordby contingent led the way. Discreetly, I tried to figure which of the two young men was Bryce and which was Brad. Both were a little over average height with light brown hair and undistinguished features. One of them had a few pimples, so I guessed that he was the younger brother, Brad. He didn't seem like a rakish seducer of young girls. But then, I didn't know what Brianna looked like. For all I knew, she might scare small children.

Vida entered with Edna Mae Dalrymple. "Ah!" Vida exclaimed. "You came! How kind!"

The praise was for the benefit of Edna Mae and anyone else who might be listening, which, given my House & Home editor's trumpetlike voice, was everybody within shouting distance. Vida, of course, knew exactly why I'd really come — to snoop, just as she was doing.

"Such a lovely service," Vida announced loudly, coming up to me with Edna Mae tagging along like a pet pup. "Dreary beyond belief," she whispered. "I almost preferred listening to the Wailers."

"What did you say, Vida?" Edna Mae asked, panting a little.

"I said," Vida responded with a flinty smile, " 'Dear me, we should defer listening to the Wailers.' "

"Oh." Edna Mae blinked several times behind her glasses.

"I didn't realize you knew the Nystroms so well," I said to her.

"I knew Elmer," Edna Mae replied. "He was such a nice man. He used the library quite often. In fact, at least once a week he'd come in on his lunch hour and read the *Williston Daily Herald.* He was always so eager to find out what was going on in his old hometown."

"Really?" I said. "I understood that the Nystroms never visited back there."

Edna Mae frowned. "That's so. Polly Nystrom couldn't stand the climate. That's one reason they moved. So hot in the summer and so cold in the winter. Very bleak, I gather, though Elmer told me he never minded it. He found a strange beauty in the land, a sense of peace, he called it."

"That's quite nicely put," Vida declared, pushing at the jet poodles on her hat to get them out of her line of sight. "It's a shame that Reverend Bartleby didn't mention it in his eulogy."

"I thought," Edna Mae said deferentially, "that the eulogy was very apt. Elmer was such a decent, pleasant man."

"We all know that," Vida retorted, shoving the hat farther back on her head. "One hopes to learn something from a eulogy. Something that wasn't common knowledge about the deceased. Take Cornelius Shaw, for instance. Such a fine, solid insurance man. Who would have thought he belonged to a nudist colony? Out of the area, of course, and Father Fitzgerald, who was St. Mildred's pastor at the time, merely said that Corny was a fresh air fiend. But we *knew. The altogether* was what he meant." Vida ignored Edna Mae's astonished expression. "Arthur Trews is another example. I had no idea he'd been a bed wetter until he was twelve — or that Cass Pidduck raised night crawlers in his basement."

Edna Mae looked surprised. "Did he really? Goodness, I don't think I'd care for that."

Vida shrugged. "Cass had always insisted he sold them to fishermen for bait. But he never did. He considered them his pets." Vida was eyeballing Ruth and Dorothy. "Are those the out-of-towners? I saw them leave the service a few minutes early."

I nodded. "Sister and sister-in-law to Elmer."

"Ah." Vida tromped over to the refreshment table.

"I suppose I should have some tea," Edna Mae said in an uncertain voice. "Perhaps a cookie as well. Excuse me, Emma."

Her departure was perfect timing for me. Polly and a tall good-looking young man I assumed was Carter were entering the hall. She was leaning heavily on his arm and fanning herself with the funeral service program. Regis Bartleby was bringing up the rear.

I felt obligated to convey my formal condolences. Apparently the receiving line had been held in the vestibule upstairs. No one was hovering around the mother and son at the moment.

"Mrs. Nystrom," I said. "I'm sorry I wasn't at the church service, but work kept me away. Again, I'm terribly sorry for your loss."

"Oh. Yes, thank you." She looked up at the man who had to be her son. There was a marked resemblance, though he was a full head taller and hadn't added the extra poundage that Polly carried on her shorter frame. "Carter, dear, I don't believe you've met Erma Land from the newspaper."

Carter's expression was quizzical as he shook my hand. "It's Emma, isn't it?" he said gently.

"Yes." His hand was very soft, almost like a baby's. "Emma *Lord.*"

Carter nodded gravely. "You and your colleague actually found my father. I've meant to call you, but there hasn't been much spare time under these tragic circumstances. You understand, of course."

"Of course." I, too, could be formal.

Polly tapped her son's arm. "I really must sit, dearest. I feel a bit faint. If you could fetch me a cookie or two, I'd be ever so grateful."

"Certainly," Carter said, smiling at his mother. "Let me settle you at this empty table."

There were plenty of those. Only a couple of dozen mourners had shown up for the reception. My glimpse of the gathering in the church had revealed about twice that many people. I assumed that the others had had to return to work, probably at the Nordby Brothers dealership.

I joined Polly as soon as Carter had her comfortably seated and she'd specified "sugar cookies only." As he walked away, she placed the funeral program on the table and smoothed it several times with her hand.

"Mr. Driggers has been very helpful," she remarked. "Is he here now?" She craned her neck, searching for Al, the funeral director. He was nowhere in sight and usually wasn't once his duties at the service had been fulfilled. I assumed, however, he'd be back on the job for the trip to the cemetery. I didn't see Deputy Doe, either.

"He's probably organizing the motorcade," I said. Maybe Doe was with him.

"Oh," Polly said, "there's no need for that. It's so damp today, and it's always windy at the cemetery. Carter insisted that I mustn't put myself through such an ordeal. He canceled the drive just before the service started. Mr. Driggers was very nice about it, Carter said. It was cremation, you know. The urn can be put in the crypt at any time."

I found it hard not to show my annoyance with Polly and her son. Even in death, Elmer seemed to be an afterthought. I also found it hard to understand why I was the only person sitting with Polly. The Nordby family was bunched together on the far side of the hall; Vida was talking to Ruth, Elmer's sister; Edna Mae had corralled Carter on his way back from the refreshment table; Regis Bartleby was attempting a conversation with the closemouthed Dorothy Nystrom; Mrs. Bartleby was chatting with a tall, lean young man in an impeccably tailored suit; and two young, fairly attractive women were talking to each other at a table near the door to the restrooms. I assumed they were Christy and Alicia, Carter's assistants. Contrary to Jessica Wesley's report, they seemed on amicable terms.

"It was good of your sisters-in-law to come out for the funeral," I remarked. "I met them just now."

"Oh?" Polly showed only vague interest. "Whatever is taking Carter so long? Who is that small woman he's talking to? I don't know her."

I explained that she was the head librarian. "She thought a great deal of Elmer. He came in to read the Williston newspapers every week."

"Did he?" Polly seemed peeved by the revelation. "He would, wouldn't he?" she murmured. "I can't think why he'd care."

"The *Advocate* has many subscribers who've moved away," I pointed out. "Former residents like to keep up with their old hometowns and the people they knew when they lived there."

"Really? I can't imagine why." She brightened. "Here comes Carter."

Here goes Emma, I thought. As much as I knew I should stick with mother and son, I couldn't stand it another minute. "Excuse me," I said. "I should talk to some of the others."

Two of the others, anyway: I made a beeline for Christy and Alicia, remembering the means of recognition from what Tara Wesley had told me. Christy was dark; Alicia had blond highlights in her hair.

"Hi," I said, trying to be friendly. "I'm Emma Lord from the *Advocate.*" I held out a hand to the brunette first. "You're Christy Millard, right?"

She nodded. "This is Alicia Strand."

I shook Alicia's hand despite her hostile expression. "Did you ever find it?" she asked.

I sat down next to her. "Find what?"

Alicia glared at me. "My grandfather's obituary. The one I mailed a week ago."

I stared at Alicia. "You're related to the Wascos who live here in town?"

"That's right," Alicia said sarcastically. "Uncle Amer told me to mail it again, but once is enough. Our office is less than a mile from the newspaper. How could it possibly get lost? Unless you people tossed it."

I was embarrassed. "I'm sorry. But honestly, we never received it. My House & Home editor, Mrs. Runkel," I said, gesturing at Vida, who had joined Polly and Carter, "will gladly run it in the next issue if you can send us another copy."

"Forget it," Alicia snapped. "The funeral was Tuesday in Seattle. It's too late now."

Judging from Alicia's hardened features, there was nothing I could do to make amends. Christy, however, seemed to be enjoying her co-worker's pique.

"Serves you right," Christy said. "You should've dropped off the notice at the newspaper. I never trust the mail." She turned as the tall, lean man I hadn't recognized came toward us. "Cool it, Alicia. Here comes the Money Man."

"Greetings," he said, standing behind Alicia's chair. "Have you tried the punch? It's pineapple and orange."

"It sounds lethal, Freddy," Christy said. "Go away."

"Don't," Alicia said. "Sit. Stay. I'm dying of boredom."

Freddy pulled out a chair next to Christy. "I may have found a receptionist for you. He's from Marysville and very efficient. His name is Geoff, with a G-E-O."

"Cute," said Alicia.

"Yuk," said Christy.

"I thought," Freddy said with a bemused expression, "you two might get along better with a male than another female. Less competition." He leered at both of them.

"That's not cute," Alicia declared archly.

Christy rested her chin on one hand and drummed the table with the other. "You're not going away, are you, Freddy?"

"Never. How could I?" For the first time, Freddy seemed to notice that I was an actual person and not part of the décor. "You should introduce me to your friend."

Alicia waved a hand as if to dismiss me. "She's not a friend. She's a reporter."

I've suffered mightily in the name of following a story, but this trio was getting on my nerves. Maybe Jessica Wesley was right, after all. Alicia and Christy were a nasty pair, and Freddy wasn't much better.

"I know all I need to know," I asserted, standing up and accidentally hitting my shin on the chair. "I'm sorry for your loss — of good manners." I stomped off toward the exit.

I'd gotten to the parking lot when I saw Vida coming out of the church entrance. "Yoo-hoo!" she shouted. "Wait for me!"

I stood in the soft rain and obeyed orders. "Those people are absolutely dreadful," I said when Vida got within hearing range. "I wish I'd never come."

"Emma!" Vida scowled at me. "When people are behaving badly, that's always when you learn the most."

"I didn't learn anything I didn't know or hadn't heard about," I grumbled. "Let's go back to the office. We can talk there."

"What about lunch? It's almost noon." She slapped again at the poodles hanging from her hat. "I'm very disappointed in the reception itself. Nothing more than a tray of cookies? Only three kinds? So stingy! I can't think how Edith Bartleby let Polly and Carter get away with that. Edith usually urges survivors to put on a more lavish spread."

"I'm hungry, too," I said. "Maybe that's why I'm so crabby. I'll see you at the Venison Inn. I can't bear to watch Ed slinging hamburgers again."

Trinity Church was on Second between Cascade and Tyee streets, which meant I might as well drive straight down to Front and park my car in front of the *Advocate*. But when I reached my destination, I saw that my usual spot had been taken by Ben's beat-up Jeep.

There was room for the Honda three spots down, by the dry cleaners. I pulled in just as Ben came out through the newspaper's entrance.

"Hey, Sluggly, want to go eat?" he shouted.

"I already have a date," I called to him. "It's Vida. Join us?" I couldn't ignore my brother, even for the sake of rehashing the funeral and reception.

"Sure," Ben said, walking toward me. "Where is she?"

I scanned Front Street. Vida had been forced to park her Buick across Fourth by the hobby shop.

"We're going to the Venison Inn," I said while we waited on the sidewalk. "I must warn you, I'm not in a charitable mood. I lost it at the Episcopal church."

"Not quite the place I'd have chosen," Ben remarked. "They're usually the soul of good manners and refined taste."

"Not this bunch," I said. "Anyway, I don't think some of them are Episcopalians."

Vida hailed my brother from half a block away. "Father Ben! How wonderful! You can cheer up your sister. She's been through the mill, I gather."

"Poor thing," Ben said dryly as we walked down the street. "Didn't they feed you?"

A snarl was my answer.

We were early enough to get a booth near the back of the restaurant. Vida sat on the aisle, of course, the better to watch who was coming in and going out, especially from the bar. The first thing she did after sitting down was to yank off the hat with its dangling poodles. Obviously, she wanted no more impediments to her people watching.

I'd gotten over my pique by the time I held a menu in my hands. "Okay," I said, "I'm not mad anymore, just unsettled. I find Polly and Carter very odd."

"Of course," Vida said. "They are." She leaned out of the booth. "Scooter Hutchins is growing a beard. He looks ridiculous. Who's that with him? A flooring salesman, perhaps. Or counter tiles."

Ben shot me an amused glance. "I assume Regis conducted a dignified ceremony?"

"Oh, yes," Vida replied. "Regis Bartleby is nothing if not dignified. But it wasn't a large turnout — mostly employees from Nordby Brothers and a few longtime customers such as the Pucketts and the Parkers and the Bartons. None of them stayed for the reception, though."

"It's a workday," I pointed out. "At least that was my excuse for missing the actual service."

"Shame on you," Ben said lightly.

"But I think I met Carter's CPA," I said.

"Whoopee!" Ben said softly, and whistled

just a little bit.

Vida, who was leaning again, swiveled around to look at me. "The man in the expensive suit?"

"Yes. His name is Freddy, and he may be an ass."

Jessie Lott, who always walked as if her feet hurt — they probably did — came to our booth holding her order pad. "Ready?" She stared at my brother. "Father Lord! I haven't had a chance to say hello. I went to Mass last Sunday in Monroe with my daughter. I spent Christmas there, too. She has a new baby."

"Congratulations," Ben said. "How have you been, Jessie?"

As usual, she looked a little glum. "Tired. I'd like to quit this job, but I won't get full Social Security for another year." She looked at Vida, taking in the black hat, the black swing coat, and the black-and-white-checkered dress. "You look like you went to Elmer Nystrom's funeral. Too bad about him. He was always good to me when I took Harold's old Blazer truck in for fixing."

Harold was Jessie's late husband, who'd died shortly before I moved to Alpine. He'd worked for the PUD and had accidentally touched a live wire that electrocuted him at the age of forty-four. Vida told me that

Jessie should have sued the county but refused because she insisted that her husband's co-workers and supervisors had always treated him kindly. She didn't want to cause them any trouble. Thus, she'd spent the last sixteen years waiting tables.

"Yes," Vida murmured, "everyone thinks Elmer was wonderful. I suppose he was. When my nephew couldn't fix my Buicks, I dealt with him, and I can't complain." The admission was astonishing. For once, Vida had no criticism to offer. "I'll have the chicken club with fries and a green salad, Roquefort dressing, and please don't let them stint on it. Oh, and hot tea." She checked to make sure there were plenty of real sugar packets in the holder on the table.

"Same for me, Jessie," Ben said. "But coffee, please."

I decided to make it easy. "Me, too," I said.

Jessie scribbled on her pad. "By the way, Father," she said, lowering her voice and speaking to my brother, "is it still a mortal sin to commit suicide?"

If Ben was startled by the question, he didn't show it. "The Church has softened its stand on suicide in recent years. Catholics who kill themselves are now allowed to be buried in sanctified ground as well as to have a funeral Mass said for them." His expression remained pleasant, inviting any confidence Jessie might want to offer.

"What about non-Catholics?" she asked.

"I'm not sure I know what you mean," Ben said.

Jessie sighed. "Never mind. I didn't go to Catholic school, so I only know what I learned in my catechism classes."

Ben smiled. "The old Baltimore Catechism, right?" He saw Jessie nod. "That got tossed decades ago, Jessie. Do you know somebody who is considering suicide?"

Jessie's round face turned pink. "Oh, not really. It's probably just talk. Excuse me. I'd better put your order in." She hurried off on her tender feet.

"Well, now!" Vida exclaimed. "Who do you suppose she meant?"

Ben's expression was no longer pleasant but somber. "I wish I knew. Maybe I should tell Kelly about it even if the person isn't Catholic. His network with the rest of the local clergy is pretty good."

"I hope so," Vida said. "It's nonsense for people to say that when someone talks about committing suicide, that's all it is — just talk, seeking attention. Usually the person is quite serious."

Ben agreed but felt there was no point speculating. "If you see Jessie at Mass on

Sunday," he said to me, "see if you can get her to open up."

"Jessie usually goes to five o'clock Mass on Saturdays," I responded. "She often works the breakfast shift here on Sundays."

"Then change your routine," Ben said. He wasn't kidding. Caring about people was, after all, part of his vocation. "So tell me more about your terrible trials at Elmer's reception."

In retrospect, there wasn't much to tell. In fact, I sounded petty as I recounted my exchanges with the North Dakota women, Carter and Polly, and the two assistants.

"Maybe my mood wasn't very good," I allowed.

"Funerals will do that," Ben remarked.

"A poor turnout," Vida remarked. "Not that many from the church itself. It makes me wonder. Did they stay away because they didn't really like Elmer — or because they couldn't stand Polly? You must recall what Maud Dodd said about Polly's rumor mongering."

I conceded Vida's point. "Carter seems innocuous enough."

"Perhaps." Vida frowned. "One person I thought might have been there wasn't."

"Who?" I asked.

"Bree Kendall. I must confess, I'm very

curious as to why she didn't come, if only out of courtesy."

"She didn't work for Elmer," I pointed out. "She may not have even known him."

"That's not the point," Vida contended. "She followed Carter to Alpine and spent two years working for him. That's what I mean by courtesy. I want to find out why she absented herself." Vida shot a steely glance at both Ben and me. "And I will do that, perhaps this very afternoon."

Sixteen

It wasn't until we were walking back to the office that Ben announced he was leaving in an hour. "Kelly won't be back until late tonight, but I've got any emergency covered by Sister Mary Joan and Sister Clare. If things really go awry, the pastor from St. Mary in the Valley in Monroe is backup."

"You tricked me," I accused him. "I thought we could have dinner before you left."

Ben shook his head. "That's why I came by to see if you were free for lunch. Follow through on that suicide thing, okay? It bothers me."

"Right." I knew I sounded uninterested. My brain was wrapped around Ben's precipitate departure and the loneliness I was already feeling.

"Hug," Ben said. "Prayers."

I threw my arms around him. Vida already had dashed into the office. My brother and

I both prayed in silence. Then he kissed the top of my head and let me go. I fought back tears as he climbed into his battered Jeep, waved once, and pulled out onto Front Street. I stood on the sidewalk, watching until he turned the corner onto Alpine Way and disappeared from sight.

Ginny was talking to someone who was buying a classified ad for a lost dog. Vida and Scott were both on the phone. Leo wasn't in sight. I went into my cubbyhole and immediately e-mailed Adam.

"Your uncle just left for East Lansing. I'm bereft. When are you going to get down here again? It seems like you've been gone for two years, not two weeks."

Mother's guilt trip, I thought, and felt suitably guilty. But I sent the e-mail anyway and waited, just in case Adam was online. After almost five minutes, I gave up. He was probably doing good somewhere with his parishioners. There were times when I wished my son hadn't become a priest. I could be surrounded by grandchildren and feeling needed. Instead, I was sitting in a room the size of a large cardboard box, feeling sorry for myself.

The phone rang. Had Adam decided to brave making a call despite the frustrating radio relay from St. Mary's Igloo?

"Yes?" I said hopefully.

"Gallstones."

"What?"

"Gallstones," Milo repeated. "You deaf?"

"You've got gallstones?" I said.

"Are you brain-dead *and* deaf?" the sheriff demanded. "Why would I say —"

"Okay, okay, I understand." I was so relieved that I laughed. "That's not very scary."

"Hell, no," Milo shot back, "but it's not funny when I have those attacks. They're damned miserable."

"I'm sure they are." *Try labor pains,* I felt like saying. *You men don't know what misery really is.*

"The operation's pretty simple," the sheriff said.

"Has your surgery been scheduled?"

"No, and keep your mouth shut," Milo ordered. "I don't want this to get out just yet. First, I'd like to wrap up this Nystrom homicide."

His statement made me curious. "Are you getting close?"

"No. Don't bug me." Milo sounded annoyed.

"I only wondered because —"

It was his turn to interrupt me. "You think I'm holding back?"

"Not really," I replied candidly. "But you can't go around having these attacks and getting hauled off to the hospital. What if it takes weeks to find the killer?"

"I have to be careful what I eat, that's all." The sheriff sounded slightly more reasonable. "That steak and the cheeseburger I had yesterday weren't good for me, Doc says."

"Probably not," I agreed. "Did Doe attend the funeral?"

"Uh . . . she kind of looked in from the back."

"I gather she has an aversion to funerals," I said, noticing that Ethel Pike had come into the newsroom to see Vida.

"Doe's half Native American," the sheriff said. "She doesn't think much of the way we other folks bury our dead. I'm not sure I don't agree with her. Anyway, that's her business, and as long as she does the job, she can think what she wants."

"Did she have any observations?"

"Yeah. She thought her part of it was worthless, since Carter Nystrom canceled the trip to the cemetery. Doe left about halfway through the service. I don't blame her — it was a waste of county time and money."

"That was Polly's doing, not Carter's," I

put in, but quickly amended my words. "That is, Carter felt his mother shouldn't have to go through a wet morning on Cemetery Hill."

"Bullshit," Milo said. "Everybody else does. What makes her so special?"

"Carter, I think. Let me tell you a little story." I lowered my voice so Ethel couldn't overhear and related Anna Maria Della Croce's account of her daughter's unintentional eavesdropping.

"Sick?" Milo said when I'd finished. "Or silly?"

"Your call."

"I've got one," the sheriff responded. "On my other line. Later."

Ethel was leaving just as I hung up. I went out into the newsroom.

"A letter to the editor," Vida said with a sneer, and handed me a single sheet of pale blue stationery decorated with a sketch of a thimble, a needle, and thread. "Ethel and Pike are upset with his care at the emergency room. They had to wait too long and insist it's because they're Medicare patients. Ethel says the doctors don't care about older folks, only younger people who pay their own way."

I scanned the three typed paragraphs. "Last night? We saw them there. What's the rush with bronchitis?"

Vida sighed. "Ethel insists they had to wait over an hour to be seen. Frankly, I don't think that's unreasonable with only two doctors in this county, and both of them are overworked as it is. Maybe you should write an editorial urging funding for a nurse practitioner, at the very least."

"I've written two or more in the last year," I said. "I suppose another wouldn't hurt. Certainly this thing with Milo might have been resolved sooner if the hospital had better testing equipment."

Vida stared at me. "What 'thing'? Do you know something I don't?"

The indignation in Vida's tone almost made me smile. "Yes. He just called. He has gallstones. But keep it to yourself." I turned to Scott, who was finally hanging up the phone. "Hear that? No tattling about the sheriff's delicate condition."

Scott nodded. "Got it." He gestured at his phone. "That was the state safety council. They don't give those type of awards. They suggested we use county funding."

"What county funding?" I shot back. "That's the problem — SkyCo is short of cash. Nobody wants to pay for bond issues and levies around here. We're lucky we can keep the public schools open."

Vida's expression remained indignant. "Alpiners are historically thrifty. A Scandinavian majority, working in the timber industry, with the town barely surviving the first big mill closure just before the Great Depression. If it hadn't been for my father-in-law, Rufus Runkel, the entire town would've been shut down."

I knew all about Rufus's bright idea to open a ski lodge. Seventy-five years ago he and another local known as Olaf the Obese had sunk their small savings into the relatively new winter sport of skiing. Their endeavor had saved the town, though growth had been minimal until the Second World War. Then, a few short years before I moved to Alpine, the timber industry had been hit hard again, this time by environmental concerns. The creation of the state community college had helped the local economy, but we seemed to be in a holding pattern of just over seven thousand full-time residents throughout the mountainous wedge-shaped county. Our tax base was small not only because so few people lived in SkyCo but because we had so little industry within our boundaries.

"We're more diverse nowadays," Scott pointed out. "Granted, Scandinavians still dominate the population, but look at the college — several ethnic groups are represented."

Vida gazed at Scott over the top of her large glasses. "A half-dozen faculty members who aren't Caucasian? Yes. But don't count the students. How many of them vote?"

The argument was pointless. I could write five miles worth of editorials and still not win over the tightfisted people who did go to the polls in Skykomish County. "Let's skip the health care concerns," I said. "This whole country doesn't have adequate medical coverage. We can't solve it at the local level if we expect the public to pay for it. As for the safety award, maybe the Nordby brothers can be conned into putting up some money for it. Certainly it'd be good public relations for them."

"I could ask Skunk and Trout," Scott offered.

"Let Leo do that," I said. "I'll write him a note."

Vida was putting her coat back on, though she had abandoned the troublesome hat and replaced it with a blue beret from her desk drawer. "Speaking of health care, I'm off to the hospital."

"Who's sick now?" Scott asked.

Vida paused at the newsroom door. "I'm not visiting any patients. I'm going to see

Bree Kendall." With a swish of her swing coat, she was gone.

Back in my cubbyhole, I read the Pikes' letter to the editor. There weren't any more typos or incorrect grammar than in most of the missives we received. At least the contents had been typed and were fairly brief. I put the complaint in my pending file along with the three other letters we'd received since the last edition had gone to press. Two, as usual, were about the potholes in the streets and roads, and the other was from the local vet, Jim Medved, in his annual appeal to people who had received pets for Christmas. He wanted the new owners to have their animals neutered. It was not only a sensible suggestion but also good for Jim's business.

Ginny buzzed me from the front office. "When's Leo coming back?" she asked.

"Ah . . . I'm not sure," I said. "He had a Chamber of Commerce luncheon, and then he was going to make some of his rounds. Why?"

"There's a Mr. Bellman to see him about an ad," Ginny said. "Do you want to talk to him?"

I didn't know anyone named Bellman, but I wasn't about to pass up revenue. "Sure. Send him my way. Thanks, Ginny."

A moment later, the newcomer walked through the newsroom. He wasn't exactly a stranger. I immediately recognized Freddy the Alleged Accountant in his well-tailored suit.

"We almost met," he said as he strolled into my office. "I'm Frederick Bellman, CPA, from Mill Creek."

I shook his hand. "Have a seat. I'm a little embarrassed," I admitted. "Sitting with Alicia and Christy felt a little like being caught in a buzz saw."

"Oh, it's very like that," he said, settling into one of my visitor's chairs. "They're rather unpleasant people. I call them the Evil Twins. They despise me because I won't let Carter give them big bonuses or huge raises every six months. They don't understand that's part of my job." He shrugged. "You'd think that pair would realize what an outlay of money it took for Carter to set up his practice."

I nodded. "Student loans to pay off as well, I assume."

Freddy shrugged again but didn't comment on my remark. Instead, he asked how many accountants worked in the county.

"Only two, really," I replied, "and one's about to retire, I'm told. Many of the local businesses keep their own books."

"Bad idea these days," Freddy declared. "It's very difficult for a layperson to keep up with all the changes in tax laws. I'm located in Mill Creek, but I have clients in Monroe, Sultan, Snohomish, and Marysville. I thought maybe I should run an ad in your paper. I might pick up a few more accounts around here."

I said I thought that was a good idea and apologized for my ad manager's absence. "We have a section on pages four and five for professional services standing ads that run every week," I went on. "But you might want to start with a one- or two-time ad that's larger and has more prominent placement. I have a rate schedule in my desk." I *hoped* I had one and also hoped it wasn't out of date. "Here," I said, finding a schedule that Leo had put together at the end of the previous August. "And let me show how the professional ads look." I also handed him a copy of the most recent *Advocate* and opened it to pages four and five.

Freddy appeared to be a quick study. "Two columns by four inches the first time," he said. "Do you think you should run a photo of me?"

"Yes. People like to know what other people look like, especially if you have a picture of yourself that oozes trust."

He chuckled. "Oh, indeed I do. Trust and accuracy. I'll send it to your ad man. Walsh, right?"

"Very good. Thank you." I paused. Freddy was looking at Elmer's obituary.

"So that's what Carter's dad looked like," Freddy remarked. "Nothing like Carter. Too bad about the way he died. Has the killer been caught?"

"Not yet," I said, "but our sheriff is very capable."

"It was probably somebody on drugs," Freddy said. He'd crossed his legs and was adjusting the sharp crease in his pants. I got the impression he wasn't in a hurry to get back to Mill Creek. "That's often the case these days. Random and crazy."

As long as Freddy wasn't going away, I figured I might as well pump him. "Why did Carter hire Christy and Alicia if they're such a pair of harpies?"

"Oh, they'd both had some experience and were highly qualified," Freddy replied. "They'd gone to school together, but I don't think they were ever friends. Of course they tone it down when Carter and the patients are around. I guess they wanted a change of lifestyle. Neither of them were city girls. Christy's from eastern Washington, around Yakima, I think, and Alicia grew up in Redmond. She didn't like that suburban scene, but she didn't want to be a city dweller, either."

"What about Bree Kendall?" I inquired.

Freddy grinned at me. "Bree. She's not just another pretty face."

"How do you mean?"

He uncrossed his legs and leaned back in the chair, looking up at the low ceiling. "Bree's interesting. Her parents were so far out, they were practically in another universe. Bree was brought up in a commune in Oregon and ran away when she was sixteen. She hasn't seen her mother and father since she left fifteen years ago. I gather they don't miss her, and she certainly doesn't miss them. You know how it is — children rebel. Bree wants order and tradition and stability in her life." He lowered his gaze and looked me right in the eye. "I'd like to give her that now that Carter's dumped her."

"Is that why she quit?" I asked, surprised.

"You bet." Freddy smiled again. He had very even white teeth in a long, lean face. "She wasted two years of her life on him. But here I am, ready and willing to let her cry on my shoulder. In fact, I'm taking her to dinner tonight at that French restaurant out on the highway." His gaze still held mine. "You find my candor astonishing?"

"Not as much as your audacity," I said. "Carter's your client. I find it odd that you'd be telling me about this in the same conversation that includes the word *trust*."

"Trust me on this," Freddy said, leaning closer to my desk. "Carter doesn't care if I make a move on Bree. As for being candid with you, I grew up in a small town — Darrington, to be exact, which is another old logging enclave much like Alpine. I know that by tomorrow morning at least fifty people will be talking about that 'tall young man who was wining and dining Bree Kendall at Le Gourmand.' And since you own the newspaper, one of those people doing the talking — or should I say listening? — will be you."

He had a point. "Fair enough," I conceded. "If Carter's not going to be brokenhearted, I assume somebody else is the object of his affections."

"Definitely," Freddy asserted. "Though he does play the field."

"The field's not very big in Alpine," I pointed out.

"Carter still has ties to Seattle," Freddy said in an offhand manner. "He spends at least two weekends a month there." At last the unexpectedly garrulous CPA stood up.

369

"I should let you get back to work. Maybe I'll go to the local Starbucks and get caught up on work over a cup of elegant Sulawesi. Are there any sights worth seeing around here?"

For somebody raised in Darrington, I couldn't think that Alpine would have anything he hadn't experienced in his hometown. "No," I said, though I was tempted to mention that Vida was our most historical landmark. "Drop in before five. Leo should be here then."

"We'll see." He saluted me and left.

Twenty minutes later, Leo and Vida returned together. "We're a couple," Leo announced. "The Duchess can't resist me."

"You smell like a smudge pot," Vida declared. "I'm so glad Buck doesn't smoke. At least not in my presence, though I believe he has the occasional cigar when he gets together with his air force cronies."

"Clearly," Leo said, "you've never smelled an actual smudge pot. Being from southern California, I know what they really smell like. I'm more of an ashtray guy."

"Disgusting, whatever it is," Vida remarked, removing her black hat and rearranging several stray hairpins. "Bree Kendall is not forthcoming. She refused to have tea with me on her break."

"What was your ruse?" I asked, coming over to Vida's desk.

"You should've offered her a cigarette," Leo said, shrugging off his barn jacket. "I've seen her smoking outside Carter's office."

Vida made a face. "Ugh." She looked away from Leo and sat down. "I told a tiny fib and said I'd left my gloves in the waiting room when I was there last night inquiring after the sheriff. Without even looking anywhere or asking anyone, Bree insisted no gloves had been found. I then tried to strike up a friendly conversation with her — how did she like her new job, was it harder or easier than her previous employment, did she find Alpine a delightful town, and so on. She kept cutting me off, even though there were only two people in the waiting room and none came in while I was there. Indeed, she was quite abrupt." Vida paused for breath.

"You haven't broken your own record yet," Leo said, tapping his watch. "You only had another eighteen seconds to go without breathing."

"Oh, hush, Leo!" Vida exclaimed. "Finally, I asked her why she hadn't attended the funeral. She got angry — imagine! — and said it was none of my business. Then she got up and stalked away. I waited — where she couldn't see me, of course, around the corner by the restrooms. After about five minutes she came back, so I apologized all over myself and invited her for a cup of tea. She refused in a most ungracious manner. At that point I gave up." Vida put her chin on her fists and shook her head. "I cannot accept failure. Obviously, that young woman is unbalanced. There can't be any other explanation."

I tensed, waiting for Leo to offer his own acerbic suggestion. But he was reading the note I'd left him about Freddy Bellman. "Is this guy serious?" he asked.

I hated to admit I'd gotten more out of Freddy than Vida had managed to extract from Bree. "I think so," I said. "Since he has Carter for a client, he's looking to pick up a few more around here. He's also looking to . . ." I winced as I glanced at Vida. "He's romantically interested in Bree, who, he says, was dumped by Carter, which is why she quit." I spoke rapidly and avoided another look in my House & Home editor's direction.

"What?" she exploded. "This Bellman person was *here?* While I was *gone?*"

I felt like apologizing for such thoughtlessness on Freddy's part and for my own role in encouraging him to speak. "Freddy and

Bree are having dinner tonight at Le Gourmand."

Vida's big bosom heaved with exasperation. "To think I wasted my time trying to talk to that silly little twit! Well, now!" She paused, obviously thinking through this revelation. "That certainly explains why Bree quit her job. It could also explain her dreadful manners and wretched disposition. A temporary state, perhaps." She paused again. "It may even explain," she said with an all-knowing gleam in her eye, "why we received the premature obituary for Elmer Nystrom."

SEVENTEEN

Before Vida could explain what she meant about the original obituary, Scott returned to the newsroom and Ginny arrived with a delivery for me from Posies Unlimited.

"There's a card," Ginny said, as excited as if the flowers had been intended for her. She set the cardboard container down on Vida's desk.

I carefully unwrapped the bright green paper. A lavish medley of yellow roses and lilies nestled among assorted greenery in a round glass vase. I opened the card.

"Feeling sorry for myself — see you sooner rather than later?"

"Ah!" Leo exclaimed after I'd read the card aloud. "Mr. AP knows how to treat a lady."

I was smiling broadly. Rolf had never sent me flowers before. In fact, I couldn't remember the last time anyone had sent me flowers. Adam remembered his dear old mother with cans of smoked or kippered Alaskan salmon. Ben sent Mass cards for my special intentions.

"I'll put the bouquet by the coffeemaker," I said, "so everybody can see it."

"I'll add more water," Ginny volunteered, dashing off to the restroom just as Kip came in from the back shop.

"Nice," he said, stroking the reddish goatee he'd grown in the last year. "Who got the flowers?"

"I did," I replied with a smile.

"Good for you." Kip, however, wasn't one to ask cheeky questions. Announcing that he was off to Sky.com to buy something I wouldn't understand if he told me, our computer genius left.

Finally, I asked Vida what she'd meant about the obit.

"I didn't have an opportunity to speak with Carter's assistants at the funeral reception," she said, "and since I'd seen you sitting with them, I assumed you'd already quizzed them. But I did have a brief conversation with Carter, who mentioned that Alicia had had a difficult week, having attended two funerals. That's when I discovered that she was related to the Wascos and had sent us the lost obituary on her grandfather, Jan. It occurred to me later that perhaps she mailed it from Carter's office."

"She did," I put in. "Christy mentioned it during our short but not so sweet chat."

"I thought so," Vida said while both Scott and Leo listened in. "The younger generation takes advantage." She glanced at Scott. "Not you or Kip or Ginny. You have higher standards, thank goodness. But I've heard so many complaints in recent years about younger employees helping themselves to petty cash, pilfering goods, taking home supplies — and, of course, using the employer's stamps as if they were their own. Carter probably bought oodles of stamps at a time — all those invoices. So he may still have had the outdated postage on hand."

"I see what you're getting at," I said, wishing it wasn't taking so long for Vida to arrive at her point. "Alicia put her grandfather's obit into the office mail, and . . . ?"

"Someone removed it, took out the grandfather's obit, and replaced it with the bogus write-up for Elmer." Vida looked around at all three of us. "The obvious suspect is Bree."

"How come?" Leo asked.

"Her last day on the job," Vida explained. "Rejection from Carter. Backbiting from Alicia and Christy. Wanting to get back at all the people she'd worked with for two years. Wasted years, in her opinion. Choosing Elmer as the subject of an obituary would embarrass Carter — if we'd run it. It was very childish, but people often act that way."

"As I recall," I said, "the obit and the envelope appeared to be typed on the same machine or word processor. But that'd be the case if both Alicia and Bree used office equipment."

"Of course," Vida agreed. "Bree would know the salient facts about Elmer's life, not only by working for Carter but also having been linked romantically with him."

Scott was shaking his head. "Dumb. Really dumb. Can Bree get arrested for pulling a stunt like that?"

"Malicious mischief," Leo responded. "In her case, it'd probably mean a fine and a long lecture but no jail time." He looked at me. "Are we pressing charges?"

"No," I replied. "It's not worth the trouble. Speaking of which, Bree's nasty little piece of revenge could cause some problems for her. If she really sent that obit — and I agree with your theory, Vida — Milo may take a more serious look at her as a murder suspect."

Scott grimaced. "Wouldn't it be pretty stupid to announce your victim's death before it happened?"

I thought so, too. "But we're talking about Milo. By the book and all that."

Vida frowned. "That's so. However, I believe Milo would be taking a wasteful detour. Bree wasn't in love with Elmer."

Leo nodded. "Bree couldn't mistake Elmer for Carter in the henhouse. Except for their height, they didn't look at all alike. Carter's got a bigger frame, lighter hair, and Elmer — well, Elmer didn't have much hair left."

"We're back to the same old thing," I said. "Who would want to kill Elmer? And why?"

Scott grimaced. "Revenge?"

I stared at him. "For what?"

My reporter looked slightly embarrassed. "I saw a TV show a while back where an auto mechanic was murdered because he'd screwed up a brake job and the customer's wife and kids got killed when the car crashed into a building." He paused. "Or maybe a family died when the car ran into their house. Anyway, the victims' father — or husband — beat the auto mechanic to death with a tire iron. Or was it a wrench?" Scott's dark complexion turned even darker. "I was watching the show with Tammy and wasn't really focused on the plot."

Newlyweds. But Scott had a point. I

looked at Vida. "Do you recall any serious problems over the years with the Nordby brothers — or even before the younger generation took over from Mr. Jensen?"

"No."

Vida's face was stiff as steel. I'd made a terrible gaffe. Her husband, Ernest, had been involved in a fatal accident caused by faulty brakes. I felt like a fool.

Leo sensed the sudden tension. "If," he said, looking at me, "you don't remember anything in the past thirteen, fourteen years you've been here, why would anybody wait that long to get back at Elmer? Besides, he didn't actually do the work, right?"

"Not that I know of," I said, unable to watch Vida's reaction. "But sometimes people misplace blame."

Scott shrugged. "Just an idea."

Still embarrassed, I retreated into my cubbyhole and immediately dialed Rolf's number at the AP in Seattle. I got his voice messaging. Not wanting to leave some sort of gushing adolescent thank-you, I hung up, doubling the proof that my maturation level hadn't gotten much past age seventeen.

Yet Scott had come up with a possible motive. Cars were such an intrinsic part of American life. Boys — and girls, for that matter — eagerly looked forward to such milestones as learning how to drive, getting that first driver's license, buying or receiving their first car. I'd spent part of my unexpected inheritance on a secondhand Jaguar; Ed's first purchase when he became a millionaire was his-and-hers Mercedes sedans; Carter Nystrom had wanted to show off his success by driving a flashy yellow Corvette. A car wasn't mere transportation for most Americans — it was a status symbol, a cherished possession, almost a living thing.

But I couldn't recall any recent incident involving a vehicle that wasn't the fault of the owner or another driver. Reports of every collision, even fender benders, were published in the *Advocate.* In the last year we'd had two vehicular-related deaths in SkyCo: One had involved a recent high school graduate on a motorcycle; the other was caused by debris falling off an out-of-town truck on Highway 2 and crushing an elderly man who probably was following too closely in the first place. The truck driver, who lived in Spokane, had been cited and given a stiff fine, but he'd had no Alpine connection other than driving past the town a couple of times a year.

Wanting to mend fences with Vida, I went back into the newsroom. "My dinner guest left town," I informed her. "I've got some frozen sockeye salmon I was going to serve Ben. Would you like to join me? I don't like to keep frozen fish too long."

Vida tapped the edge of her desk and thought for a minute. "That would be very nice. I'm sure you're already missing your brother. I had no idea he was leaving right after lunch."

I smiled, grateful for what I assumed was her forgiveness for bringing up painful memories. "You can follow me home," I said.

"No, no," Vida responded. "I must put Cupcake to bed. He gets fractious if I don't cover him up as soon as it gets dark. Thank goodness the days will start getting longer now."

"That's fine. I'll serve around six or so," I said, though I often wondered just how fractious her canary could get since he was kept in a cage. Maybe he spit seeds at her or warbled off-key.

On my way back to my desk, I asked Scott to join me. "I've got a job for you," I said. "Can you check through all the traffic and vehicle citations issued in the last year? Just in case. I think you raised a good point. Or do you recall anything from the police log off the top of your head?"

Scott roamed the short distance between my file cabinet and the map of Skykomish County on the other wall. "Wow a whole year's worth of citations. That's a lot." He grinned at me. "Wish I'd been here when old Durwood Parker was getting arrested every other month for some seriously bad driving."

"Be glad you weren't," I said. "Durwood was lucky he never killed anyone — or himself. He came close, though, especially the time he drove right through the annual Loggerama picnic at Old Mill Park and ended up on the bandstand. Luckily, the band hadn't been playing. Come to think of it, everybody was lucky when the band didn't play. They were terrible."

"I'll go over to the sheriff's and look through the log," Scott said, glancing at his watch. "It's after three. I may be gone the rest of the day."

"That's fine," I told him. "It's Friday. Go home early, say, around five to five."

With another grin for his not-so-witty boss, Scott left. It occurred to me that I didn't know what Scott was looking for among the dozens of tickets the sheriff and his deputies handed out every year. The state patrol's tickets also showed up on the local blotter if the stops had been made within the county. It also dawned on me that Scott, being younger and thus less experienced with the vagaries of human nature, might overlook something of interest. Maybe he could use some help.

By the time I got to the sheriff's office, Scott was sitting at the far end of the counter with the police binders in front of him. The only other person on hand was Lori Cobb.

"Got a spare chair?" I asked her. "I'm going to join Scott."

"I can get you a folding one from the back," she offered.

"Thanks. How's the sheriff this afternoon?"

Lori shrugged. "Okay. He went on patrol this afternoon. He said he needed to get outdoors."

I understood. Walking over to Scott, I asked how far he'd gotten.

"End of January," he replied. "Why couldn't we do this from our own files? We list all the traffic stops in the paper."

"Because," I explained, "we don't run all the little stuff. Broken taillights, unsecured loads, expired license tabs. You don't usually take down those citations unless the offender has given the deputies a bad time or caused a serious problem."

"True enough," Scott conceded. "What about chronic DUIs?"

"This state's laws are pretty tough," I said. "Besides, we always run those. Let's concentrate on some of the less flagrant violations. We should be looking for something to do with vehicle maintenance, a connection to auto repair or somehow to Elmer."

Lori brought me a chair and set it up. I took the binder for March, since Scott was about to start on February.

"What," Scott asked, "about citations for not having traction devices? There's a half-dozen of those in January and early February."

"That's not a big deal," I said. "Most people around here know how to chain up, and Cal Vickers usually puts on snow tires for customers."

Scott nodded once and kept reading.

During the third week of March, I found an unsecured load citation for Bickford Pike and his pickup. Ten days later Christina Milland was ticketed for a broken headlight. I made notes on both of them.

Scott was already into April, so I moved to May. "Hey," he said, "how about Nicholas Della Croce getting pulled over for having studded tires after the removal deadline before April first?"

"He has himself to blame for that," I replied, "but since he lives next door to the Nystroms, I'll put him down."

"Same thing for Elmer Kemp a week later," Scott said. "Those fines are over seventy dollars each. Wouldn't you think people would remember to switch their tires on time?"

"I'm not unsympathetic," I responded. "Historically, we've had snow well into April in Alpine. But not, I admit, lately. Frankly, I hate to have Cal take my studded tires off at the end of March. With all the rain, the hills around here are still dangerous."

"But those studs are so hard on the roads and freeways," Scott pointed out. "Not to mention in the bigger cities, where all that traffic really chews up the streets."

"More broken headlights and taillights in May," I noted. "Bebe Everson, Mike Corson, Walt Hanson." I looked at Scott. "Do any of them have a connection to Elmer?"

"The Eversons live out that way off the Burl Creek Road," Scott said after a pause. "But not that close to the Nystroms. Roy Everson runs the post office, and Mike Corson's a carrier for the mail that goes outside Alpine's boundaries. Walt Hanson drives a Toyota. He'd take his car to that dealership, not Nordby Brothers."

"I'll put them down, just in case," I said, closing the May binder. "You're Mr. June, I'm Ms. July."

We finished our task just after four-thirty. We'd collected a grand total of thirty citations, none of them involving an injury or an accident. Only four people had more than one ticket. Bickford Pike, Bebe Everson, and Nick Della Croce had three apiece. The winner with five citations — all for faulty equipment — was the Alpine Chamber of Commerce manager, Rita Patricelli. Maybe she felt it was her duty to put money into the county coffers. The prickly Rita wasn't one of my favorite Alpiners, but she drove some kind of Ford van. I couldn't think of any link between her and Elmer except, of course, for chamber meetings.

"Waste of time?" Scott asked as we left the sheriff's office.

"Probably." I shrugged. "Go home. I'll check your in-box and voice mail to see if you've missed anything important. If you haven't, I won't pester you. Enjoy the weekend."

When I returned to the office, Freddy Bellman was talking to Leo. Vida was on the phone. I nodded at Freddy and went into my office. If nothing else, all the vehicle research I'd been doing had given me an idea for an editorial. It was a subject I'd harped on ever since I'd been the *Advocate*'s editor and publisher: There was nothing to be done about Americans owning cars. It was a love affair that would never grow stale. But while the state searched desperately for ways to raise money, vehicle license tab fees had decreased, not increased. Granted, some families genuinely needed two cars, but three or more vehicles were superfluous. Still, if that was what drivers wanted, fine. Then let them pay for their excess by tripling or quadrupling the fees to help fund for highways and roads. Maybe some of that money could even trickle down to the counties and municipalities.

I knew I didn't have a prayer of getting through to the politicians. The idea made far too much sense. Some people would have to get rid of a vehicle or two or three because they wouldn't be able to afford the annual fees for license tabs. Thus, there'd be fewer cars to guzzle gas, congestion would be eased, and insurance rates might go down. Crazy Emma, blowing her ideas into the wind.

I'd gotten to the third paragraph when Freddy strode into my cubbyhole. "I've cut a deal with your Mr. Walsh," he announced. "Two three-column by four-inch ads running in the next issues, placement in the professional services section for three months, and another, larger one-time-only ad in mid-March before the income tax deadline. Do you feel richer already?"

"My middle name is Wealth," I replied. "Thanks. Leo will do a good job for you."

"And I shall do the same for my new clients." He sat down. "In fact, I've already acquired one."

"Who?" I asked idly.

"A fellow named Ed Bronsky. I ran into him at that burger place across the street."

I tried not to gape at Freddy. "Ed wants you to be his accountant?"

Freddy chuckled. "You think I'm foolish to take on some guy who's slinging hamburgers at a greasy spoon? Self-employed pros like me know you have to start small and expand your base when you plunge into new territory. If I can help this poor sap out of his tax mess, he'll spread the word and help me get new, more prosperous clients." Freddy shrugged. "It's a simple theory, like throwing a rock in the water and watching the circles move ever outward."

I decided not to say anything more about Ed, let alone divulge his background. "Sensible," I remarked, and promptly changed the subject. "What time is your dinner reservation?"

"Seven-thirty." Freddy stretched and yawned. "Bree doesn't get done at the hospital until six. She has to go home and change."

Judging from Freddy's relaxed attitude, he'd decided that the *Advocate* office was his personal waiting room. I was about to remind him that we would shut down in another ten minutes, but instead I inquired if Bree had a sense of humor.

"Interesting query," Freddy responded. "Yes, sort of. Why do you ask?"

"I think it's important in relationships."

"It is." He regarded me with curiosity. "Are you matchmaking?"

"Never," I said. "I was just wondering why she and Carter broke up. I don't really know her, and I met Carter for the first time today at the funeral reception. That's hardly an occasion to probe for somebody's funny bone."

"Don't bother yourself about Bree's heart-break," Freddy cautioned. "She could be Venus reincarnated and it wouldn't matter to Carter. I could have told her that before she ever followed him to Alpine. But I didn't know her back then."

"What do you mean?"

He chuckled, a rather unpleasant sound.

"You know what I mean." He slapped his hand on my desk and stood up. "I should be going. I imagine it's quitting time around here. Enjoy your weekend." He strolled out of the office, whistling.

EIGHTEEN

Vida showed up at my house a few minutes before six. She'd gone home just before Freddy Bellman made his exit. Naturally, she wanted to know if he'd told me anything interesting.

"I think so," I said, melting butter to drip over the salmon steaks. "But I almost hate to repeat what he implied. Carter may be gay."

Vida considered the statement. "Well . . . that would hardly reflect on his ability as an orthodontist. Still, it's not something that Carter might want known in a small town." Vida grimaced. "I despise saying so, but some people harbor peculiar prejudices."

Vida's broad-mindedness might surprise most people, but not me. I knew her too well. As a student of human nature, she considered any deviation from the norm as "interesting" and therefore worthy of endless speculation — and, of course, scathing criticism. In this case, however, she seemed unusually benign.

"Still," she went on, tracing the daisy pattern on my kitchen tablecloth with her finger, "it might explain Carter's behavior toward his mother. An Oedipus complex of some sort."

"I don't know much about Freud," I admitted, "though I recall from Psych 100 in college that young boys who fixate on their mothers often show homosexual tendencies in later life. Or not," I added lamely.

Vida frowned, obviously thinking hard. "Really, I have so little faith in psychology and psychiatry and such. Common sense is much better as well as cheaper — yet rare. Still, such fixations exist and must be called something. Oedipus complex will do."

I was still trying to remember anything specific from my long-ago freshman course at the University of Washington. What I recalled most vividly was trying to stay awake during early morning lectures. "This may sound crazy, and excuse the expression," I said, "but I think I read or heard in class that early on the overwhelming love in boys for their moms is accompanied by a death wish for their dads."

Vida nodded. "Yes, of course. That's why the complex is named for Oedipus, who killed his father and married his mother. Honestly, even in Alpine that would be a scandal! It's bad enough that I know at least two sets of first cousins who married each other. It's no wonder their children are extremely odd! They're also rather homely."

I wasn't sure who Vida meant, nor did I want to find out. The salmon was under the broiler, and the potatoes and Brussels sprouts were boiling on the stove. Vida was drinking ice water; I sipped a Pepsi.

"So," she said after I'd told her about the search Scott and I had made at the sheriff's office, "you aren't much wiser."

"No," I said, lifting the lid off the potatoes to see if they were done. "Maybe it *is* a random thing. The railroad tracks run fairly close to the Burl Creek Road along that stretch. The trains always slow down when they approach Alpine. A vagrant might have jumped off and spent the night in the hen-house. Elmer could have surprised whoever it was, and the guy put up a fight. It happens."

"True." Vida folded her hands in her lap. "Tell me again who received those citations."

I ran down the list from the notes I'd brought home with me. Vida, of course, needed no such visual reminders of who was who and who did what to whom. I've never known her to make notes of any kind. Her local lore was encyclopedic — and infallible.

"Nick Della Croce," she murmured after I was finished. "That's the name that intrigues me most. Yet the offense of not removing his studded tires on time isn't connected to Elmer, even if the Della Croces do live next door to the Nystroms."

"I've never met the man," I said, "though I vaguely recall seeing him a couple of times at St. Mildred's. Solid build, mustache, receding wavy dark hair going gray. And his wife is an orthodontist's assistant who didn't get a job with Carter."

Vida nodded. "No doubt Mr. Della Croce is very protective of his only child. Gloria might shrug off the strange relationship she's overheard, but her father may not have done the same." She unclasped her hands and clapped them together. "Ah! We must pay a call on the entire family after dinner."

"Vida . . ."

"Don't argue. Let's see . . . our pretext . . ." She shoved a hairpin into her unruly gray curls. "Car trouble? No. Too obvious. A readership survey for the paper? No, no. Not in person. You mentioned your editorial for the next issue . . . Burl Creek Road needs to be resurfaced. Perhaps we could say we're asking residents who live along there to —"

"Vida!" I all but yelled at her. "How about the truth?" My House & Home editor was the soul of integrity, except when she resorted to subterfuge in the name of the job. Then she relished dreaming up plausible excuses for snooping. "We're still working on the murder investigation story," I said in a reasonable tone. "We haven't yet talked to the father and the daughter. They could be witnesses."

Vida looked disappointed. "Well, now . . . I suppose that would do."

I smiled and shook my head. "Maybe you should have become a spy."

"I think not. Spies can't wear hats that get noticed." She sniffed at the air. "My, my — something smells delicious."

"I put some liquid smoke on the salmon to give it that alder flavor," I said. "We're almost ready to eat."

"Very kind of you to invite me to dinner," she said in a relatively quiet voice.

"You were right," I told her as I drained the potatoes and the Brussels sprouts. "I definitely miss Ben already. Furthermore, I haven't heard from Adam since I e-mailed him earlier today. I always worry when he doesn't respond right away."

"He's busy," Vida stated with conviction. "His duties as a priest must take him far afield in a remote area such as St. Mary's Igloo. Doesn't he spend some time in Nome?"

"Yes," I said, placing a salmon steak on Vida's plate, "but he usually tells me when he's going there." Suddenly I remembered something Vida had mentioned earlier in the week. "I thought you were going to have Roger come tonight for a sleepover."

Vida frowned. "He told me he had too much to do. Studying, I suppose. Now that he's a college student, his time is taken up with class work and activities and his friends. I don't see as much of him as I used to. But," she added hastily, "that's hardly his fault. Roger is virtually an adult these days."

The use of *Roger* and *adult* in the same breath struck me as incompatible. "How soon will he get his associate of arts degree?" I inquired as visions of a frozen hell played in my mind's eye. I even pictured Roger's chunky body in a red suit with icicles on his pitchfork.

"I'm not sure," Vida replied, looking away from me. "He's had to drop some courses along the way. So much stress, you know, and some faculty members are very dense. They have no imagination, particularly when it comes to writing papers. Just last week Roger's history professor assigned a paper on the Civil War. Roger wrote his about a football game he'd watched very recently . . . some sort of bowl contest . . . fabric in the name . . . yes, Cotton Bowl. Anyway, Roger wrote how these two teams from the Southern states never used to have black players, but now they did, and the games were so much better because Lincoln had freed the slaves. I thought it was a very inventive premise. The professor didn't agree. But then, Grams doesn't know much about sports."

As usual, Vida was wearing blinders when it came to her grandson. Her innate common sense and good judgment had flown out the window. If she'd been talking about any other college student, her criticism would have slashed the poor kid into bite-sized ribbons.

I avoided commenting on Roger's essay. "You must miss not having him around so much," I said, sitting down across from Vida.

"My, yes," she replied. "The other grandchildren are just far enough away that it isn't easy to visit back and forth. That traffic in Tacoma is so bad, and of course I-5 going either there or up to Bellingham is usually bumper to bumper on weekends. Not to mention that Beth and Meg are so busy with all their children's activities. Gymnastics, swim meets, soccer — they're constantly on the go. Unfortunately, they don't often come to Alpine. It's not on their schedules."

Vida made the statement without expression. Of course I knew what she was thinking: Her two daughters who lived out of town simply had no spare time to visit — or to entertain. I began to understand why Vida had confessed to feeling alone.

"Parents are on overload these days," I said. "As a single working mother, there was no way I could get too involved in Adam's extracurricular activities. I felt I short-changed him, but I had to put food on the table."

"Speaking of food," Vida said, pointing her fork at her plate, "this is very good, Emma. I must mention that smoked alder flavoring in one of my cooking columns."

I realized she wanted to speak of other things. Despite being an inadequate cook, Vida felt no compunction about telling other people how to prepare food, blatantly stealing advice from one of our syndicated columns yet never applying it to herself.

We spent the rest of the meal discussing mundane matters such as the cost of groceries, housing, and gas. Vida helped me clear the table and load the dishwasher. I insisted that we call the Della Croces before going to see them. Vida quibbled but gave in.

A youthful female voice I assumed belonged to Gloria answered the phone. "I'll tell them you're coming," she said rather timorously, and hung up. Her mother's pride had given me the impression that the daughter oozed self-confidence.

We arrived just after seven. Anna Maria greeted us at the door, her round face slightly florid and her brown eyes wary. "This isn't going to take long, is it? Nick has a TV program he wants to watch in a little while."

"No," I assured her as we went into the living room. "We only have a few questions."

"We might have answered them over the phone," Anna Maria said. "This is my husband, Nick."

Nick Della Croce made an effort to hike his burly body off the recliner but managed to make it only halfway and gave us a desultory wave. "I've seen you both around town," he said, not sounding convinced that he was pleased to see us again.

Anna Maria indicated that we should sit in a couple of side chairs. Apparently the sofa was her domain. She settled back down on its corduroy cushions and pushed aside the jumble puzzle she'd apparently been doing. "I could make some coffee," she said in an uncertain tone.

"Please don't trouble yourself," Vida insisted. "This is business, not social." She smiled in her toothiest manner.

"We were hoping to talk to Gloria as well," I put in. "I assume she's home. I thought she answered the phone."

"She's in her room," Anna Maria said. "Gloria has a phone in there. She's got company, so she won't be joining us."

"Oh, dear!" Vida looked upset. "It's terribly important that she should be here, too. So mature and perceptive — at least that's what I'm told. Surely her chum could spare her for fifteen minutes."

Nick and Anna Maria exchanged glances. I sensed that the husband deferred to the wife when it came to issues regarding their daughter.

But I was wrong.

"As long as you don't embarrass her," he warned, and rose from the recliner. "I'll go get her."

Anna Maria didn't look pleased. "This is all so sordid," she declared after Nick had left the room. "I don't like Brianna being left alone." She got up from the sofa and followed her husband into the hallway. "Nick, tell them both to come."

At the mention of Brianna's name, Vida stared at me and mouthed the name "Phelps?" I shrugged.

The parents returned to the living room. "They'll be along in just a moment," Anna Maria said, still looking out of sorts. "Can we get started?"

"Certainly," Vida said. "Mr. Della Croce, did you know the Nystroms very well?"

He moved the recliner into a sitting position and frowned. "Not really. I probably saw more of Elmer than Mrs. Nystrom or the son. Nice guy. I'd see Elmer out in the yard sometimes, especially in the spring and summer. He liked to work in the garden. Kind of fussy about it — everything neat as a pin."

Vida nodded approvingly. "I enjoy yard work myself. Did you ever have dealings with Elmer at Nordby Brothers?"

Nick nodded. "My truck's a Chevy Colorado. Great service at Nordby. Elmer was the best."

A pretty dark-haired young girl entered

the living room, followed by a shorter and not quite so pretty blonde. Anna Maria introduced us.

"Gloria," she said, moving over to make room on the sofa for the girls, "this is Mrs. Runkel and Ms. Lord from the newspaper."

The dark-haired girl smiled faintly. "Hi." She put a hand on her friend's arm. "Meet my friend, Brianna Phelps."

Brianna also said hi, though there was no smile. She seemed suspicious. She might have been pregnant, though it was hard to tell with the baggy Seattle Pacific University sweatshirt she was wearing.

"Of course!" Vida exclaimed. "You're Reverend Phelps's daughter. I remember when you were a baby. We ran your picture in the paper."

Brianna didn't respond. Maybe the word *baby* put her off.

Anna Maria did her best to cover the awkward moment. "Gloria and Brianna are what they call 'buddies' at the high school. Seniors befriend sophomores to make the transition from junior high easier. Our daughter was lucky. She and Brianna have become genuine pals."

"Oh, yes," Vida said enthusiastically. "I recall when my grandson, Roger, had a sophomore buddy. Ryan Post. Roger always called him 'Lamp,' no doubt because Ryan was so bright."

I figured that wasn't the reason behind Roger's nickname and that poor Ryan probably had suffered mightily at his "buddy's" chubby hands. Naturally, I kept my mouth shut.

Nick was drumming his fingers on the arm of his recliner. "Get on with the questions, okay?"

Vida's expression turned severe. "Very well. Gloria, how often did you overhear those silly conversations between Mrs. Nystrom and her son?"

"How'd you know about that?" Gloria asked, with a sharp look for her mother.

Anna Maria avoided her daughter's gaze and kept quiet.

I intervened. "We've been conducting our investigation ever since we discovered Mr. Nystrom's body. Any information we can get will help find his killer and keep this neighborhood safe."

Gloria frowned but seemed appeased. "Okay, that makes sense. I heard quite a lot from those two next door," she went on. "I mean, off and on during the summer, maybe a couple of times a week. It was totally gross. I felt like yelling out my window and telling them to shut up."

Now that Gloria had spoken at length, I realized that she hadn't been the one who had answered the phone when I called. Brianna had picked up the receiver, perhaps expecting a call from Brad Nordby with a marriage proposal. *Good luck,* I thought. When I'd gotten pregnant without benefit of having a husband, I knew that call would never come. Tom Cavanaugh's loyalty to his crazy wife was stronger than his love for me.

"But it was all talk," Vida said with a question in her voice.

Gloria rolled her eyes. "I guess. After a few minutes he'd turn the bathroom light off and go into his own room. Then they'd both be quiet and I'd be left in peace." She gazed from one parent to the other. "If I had a TV in my own room, I could tune them out when they open the windows later on this year."

Nick chuckled. "Maybe you'll get one for graduation. But you can't take it with you if you go away to college."

"I'm going to the UW for sure," Gloria asserted, "but fall quarter doesn't start until the end of September."

Her father shook his head. "You know what I think. You should spend at least one year at the community college here. The UW has thirty or forty thousand students.

Don't make it harder on yourself than you have to."

"Dad . . ." Gloria's withering glance told me that this was an old argument.

"We'll talk about it later," Anna Maria said in a weary voice. She turned to Vida and me. "Is that it for Gloria?"

"One thing," Vida replied. "Monday morning — when Elmer was killed — did you hear or see anything unusual? Anything at all?"

She'd posed the query to Gloria. The girl wound a strand of dark hair around one finger. "No . . . I don't think so. I caught the school bus at seven-forty. I wait for it a couple of houses up the road, by that old barn that's falling down."

"Do you wait alone?" Vida inquired.

"Not usually," Gloria said, "but I did that day. Both of the Sigurdson kids were sick."

"No one was walking along the road?" Vida asked.

Gloria shook her head. "I wasn't standing there very long. I time it so I don't have to wait when the weather's cold and wet." She stopped twirling her hair and made an impatient gesture. "Is that all?"

Vida pursed her lips. "Yes. Unfortunately. I was so hoping that being a bright young person, you'd have noticed something."

Gloria seemed to know she was being conned. "Shall I make up something?"

"Certainly not," Vida retorted.

Gloria got up from the sofa. "Come on, Brianna. Let's see if I can find that Black Eyed Peas CD you like."

Brianna held back. "What about that old Elvis record you found?"

Gloria looked puzzled. "I didn't think you were into Elvis."

"I mean the one you found while you were waiting for the bus."

Gloria struck a hand to her forehead. "Oh! I forgot!" She uttered a lame little laugh. "There was a really, really old Elvis Presley album — vinyl — in the ditch by the bus stop. I know that vinyl is coming back in, so I stuck it in my backpack. I thought I might sell it on eBay if it wasn't ruined. Or take it in to Platters-in-the-Sky. They sell used recordings."

Vida leaned forward in her chair. "Was there a name on it?"

"You mean the album itself? It's like *Elvis' Forty Greatest Hits.* Do you want to see it?"

"No," Vida replied. "I meant the name of who owned it."

"Oh." Gloria looked apologetic. "Sorry. Nothing like that. The album cover's kind of faded and worn, but the record seems fine."

"Interesting," Vida remarked. "Thank you, Gloria. And you, too, Brianna, for reminding your friend."

The girls scampered back into the hallway. Nick was scowling. "I wish Gloria had left that thing where she found it. These days you never know what kind of germs you can pick up off of stuff that's been lying around. We live in a really terrible world. It's a bad place to bring up kids."

Vida lifted her chin. "You could, I suppose, move to Jupiter."

Nick stared at Vida and laughed. "Yeah, right. We don't have much choice, do we? Still, I hate to think of Gloria going to college in a big city like Seattle. Everything's worse there. She'd be better off in Pullman at WSU."

"I don't think," Anna Maria said with an edge in her voice, "we need to get into that argument again. That's not what Mrs. Runkel and Ms. Lord came to hear." She turned toward the two of us. "Are you done?"

"No," Vida answered. "I don't believe either of you mentioned what you were doing Monday morning around the time that Elmer was killed."

Nick practically bolted out of the recliner. "Hold on! You aren't cops. It's none of your damned business what we were doing Monday!"

Vida shrugged her wide shoulders. "It is if you noticed anything. I'm trying to figure out how you could not. That is, everybody sees or hears things that aren't routine. If, of course, you're paying attention to the world around you."

Anna Maria looked anxious. Nick sat back down. "We're not robots, you know," he said.

"I'm sure you're not," Vida responded in an agreeable tone.

Nick sighed. "Okay. Let me think back. I had to be on a surveying job by eight o'clock at the Foss River campground. I left here around seven-fifteen. The drive up there can be tricky this time of year. I didn't see anybody or anything that was out of the way." He folded his arms across his barrel chest and tried to stare down Vida, never an easy task.

She turned to Anna Maria. "Yes?"

Anna Maria sighed. "I suppose I was finishing breakfast and getting Gloria off to school. Caroline Sigurdson called to tell us her kids had flu and wouldn't be at the bus stop. Then . . ." She paused. "I turned on the TV after Nick and Gloria were gone and watched one of those morning programs until nine or so. I'm a slow starter, especially on a Monday. The next thing I remember was when I noticed several cars parked by the road. They weren't for us, and the Nystroms rarely had company." She grimaced. "That's the first I knew of anything happening next door."

The Della Croce accounts sounded reasonable but were not very helpful. Vida was getting to her feet. "Thank you," she said stiltedly. "We're sorry to take up your time. Good night."

In my usual stoogelike way, I followed her to the door. Anna Maria saw us out but murmured only a terse "Goodbye."

"Honestly," Vida said when we reached my car, "it's so maddening when people are oblivious to their surroundings! How can they be so self-absorbed?"

I didn't respond until I got behind the wheel and was fastening my seat belt. "I didn't think the visit was a complete washout, though."

"My, no," Vida agreed. "Nick Della Croce is very protective of his only child. As much as if not more so than Anna Maria. Strange," she went on in a musing tone.

"The two families mirror each other, don't they?"

I made a cautious U-turn on Burl Creek Road. "Uh . . . yes, you're right. Two sets of parents, one child apiece. But very different dynamics."

"I can't say I like the Della Croces very much," Vida said, "but they seem to be much more like a normal family. Then again, how do you define *normal?*"

"Good point." I laughed softly. "I don't think Gloria's in love with her father. But she'll like him better if he buys her a TV and lets her go to the UW."

"I see Nick's point," Vida said. "Gloria would be much better off attending Skykomish Community College. Cheaper, too. I hate to think of Roger going on to the UW in Seattle."

I was sure the administrators at the UW would hate to think about it, too. But as usual, I kept my mouth shut.

When we got back to my house, Vida went straight to her car and left for home. She told me she had some phone calls to make. I wanted to check my e-mail to see if Adam had responded.

Happily, there was a message.

"Hi, Worried Mother," Adam wrote. "Spent the afternoon helping the local ladies figure out how much they'll make off of their Christmas knit sales. The harpoon and the diamond patterns did really well in the Lower Forty-Eight gift shops and on-line. You asked what a *kuspuk* was — it's a women's lightweight parka for warmer weather than the below temps we have now. Tomorrow I go island hopping to say Saturday Masses. Did I leave my digital camera in my old room? I can't find it anywhere. Love and prayers, Your Son the Popsicle Priest."

Some things never change. Adam remained careless about his material possessions. I couldn't help it — the trait proved he was still a child in some ways and thus needed his mother. I was smiling as I went into his room and searched for the camera.

I'd cleaned house after he'd left but hadn't spotted the camera then. Having already checked under the bed, I knew it wasn't there. The closet was another matter. I used it for storage and kept promising myself I'd sort through the items that neither Adam nor I had used in years. Of course I'd never gotten around to it. I keep a reasonably tidy house, but I tend to clutter, never embracing the old saw that cleanliness is next to godliness. If I had to spend time with a neat freak like Elmer, I'd go nuts.

The camera wasn't in the closet. But as I delved into the useless items I should've gotten rid of years before, an idea popped into my head. Had Elmer's penchant for tidiness, method, and order driven someone to madness? And to murder?

I continued the hunt. Finally, I managed to move the bureau a few inches out from the wall. Sure enough, the camera was on the floor. I immediately e-mailed Adam and told him I'd mail it to him on Monday.

Finding the camera pushed the idea about Elmer to the back of my brain.

But it would come back to haunt me.

NINETEEN

The sun made a brave attempt to break through the clouds Saturday morning. After breakfast, I called Milo. He didn't answer on either his home phone or his cell. Maybe he'd gone steelheading. I hoped he'd taken someone with him in case he had another gallbladder attack, but I guessed he was alone. Fishing isn't a social event. It's more like a spiritual experience with silence as its golden rule.

I tried to phone Rolf next. No answer there, just his voice mail. Again, I didn't leave a message. He'd often walk to the Pike Place Market on Saturday mornings and buy whatever delicacy appealed to his mood. I'd gone with him a couple of times, though I wasn't keen on the walking part. The last time, in mid-October, I'd insisted we take the bus back to his Lower Queen Anne condo.

I stood staring out my front window where

the pale sunlight had turned Fir Street's rainy pavement from shiny black to dull gray. Ben was cruising along I-90 in Montana by now. If he'd driven most of the night, he should be past Butte. I tried not to worry.

But the only way I could do that was to worry about something else: Milo. On a whim, I called the sheriff's office. It was officially closed on Saturdays, but someone would be on duty. Sam Heppner answered.

"You're right," he said. "Dodge went fishing. He thought he'd head for the Tye just below where the Foss River comes in."

"He didn't answer his cell," I said. "I can't help but fuss."

"The cell may not work up there," Sam said. "Maybe he turned it off. Dodge wanted to get away from it all or some damned thing. Can't say as I blame him. He's had a crappy week."

I thanked Sam and hung up. As the crow flies, the sheriff was only about three miles from my house. The whim and the worry were still upon me. I put a cable-knit sweater over my cotton turtleneck, donned my car coat, and headed out into the morning.

Driving down Alpine Way, I felt foolish. I needed a better excuse to interrupt Milo's solitary steelhead adventure than my concern for his health. If I even hinted that I was fussing over him, he'd be angry. At Front Street and Alpine Way, I pulled into Starbucks. Even the sheriff wouldn't turn down good coffee. Not that I believed he'd know the difference after the sludge he'd been used to drinking while Toni Andreas worked for him.

The line was ten deep at the counter. While waiting my turn, I gazed around at the gathering seated at tables or in armchairs by the fireplace. At least two-thirds of the clientele were college-age students or under forty. I seemed to be the oldest person in the coffeehouse.

Then I spotted Bree Kendall sitting by herself at a small table and reading a book.

I couldn't resist. I got out of line and went to her table, sitting down in the empty chair across from her. She looked up from her book and glared at me.

"What do you want?" she demanded.

"An apology," I said.

Bree closed the book, which was the latest Margaret Atwood novel. "For what?"

"I think you know."

Bree's chilly gaze faltered. She leaned back in her chair and sighed. "It wasn't my idea."

I was surprised. "What do you mean?"

"Carter asked me to do it." She looked disgusted.

"Why?"

"Somebody he knew in Seattle had died recently." Bree stopped. "Why do I have to explain this to you?"

"Because if we hadn't known better, we'd have run the obit on Elmer and looked like idiots."

She uttered a hollow laugh. "You did run it."

Bree had a point. "But Elmer was alive when it arrived in the mail. Are you saying Carter knew his father would be dead by the time the paper came out?"

Bree looked up at the ceiling. "Maybe."

I tried to gauge Bree's mental state. Was she nuts? Was she lying? Was she vindictive? I couldn't tell. "Did Carter give you a reason for writing up his father's death notice?"

"Oh, yes." She smirked at me. "Carter could be *so* sincere. Or pretend to be. This friend of his who'd died a couple of weeks before Christmas had no surviving relatives in the area. Carter had gone to see him — his first name was Connor, but I don't know his last name — a few days before the end. Carter had asked to be notified if — when

— Connor died. The hospice people forgot to let him know, and Carter found out only because there was a very brief notice in the Seattle paper."

None of this was making much sense. "So?"

"It upset Carter that Connor had died alone. There was nothing about his life in the obituary — only his death. Connor was a successful sculptor. Carter said —" Bree stopped, a glint of tears in her eyes. "Why," she whispered, "couldn't he have cared that way about me?"

"Only Carter can tell you that," I said. "So why did he have you write up the obit for his father?"

Bree clenched her fist around the paper napkin she'd been using to hold her cup. "He had me write up both of his parents so they could be kept for future use. The one for Mrs. Nystrom was much longer, and he wanted to go over it before he gave it to me. He planned to write his own, too." She snorted in contempt. " 'Be prepared' was his motto. The way he talked about his mother and how wonderful she was — it made me want to puke. I'd have rather sent that one in, but I never got it, so I used that backbiter Alicia's envelope with those stupid animal stamps. I tossed the notice for her uncle or grandfather or whoever the old coot was and mailed Elmer's, just to piss him off as a farewell gesture. Oh, hell!" She scooped up her book, clutch purse, and car keys. "That's where they can all go as far as I'm concerned," she mumbled, kicking the chair out of her way and rushing for the door.

Bree's explanation about the obituary seemed credible. She was clearly an emotional mess. People do strange, even childish, things when they're faced with rejection. Dinner with Freddy Bellman at Le Gourmand didn't appear to have cheered up Bree. The accountant had an uphill struggle to win her affections. He thought she was worth it. I wasn't so sure.

Standing up from the table, I saw that the line had dwindled to only a couple of people. Five minutes later, I was out the door carrying two decaf lattes and a couple of bran muffins. I assumed my purchases wouldn't set off another of Milo's gallbladder attacks.

I had to take the Burl Creek Road to get beyond Cass and Profitts ponds. I slowed as I passed the Della Croce and Nystrom properties. A truck was parked in the first driveway; a yellow Corvette was pulling out of the garage at the second house. Foiling common sense and good manners, I pulled over to block the 'Vette's exit.

The driver had stopped about ten yards from the road. He was probably used to people turning around in his wide, neatly tended driveway. The sports car's windows must have been tinted. I assumed Carter was at the wheel, but I couldn't really see him. Turning off the engine, I got out of the Honda and approached his ostentatious new toy.

He rolled down the window on the driver's side. "Ms. Lord? Are you having car trouble?"

"I'm having trouble," I said, "but not with my car. I have to talk to you. Have you got a minute?"

Carter frowned slightly. "I was going to grocery shop," he said.

"It won't take long."

Reluctantly, he turned off the engine. "V8," he murmured.

"Very nice."

"Well?" He looked at me curiously.

I would have preferred not standing next to the car. It wasn't conducive to making me feel at ease. Of course Carter knew that.

"I have an awkward question," I said, and paused, waiting for a reaction. There wasn't any. "What time did you leave for work

Monday?"

Carter looked slightly affronted. I didn't blame him. "Just before seven-thirty. Why is that important to you?"

"I've been asking several people in the vicinity," I explained, "to find out if anyone noticed some unusual occurrence."

He seemed vaguely amused. "Journalist plays detective? To think I always believed that small-town newspapers were interested only in rescuing kittens from trees and baking cupcakes for the church bazaar."

"Odd," I remarked. "I don't recall your mother ever making cookies for the Episcopal church."

"She seldom bakes," Carter replied. "She has a skin allergy to wheat flour. Working with it gives her a rash."

"A shame." I waited despite the fact that I was getting a kink in my neck from looking down at Carter in his comfortable bucket seat. "Well?" I finally prompted.

He frowned. "Well what?"

"Monday morning. Anything unusual. My question."

"No. Nothing. Don't you think that if I had seen anything, I would've informed the sheriff and his deputies? It was an ordinary morning."

Not, I thought, *for your father.*

"You didn't find it odd that your dad hadn't left for work?"

Carter shrugged. "He often left a few minutes after I did. My routine varies from day to day, depending on my bookings. Is that all?" He started the engine again.

I felt stymied. Carter was very smooth. Bree had told me he had a knack for seeming sincere. I didn't know what to make of him. "Yes. Thanks."

"Thank you as well," he said, "for coming to the funeral reception. My father was well liked and well remembered," Carter added, his features softening slightly.

I frowned. Who was Carter describing? I wondered. Willy Loman in *Death of a Salesman*? Perhaps he was and didn't realize it. Like Willy, Elmer Nystrom might have been chasing the American dream, becoming "well liked" only to end up murdered in a chicken coop.

I started to turn away but saw Polly in the front doorway. "Is something wrong?" she called. "Is Carter all right?"

"Yes," I shouted. "He's fine."

I turned away abruptly. A moment later, I pulled my Honda out of the drive, allowing Carter to reverse and head for town. Polly had gone inside, but she wasn't the only one who'd been watching. I was about to drive away when I saw Gloria Della Croce running from her porch, waving frantically.

It was my turn to roll down the car window. "Hi," I said. "What's up?"

"I feel so dumb," Gloria said after catching her breath. "I should've remembered about that Elvis album. Sorry."

"No problem," I assured her. "Your buddy reminded you. How's Brianna doing, by the way?"

Gloria pushed the long dark hair away from her face and sighed. "It's tough. She doesn't want to marry Brad. They're both too young. But her folks are giving her kind of a bad time. That's why she stays with us quite a bit. You'd think being a minister would make her dad more understanding."

"That's not always the case," I said. "Reverend Phelps probably thinks his daughter should practice what he preaches."

"Easy to say," Gloria remarked, looking unusually wise for a girl of her age. "Dads with only daughters can be a pain. I ought to know."

"Overly protective?"

Gloria nodded. "That's the other thing. I wanted to tell you my dad isn't always a complete butt. He came on pretty strong last night. I've gotten so I just tune him out."

"He only wants what's best for you," I said.

"I know . . . but sometimes . . ." She hesitated. "Hey, I've got to go. Brianna spent the night. She was just waking up a few minutes ago. I don't want her to think I ran off without her."

"She's lucky to have you for a friend — like a big sister, I imagine."

Gloria uttered a self-deprecating laugh. "Maybe. I haven't had much practice." She ran back toward the house.

I drove off down the road, leaving the occasional house, abandoned cabin, and dilapidated shed behind. I'd slowed down by Roy and Bebe Everson's place. She had received a citation for broken head- or taillights, but that was no motive for murder. I'd also passed Ethel and Bickford Pike's property. The pickup truck Pike used for hauling his junk wasn't parked by the house. Maybe they'd gone into town to shop or to Everett to sell some of his loot. His ticket for an unsecured load loomed larger in my mind, though it hardly seemed like a reason to kill Elmer.

I drove on. There was no snow at this level, not even as I craned my neck to look up at the face of Tonga Ridge. I thought about the two families I'd just encountered.

Carter was something of an enigma to me. Or maybe I was trying to read something into him that wasn't there. He was intelligent, was a professional man, had a mother fixation, and perhaps was gay. None of those things made him evil, just a little different. Certainly it didn't convince me he'd commit patricide.

Nick Della Croce was a very protective father but appeared only to have his daughter's welfare at heart. I hardly thought he'd kill Elmer because Gloria had overheard the poor man's wife and son making verbal love.

The problem, I realized, was motive. What incited people to commit murder? Certainly, I thought as I watched for the turnoff to the gravel road that led to Milo's fishing hole, I'd come across several killers in my career as a journalist. Greed, fear, revenge, jealousy, and just plain insanity had provoked those murderers. I also knew that the victim often revealed a great deal about the killer's identity. Yet in kindly Elmer's case, that didn't seem to be true.

I spotted the gravel road to the fork in the Foss and Tye rivers. Just beyond a slight bend, I saw Milo's Grand Cherokee. I pulled up behind it and got out of my car.

The air felt damp despite the sun's flirtatious appearance. My boots sank slightly into the dirt path that led down to the river. Through the bare vine maples, I could see Milo about twenty yards downstream, standing like a statue with his back to me.

There wasn't much bank this time of year, and I had to be careful not to slip on the smooth rocks or trip over the tree branches that had blown down earlier in the winter. I didn't shout at the sheriff. That would've broken the rules of fishing etiquette, the equivalent of mooning the guest of honor at a formal banquet.

As I got within fifteen feet of Milo, I stopped. He had reeled in his line and was about to cast again. I didn't want to get hit with a hook. He moved a few steps farther down the river and waded out until the water came to within a few inches of his boot tops. The current was moving more slowly here, not the kind of noisy torrent that signaled heavy rain or rapidly melting snow. I moved a little closer.

The sheriff was tugging on his line. At first I thought he might have a fish on, but after the second or third pull, I realized he'd gotten snagged on the river bottom. As he struggled to free his line, he turned and saw me. I could tell he was scowling, so I didn't say a word. At least another minute passed before the sheriff swore out loud as the line broke and dangled over the rolling current.

"Second leader I've lost today," he called to me, wading toward the bank. "That's the trouble with fishing here. Too much crap gets swept to the fork."

"How about a coffee break?" I asked, holding out the paper cups and the bag with the muffins.

"How about telling me why you're here?" Milo said, opening his tackle box.

"I was bored," I said, setting my Starbucks offering on a flat rock. "I needed to get out and listen to the river without the sound of cars and trucks and jerks who don't like my editorials."

It was true. It was also a language that Milo understood. "I don't know why you don't do some fishing yourself," the sheriff said, taking out a shiny green lure from his tackle box.

"I don't have the patience anymore," I said. "At least not for winter steelheading. And frankly, the rivers around here don't produce like they used to. Any luck so far?"

He shook his head. "Not even a bump. The river's off-color. I've lost three of these babies at five bucks a pop," Milo complained, pointing to the lure. "I'm going to try one more shot and then pack it in." He frowned as I took the muffins out of the paper bag. "They didn't have bear claws?"

"Gee," I said, handing him a muffin, "you must enjoy getting hauled off to the hospital. Have you got a crush on one of those bulky nurses?"

The sheriff sighed. "I'll be glad to get this damned thing over with. Maybe I'll schedule the surgery for early February." He took the muffin and picked up the paper coffee cup. "We might have this Nystrom case wrapped up by then."

"You think?" I sipped my latte, which had grown lukewarm. "Do you know something I don't?"

Milo shook his head. "Nope. But without any real leads, I figure it's a random thing. Somebody stole eggs from the henhouse. Maybe a chicken, too. We're probably dealing with a nut job of some kind." He shot me a sidelong glance. "Anything new with you?"

"About the case?" I shook my head. "Not really."

"I meant in general."

I figured it was Milo's way of asking why I'd come to the fishing hole. "Not particularly."

He didn't say anything but sipped his latte and gazed out at the river. I assumed his curiosity about my arrival had been satisfied.

"I should head back to town," I said.

The sheriff nodded once. "See you."

He seemed detached, but I assumed his mind was back on his steelhead quest. I finished my muffin and collected our litter. Milo was still drinking from his cup as I turned to leave.

I stopped short when I saw Dustin Fong picking his way along the riverbank.

"Sheriff!" Dustin called. "We got trouble!"

Milo gulped down the last of his latte and scrunched the cup in his big hand. "What now?"

"Polly Nystrom," Dustin said, stopping next to the gnarled roots of an uprooted cedar tree. "She called to say she was being attacked."

TWENTY

The sheriff picked up his fishing rod as carefully as he'd hold a baby. "Well?"

"Sam and I went over there, but she wouldn't let us in," Dustin explained, reverting to his usual calm, careful manner. "Carter wasn't around as far as we could tell. Nick Della Croce came out of his house and said he'd heard a commotion but hadn't seen anything. We finally got Polly to come to the door, but she refused to open it. She claimed her attackers were gone and said she'd wait for Carter."

"Did Sam stay at the Nystrom place?" Milo asked, looking annoyed.

Dustin nodded. "I left him there to come get you. Your cell's not working."

Milo heaved a big sigh. "Just what I needed," he muttered, starting to dismantle his rod. "Is the old bat nuts?"

"I don't know," Dustin replied. "There was no sign of forced entry that we could see — just some tire marks on the front lawn, like somebody drove over it."

I finally spoke up: "Those marks weren't there an hour ago," I asserted. "I'd have noticed them. The Nystroms have a tidy yard, even this time of year."

"Not now," Dustin said. "There's some old tin cans and broken plates out front." He frowned. "You're right — that's not like them."

The idea I'd had while rooting around in Adam's closet suddenly came back to me. It burst full-blown inside my brain, but it was too off-the-wall to mention. Milo would disparage my notion, and I'd feel like a fool. Still, a sense of urgency overpowered me.

"This is serious stuff," I said.

Both men stared at me — Dustin curious, Milo skeptical.

"Like how?" the sheriff asked, placing the rod in its case.

"Polly must know who came to her house and drove over the lawn and —" I stopped, noticing that Milo wasn't listening. He had his back to me and was collecting his gear. "Fine," I said sharply. Turning around, I moved past Dustin and made my way as fast as I could along the obstacle-covered riverbank.

When I reached my car, I saw that Dustin's cruiser was barring my way. Frustrated, I got behind the Honda's wheel to see if I could maneuver around the other vehicle by reversing into the ferns and salmonberry vines alongside the road.

But the ground was too soft from all the rain, and after the first couple of feet in reverse, I knew I'd get stuck. I sat in the car, anxiously tapping my fingers on the steering wheel. Only a couple of minutes passed before I saw the deputy coming up from the river.

"I'm leaving," Dustin shouted. "Sorry."

I watched him in the rearview mirror. He got into the cruiser just as Milo appeared, carrying his fishing gear. He set his belongings down by the Grand Cherokee and loped over to my car, motioning for me to roll down the window.

"Where do you think you're going?" he demanded.

I almost didn't tell him. But candor and common sense forced the words out of my mouth. "To the Pikes'," I said.

"Why?"

"Because . . . I want to talk to them," I replied. I couldn't explain my foreboding. The sheriff wouldn't understand.

"Go ahead," Milo said, and shrugged.

Dustin had reversed into the turnaround

by the Burl Creek Road. He drove off toward town. I did the same and had to be careful to keep my foot off the gas pedal so that I wasn't tailgating him. The deputy didn't seem to be in any hurry, but I was.

Ethel and Bickford Pike's house was modest, a four-room bungalow some fifty or more years old where they had raised their only child, a son named Terry who lived in Orlando with his wife and children. It occurred to me that like the Nystroms and the Della Croces, they were another set of parents with a single offspring.

There was still no sign of Pike's battered pickup. The small front yard was choked with dandelions, thistles, moss, and an occasional patch of long grass. I couldn't remember if Ethel and her husband had a second car. I hesitated, then steeled my nerve and got out of the Honda. I walked along the rutted dirt driveway, avoiding puddles that had not dried up from the last rainfall. The dilapidated garage was closed, but there was a window on one side. I went up to it and tried to peer in through the grime and cobwebs. It appeared to be a storage area, probably for all the junk Pike collected.

Going around to the other side, I saw an

old rusted-out Pontiac up on blocks with its wheels missing. It stood derelict under the bare branches of a sickly apple tree. How fitting, for people like the Pikes had no place to go and no way to get there. Their wheels had fallen off long ago; their hearts — their engines — had worn out. That was true, too, in a different way of the Nystroms, but they had a facade, eloquently expressed by Carter's bright and shiny new Corvette.

There was no point knocking on the door. I knew the Pikes weren't home — an inappropriate word for their house. It seemed more like a prison, made off-limits to others by all the junk that might as well have been iron bars. I started back to my car as Milo pulled up on the edge of the road.

"What the hell are you doing?" he demanded, opening the door on the driver's side but remaining behind the wheel.

I stood in the driveway with my hands shoved into the pockets of my car coat. "I'm not sure," I said. "What's going on with Polly Nystrom?"

The sheriff shook his head. "Nuisance stuff, nothing serious. I'm on my way there now. Dustin's up ahead." Milo gestured down the road.

"I know," I said, my voice sounding hollow. "Sam Heppner's there, too."

"Right." Milo paused. "Come on, Emma. Get moving."

"Okay." I opened the car door, but before I could get in, I heard Milo's cell phone ring. And then I heard him swear.

"Meet you there," he said. Or something like that. I wasn't close enough to catch the exact words. He slammed the Grand Cherokee's door shut and started the engine.

I hurried to follow him. He was heading toward town but took a left about a hundred yards from the Pike property. As I twisted the wheel to make the turn, I realized we were by Bebe and Roy Everson's house. In a blur, I saw them standing by the split-rail fence that separated their yard from the dirt track on which I was now traveling. I wasn't sure where we were going, but I had a sickening feeling that I knew why.

The winding road led to Burl Creek, just a short way from Cass Pond. I could see that it had been used by locals as a dumping ground. Car parts, kitchen appliances, garbage, and even an old toilet were heaped in piles and strewn about the small clearing. A NO DUMPING sign had been riddled with bullets.

But none of this rubbish riveted my attention like the old Silverado pickup truck parked at the edge of the creek. Milo had gotten out of the Grand Cherokee and drawn his sidearm. He approached the pickup slowly. If he knew I'd followed him, he didn't turn around to look in my direction. Even I had sense enough to stay in my car.

With dread, I watched him peer into one side of the pickup's cab and then into the other. He put his gun away and opened the door on the driver's side. I held my breath as Milo leaned inside for no more than a minute, though it seemed like forever.

Finally he turned to look my way. Shaking his head, the sheriff came up to the Honda. I rolled down my window.

"They're both dead." Milo bit his lip. "Ethel and Pike. Shotgun on the pickup's floor. Poor old coots."

I cleared my throat. "Murder-suicide." It wasn't even a question. The Pikes had chosen well for the site of their deaths. No doubt they'd seen themselves as old, useless, and broken, just like the rest of the trash at the dump area.

The sheriff nodded at me before looking over his shoulder. "Here come Dustin and Sam. Go back to town, Emma. I'll see you at my office."

I passed the police cruiser on my way back to the Burl Creek Road. It'd take Milo and his deputies quite a while to accomplish their pathetic task. I didn't go to the sheriff's office but kept driving along Front Street until I got to Sixth and turned up the hill to Vida's house on Tyee. I didn't know if she was home, but for now I couldn't be alone.

With relief, I saw her in the front yard, energetically chopping off branches from a leggy forsythia bush. She looked around when she heard the car pull up.

"Emma!" she cried. "How nice! I was about to go inside for a bite of lunch." Seeing my stricken expression, she put a hand to her cheek. "Oh, no! What is it?"

"Wait until we get in the house," I said.

Once we were in the kitchen, Vida immediately put the teakettle on. "So." She sat down opposite me at the kitchen table. "What's happened? You're quite pale."

"Ethel and Bickford Pike are dead."

Vida sucked in her breath. "Oh, my!" she exclaimed after a long pause. *"Oh, my!"* she repeated more softly. "How?"

I admitted I wasn't sure. "I assume Pike shot Ethel and then himself. Pike must have been the only person in Alpine who didn't like Elmer."

"The junk," Vida murmured. She didn't seem shocked, only surprised. Maybe she, too, had guessed that Pike had killed Elmer.

436

"Those so-called collectibles that fell off of his truck would've annoyed Elmer no end. He headed up the Kiwanis Club's litter collection along a section of the Icicle Creek Road. Tsk, tsk. Such a tidy man."

"Pike may have scavenged — or collected, as he'd put it — more than junk. Pilfering must have become second nature to him. I'll bet he'd been stealing eggs — and probably that missing chicken — for some time." I shook my head. "Elmer caught Pike that morning in the henhouse. He probably threatened Pike with calling the sheriff. Maybe the two men got physical. Pike simply reacted and whacked Elmer with whatever was at hand."

Vida nodded. "Being a simple man, committing a simple crime."

"But not really simple," I pointed out. "People, even the Pikes of this world, are very complex."

"Oh, yes. They — we — all have our opportunity to be part of humanity despite our troubles and tragedies." Vida gazed up at Cupcake, who was honing his beak on a cuttlebone. "Of course the Pikes were lonely, but they could have been otherwise. Strange," she mused, removing her glasses and rubbing her eyes with less than her usual zest, "that Ethel complained about so many things — except what truly bothered her. Their only child thousands of miles away in Florida, hardly any other family close to them unless you count Pike's sister, and they fought like cats and dogs. I suppose Pike took the easy way out by killing himself and Ethel."

"Well . . . it doesn't seem right. Oh," I went on, "I know that loneliness is like a cancer and can eat at you until —"

Vida interrupted me with a shake of her head. "I don't mean just that, or even being arrested. I'm talking about actual cancer. It wasn't bronchitis that Pike had. I called Marje Blatt last night after I got home from your house. She confided — bless her — that Pike was dying. Marje and Doc Dewey were worried about what would happen to Ethel because of her diabetes. She was beginning to lose the feeling in her feet. That's why she limped so badly. Marje and I talked about what would happen to Ethel after Pike died."

"She could've gone into a nursing home," I said.

"Not Ethel!" Vida smiled grimly. "Too proud, too ornery." Her smile softened. "She could be a pill, but I rather liked her."

I'd never have guessed it.

"You know," Vida said, as the teakettle

whistled, "some people can't bear to live alone." She stood up and went to the stove. "The rest of us put one foot ahead of the other and keep going."

"So," Milo said to me later that afternoon when I reached the sheriff's office, "what put you on to the Pikes?"

I leaned back in the visitor's chair. Scott was out front, talking to Dustin and Sam. I'd decided to let my reporter wrap up the story. He needed the experience, and I was tired — tired, I suppose, of having had too much experience.

"It was that Elvis album," I said.

"What Elvis album?" he asked.

I explained about how Gloria Della Croce had found it by the road. "All along, I kept thinking that Elmer couldn't have been liked by everybody. Nobody is, not even saints. What would make someone dislike him? His apparent perfection, for one thing. Elmer was helpful, kind, and tidy. He embodied so many American virtues. But he also chastised people when they didn't live up to the high standards he'd set for himself. Ethel mentioned Pike's truck once, but she called it a 'Silvery' something-or-other. It didn't dawn on me that it was a Chevrolet brand, a Silverado. It was an old beat-up thing, and I can imagine that Elmer and Pike had gone head-to-head over that truck for many years."

"But it still ran," Milo pointed out. "Maybe Pike worked on it himself."

I nodded. "He probably did. He was handy, according to Ethel." I smiled faintly at the memory. "I can imagine how annoyed Elmer — and Polly, who is a terrible complainer — could get when Pike would go by in his rattletrap truck and stuff would fall off all over the place. I suppose half the time Pike didn't know it and wouldn't bother to collect it. It may have seemed like a minor feud to everybody else, but it was very serious to someone like Pike, who must have seen Elmer as the ideal family patriarch. But that was only the facade. The reality was quite different in terms of the Nystroms themselves."

"Reality." Milo shook his head. "It always comes down to that, doesn't it?"

"I'm afraid so." I traced a groove in Milo's desk with my fingernail. "There's no happy ending for most of the people involved."

"Bunch of screwed-up lives," the sheriff remarked.

"Whose isn't?"

Milo shrugged. "Dustin and Sam should've guessed Pike and Ethel were up to something when they scared the hell out of Polly by dumping more crap on her lawn. It's a good thing Roy and Bebe Everson called in about the gunshots. They'd seen the Pikes go by in the pickup and thought they were either dumping stuff or salvaging it. I guess Pike went down to that site fairly often. They heard the shots and got worried when the truck didn't show up in the next half hour."

I rose to my feet. "I'd better go home."

"Yeah. I've got paperwork to finish up. Hey, thanks for the coffee and that damned muffin."

I swiveled around with my hand on the doorknob. "Oh, sure. Emma's fast-food delivery service."

"Your turn," Milo said.

My hand fell away from the knob. "To do . . . what?"

"Say thank you." Milo looked curious.

"Ah . . . for . . . ?"

"The flowers."

"The . . . oh!" I gaped at him. "You sent me that beautiful bouquet?"

"Didn't the card say so?"

"No. There wasn't any name. I thought . . ." I felt like a moron.

Milo's long face showed no emotion. "I thought it'd make up for getting sick after I ate your dinner. Whoever's filling in at Posies Unlimited while Delphine Corson's on vacation must have forgotten to put my name on the damned card. Oh, well."

The sheriff's phone rang. He raised his hand in a halfhearted wave and picked up the receiver. "Dodge here."

I left.

Sunday night Vida asked me to go with her for a little ride. She didn't explain. I didn't inquire.

It was dark by seven that night, with a light rain falling and only a faint breeze blowing down from Tonga Ridge. She chattered about many things as we drove down Alpine Way and turned toward the Burl Creek Road.

"Now about my 'Scene Around Town' column this week. I've not put my mind to it with everything else happening . . . Delphine on a ski trip to Sun Valley, of course. I'll interview her when she comes back. Edna Mae gathering used romance novels for a special St. Valentine's sale to benefit the library. Or is that a small story? I suppose it is. Dare I mention Ed working at the Burger Barn? Perhaps not. He won't last."

We pulled up in front of the Nystrom house. Vida grunted as she twisted around to reach into the backseat and pick up a Grocery Basket bag. "You were right," she said. "I checked my files — and my memory. In all the years Trinity Episcopal has had bake sales, Polly Nystrom never contributed so much as a batch of biscuits. Nor was she active in any of the church's activities."

"So?"

She handed me a white paper bag. "I hate to waste good food, but needs must."

I peeked into the bag. It contained a couple of dozen vanilla wafers from the store's bakery section. I was still puzzled. "Now what?"

Vida had taken out a brand-new cookie cookbook encased in plastic wrap. "It's our turn to decorate the Nystroms' lawn. Come, let's hurry. It's raining harder, and I didn't wear my galoshes. Very foolish of me. I don't know why I didn't . . ." The rest of her words were lost as she got out of the car.

I got out, too. Even in the dark, I could see the crescent-shaped tire treads left in the carefully groomed lawn. Carter must have picked up the debris left by the Pikes. Our mission took less than a minute. I suppose it was foolish of me to obey Vida so blindly, but I knew she had a method to her madness.

We simply tossed everything from the side

of the road and hurried back to her Buick. Although the lights were on in the Nystrom and Della Croce houses, no one seemed to notice us. That was lucky. Vida would have been easily identified by her big green hat with its acorns and oak leaves. I smiled to myself, wondering if she'd thought about the symbolism: green for hope, the acorn for strength, oak for endurance — and forgiveness. I took one last look at the round little cookies haphazardly strewn around the yard. They reminded me of Communion wafers. Ironic or appropriate? I wondered.

"Okay," I said as Vida started up the car. "Why did we just commit a crime that could get us arrested?"

"To remind Polly and Carter that they're still alive." She glanced over at me before pulling back out onto the road. "To never retreat from the rest of the world."

We followed the dark road back to town, where the rain-blurred lights in the houses and shops along Alpine Way welcomed us home.

ABOUT THE AUTHOR

Mary Daheim is a Seattle native who started spinning stories before she could spell. Daheim has been a journalist, an editor, a public relations consultant, and a freelance writer, but fiction was always her medium of choice. In 1982 she launched a career that is now distinguished by more than forty novels. In 2000, she won the Literary Achievement Award from the Pacific Northwest Writers Association. Daheim lives in Seattle with her husband, David, a retired professor of cinema, English, and literature. The Daheims have three daughters: Barbara, Katherine, and Magdalen.